PRAISE FOR GLASS MOUNTAIN

A heck of a good tale about tenacity, resilience, and the choices we make. I read Glass Mountain in one sitting, and from the first page I was rooting out loud for the characters.

— JEANNETTE WALLS
AUTHOR OF THE GLASS CASTLE

Like the prospectors of old, Laura Treacy Bentley finds gold in the hills — in the rugged, distant places on the far horizon. The treasure lies in her stories. You'll love Twyla Townsend, the unforgettable heroine of Bentley's new novel. Filled with heart and soul and sass, Twyla discovers strength and peace — and solves a mystery — in a remote cabin in this warm, funny, captivating tale.

— JULIA KELLER
PULITZER PRIZE-WINNING AUTHOR OF
A KILLING IN THE HILLS

You've done it again . . . Making me double-check that all doors are locked and curtains shut tight! Another truly "gripping" novel.

Waitressing, trying to take care of her 10-year-old half-brother, hounded for money she doesn't have by her substance-abusing mother and boyfriend, and now that her young waitress friend is missing, Twyla Townsend, 21 years old, fears she is the one meant to be targeted.

Just as in Laura Treacy Bentley's, first novel, The Silver Tattoo, suspense builds layer upon layer with Twyla risking everything when Sam, a talkative elderly customer offers her $20,000 if she'll house-sit his cabin on the isolated top of Glass Mountain. Snowstorms, bears, and strange happenings ratchet up the tension in this haunting, impossible-to-put-down novel.

— Anna Egan Smucker
Author of nine award-winning books

GLASS MOUNTAIN

LAURA TREACY BENTLEY

The Henlo Press
P.O. Box 1694
Ashland, KY 41105
www.thehenlopress.com

For my brother, Denny.

The eye, like a shattered mirror, multiplies the images of sorrow.

— EDGAR ALLAN POE

PROLOGUE

CORKSCREW SWAMP, WEST
NAPLES, FLORIDA AUGUST 2018

R*ebecca applied bug repellent to her excited 8-year-old twins, a boy and a girl, who were wearing their new Ghost Orchid t-shirts. Ben waited impatiently for them at the entrance of Corkscrew Swamp so they could begin their self-directed tour. Rebecca hurried the twins along, but Sophie lagged behind Shane for a second and put something in her pockets.*

A tropical paradise awaited them, so they silenced their phones, readied cameras, and draped binoculars around their necks in anticipation. Rebecca and Ben warned the children to whisper so they wouldn't scare away the wildlife. Obediently, they crept single file behind their parents, following the bends and curves of the elevated boardwalk, listening to songbirds mixed with creepy jungle sounds they'd only heard in movies. After passing by pine flatwoods, marsh wetlands, and pond cypress, they ended up near the ancient Bald Cypresses that towered above them. The trees created lacy shadows as they all kept a careful watch for alligators, Snowy Egrets, and the illusive Painted Bunting with its dazzling red, blue, and yellow plumage.

Ben pointed to two sleeping alligators on a nearby bank. After a flurry of camera shots, Rebecca spotted a cluster of Ghost Orchids blooming about fifty feet up in one of the Bald Cypress trees. They zoomed in with their binoculars to get a closer look when Shane spotted a Roseate Spoonbill in the same tree. He had just seen a photo of that goofy bird in the guidebook. When he burst out laughing, a startled Wood Stork took flight.

As they approached the end of the two-mile boardwalk, the twins were hot and sweaty and thirsty. They rested on a bench overlooking the murky swamp water with red-bellied turtles sunning on a fallen log. Their parents, just a few yards away, soaked in the lush green wonder and cathedral quiet of this 5,000-year-old sanctuary.

Sophie secretly reached into her left pocket, nudged her brother, and put a few pieces of gravel in his hand. Shane grinned and took dead aim at the turtles, and they plopped, one at a time, into the still water. He pitched the last stone at what looked like a shiny black mirror floating on the surface of the tea-dark water, but it just pinged when it hit its mark. Sophie tugged a big rock the size of a paperweight from her other pocket and hurled it with all her might toward the large mirror that had snared the cypress shadows, clouds, and glinting August sun in its shiny web. The rock hit hard and detonated the silence like the blast from a shotgun. The swamp creatures went mute and nothing moved except the unbroken mirror that rocked on the gentle swells and a cottonmouth slithered away on top of the water.

1

JULY 2018

SAM

"I like my coffee strong, baby sister," Sam said, eyeing my red cowboy hat and silver cap guns tucked safely inside their holsters. He got a kick out of my uniform. I did, too. It was fun to dress like a cowgirl every day—like Halloween without a mask, but I could cover my face with a bandanna if I wanted to. At least I didn't have to wear nurses' shoes, a ruffled apron, and a hairnet.

"I always add an extra scoop of French roast in the pot when I see you parking your big red truck."

"It's a Silverado," Sam said proudly.

"Shouldn't you have a *silver* Silverado?" I teased.

"I'm partial to red," he said.

I filled his mug with freshly brewed coffee.

"And my dessert, I . . ."

"Like it homemade. Nothing artificial, right?"

"Right, Twyla. None of that sugar-free, fake whipped cream, and decaffeinated slop with powdered creamer for me."

I'd already memorized Sam's daily banter. It was easy since he always said the same thing. Ruggedly handsome for an old man—trim, tan, and he had a thick head of white hair, imprinted with a crease when he took off his Stetson. Sam wore alligator cowboy boots and often bragged about his snakeskin belt and the Western bolo he wore with its beige rope tie, silver tips, and fat, jade-green stone.

"It once belonged to a world-famous movie star named John Wayne. Have you ever heard of him?'

"I'm not sure," I said.

Sam just shook his head.

"After much deliberation, Twyla, I've decided on the coconut cream pie. Don't forget the extra whipped cream."

I cut a big wedge and put it on a plate in front of him. Then I shook a canister and turned it upside down, filling a soup bowl with a mountain of whipped cream.

"All our pies are made from scratch," I said, admiring the coconut cream's egg-rich custard topped with three inches of glistening meringue and toasted coconut.

"Choosing the perfect slice of pie is crucial," Sam said.

His eyes were trained on the French apple crumb, lemon meringue, banana cream, and fresh peach pies that still seduced him from the refrigerated display case.

"Crucial?"

"Comfort food calms your soul," he said.

I placed the bowl of whipped cream beside his plate. Pie wasn't a matter of life or death, but finding Ashley could be. Ever since her mom called me early this morning, I couldn't get her out of my mind. When I looked out the window, Ashley's bike was still locked in the bike rack just where she had left it.

"You just never know when you're going to kick the bucket, Twy, and I'm sure as shit not gonna miss the best dessert of the day, pardon my French."

"You look pretty healthy to me. There's always tomorrow and plenty more choices. Louise plans on whipping up a wicked chocolate silk pie and strawberry shortcake tonight," I said.

I didn't want to think about death. Not now, or ever. Sam had terrible timing, but he didn't know how worried I was about Ashley. I glanced at my watch. It wasn't like her to not show up or forget to call.

"I'm partial to strawberries. Fresh-picked strawberries, that is. You got some cinnamon handy?"

I popped open the lid of a small red tin, set it next to his plate, and pushed a tiny pitcher of cream closer to him. I had learned the customer was always right and not to skimp on flattery. So had Ashley, and our tips got much better.

"How come you never seem to gain any weight, Sam?"

"I have a fast metabolism, like a ruby-throated hummingbird. Inherited it from my Pop. He ate everything he wanted and stayed slim and trim all his life."

"You're one lucky guy," I told him.

After filling a carafe with water, I made another pot of coffee. Decaf this time. We always kept one regular and one decaf on hand for our senior citizens. After two months on the job, I knew the routine here at Calamity café, and all the regular customers, especially Sam.

I used to work a part-time job at the newspaper writing obits and was hired full-time at Calamity. It's an old restaurant on a side street that seniors on fixed incomes and the locals like. Big servings and affordable prices were the draw. I made decent money with the overtime and tips. My chaps, vest, hat, holster, spurs, and cap gun were provided by the management. The only items I needed to buy were my black Laredo cowboy boots, white jeans, white t-shirts, and some red bandannas. Charged them at Walmart—another bill I didn't want with my car needing a lot of work and the rent coming due.

Sam watched me as I collected a few stray tips.

"You missed one." He pointed at a dollar placed under a mug at the end of the counter.

I walked over and folded the bill into my shirt pocket. I remembered a middle-aged woman had sat on that stool earlier. She didn't have a suntan, so she must have been passing through. Everyone ended up with a tan after a week in Naples,

Florida, whether they wanted one or not. Maybe she was a movie star. She didn't remove her sunglasses and wore a New York Yankees ball cap with her ponytail fished through the back.

I poured Sam another mug and refilled his cream pitcher.

"What else can I get you?" I asked. "I mean, what do you want for breakfast?"

"Give me a minute. I've only ordered lunch," he said.

As I handed him a menu, a car suddenly backfired and a beat-up, white convertible peeled into the parking lot.

"What the hell?" Sam said, jerking around for a better look.

The car came to an abrupt stop, and a woman slipped out of the passenger side. She hobbled barefoot across the gravel lot, stopping once to steady herself. Her long blonde hair was wind-blown from the ride, and she wore a hot pink mini-skirt.

I knew her hair and that stupid walk of hers. I'd seen it too many times. I felt sick and wanted her to magically disappear.

The woman came in through the sunroom door and the five seniors having their morning coffee klatch went church silent. She stopped, leaned against the wall to brush the dirt from her feet, and smiled at them. Even from here, she looked pretty. Pretty drunk. She set her sights on the counter about ten feet away and spotted me.

"Who's that?" Sam asked.

"My mother. I haven't seen her for a while."

"Your mother? She can't be more than 30!" he said.

"Joy's 36. She had me when she was 15."

I watched as she wove her way toward the counter holding on to a chair or two. A slippery red smile was glued on her face.

"Let me help you there, miss," Sam said, offering his hand to steady her.

Joy sat at the counter and tugged at her skirt, as if that would help cover her sorry ass.

"Hey, Twyla. You're looking really good, honey."

I pretended I didn't hear her.

"Can't stay long, sweetie," she slurred. "Randy's waiting on me, and he won't wait for long. He's a busy, busy man, you know. A mountain man of few words."

I glanced out the window and could see her latest boyfriend waiting in the car. Two bushy squirrel tails dangled from his rearview mirror.

Joy's breath stank of alcohol, and her blue eyes were blood-shot. Another all-nighter, no doubt.

"How's my baby boy, Chase, doing?'

She picked up Sam's coffee with both hands and took a big sip.

"He's doing fine, especially without you," I said.

"Don't you goddam talk to me like that!" Joy slammed the mug on the counter and his coffee flamed up just before it hit the floor.

Sam scrambled out of the way lightning fast, and when Randy laid on the horn, the customers jumped a second time. I grabbed a couple of hand towels and tried to mop up the counter as steaming liquid poured near my feet.

"See, I told you my boyfriend's not much of a talker, just a honker," she said, laughing loudly at her own joke. "Sorry about your coffee there, mister. Twyla will get you a fresh cup."

"I've had enough for today," he said, standing back from the counter.

Joy smoothed her hair and pulled it over one shoulder. It was tangled, but clean. Sam finally took a seat two stools away from her.

"Listen, I need a favor, Twyla," Joy whispered, staring down at me on my hands and knees picking up pieces of the shattered mug.

I tried to ignore her, but she just got louder.

"This kind gentleman will help me get to my car, won't 'cha darlin'?" she said, twirling a strand of her hair around her finger and standing right behind Sam. "But first, I need a favor from my beautiful daughter. We don't look a thing alike, but she's beautiful to me," she boasted, leaning closer to Sam.

"What do you want?" I asked.

"Just an itty-bitty loan to tide me over. I'm in a rough place right now, sweetie. I'll pay you back next week."

"What about Randy? Isn't he good for a loan?"

"She's a spitfire, don't you think? What's your name, handsome?" Joy asked as she rested her hand above Sam's knee.

"Sam. Just Sam," he said, gripping both of her hands now to keep them from wandering.

"Sam. I like that name. It's strong sounding, like my first husband's name. Buck. Buck Townsend. He's Twyla's daddy. We met at a party, and he didn't know I was just a kid. I never saw him again, and nine months later, Twyla was born."

"How much do you need?" I asked, trying to stay calm.

"Five hundred would help tide me over, sweetie. You got five hundred handy?"

"You know I don't have that kind of money. Here's a twenty. It's all I've got right now," I said, pulling a bill from my pocket.

Randy blasted the car horn again, only this time he didn't give it a rest. The customers exchanged nervous glances and quickly gathered their things to leave.

"Shut the fuck up!" Joy yelled toward the window as if Randy could hear her, and then she smiled sweet as honey as she steadied herself on Sam's shoulder, tucked the $20 into her cleavage, and took a deep breath. "I'll take this as a down payment."

Sam escorted her to the side door as she half shuffled, half leaned on him for support, and then she craned her neck and yelled.

"Tell Chase I love him! Tell him Joy will take him to Hawaii when she wins the lottery! I don't look like I have two kids and a daughter *that* old, do I?" she asked Sam and the five bug-eyed seniors, as she pointed her finger directly at me.

"No, ma'am, not at all," Sam said, answering for everyone.

He stood in the doorway and watched her as she side-winded her way over the gravel to the convertible.

"Some people don't deserve to be mothers," I said.

Sam looked down and cleared his throat. For once, he had nothing to say.

"I'm glad I don't look like her. I think I'd kill myself if I did," I said.

"She's pretty and so are you, Twy."

"I have a different dad than my brother. I've never met the man. You heard Joy say his name was Buck. Chase gets his blue eyes and blonde hair from Joy. At least he's a boy, so he won't be compared too much to his druggie mother. Joy's been trouble all my life. I don't owe her anything. Chase doesn't either."

Randy revved the engine and smoked the parking lot with exhaust fumes. She crawled into the passenger side and closed the door. The seniors didn't move as they watched him back up and make a U-turn onto the highway to avoid the stoplight. The squirrel tails swung like mad as he sped past a car and disappeared down the road.

2

ASHLEY

Sam glanced over his shoulder to check on Cali. He brought his dog here every day. She rested on the cool slate floor of Calamity's small attached sunporch, which was furnished with five bistro tables. A few early risers liked to gather there before work each day. Meeting Sam's gaze was a beaut of a dog with soft brown eyes, long golden fur, and silky ears. She didn't lift her head from her paws—just swept the floor with her wagging tail.

After grabbing a mixing bowl from under the counter and putting a scoop of crushed ice into it, I filled it halfway with tap water. I'd saved some bacon and sausage scraps, half-eaten scrambled eggs, and hash browns on a Styrofoam plate—leftovers from my morning customers.

"In two short months, you've managed to totally spoil my dog," Sam grumbled.

He poured a thin stream of creamer into his coffee. After he dusted cinnamon on top of his whipped cream, he scooped a huge bite into his mouth with a soup spoon. When he closed his eyes, he seemed transported for a second, savoring its sweetness. He always took his time—ate his pie first, then his whipped cream.

"Maybe I *want* to spoil her," I teased, knowing I couldn't deny that dog anything.

When Cali spotted me coming, her tail ticked faster. A few flies buzzed as they inched around the perimeter of a plate glass window overlooking the parking lot. They were those pesky drunk kind of flies that lingered instead of dying, bumped into your face in slow motion, and shadowed your hand when you tried to bat them away.

Looking out the window, I stared at Ashley's lavender and pink beach bike glimmering in the morning sun. The sight of it upset me all over again. When her mom said she didn't make it home after closing last night, I knew something was wrong, terribly wrong. Josh told me he gave Ashley the money bag to drop off at the bank instead of me. Then she just disappeared. She didn't take her bike and ride the six short blocks to her house afterward like she always did or wake her mother, who often fell asleep on the couch in front of the TV. When she discovered her daughter wasn't in her bed this morning, she freaked out.

"Did Ashley tell you where she went?" I heard the panic rising in her strained voice.

"Maybe she went to a friend's house or out with Brad. Did you call Brad?"

"She didn't leave me a note or anything, Twyla. I'm so worried! Where would she go alone at night on her bike? Maybe she got sick or something and went to the emergency room, but someone would have contacted me by now. Maybe she..."

Maybe she ran away, I wanted to say, but I knew she'd never do that. She loved it here, loved her mother, loved Brad, and was saving all her money so she could go to the community college to become a practical nurse and get a good job at the hospital. She had worked at Calamity since she turned sixteen and was dependable. Everyone liked her, especially Sam. So where would this shy high school girl be right now? I didn't have a clue.

"Call the police and report her missing. I'll check and see if anyone at work has heard from her," I promised. But when I had pulled into the lot early this morning, Ashley's bike was still padlocked in the rack where she had left it. And no one had heard a word from her.

Just then, a siren shattered my thoughts when a fire truck came screaming down the highway with its red lights flashing. Cars pulled over to each side of the road to let it pass. I froze as it blasted its foghorn three times and sailed through the intersection. An ambulance and squad car followed close behind. Cali raised her head and howled, a low and mournful sound until the sirens faded away in the distance.

"It's okay, girl," I said, trying to calm us both. I walked toward her with the Styrofoam plate balanced on top of her water bowl and reached into my jeans pocket with my free hand. Cali stood in anticipation and sniffed my fist.

"Sit, Cali," I said, and she obeyed. I knelt in front of her, carefully avoiding the spurs attached to my new Laredo boots. I patted her head and smoothed her long, curly ears between my fingers. "You're a good dog."

Never gushy, simply loving and serene, she licked my face. Just once.

"Shake," I commanded.

Cali placed her golden paw into my hand. I rewarded her with a few miniature marshmallows I had taken from a small bin near the hot chocolate dispenser. Cali tilted her head and licked them slant-wise, one at a time, from my sticky palm. She smiled, or at least it looked like a smile, and waited for me to put the bowl of ice water and food scraps on the floor.

"There must be another bad wreck on the Interstate or another overdose," Sam called out. "It seems like there's something every day now."

Call me, Ashley. Call me now!

The humidity built up fast, so I turned the thermostat down and yanked the ceiling fan's metal chain to make the blades spin faster. Cali's fur and the fringe on my red vest and chaps fluttered in the draft.

Red and white were Calamity's signature colors. The red walls were decorated with lassos, branding irons, rusty horseshoes, and old saddles. Ten white tables and chairs filled the main dining room, a red buffet table with a wagon wheel mounted at each end, and red Naugahyde bar stools lined the counter where I was stationed most of the time. The white countertop showed every smudge, but I managed to keep it spotless.

I wiped my hands on a dish towel I kept tucked in my belt. When I took off my cowboy hat, I could feel my earrings fluttering against my neck. I kept my hair really short now—almost a buzz cut with shaggy bangs. I wanted to streak it purple and pink, but I couldn't afford it right now. Sam said I looked like a boy who liked to wear dangly earrings, but I didn't care what he thought. The overhead fan cooled my face as I raked my fingers through my bristly hair. I could hear the jukebox blaring "Pretty Woman" and Sam singing along at the top of his lungs.

"Lots of money here in Naples, Twy. Bet a *pretty woman* like you could find a multi-billionaire if you were looking for one."

Coming from an old man, Sam's attempt at a compliment felt creepy.

"Like you? Are you a billionaire on the prowl?"

My questions killed his smile. I was in no mood to flirt, tip or no tip. I tried to keep my questions short, so he'd just answer yes or no.

"Are you crazy? I'm not a billionaire, and I'm never getting married again! Lydia and I were married for fifty wonderful years and nobody will ever replace her."

"I don't know anyone who's been married longer than five."

Sam just rolled his eyes.

"It's the truth. Most of my friends live together or the ones who do get married split up after a year or so."

"Yeah, people told Lydia and me all the time we were dinosaurs, circus freaks, but we were inseparable. Siamese twins," he said with a wink.

The phone in the kitchen echoed off the walls, and Sam and I both jumped. I ran to answer it before Josh did.

"Ashley? Is that you? Ashley?"

I could hear people talking in the background, so it had to be a robocall. When no one answered me, I hung up.

"Probably a wrong number," I said in a controlled voice as I approached the counter.

"Jesus H. Christ, that phone would wake the dead," Sam yelled.

I began rolling silverware inside red dinner napkins and stacked them in a wire basket.

"Sorry, I'm expecting a call. I'll turn the ringer down now."

I went and adjusted the lever on the old greasy wall phone. Calamity still had a landline with an extra-long cord that pooled onto the linoleum floor.

"Hot date or something?"

I continued stacking the silverware like I didn't hear him. Sam was getting too friendly.

"What kind of dog is Cali?" I countered, squaring the cowboy hat on my head and carrying the wire basket over to a table.

"The vet said she's part Cocker Spaniel and Golden Retriever. I found her wandering on an interstate median where some idiot had dumped her. The poor girl kept searching for her master in every passing car, and she cowered if drivers laid on their horns when she tried to cross the road."

Sam scraped the bowl with his spoon and polished off the last of the whipped cream.

After the place settings were distributed, I turned and saw his familiar black Stetson with a silver buckle on the hatband hanging on a hook underneath the counter. When the café was full of customers, ratty ball caps and purses usually hung there, not fancy Stetsons.

"Gut wrenching, all right," he continued. "I pulled onto the berm and grabbed some nylon cord I keep in the bed of my truck, thinking I could lasso it over her head like a makeshift leash, but I didn't have to use it. When I approached, she practically leapt into my arms, so I carried her across the Interstate and put her in the cab. I fed her a couple of cookies I just happened to have in the glove box and covered her with an old army blanket I keep for emergencies. She curled up on the passenger's seat and quivered until she fell asleep."

"You're a hero, Sam," I said.

"Nah, nothing like that. I just did what any animal lover would do. Cali had a bad scare and needed a bath, but otherwise checked out okay. I figured she was about seven or eight months old and had been living with some asshole. She's one smart, big-hearted animal, that's all I know, and a damn good watchdog. In five years, she's spooked deer, a rabid fox, and a bear or two. She's fearless, just like her namesake there," Sam said, staring at the life-sized mural of Calamity Jane on the wall behind the counter. "Marthy was a real sharp-shooter. Her real name was Marthy Canary, you know. She had just turned 51 when she died, but looked a hell of a lot older. A lifetime of drinking and carousing finally caught up with her."

"Poor Cali's lucky to be alive," I said, looking at the golden dog sleeping peacefully on the sunroom floor.

I hoped Ashley was lucky, too. When a young girl suddenly disappears, I always think the worst. Rape, murder, or both. I tried to keep from imagining a grisly crime scene, but I failed. She'd only been missing for about twelve hours. What could possibly go wrong?

3

CALI

When a shiny police cruiser pulled into the café's parking lot, I was jolted back to reality. Somebody must have reported Ashley missing, or Joy was in trouble. Again.

"How come you know so much about Calamity Jane?" I asked quickly, trying to distract Sam.

"For an old codger, you mean?"

He was playing martyr, and I knew it.

"No, that's not what I meant at all, Sam. I'm just curious."

"The wild west is a hobby of mine. Since law school."

I tried to imagine Sam swaggering into a courtroom, tipping his Stetson at the jury before he held it over his heart for effect when he began his closing remarks.

"Think, Pilgrims. Remember what it felt like to be young and carefree? When a childish prank was just that. A prank. Not a felony."

I slipped two laminated menus between the nearest metal rack that held salt and pepper shakers and squeeze bottles of mustard and catsup. I could hear running water and the clatter and clang of dishes being hand washed by Josh in the kitchen.

I stared for a second at the shiny new Rolex strapped on

Sam's wrist. I'd seen pictures of them in slick magazines with huge price tags. Maybe he really was filthy rich. A lot of well-to-do people lived in Naples, but not many of them came to the diner. The Mercedes and BMWs were always parked in front of fancy restaurants.

"Did you know Marthy wrote a book before she died?" Sam asked.

"I'd like to write one someday," I said softly. The words spilled out before I could stop them.

"Listen, you've got plenty of time to write a cookbook and eat dessert every day. No man wants to marry a skinny super-model—just ogle them, that's all. My wife never watched her weight, and she was beautiful. If Lydia were alive, she'd let me buy her a big slice of that fluffy lemon meringue that's calling my name. If she'd known she would die in her sleep before her first grandchild was born, she might have done a lot of things differently."

"I'm sorry about your wife."

I couldn't bear the sadness in his eyes. I wished he'd imitate John Wayne or even flirt with me again. Anything but this.

"Aneurism—no fucking warning," he muttered under his breath before taking the last bite of his coconut cream. "She died a year ago on the Fourth of July, but it seems like yesterday."

A policeman pulled into Calamity's parking lot and stopped beside the front entrance. Two other cruisers suddenly appeared. The first officer must have called for back-up.

I wondered if Marthy had to buy her boots and jeans on time, raise her half- brother, pay rent, buy food, and take out loans to pay off credit cards.

"Now don't take this the wrong way, but you seem a mite older than 21, Twyla."

"It must be all that drinking and carousing. It ages a woman, right?"

"You just don't act 21, that's all. You're an old soul, and that's a compliment."

"So, how's the condo-sitting going?" I asked, changing the subject.

I stared at the cruisers with their dark tinted windows and made a mental note to exercise, get more sleep, and splurge on some expensive multivitamins with iron at the health food store when I got paid. I didn't want to be an old soul.

The other officers got out of their cruisers and walked over to the first one on scene. He lowered his window, and they talked for a few minutes.

Two of the officers left, and one wearing mirrored sunglasses and holding a folder got out of his cruiser and touched the radio on his shoulder. He said something into it, and then put his hat on and walked around the corner until he disappeared from sight.

"Tell me about your cabin, Sam," I said in a rush.

"You feeling okay there, Twy?"

"I'm fine. It's a stupid caffeine headache, but I'm feeling better. Tell me more about your place."

"Well, if you insist," Sam said, sitting straighter and clearing his throat. "The elevation's over 3,000 feet on top of Glass Mountain. It kisses the night stars, and the woods are thick with mountain laurel, pine trees, and white-tailed deer. It's my log palace with a billion-dollar view. Lydia and I lived there year-round after I retired ten years ago. Sunrises and sunsets to *live* for. A painter would never lack for inspiration."

I remembered another Palace. It was the name of a community theater where I watched my high school teacher, Alexandra, direct a play. Sam's palace, though, began to frame up around me, log by log, in slow motion. I imagined him sitting on the porch with his wife, drinking a beer, and staring at the Milky Way with Cali curled at his feet. When the officer reappeared and walked to his cruiser, the logs came crashing down.

"Why is it called Glass Mountain?"

"We get lots of ice storms, so that's part of it. The house site was cleared years ago, and it's pretty bald except for a pin oak and some scrub pines. The road gets slicker than glass in the winter. Sometimes no one goes up or down my mountain for weeks. My buddy Caleb looks after the place when I'm gone. He's a good ole boy, but set in his ways and a mite superstitious. Well, maybe more than a mite. He's been to hell and back, so nobody really cares how he acts anymore. He just loves living in the mountains—being close to the sky."

"How do you get to your cabin?" I asked.

"My truck has four-wheel drive, so I haul firewood, ford streams, and wrangle that goat farm of a road that leads to my place."

"You're kidding, right?"

"Dead serious. I lay in supplies every winter and rely on Caleb if I have to leave the mountain. I've got a generator, tins full of candy, canned goods, and a stocked wine cellar, plus plenty of whiskey, beer, and bottled water. I don't touch that cistern water, though—found too many dead rats and snakes floating in it over the years. You know what a cistern is? Rainwater corralled in a big holding tank," he said, answering his own question. "I put bleach in it every few weeks when I'm there, but algae can build up fast. We use it for flushing the toilet, watering flowers, or washing off my truck. The road to my cabin is too steep to haul a tanker full of water up there, and digging a well is out of the question on top of Glass Mountain."

"Don't you ever get lonely?" I asked.

"You're sure full of questions today, Twyla. I haven't been to Glass Mountain since Lydia died last year, so my son, Robert, kept me busy by house-sitting his condo in Naples this summer. He and his wife have a nanny for my grandson, Blake, and they take him everywhere. He's a real good-natured baby with big blue eyes. Blake was a year old in July. When he gets older, I want to take him to the cabin and go squirrel hunting. I'll tell him all about his grandmother, too."

"Sorry, Sam," I said.

"Lydia left a gaping crater in my heart, but I've still got Cali to keep me company. She's all I need right now. And a Colt 45, but I've never had to use it. Keep it loaded, though, and I've got a drawer full of extra bullets."

"So, you're a survivalist with a sweet tooth," I said slowly as I kept my eyes peeled on the officer. Sam's eyes widened as he mulled my words over for a second.

"Cell service is pretty spotty on top of Glass. You don't see people praying to their infernal cell phones and shouting out their dirty laundry in public."

"Here, let me freshen your coffee," I said, reaching for the carafe.

My hand trembled as I refilled his cup, and a few drops splattered on the counter. I smeared them away with my thumb. I caught Josh's eye, and he flashed that shy smile of his at me through the window where I placed my orders. He looked cute standing there with his white butcher apron on. His face was a bright shade of pink from rinsing the breakfast dishes with boiling water. He wanted to take me to the movies this weekend, but I had put him off. I nodded toward the policeman standing beside his cruiser.

"We'll probably have to answer some questions," I whispered. "Maybe we could talk on the sun porch. If a customer comes in, I'll wait on them, and then you could stay with the cop."

"How's your old teacher friend doing?" Sam asked. "Are you going to her place tonight?"

"Remember, my shift ends early on Mondays and Tuesdays."

"Is Ashley in the kitchen? I just wanted to say hello. I saw her bike out front and figured she must be helping Josh," Sam said.

"No, Louise will work the lunch shift today," I said, trying to stay calm.

Sam looked at me and narrowed his eyes.

"Ashley's a good kid. Kind of like you, only prettier. It's her blue eyes and long blonde hair," Sam said, in his now annoying John Wayne twang.

"I've heard that before," I muttered as I rolled my eyes.

"Just kidding, Twy. You *know* I am."

4

CHASE

The policeman leaned over and studied the blacktop like he had lost a contact lens. His sunglasses reflected the blinding sun when he stood in front of Ashley's bike for a minute—it was still padlocked to the rack. He took photos of it with his cell phone, jotted something down in his folder, and then entered Calamity.

When he walked over to the counter, I stared at two tired faces in his mirrored sunglasses. They were mine.

"What can I get for you, officer?"

"I'm Officer Lancing, ma'am. I need to talk to Twyla Townsend and Josh Patton for a minute," he said, glancing at his notepad. "Do you know them?"

Maybe he found out more about Ashley or Joy was in jail. I didn't have enough money to bail her out, let alone pay my water bill this month.

"I'm Twyla Townsend. Josh is in the kitchen," I said, trying not to stutter. "Why don't you take a seat in the sunroom, officer? I'll get Josh and bring you a glass of iced tea. It's getting really hot out, isn't it?"

"Sure is. I could use a cold drink. Thanks," he said, turning to face the sunroom before he took off his hat and headed toward Cali. She never knew a stranger and stood up immediately and wagged her tail. The officer scratched her head until she closed her sleepy eyes.

Sam soaked it all in, and I knew his mind was spinning with questions.

"We'll just be a minute, Sam," I told him, slipping a slice of lemon onto the lip of the glass of iced tea.

I handed it to the officer, and we sat at a table in the sunroom. He looked too young to be a policeman.

"Thank you, ma'am," he said. I tried to steel myself for bad news.

Cali lay at my feet and rested her head on my boot. Josh hurried over and dried his hands on his apron before he sat down.

"Did you find Ashley?" I blurted out.

"Not yet, but I'm sure she'll turn up. Are you close friends?"

"Just co-workers, but everyone looks out for her. She just turned 18."

"How long have you known her?"

"About two months. I haven't worked here very long."

"I've known her for over a year," Josh volunteered.

"Ashley's mother gave me this photo, and we're intensifying our search," the officer said, sliding a 5x7 of her senior picture from his folder.

I had seen her photo posted beside mine and Josh's on the employee bulletin near the cash register, but now her sweet smile and baby blonde hair sent a chill through me. It reminded me of some of the photos I had published in the newspaper last year: teens and people in their early 20s who had injected a fatal shot of heroin. If their obits didn't say they had died from meth or opioids or heroin laced with fentanyl, their young faces on the same page as grandmothers and great-grandfathers were giveaways.

"Tell me about Ashley. What she does, where she goes, who her friends are?"

We told him everything we knew in less than 10 minutes. Josh had more information than me, so I didn't help much.

"Did Ashley deposit the money bag by herself yesterday evening, Josh?"

"Yes, sir. Twyla usually drops it off after we close, but she doesn't work the evening shift on Mondays and Tuesdays, so I do it then. I had just worked a double, and Ashley begged to help out. Since she's eighteen now, I let her deposit it for the first time. She knew the ropes and wanted more responsibility. After she put the deposit bag inside a black plastic bag, she set it in her bike basket. She took off her cowboy boots and put on her pink running shoes. I saw her stuff her boots in her backpack. The bank drop-off is only a half a block away, and it was still light out."

"Did you actually see her unlock her bike and leave the parking lot?" the officer asked.

"Well, no. I was busy securing the doors and turning out the lights. I left by the kitchen door since I parked my truck in the back."

The officer lowered his head and peered over his sunglasses at Josh.

"I didn't pay much attention to Ashley after I locked the front door behind her."

"How much money do you usually deposit each day?"

"On a good day, as much as $1,000, but most of the time it's about $500 or $600," Josh said.

"How much money was in the money bag you gave to Ashley yesterday?"

"Five hundred and fifty dollars. I log the amount each evening into a notebook I keep in the safe. It was an average day's take."

"Ashley never made it to the bank. There's no record of the

deposit," the officer said. "That's why her bike is still in the bike rack."

Josh and I just sat there stunned.

"What did she have on?"

"Her uniform," Josh managed to say after a minute. Just like Twyla's there: red cowboy hat, white jeans, red chaps, and black boots with silver spurs. And her pink backpack. She wears her running shoes when she rides her bike and puts her cowboy boots inside the pack."

The policeman glanced at me and drew a crude stick figure of Ashley and labeled it. He took another drink of his iced tea before he continued.

"I need to take a picture of you in your uniform, Ms. Townsend, in case someone might spot her. Stand beside your chair, please."

I hesitated, and then slowly stood. At least he didn't say *ma'am* again. The double image of my red face reflected in his sunglasses was unnerving. After he snapped several photos, he motioned for me to sit.

"There's no sign of a struggle in the parking lot. Maybe someone she knew gave her a ride. Does Ashley have a cellphone?"

"Yes, but she doesn't bring it to work. Walter, our boss, doesn't allow us to talk or text while we're here. He's old school. He keeps a landline in the kitchen, but I leave my cell in my car and check it on breaks."

"Does she have a boyfriend?"

"Yes, Brad Fetty. He's her high school sweetheart, but he graduated a year before her. He's 19 and lifeguards at the Surfside Pool. I think he works most days from 10 a.m. until dusk," I said.

Josh nodded his head in agreement.

"Any other distinguishing characteristics? A tattoo? Does she have any jewelry or rings?"

"No tattoos that I'm aware of, but she always wears a necklace with a gold heart. Brad gave it to her for her eighteenth birthday," I said.

The officer jotted it down in his notes and drew a necklace around the stick figure's neck. I felt like I was playing a deadly game of Hangman and I had guessed the wrong letter.

"Do you have video surveillance here?" he asked, scanning the perimeter of the ceiling for cameras.

"No, but the auto body shop next door does. They got one after they were robbed last year," Josh said.

"I'll file a missing person's report after 24 hours if Ashley doesn't turn up by then. Maybe sooner. Does she get along with her parents? Any enemies or overly friendly customers that you know of?"

"Ashley never complained about anyone bothering her. She's super close to her mother since her parents separated, so her mother would know," Josh said.

"If she shows up, call me. Here's my number." The officer gave each of us his business card.

"I'll stop by the auto body shop and then drive over to the pool and talk to her boyfriend. Maybe he left work early yesterday, and they eloped and needed the money. It could be something that simple. She's 18, so there's nothing we can do if they got married, but we could arrest them if they stole the money."

When Officer Lancing shook my hand, my elbow bumped his half-filled glass of tea. It crashed to the floor, splintering into jagged pieces. Cali bolted away to Sam's side and hid underneath his barstool. Josh hurried to the kitchen to get a broom and a trash can.

"It's all right, girl," Sam said, craning his head to stare and petting Cali until she stopped shaking.

"I'm so sorry, Officer," I said, picking up the lemon slice and raking the big pieces of glass together into a pile with the toe of my boot.

"It was an accident. Here, let me help you," the officer

offered, mopping the spilled tea on the table with a handful of red napkins.

When the mess was cleared, Josh took the trash can away. I noticed Cali was still trembling underneath Sam's barstool, so I dug a few leftover marshmallows from my pocket, and she came running right over to me like she always did.

Just then, the front door swung open, and my little brother stepped inside, bringing a heat wave along with him. The two palm trees that flanked the entrance were motionless, and the Florida sun flashed off the plate glass door. He held a helium balloon by its string. Ashley's beach bike sat framed in the doorway as the officer put on his hat. Chase just stared at his shiny badge, the handcuffs dangling from his belt, and the gun in his holster. He held the door open until Officer Lancing tipped his hat and exited.

My brother stood under the signed photograph of Buzz Aldrin for a few seconds, bobbed the pink balloon up and down, and scanned the dining room. He pushed his hair out of his eyes as he wrinkled his nose at the smell of kale and salmon cakes. Chase was small for a 10-year-old boy. It seemed like he was a block away from me instead of just a few yards. He shielded his eyes from the sun and then checked the old pay phone for change. He spotted Cali on the sun porch and ran to sit on the floor beside her. The ceiling fan blurred sleepy shafts of sunlight and shadow, and Chase looked like an impression-istic painting: a golden-haired boy with one skinny arm wrapped around a golden dog and the other holding a floating balloon.

Sam motioned for him to come, and patted an empty bar stool.

"Hey, boy, come and sit beside me!" Sam said, giving the stool a healthy spin. "Twyla will rustle you up a plate."

Chase hugged Cali one last time, shuffled toward the counter, and stopped the spinning stool with his free hand.

"Any black bears lurking out there? Twy's got cap guns, you

know! Pow, pow, ker-POW!" Sam said, pointing his finger like an imaginary gun at Chase.

"Just lizards and mosquitoes. Wish we did have some bears," he said.

"Where did you find that balloon?" I asked. "Did you have a party at school?"

"No, I just found it," Chase said.

"Hey, where'd you get a shiner, boy?" Sam asked.

"It's nothin'," Chase mumbled as he turned away from Sam and me.

"Have you been in another fight?" I asked, turning him around so I could look at him. His eye was swollen and a dusky shade of blue had formed under it.

I scooped some crushed ice into a zip-locked bag and handed it to Chase.

"Hold that on your eye to keep the swelling down. Now, tell me what happened?"

"A kid tripped me in the hall, and I punched him. He punched me back," Chase said, gently pressing the ice pack against his eye.

"Did you report him or tell your teacher?"

"Nobody saw it happen, so I left. I socked him pretty good. He won't be bothering me again."

"You're one tough hombre, Chase. Never give those bullies an inch," Sam said, patting his shoulder.

"Don't encourage him. He's in enough trouble already. So, what really happened?"

"I already told you," he said, setting the ice pack on the counter.

"Where did you find that balloon?" I asked again.

"It was tied to Ashley's bike."

My stomach dropped.

"You need to put it back right now," I sputtered. "It's not yours."

Chase frowned, but he obeyed.

He came to the café for a late lunch every day after summer school. In eight short weeks at my new job, Sam had practically adopted him. I watched through the windows as the policeman walked next door to the auto body shop.

When Chase came back inside, he took a salt and pepper shaker out of its metal rack and turned the molded glass over and over until salt dusted his hands and a little fell on the floor.

"How's summer school going? Any cute girls at Lake Park?" Sam asked.

Chase looked down and scuffed the white crystals into the floor.

"Go wash your hands, and I'll have Josh fix you a grilled cheese sandwich and a bowl of tomato soup," I told him.

"Is Joy in trouble, Sis?" Chase asked, watching the officer move toward his cruiser.

He knew all about trouble. Our mother had been arrested a few times for DUIs, bounced checks, and possession of a controlled substance.

"The policeman just had some questions about someone I know, that's all."

"About Joy?" Chase asked.

"No, it didn't have anything to do with her this time, so relax."

He dropped the salt and pepper shakers into their slots and headed for the restroom near the EXIT sign.

"This is all about Ashley, isn't it?" Sam asked. "I couldn't help but overhear you and Josh earlier."

"Yeah, she didn't make it home last night, but I'm sure she'll turn up soon."

I didn't feel like talking, so I was glad Sam kept rattling on.

"Why, when I was Chase's age, I was catching bluegill and skinny dipping all summer long. It's a shame he flunked fourth grade."

"When I was ten, I was taking care of Chase," I said.

Sam squirmed a little and took a sip of his coffee.

"Sorry, Twy, I had no idea. Is there anything I can do to help?"

"He doesn't care much about anything these days," I said, trying to think of an answer to his question.

Chase came over and sat on a barstool. After I examined his hands to see if they were really clean, I lifted the salt and pepper shakers out and wiped them with a soapy dish rag.

"You better throw some salt over your left shoulder. You don't need any more calamities in your life," Sam warned.

"Are you superstitious?"

"A little. I guess I've been around my mountain buddy, Caleb, too long," he said, taking the salt from me and shaking it over his shoulder a couple of times. "There, that should do it. Now, what kind of ice cream do you like, Chase?"

"Oh, no you don't! He won't touch his lunch if he eats ice cream first."

"Are you his mother?"

"Something like that."

I fished the tips out of my shirt pocket to pay for Chase's lunch and counted out five one-dollar bills but stopped when I came to the last one—a new hundred-dollar bill. I held it up to the light and saw something had been written on it. Then I turned it over and read these words: *I've got your back.*

After carefully folding it in half, I slipped it into my jeans pocket. *Finders, keepers.*

5

KRISPY KREME

"Shit!" I released the lever and jerked the nozzle from the tank. Gasoline gushed over my hand and down the side of my ancient VW Super Beetle.

A man wearing a Dolphins' ball cap in the next bay over grabbed a wad of paper towels from a dispenser and handed them to me after I slammed the nozzle into its station. I reeked since my jeans and cowboy boots were drenched. At least I had tossed my holster and cowboy hat on the back seat before fueling up.

The guy watched me try to wipe the oil stains from my white jeans and chaps with the paper towels, and then his eyes fixed on my silver spurs.

"Anything I can do to help?" he asked, as his eyes slowly found my face.

"I only pre-paid for 4 gallons," I mumbled, sweating more from the sudden scare than the heat. The smell of gasoline was overpowering.

"Something must be wrong with the shut-off valve, sugar. I'm heading inside, so I'll tell the cashier what happened. At least you got a full tank of gas out of the deal. I'll make up the difference if he doesn't take my word."

"Thanks, I owe you."

I rubbed at the spots on my gasoline-soaked boots and then tossed the oily paper towels into the bin. I grabbed another towel from the dispenser and tried to dry my hands before I reached into my pocket to see if the hundred-dollar bill was still there.

When the man returned to his car, I had taken off my boots and socks and set them on the floor mat. He watched as I slipped my bare feet into a pair of pink flip-flops.

"Thanks again," I said. "I really appreciate your help."

"I noticed your fancy cowboy boots. If you don't mind me asking, how long have you been stripping at The Carousel?"

"Go to hell."

I got in and started the engine, hoping it didn't spark a fire from the gasoline slick that had formed under the car. As I peeled out of the gas station, I hoped the man choked on the cloud of black smoke I left behind.

"Asshole."

Fury masked my fatigue, and it sped me over the highway toward my apartment. I rolled the window down and blasted the air conditioner on high. The gas fumes from my saturated boots started getting to me before I reached the first stoplight.

It had been a long, rough day at Calamity. My feet didn't ache from dancing at a damn strip club, but from never finding any time to sit down. Senior citizens got their 15 percent discount every *All-You-Can-Eat Italian Monday,* starting at 2:00 in the afternoon until closing at 8:00. I usually missed most of the excitement since I only worked until 3:00 p.m. on Mondays and Tuesdays, but I had to stay three hours over today until they got someone to cover Ashley's shift. My back hurt; my feet throbbed. And now my boots were stinking up the car.

Like always, the seniors had crowded into the restaurant right on time, waving their neatly cut coupons at me. Most of them were really sweet, like Sam, but some found fault with everything. The coffee—too hot or not hot enough. Their tables—too close to the front door or the kitchen. They needed more spaghetti or lasagna or manicotti, parmesan cheese or catsup, or salad and garlic bread sticks. Even though the sign on the buffet read *No Take Home*, they usually filled their plates one more time after they'd already stuffed themselves and then asked for a doggie bag. I knew they lived on fixed incomes, and I understood poverty all too well, so I always let it slide. I'll probably do the same thing when I'm their age.

When I brought the checks, a few seniors pushed their reading glasses lower on their noses and studied the bill like cranky accountants. They always asked if I remembered to take their 15 percent off, so I learned to highlight the discount with a yellow marker. I'd usually find two or three quarters slipped under a plate for all my trouble. At least they didn't leave pennies. I kept the tips in an empty coffee can in the trunk of my car for emergencies. Every time I made a hard turn, I could hear the reassuring rattle of coins inside the tin can. I told Chase I had a pair of tire chains in there just in case we'd have a snowstorm. In Florida. He believed me.

I pulled in front of Ocean View and spotted the lights on in my apartment on the tenth. Hurrying inside while carrying my boots, I caught the elevator just before the doors closed and held the button down so it wouldn't stop on each floor as it slowly creaked its way up. Three loud knocks on my apartment door let Chase know it was me before I unlocked it.

"I'm home!" I yelled, as I opened the bi-fold doors of my laundry closet.

I removed the spurs from my boots and rubbed the stains with a dry rag, but it didn't help. After stripping off my clothes and taking the hundred-dollar bill from my jeans pocket, I put it on top of the dryer. I shoved everything into the washing machine, poured in two capfuls of detergent, and let the cold water fill the tub before turning it off and closing the lid. Maybe soaking things overnight would help the stains come out. I washed my hands with liquid soap and added some baking soda to make a thick paste like I did for Chase's dirty hands, dragging my fingernails through the grit to try to dull the gasoline smell. I dusted myself with baby powder and put on a clean pair of shorts and a t-shirt, and then I picked up the bill and read it again.

"At least somebody's got my back," I whispered.

Chase sat on the living room floor in front of the blaring TV with every light on in the apartment. He wore baggy sweat-pants, one of my plus-sized t-shirts from the Dollar General Store I liked to sleep in, and a pair of tube socks. A couple of old blankets were spread end-to-end in front of him as he inhaled a bowl of microwave popcorn. He liked to get a running start and slide in from the kitchen to an imaginary first base in the living room, so he wore my sweatpants and pulled the drawstring tight. He looked like a child clown with one black eye. All he needed now was a goofy top hat, gigantic shoes, and a shiny red nose.

"You're late." He kept eating the popcorn and didn't take his eyes off the TV. His flashlight rested in his lap.

"Sorry, I had to work over." I grabbed the remote and turned down the volume.

"Oh, yeah. All-you-can-eat day. Did you bring me some?"

"I've got boxes of mac and cheese in the freezer. You know how to use the microwave."

"Can I cook two?"

"Sure. Is your homework done yet?"

"I'm going to do it right after this show goes off."

"Keep the volume down or you'll get us evicted. I'm lucky to get this efficiency in senior housing, so don't blow it."

"The lady next door is deaf," Chase whined, sucking salt from his fingers.

"Just do as I say. Lock the door when I go, and don't let anyone in. Leave your homework on the kitchen table. I'll check it later tonight. When Joy comes to take you home, be sure and lock the door behind you."

"What if it's her boyfriend, Randy?"

He looked at me with those sad blue eyes, and I hated myself. Again.

"He's a stranger, so *don't* open the door."

"What's that weird smell?"

"Baby powder. Listen, I'll bring you some donuts tomorrow at Calamity— Krispy Kremes—if you do all your homework," I promised, carrying my boots. He followed me and locked the door. I waited a second and knocked three times—our secret code.

"I love you, too, Sis," Chase whispered from the other side of the door.

"Call or text me on your Tracfone if you need me, and remember, don't open the door for anyone."

"Even Joy?"

"You know what I mean. Keep the volume way down on the TV, and always look through the peephole first."

"Okay."

"I'll be back, Chase. I always come back."

My eyes began to tear as I waited on the elevator and got in when the doors slid open. When it reached the ground floor, I went outside and set my boots beside the stoop under a low hedge to air out overnight. My flip-flops slapped against my heels as I headed toward the car. I needed to see Alexandra one last time and wouldn't get another chance. I'd call and check on Chase in an hour. Maybe a half an hour.

Even with all the windows down now and my boots gone, the VW still reeked of gasoline, so I dragged the floor mat out, slung it like a rubber stingray, and watched it skid to a stop under the hedge. I hoped the other tenants wouldn't notice and report me. I glanced up at my windows on the tenth floor of Ocean View that didn't even have a filtered ocean view. False advertising, but who cares? The price was right.

I unlocked the glove compartment to see if my one-shot derringer was still loaded and wrapped in one of my red bandannas. It was. It held three bullets, but I always just inserted two and left the first chamber empty. I didn't want to shoot a friend by mistake. I usually kept the gun in my purse or the apartment, but at work or when I knew I'd be out at night, like tonight, I kept it in my car.

I glanced at *F* for full on my gas gauge. This wasn't my plan. Even if it was free gasoline, it didn't make me happy. They might send the cops after me for the unpaid balance anyway. My mysterious big tip didn't make me happy either, but I definitely planned on keeping it. On the way to the Hi-Life Liquor store, I thought about how a half tank of gas kept me honest. It stopped me from running five separate errands instead of one.

I parked, popped the trunk, walked to the front of my VW, and counted out enough change from the coffee can. I dropped the hundred-dollar bill on top of the remaining silver quarters and dimes and nickels, and snapped the plastic lid shut.

"Robbing your piggy bank again?" the clerk asked as she counted the coins. "I need to see your license, sweetie."

"I've been coming in here every Monday for months, Nancy," I said, reading her name tag. I had a death grip on the bottle of whiskey like she might try to steal it from me.

"You know I have to see your driver's license or I'd lose my job."

"Whatever," I muttered, taking it out of my wallet and looking at the clock over the counter.

At seven o'clock, I parked in front of Alexandra's house. When I turned off the ignition, the engine chugged backward, rocking and shimmying for a few seconds until it went dead. A plume of black smoke drifted over the top of the car, and I felt myself giving in. A wave of pent up emotion surged through me. I needed to ask Josh if he would look at my car and change the oil. I knew I'd have to return the favor and go to the movies with him, but it was worth it.

I thought of Ashley's bike with the pink balloon, and Chase all alone in my apartment. He was afraid of the dark, so I always let him leave the lights on when I was gone and kept him supplied with fresh batteries for his flashlight. I don't remember being afraid of anything when I was a kid. No time to be afraid. Sometimes when I think about it, I don't know which of us had it worse growing up. Chase or me.

6

SUMMER 2011

TWYLA & CHASE

The power went out again last night. So when it got too hot inside, I followed the smell of Joy's cigarettes and went outside on the side porch with her. "It's our 'crow's nest,'" she always said. "Our secret look-out on the high seas." It was just big enough for the two of us to lie on the floor and stare up at the stars.

Chase found me there the next morning after Joy had taken off again. His pajama top was missing, and he was sucking his thumb and rubbing the top of his nose with his pointer finger. He'd been eating a Reese's Cup that Joy must have hidden somewhere in her room. His hands were covered in chocolate and peanut butter, and he had a funny milk-chocolate mustache. I told him to lie down, and he put his head on Joy's pillow. Peering through a narrow gap between the porch floor and a slatted half wall, I watched headlights spark and flicker as cars sailed down our street toward town, listening to the swooshing waterfall sounds they made. "White noise," Joy called it.

After Chase fell asleep, I wanted to turn over without waking him, but his skinny arm squeezed me tighter. His hair felt like a scrub brush against my cheek, so I tried again and slowly lifted his *arm off of me. Joy shaved his head in hopes he wouldn't get lice again, and she kept mine so tightly braided my head ached.*

After a few minutes, he woke up crying for Joy, and I had trouble making him stop. I was getting better at it, but I wasn't his mother. I led him to the bathroom where his pajama top lay in the middle of the floor. We went downstairs, and I found a can of Pepsi behind a six-pack of beer and poured the soda into two small mugs. When it stopped fizzing, we sipped it through paper straws so it would last longer. I spotted some money Joy had left under an ashtray on the coffee table. I knew what I needed to do.

After I washed the chocolate from Chase's face and hands, I dressed him in a clean shirt and pair of shorts. He kicked his feet when I tried to put on his shoes, so I gave up and we walked outside. He held my hand, and we headed toward the grocery. Chase only made it about two blocks before I had to carry him piggyback the rest of the way. Inside the store, I helped him into a shopping cart. He already knew how to climb into the baby seat.

He loved going shopping with me and happily swung his bare feet. I was all sweaty, so the air conditioning felt good. I took my time walking up and down the aisles with five dollars in my pocket. We stopped by the deli for free samples of cheese on tooth-picks, and the bakery had tiny samples of powdered donuts. Chase wanted to buy Fruit Loops, but I knew I didn't have enough money. I handed him a small bunch of bananas to hold on his lap and put a dozen eggs, a box of dry milk, a jar of peanut butter, and a loaf of day-old bread into the cart. Promised him if he was good, he could eat one of the bananas on the way home. I didn't have enough money, but the nice cashier said it was close enough, so I wheeled our cart through the automatic doors.

Chase ate the top half of the banana, and then I crisscrossed the strips of peel around the rest. I'd let him eat it when I returned the cart. We stopped on our way home by the Freewill Baptist church that had big red doors. They gave out free lunches and cartons of cold milk to kids in the summer.

"Two boxes, please, one for Chase and one for me."

A blue-haired lady with sparkly earrings smiled and slipped three boxes inside a big plastic bag.

"Thank you, ma'am."

"You're welcome," she answered, staring at Chase's dirty feet. "How old are you, sweetheart?"

"Ten. Chase will be three next month," I said.

"You know, you ought to put some shoes on that baby. He might step on broken glass or get stung by a bumblebee."

"He won't wear his shoes. They're too small for him anyway, but Joy says she's going to buy him a new pair real soon."

He raised his arms for me to pick him up. He wouldn't look at the blue lady and started sucking his thumb and stroking his nose.

"He's almost as big as you! Here, let me help."

Chase squeezed me tighter and turned away from her.

"He's afraid of strangers. And, the dark."

"Most children are," she said. "I was afraid of the dark when I was a little girl."

"I'm not afraid of anything," I told her.

"I'd love to meet your mother and father sometime. And Joy, too. Have them bring you to Bible School next Monday. Lots of Kool-Aid, hot dogs, popsicles, and crafts. We might make crucifixes with popsicle sticks. And free Bibles. Would you like to own your very own Bible?"

I wasn't sure what a crucifix was, but if it was made of popsicle sticks, it must be something fun to make. And a free Bible sounded good, too. My friend Amanda had one with her name printed in gold on the cover, so I nodded my head yes.

The lady scratched her thigh, and I wondered if she had a patch of poison ivy like I did last summer.

"Have you and your brother been baptized?"

"What's that mean?"

"Oh, mercy, child! It's when all your sins are washed away and you are saved by Jesus. You want to be saved, don't you?"

Chase patted my cheek and gently turned my face toward his.

"I wanna go home," he whispered.

"I have to leave now," I said, putting Chase on the ground.

"Come to Bible School. It's so much fun. Tell me your names, honey, and we'll be sure and save a place for you."

"I'm Twyla and this is my baby brother, Chase."

He hugged my legs and looked up at me.

"Home," he said, popping his thumb into his mouth.

"It's his nap time," I explained.

The lady smiled an understanding smile and followed us down the steps.

"You'll have to walk the rest of the way," I told him, taking the big plastic bag with the three lunches from the lady who scratched her neck now. When we reached the corner, she was still standing there, so I waved.

When we got home, the power was still out, but I put the eggs in the fridge anyway and set the rest of the stuff on the kitchen table. I left the front door open and raised some windows, but it didn't help much. I took Chase to the crow's nest and sang to him, but he didn't want to take a nap. We played Hide & Seek instead and colored in his coloring book until he got thirsty. I took one of the three cartons of milk from the bag, and he drank it while I read a couple of story books to him I had gotten at the library. He liked Clifford the Big Red Dog the best. I gave him a bath, and the water turned a muddy shade of brown. We ate our boxed lunches of bologna and cheese sandwiches, an apple, potato chips, and drank the last two cartons of milk. I ate Chase's leftovers and put the third box in the fridge for my friend, Amanda. I hoped the power would come on soon.

When it got dark, Chase started crying. I switched on the flashlight I kept under the sofa bed and gave it to him. He stopped crying like magic. He liked to hold the flashlight and dance the beam across the ceiling. I carried our pillows to the crow's nest, and we lay down, listening to the shushing noise of the waterfall traffic and staring up at the North Star until he fell asleep.

I wished I could follow that star. I wondered if Amanda could see it from her house.

7

ALEXANDRA

The price of admission was Jack Daniel's. When I first arrived at Alexandra's house six months ago with a nice, but cheap, bottle of wine, she wouldn't even open it. Much less keep it. Now I always bring a fifth of the good stuff.

A quick check to see if anyone was following me, and then I got out of the car. Three concrete steps led me to her porch, and I rang the doorbell. A mosquito landed on my arm, and I smashed it flat. A spot of somebody else's blood remained, and I smeared it away. It felt extra muggy outside, even for Florida, and I waited patiently while Tristan barked like buckshot and Alexandra slowly opened the storm door.

"All bark," she reassured me every Monday about her Pomeranian, who looked like a stubby red fox. "Come IN!"

Alexandra was 75 and Greek. She'd never been an Alex or an Allie in her life. Although petite and thin, her noble presence commanded attention. Even now, after a minor stroke, as if any stroke can be minor, her dark eyes flashed with wit and intelligence. She didn't believe in retiring, but time had finally won out, and she quit teaching five years ago when she turned 70. After picking up a now quiet Tristan, she led me into her cozy living room.

"Merlot?" she asked.

I nodded, knowing this might be our last communion—I tried not to think about it.

"Have you been siphoning gas and powdering a baby's bottom?" Alexandra asked, sniffing the air.

"There was a faulty shut-off valve on my gasoline pump. I tried to clean up before I came."

"Sorry about that, Twyla." She disappeared down her carpeted hallway with Tristan tucked under one arm.

Settling on the couch, I took out my phone, slid off my flip-flops, and tucked my feet under me—working late had done me in. Alexandra hated cell phones, but I had to be available if Chase needed me and made a mental note to call him at 7:30. I glanced around the small room: woodcuts, old books and new filled the bookshelves, and small serpentine elephants from Zimbabwe grazed on the mantel. I stared at a pen and ink drawing on the far wall. I always stared at it. It was a drawing of Alexandra when she was about thirteen, a *regal* thirteen. She looked like a young Greek Joan of Arc. Alexandra told me once she had been cast as St. Joan when she was in high school. *Typecasting*, I thought: *intense, fearless, and ready to fight to the death for a higher cause.* If only I were a time traveler and witness to her performance.

When Alexandra returned, she held a glass of wine and a shot glass filled with old #7.

"Why do I feel like a criminal when I hand my second favorite student a drink?"

"It's okay. I'm 21 now," I said.

"But you still look young."

"Sam doesn't think so."

"Who?" she asked.

"He's a regular at Calamity."

Alexandra stared at my flip-flops on the floor beside the couch.

"I told you it's not safe to drive a car, especially a stick shift with sandals on."

"Flip-flops," I corrected her. "I do it all the time."

"You'd be better off to drive barefoot, but you know that already."

"At least I don't ride a horse wearing flip-flops like my friend Stella does."

"Are you planning on trading your VW in on a pony?" she asked.

"Only if I can wear my pink flip-flops."

"So, are you working on your novel, Twyla?"

Alexandra switched on the milk-glass lamp with a large brass key. The globe was etched with delicate pink roses and the base was gray marble.

"You're one of the characters—a serial killer," I teased.

"I'd escape in the first chapter. When are you going to finish it?"

"As soon as I save some money."

"You don't need money to write, child. Just inspiration."

"But money buys me time," I said.

"What chapter are you on?"

"Maybe ten or eleven. I haven't been paying much attention."

"You're lying." She leaned in really close to study my eyes. So close that I could smell the musk of old cigarette smoke locked in her hair. "Your pupils are dilated. You haven't started writing it yet, have you?"

"I, well, I have an outline," I mumbled.

"Nobody can fool me. Not even you."

"I think I see Diana's headlights," I said, changing the subject.

Alexandra moved toward the picture window and parted the curtain. For a second, she looked strong and vibrant, like the first time I saw her directing a play at the community theater. She chain-smoked unfiltered cigarettes as she gave stage directions to three actors who scribbled every word down in their scripts. The theater was a crumbling former movie house, called The Palace next to an alley and across the street from a bread factory.

I went there after work one evening and watched from the last row. One of the new reporters from the newspaper had a part in the play and had invited me to a rehearsal. When Alexandra's gravelly voice filled the theater, every word seemed important. Just like they did in her English class.

Diana tapped on the front door, and Alexandra ushered Diana into the living room. They laughed together at yapping Tristan, who appeared as if on cue.

"Sorry, I'm late. I had an emergency at the hospital. You don't want to know about it. Believe me."

"Chablis?" Alexandra asked as she scooped Tristan into her arms.

"Yes, please." Diana sighed as she dropped into the nearest chair. "I'm *so* tired."

"Me, too." I leaned my head against the couch and stared at the ceiling.

"This is our *last* time, isn't it?" Diana whispered, almost to herself.

Alexandra was moving next week to live with her son in Hawaii. She couldn't drive anymore and didn't feel safe living alone.

"I still can't believe she's really leaving," I said, trying to memorize each object in the room.

"I know," Diana said.

"We promised we wouldn't be sad, but I'm not any good at goodbyes."

"Who is?" Diana asked.

We sat unmoving until Diana's cell phone broke the silence with a piercing rendition of "Ode to Joy." I flinched when I heard it; my mother had that same annoying ringtone. Diana let it go to voicemail and set her phone on mute.

"I'm officially off duty now. So, what are you reading these days, Twyla?" I glanced at my watch. It was 7:20.

"Well, I finally finished *Cold Mountain*, and I just checked out *Running to the Mountain* from the library. I'm a slow reader."

"Maybe you should go to the…"

"Mountains for a few days," I said, finishing her sentence. "Maybe I should."

8

GAMES

Alexandra placed a brimming glass of wine into Diana's outstretched hand. She was a doctor—the first Black female doctor in Naples. She went to med school after her son graduated from high school. And now, at 44, she was a respected internist.

Alexandra sat across from us and took a long drink. Playing hostess had taken its toll. She looked tired and much older than she had last Monday.

"So, how did it go today, Twyla?" she asked.

"Pretty busy. I got a big tip this morning. A hundred dollars."

"Who from?" she asked.

"Some lady. She didn't stay very long, but she must have been happy with the service. I never got tips at the newspaper."

After high school, I worked weekends at *The Florida Sentinel*. I answered the phone in Circulation, made sure people got their papers, took complaints, and talked people into subscribing. My boss liked me, so after a month I got promoted to writing obituaries part time.

"Do you ever see anybody from the paper at the café?" Diana asked.

Alexandra lit an unfiltered cigarette and switched on her portable air purifier.

"Yeah, it's strange. They think I got fired, because they stop talking before I take their order. I don't try to explain—just smile and make conversation. They play along because beer and Buffalo wings with a side order of ranch dressing are the only things really on their minds."

"Alexandra, do you care if I refresh our drinks? I knew you wouldn't," Diana cooed.

"I need to call Chase. I'll be right back," I said in a rush.

I went outside and sat on the porch steps. The phone rang four times before he answered.

"What took you so long?"

"I was in the bathroom. I tried to hurry," he said.

"Turn the TV down!"

"Oh, I forgot. Hold on," and in a second it was quiet.

"Have you started your homework yet?" I asked.

"Did you buy me Krispy-Kreme donuts?"

"Don't answer my question with a question, Chase."

"I'm almost done. I just have to study my spelling words."

"Okay, call me if you need me. I'll stop by the *7-Eleven* on my way home," I told him.

"Cream filled?"

"Maybe. If they have any left. Remember, don't open the door to strangers," I said.

"I'm ten years old, Twyla. Stop reminding me," Chase whined.

When I came inside, I watched Alexandra finish her cigarette and snuff it out in an ashtray. Nobody had ashtrays anymore. I could hear Diana in the kitchen as we sat in calculated silence, trying to decide who should speak or ask the first question. It was part of the game.

"What play, of all the plays, is most like your life?" I finally asked.

"What? Oh, that's a tough one. Let me think. What about you?" Alexandra stalled.

"I asked you first."

Alexandra peered at me over her drink. She was used to my questions.

She leaned in closer. "King Lear," she said, staring at me with unblinking eyes.

"Are you the king?"

"I am," she said, "because I'm..."

"*Blind to the love of one and betrayed by two*." I said, finishing her quote.

"You've cut to the bone again." Alexandra smiled her Cheshire-cat smile. "You must write one true sentence. Write the..."

"Truest sentence you know," I echoed. "Ernest Hemingway."

"No wonder you were my favorite student in high school, Twyla."

It was a game Alexandra and I liked to play. We tried to capture a life in one sentence.

Decades ago, after she had moved to New York, she discovered a homeless man sleeping in a cardboard box near The Plaza Hotel: *He lost his soul in Vietnam,* she told me. Later, she watched an aspiring actress at a restaurant wait on her customers like she was a Broadway diva: *Her cartoon life became a play within a play.*

Alexandra invented the game, but I liked the challenge when I wrote obits for the newspaper. How do you crystallize a life into one long paragraph? And then into one sentence? It was easier than I thought.

Diana returned with two bottles, and I covered the top of my wine glass with my hand.

"You said I was your favorite student!" Diana said, pretending to be hurt.

"You were my *first* favorite," Alexandra said, "but Twyla was my second."

"So, what did I miss?"

"Alexandra says the play *King Lear* is most like her life," I said.

"How in the world did you get to that? I was only gone for a few minutes."

"Long live the King." I raised my half-filled glass.

"Wait!" Diana rushed to the kitchen and returned with a full wine glass.

"To the King," she chanted, and we chimed our glasses together.

We were an odd trio of women. Each separated by ethnicity, creed, and age. Who would ever think a 75-year-old Greek-American, a 44-year-old African-American, and a 21-year-old Florida girl of unknown origins would become fast friends? All together, we were a daunting 140 years old.

"So, what play are you, Diana?" I asked.

"Let the games begin," Alexandra challenged in her husky voice, eternally hoarse from a lifetime of smoking. "You're up next, Twyla."

I smiled and stole a quick glance at my cell phone. No messages.

"Mine has to be the Tennessee Williams play we studied in your class. *The Glass Menagerie.* I never identified with Laura because she felt so pitiful, so Emily Dickinson. I mean, how could anyone mistake the word *pleurosis* for blue roses? But I thought it was cool that the photo of the absent father became part of the cast. I loved Amanda's line, '...I fell in love with long distance.' Okay, enough about me; it's your turn, Diana."

"Let me think. I've always loved *Our Town*. Not that it was anything like my life, but maybe because it portrayed what I imagined a normal life *should* be. I wanted to play Emily in high school, but I didn't have a chance. A black Emily would have brought the Klan out for sure. But yeah, *Our Town*. It gets to me every time. Maybe I'm the real Emily."

Time flew by after that. I left early and didn't even say a final goodbye to Alexandra. She knew I wouldn't leave Chase alone in my apartment for very long, so she understood. And sometimes that word *goodbye* means forever, and I wasn't ready for forever.

Driving home in the dark, headlights seeking the promise of intersections and more roads ahead, I kept thinking about our conversation. We always managed to talk about something important on Monday, but I didn't mention that Ashley went missing, not even once, and she was definitely important. Her bike remained locked in the bike rack at work. Maybe if I didn't say her name out loud, I could pretend things were normal, that she wasn't in any danger.

I headed to the nearest McDonald's and ordered a small coffee with three creams. A girl took my money at the first window, and I drove to the second to get my order. I loved the ritual. No mixing of dirty money and fast food. A skinny boy with acne carefully handed me a cup with the creamers stacked on top.

I set my coffee in the cup holder and stopped at a red light on my way to the *7-Eleven*. I peeled off the plastic tab and emptied two of the creamers into the V-shaped opening. Before I could open the third creamer, my phone vibrated. It was an unfamiliar number, probably spam, so I ignored it. Right after that, I got a text from Chase.

It started to rain, and heat lightning spidered a soundless sky. The delayed thunder behind me felt like a feeble afterthought. I glanced in the rearview mirror, but nothing was there. No cars waiting for me to move on, so I sat through the green light, took a sip, and opened the text.

Did you get the donuts yet? I whispered to myself, predicting Chase's words.

But, just one chilling word appeared on my glowing screen:
Stranger.

9

ER

Emergency rooms are scary places like Walmart at midnight. It was not my room of choice, especially not knowing how I got there and wearing a faded gown that tied in the back. I heard people coughing and babies screaming and smelled that hospital smell—a sickening cocktail of rubbing alcohol and Band-Aids. A tall nurse entered my curtained-off space. She held a compress, a tiny paper cup, and a glass of water.

"What happened?"

"You'll be good as new, honey. Unfortunately, you were the victim of a hit and run this evening. Your car was rear-ended at a stoplight, and you passed out. You've got a nasty bump there on your forehead and a few cuts and bruises, so we're going to keep you overnight for observation," the nurse said, placing the cold compress on my throbbing forehead. "I'll take you to a hospital room as soon as the next one is available."

"What time is it?" I asked.

"Midnight. The EMTs brought you in at 9:30 p.m."

"I don't remember anything," I said, searching the room for answers that weren't there.

"You came to in the ambulance, but they gave you something to help you rest."

"Where's Chase?"

"Who?" the nurse asked, setting the glass and the paper cup on the nightstand.

"My little brother. He's alone in my apartment."

"How old is he?"

"Ten. I've got to leave right now!" I said, sitting up and pitching my blanket to the floor.

"Hold on there, honey," the nurse said, gently easing me onto the bed and placing the compress back on my head. "Who can we call? A relative? Your parents?"

"My mother's name is Joy, but don't call her, and I have no idea where my father is."

"Who then?" the nurse asked.

"Donuts," I muttered. "Chase was waiting for me to bring donuts."

"Listen, everything will be okay, sweetie," the nurse said slowly, putting the blanket into a hamper and covering me with a fresh one. "We'll make sure your brother is safe. I'll call the police and tell them to go to your apartment and check on him. What's your address?" she asked.

"1014 Ocean View. It's on the tenth floor of a senior high rise."

The nurse quickly called 911 and gave the dispatcher my address.

"The police are on scene right now. Someone must have already called," she told me. "Is the boy okay?" the nurse asked the dispatcher.

"Chase, his name is Chase," I called out.

"The boy's name is *Chase*," the nurse said. "He's fine? Good! I'll let Twyla know. No problem. She'll be here."

"Let me know what?" I asked.

"An officer needs to ask you a few questions."

"Why does he have to talk to me?"

"It's standard procedure," the nurse said. "Don't you have any other family in Naples? What about your sister?"

"Who?" I asked.

"Your sister called earlier. She didn't leave a number."

"Maybe it was Diana. She's a doctor here," I said. "Dr. Diana James."

"Dr. James is your sister?"

"No, just a good friend," I said. "I don't have a sister."

"Okay, is there anybody else we can call?"

"Sam," I sputtered. "His number is in my phone."

"Just try to relax," the nurse said, handing me the cup with a pill inside and a glass of water, before unsealing a large plastic bag with my purse, flip-flops, shorts, and t-shirt inside.

"What's his last name?" she asked.

"I don't know. Sam, just Sam. Here, give me my cell phone," I demanded, setting the water and pill on the metal serving tray at the foot of my bed.

My hands trembled as I scrolled through my contacts until I came to the S's. "He's staying at the Palmettos," I said, pushing *Call* before handing my phone to the nurse. "Where's my car?"

"It was towed. We found an emergency card in your purse when the EMTs brought you in, but we couldn't reach someone named Alexandra, so we left her a message."

"Maybe Alexandra called and said she was my sister," I said weakly, trying to make sense of things.

"Sam's not answering," the nurse said. "I'll try him again in a few minutes, but you have a text."

"Let me see it," I said, sitting up again and taking my phone. "*Stranger*," I read aloud in a shaky voice.

Then it all came flooding back. It was the text Chase had sent before my car was hit, before I blacked out, before the flashing red lights, and an ambulance's siren that must have filled the night.

I tried to stand, but I sank to the floor instead.

"You have to lie flat until we can do an MRI," the nurse said in a firm voice. "Doctor's orders."

"Chase is in trouble!" I cried, clutching my phone.

"Try to stay calm, honey. The police will make sure your brother is taken care of," she reassured me.

The nurse tried to help me stand, but I pushed her away. She pressed a button on my bed and a male orderly quickly appeared in my room. He stood in front of me and crossed his muscular arms. The nurse handed me the glass of water and shook the pill from the cup into my hand and both of them watched until I swallowed it. Then the orderly lifted me off the floor in one try, like I was a life-sized doll made of Styrofoam, and put me on the bed.

10

ONE SENTENCE

Dr. Diana popped into my room at 7:00 a.m. on her morning rounds. I was already dressed and talking to Sam on my phone.

"What ever happened, Twyla?" she asked, concern clouded her eyes.

"Someone rear-ended my car at a stoplight," I said. "How did you know I was here, Diana?"

"Hold your horses, girl. I just ran into your doctor five minutes ago—that's how I knew. And why didn't you call me? You know I would have rushed right over."

"I wasn't thinking straight last night," I said.

"Going somewhere?" she asked, eyeing my clothes.

"Home. Randy kicked in the door of my apartment last night when Chase wouldn't open it. Thank God, he called 911 like I had taught him, and the police rushed right over and arrested Randy. He's in jail now. Chase is still terrified, but safe with Sam."

"Oh my God!"

"Sam says he's fine. Just shook up. Randy was charged with attempted kidnapping and drug possession. He told the police he had come to take Chase to Joy's place, but they didn't believe him. He even bragged that Joy would bail him out of jail as soon as she got sober."

"How can I help?" Diana asked.

"Do you have a one-way ticket to Mars?"

"That's not a bad idea. Maybe you should go somewhere else until things settle down. Do you have any relatives who could help out for a while?" she asked.

"Are you kidding?"

"Don't worry. We'll figure something out, girl," Diana said.

"I have to replace the front door first. The deaf lady across the hall never saw or heard a thing, and the other tenants either slept right through it or were afraid to come out. I forgot about Chase's homework, too. I planned to check it that evening and leave it with the school's secretary the next morning."

"Under the circumstances, I'm sure his teacher will understand. That's the least of your worries right now," Diana said. "It says here on your chart you have a mild concussion, so you're not going anywhere until your doctor discharges you."

Diana slid the chart into its slot at the foot of my bed.

"You'll be fine, Twyla. Just follow the doctor's orders. I hate to tell you this, but you look like a victim of domestic abuse. Stay away from mirrors for a while. I'll be sure and check on you again after my rounds. Get back in bed, *Blue Roses*," she said. "No excuses now."

After Diana left, a nurse came in and took my blood pressure, shone a light in my eyes, and stuck a thermometer in my ear. Everything was normal, but I didn't feel normal at all. The nurse told me to put my hospital gown on, get in bed, and press the button on my bed when I needed to go to the bathroom.

"Tell the doctor I *have* to go home today. I don't have any insurance," I muttered.

As soon as the nurse was gone, I stood up. The room wobbled a little, and I pressed my fingers against my temples. I slowly inched my way to the bathroom and avoided the mirror, just like Diana had said. *One crisis at a time*, I thought. I climbed into bed before a young volunteer carried in my break-fast tray. A dark braid hung below her waist—her hair had probably never been cut.

"Hi, my name is Starla," she said. She didn't look older than 16.

She set my food on the bedside tray, elevated the bed so I could sit up, and then moved the tray closer to me. I pulled the blanket to my chin to hide my clothes.

Her face was a mask of heavy make-up. Each eye was heavily outlined with kohl, her lids were dusted with deep purple eyeshadow, and her eyelashes looked like clumpy spiders coated with a week's worth of waterproof mascara.

When Starla left, I whispered, "*She disguised her youth so well, she was never young.*" Alexandra would be proud of my latest distillation.

Poking at the powdered scrambled eggs on my plate, I took a sip of the lukewarm decaffeinated coffee. I needed a cup of McDonald's coffee with three creams. I managed to eat the dry toast cut in perfect triangles after I spread on some butter and two packets of grape jelly.

When the hospital phone rang beside my bed, I jumped and fumbled for the bulky receiver.

"Hello?"

"Twyla? Are you all right?" Alexandra said. "I just listened to a voice message from some nurse at the hospital. Sorry I didn't call you earlier, but you know I can't hear a damn thing after I go to bed and turn on my sound machine."

"I'm fine, just a little banged-up, that's all. I got rear-ended at a stoplight. Did you call me here last night?"

"I didn't get this message until just now. So, no, I didn't call you last night. Why?"

"Everything is crazy. First, the accident and then someone called the ER and claimed to be my sister," I said.

"It wasn't me. I'm too old," she said with a weak laugh. "Maybe the person who rear-ended you had a guilty conscience and wanted to see if you were all right. Try to forget about it and get some rest. I know you won't, Twyla, but try. I'll talk to you later," Alexander said.

After I hung up the phone, another volunteer entered my room, pushing a cart full of reading materials and snacks.

"Would you like a magazine or a book to read?" she asked.

"Do you have today's paper?"

"I've got two copies of *Chicken Soup for the Soul*," she chirped.

"I'll take a Snickers and a cup of strong coffee with cream if you have it," I said, letting the blanket slip to my waist.

The doctor walked in just then. The perky volunteer gave me the candy bar and wheeled her cart into the hallway.

"Well, I can see we're dressed and ready to leave, Miss Townsend. Your MRI is fine, so you're safe to go home. The nurse will get you the release forms to sign. Here's a prescription for some pain medication if you need it. No refills. I've scheduled a follow-up appointment for next Monday at 2:00 p.m.," he said. "Any questions?"

I shook my head no, and the doctor smiled a plastic smile before he left.

"*His life became a series of sterile rooms, and then he died*," I whispered.

When the nurse arrived, I signed the forms and put the prescription in my purse. I'd throw it away later. She asked if someone could drive me home.

"Just call a taxi," I demanded, as Starla, with the long braid and clumpy eyelashes, pushed a wheelchair into my room. "Who's that for?"

"It's standard procedure, Sunshine. We don't want you to have another accident before you leave the hospital grounds. Oh, and your sister called again to see if you were all right, but I had some trouble understanding her," the nurse said, reading from a Post-It in her hand.

"I don't have a sister," I said.

11

TAROT / SOLITAIRE

When I got off the elevator, my battered door leaned against a wall and another door had already replaced it. I wondered how much it would cost me, but I was too tired to care. One of the white-haired residents named Pearl opened her apartment door and shuffled down the hallway toward me. She must have spotted my taxi from her front window.

"Sorry about your door," she said with a nervous laugh, touching the white opera glasses she always wore around her neck like double vials of smelling salts. "I've been bird watching this morning and spotted two robins building a nest in a tall pine tree out front."

"That's nice," I said, knowing robins flew north to breed, wishing she'd join them. "The landlord said you'd need this to get inside your apartment now."

She handed me a small envelope with two keys inside.

"Thanks, Pearl," I said, unlocking and then tugging on a door that didn't quite fit the doorframe. "Did you hear any loud noises two nights ago about 9 p.m.?"

Pearl shook her head.

"Chase was alone when someone kicked in my door," I added, studying her face.

"I leave my TV on all night. It makes me feel safer somehow. I sleep much more sound that way, and I'm always in bed by 8 p.m., so I'm sure I didn't hear anything. If one of the other tenants saw anything, I'll be sure and let you know," Pearl said shyly, fondling her opera glasses as she moved down the hall to her apartment. She waved her fingers at me like a little girl before she went inside.

She heard and saw everything, I thought, *but didn't want to get involved.*

I needed to clear my head: a hot shower and a nap would help while the pain killer the nurse gave me was still working. I locked the door behind me and saw my apartment was a wreck. The kitchen drawers were open and their contents emptied, and my clothes were scattered all over the bedroom floor. I quickly checked the freezer where I had hidden a fifty-dollar bill inside a bag of frozen blueberries. The money was still there.

After I cleared a path and threw my clothes on my bed, I listened to a voice message Sam had left. Chase wanted to spend another night with him at Palmettos—go swimming and watch old Clint Eastwood movies.

"I promise to feed him real good, Twy. Rest now and don't you fret," his now familiar voice said. "Are you okay?"

Someone's trying to kill me, I almost said.

I wanted to see Chase, but I needed more time to recover since I was pretty beat up, so I texted Sam.

"Thanks, I'll get Chase tomorrow morning and drive him to school."

"But your car's been towed," Sam responded.

"Sorry, I forgot. I'll call Josh and see if he can help me out. How's Chase doing?"

"He's still shook up, but I told him he was safe since Randy was in jail. I've been keeping him busy, but he had a big scare," Sam said.

"I don't know what to do, Sam," I whispered. "Tell Chase I'll call him later."

I sat on the couch and rang Josh's number. He answered on the second ring.

"You want a lift tomorrow?" he offered before I could speak. "Sam told me about the wreck. I can swing by your place on my way to work."

"That would be great. Could you take Chase to school, too?"

"Sure, and then we can stop by the junkyard after work and see if your car can be repaired," he said.

"Thanks, I'll be ready in the morning," I told him, heading toward the shower.

The thought of going to work was a mix of dread and grateful anticipation for a normal day filled with cheeseburgers and French fries. Even the thought of refilling those red-and-yellow plastic bottles with Heinz and French's seemed like Zen therapy.

After a long shower, I took out the order pad from work I'd stowed in my purse. I had already scrawled a few pages of single words: *Loner. Alcoholic. Misfit. Meticulous. Betrayed. Generous. Abandoned. Suicidal.* I played a new word game this time, but instead of summing up my customers in one sentence, they just got one word each—like reducing fractions to their lowest common denominator.

Alexandra wouldn't approve. She said everyone was entitled to a complete sentence. I sat on the couch, opened my laptop, and typed fifty-two words from my order pad in all-caps—two columns of twenty-six words each, and then printed it out. After centering the paper on the refrigerator, I placed a black magnet neatly in each corner.

Stress does strange things to people. After my aunt died, her daughter cleaned and re-cleaned the house. She vacuumed, scrubbed the bathrooms, and waxed the kitchen floor. She even washed and dried a bar of soap each time before and after she used it. There's a strange comfort in ritual: organizing monthly magazines in neat January to December stacks, counting steps, waxing the car every Saturday with a chamois cloth, making dollar bills line up George Washington perfectly.

I lay down on the couch for a short nap but slept for hours instead and woke the next morning sore and stiff. I swallowed some aspirin, got dressed, and waited outside on the stoop for Josh.

"Don't take this the wrong way, Twy, but you look like you've been in a cockfight," Josh said after I got into his truck. "I hope they lock that Randy creep up for a long time. Breaking and entering is a serious crime."

"I'm filing for custody of Chase," I blurted out. "Sam told me he could speed it through the courts."

"You need any money?" Josh asked.

"No, Sam said he'd take care of it. Could you drop me off at work first before you take Chase to school? I need more time before he sees me like this. Sam will pick him up later today."

"No problem," Josh said, staring at my black eye before pulling out from the curb.

After an endless day at Calamity with few breaks, Josh and I went to Lucky's junkyard. My VW was totaled, and I felt really lucky I hadn't been seriously injured. After unlocking the glove box, I took out my registration card, opened the hidden compartment, and slid my bandanna-wrapped derringer into my purse. No one knew I had a gun. The rear bumper of my car was gone, and the trunk looked like a smashed tin can, but Josh lifted the lid without any problem.

"Someone stole my money," I said, shaking the coffee can before I took off the lid. "At least a hundred dollars in change and a new hundred-dollar bill," I said, peering into the empty can.

"I didn't know you hid money in there."

"Nobody does. Not even Chase. I just use it for emergencies and Jack Daniel's."

"Looks like somebody discovered your stash," Josh said.

"Do you think you can fix my car?" I asked, tossing the coffee can back in the trunk.

"Believe me, it will cost much more than it's worth. Do you have car insurance?" Josh asked.

"Are you kidding? It's all I can do to keep the car running and put gas in it. For once it has a full tank."

"A full tank? That doesn't sound like you," he said, trying to lighten my mood.

"It's a long story," I said.

"Hey, you can use my truck for a while. I'm painting my landlord's apartment on my days off, so I won't need it anyway."

"Are you sure?"

"He just lives down the block from me," Josh said.

Now I was really indebted. I knew I shouldn't delay our movie date for much longer.

"It's easy money, so I can't pass it up. One of my buddies will follow me over to your place in the morning, and I'll park out front and put my keys in your mailbox."

I called Sam after Josh took me home. I told him I had borrowed Josh's truck for a few days and could take Chase to school. Everything was settled, at least for a while.

I tried to sleep that night, but it was useless. The wreck, the strange phone call, Chase, my ransacked apartment, Ashley, my totaled VW, and my stolen money kept rewinding in my brain. At least my tips were good today because I got a lot of sympathetic stares. I'd tried to cover my black eye by wearing sunglasses, but it didn't help much. After an hour, I finally stopped explaining and let my customers think whatever they wanted to think. Domestic abuse, cat fight, a fall, I didn't care as long as the tips kept coming.

After tossing in bed for a couple more hours, I went into the kitchen, poured a glass of milk, swallowed some pills, and finally fell asleep. Then my phone rang. I bolted awake, thinking it was Sam, that something must be wrong. It's always bad news after midnight.

"I'm sorry to wake you, Twyla, but I just found out I have to leave tomorrow, and I wanted to let you know," Alexandra said.

"What time?"

"Don't come. I might cry," she said, ignoring my question. She was lying because she never cried. "I'll write as soon as I get settled in Hawaii."

I knew this day was coming, but it still felt like sudden death. Not just her leaving, but she would be more than an ocean away. Endings were always hard for me, but the speed of her departure was mind-boggling. She was the only one I felt I could trust. No time now for one more Monday meeting, one more glass of wine, or one last question.

I managed to go to sleep, but anxiety kept me checking the time on the alarm clock every hour or so. Finally, at 5 a.m., I gave in, stumbled into the kitchen, and made a pot of coffee. After switching on the TV, I stared at an exercise show for an hour. The muscled 60-something instructor made it look so easy, all the repetitions, the yoga poses, and deep cleansing breaths. I used to watch that show with Joy when I was little. I remember the cool rock music playing in the background. We didn't try to do any of the exercises—it just became a morning spectator sport for Joy to watch and recover from her latest hangover.

After I toasted a cinnamon and raisin bagel, I smeared peanut butter on top until it melted and poured myself a cup of coffee.

I found a pack of 3x4 note cards in the junk drawer to make flashcards for Chase. It helped him learn his spelling words, and we had fun sitting and laughing together on the floor while I quizzed him. Sometimes I created card games for us to play, like *Concentration*. We'd cut two apples, two hats, two shoes, etc., from old magazines and glue them to one side of the cards until we had enough to play. I'd set the kitchen timer, and we'd each get one minute to try to find a match.

I took the worn paperback copy of *Naming Your Baby* from under the coffee table. It belonged to Joy. I'm not sure how I ended up with it, but there it was, sandwiched between the old magazines she gave me when I first moved to Ocean View. Some pages were dog-eared and others had names starred and high-lighted with a yellow marker.

Chase was short for the French word chasseur, which means hunter. Twyla wasn't even listed, but Joy had written it in herself along with its meaning above the name Tzigane. *Twyla: twilight, a character in the novel Pilgrimage, the dancer, Twyla Tharp.*

Joy said she had recurring dreams before I was born about dancing on Broadway, so she settled on the name Twyla. She couldn't afford lessons, but we used to dance barefoot on the living room rug with the radio blasting. Joy would applaud, curtsey, and give me a bouquet of plastic daffodils she kept in a vase on the mantel. I liked the name Tzigane better. It meant gypsy—a Romani maid whose heart was filled with music and adventure, but Twyla was pretty good, too. Nobody else had a name like mine, so my teachers always remembered me.

I lifted the magnets from my list on the refrigerator and put the paper on the kitchen table. I carefully printed the words in blue ink on one side of the notecards and random names from the baby book on the other side with a red marker. The routine was comforting, like coloring in a coloring book. Like I said, stress can make you do strange things. Then I shuffled the cards like Joy had taught me, just like a professional poker player, and laid them on the table in long, straight rows, red baby name side up. I chose the card with Cordelia, the faithful daughter of King Lear, and flipped over seven other cards like a strange game of Tarot/Solitaire. I read Cordelia's name out loud along with *intrepid, humble, loyal, creative, caring, honest, saint.*

12

LEAR

I climbed into Josh's truck the next morning, pushed the seat forward so my feet would reach the pedals and adjusted the rearview and side mirrors. When I started the engine, the truck sputtered to life, and I let it idle for a few seconds. The upholstery smelled like cigarette smoke, and a crushed can of beer leaned to one side in the cup holder. I lowered the windows with one click of the controls and drove to Palmettos, enjoying the balmy air, gliding the stick shift into gear, and thundering the glass pack muffler when I revved the engine. *Maybe I could find a used truck and have Josh add a cool muffler*, I thought, savoring the rumble of power when the light changed to green.

Chase stood in front of Sam's condo. I spotted the red swoosh on his new Nike sneakers first and a shirt I didn't recognize. After I honked the horn to get his attention, he raced toward the truck, climbed in, and gave me a hug and wouldn't let go.

"Did you have a good time?"

He smelled like Ivory soap, and his hair was still wet and seamed with comb marks. When he looked up at me, his eyes welled with tears.

"I'm fine. Don't worry. Just a little battered, that's all,

68

Chase. You better close the door before a bumble bee zooms in here. You know I'm allergic to bees.

Chase nodded and very gently touched my black eye before he strapped his seatbelt on.

"What are you doing with Josh's truck?" he asked.

"My car's totaled."

"What's that mean?" he asked.

"It can't be fixed."

We both waved at Sam, who had stepped outside when Chase headed my way. Sam squinted at us, so he put on his sunglasses and tipped his new cowboy hat. The brim was curled up, and it was made of brown felt with a leather band. He looked like an aging movie star. When he walked toward us, I lowered the window.

"You doing okay there, Twy? I can keep him another night if you want. No trouble at all," he said, giving my face the once over. "The police are still looking for your hit-and-run driver. Not much to go on with no witnesses."

"I'm fine. Thanks for watching Chase. I'll be good as new in a few days."

"Let me know if there's anything else I can do. Call me anytime," Sam said.

"I will. When did you buy that hat?" I asked.

"What?" Chase answered, instead of Sam, while rifling through Josh's glovebox.

"Your new cowboy hat, *Sam*," I said, reaching over Chase to shut the glovebox with a snap.

"Sam said he wanted one just like Clint Eastwood wore in *The Good, The Bad, and The Ugly*. It's really cool!" Chase said.

"What's with all *your* new clothes?" I asked, tugging on his shirt.

"Sam bought me four pairs of Levi jeans, four shirts, and these Nike running shoes. They weren't on sale either!" he said, lifting one foot so I could see.

I rolled my eyes and wondered if that was how Chase would

remember his cheap sister twenty years from now—always trying to make ends meet. I glanced at his dancing eyes, his sunburned cheeks.

"Well, we'll have to make him a cake or something. Maybe clean his condo for him one day next week?" I said, trying hard to think how I could repay Sam for his kindness.

"He's already got a cleaning lady. And a pool boy comes and cleans the swimming pool every day. He lets me watch him sweep the pool and add chlorine tablets. I got to fish out a big bullfrog with a net, too. I wanted to keep it, but Sam said no."

"Did you do your homework?" I asked.

"All of it. Sam helped me. He promised if I got an A on my spelling test, he'd take me to see the alligators wrestling tomorrow."

I glanced at his beaming face.

"If it's okay with you, Sis," he added softly.

We rode the rest of the way in silence. Chase put his hand on top of mine when I shifted the gears, as if he were memorizing the exact motion. Josh was the only other person I knew who drove a stick shift. In five years, Chase would have his driver's permit, but I didn't want to think about that. Maybe I'd be able to buy a truck by then and afford some insurance. I stopped in front of the elementary school and Chase climbed out. He seemed really happy, almost excited.

"Meet me at Calamity after school. Meatloaf and mashed potatoes is the special today. Maybe we can go to a movie tonight after work and buy buttered popcorn."

"A Western?" he asked.

"We'll have to see what's playing first, okay? Love ya, Chase."

"Love you more," he responded automatically before shutting the door and running toward the school's entrance.

"That's a first," I said to myself.

Sam must be working some of his cowboy magic, since

Chase always hated school—until today. I made a U-turn, drove to the public library, and parked on a side street. I fed two quarters into the meter. That gave me plenty of time to browse the stacks before work. The quiet of the library was always healing, and I made time today for this luxury.

I rode the elevator to the second floor, made my way to the art section, and found three volumes on Rothko. Last week it was Mary Cassatt. The week before that, it was Picasso. Maybe I could get a job at an art museum someday, but I'd have to go to school. No time or money for that now.

I claimed my favorite wooden table, hidden away from the computer junkies and sleeping winos. Today, a homeless man with a scraggly beard sat on a worn-out couch. He had on a scratched pair of Liz Claiborne sunglasses with LC printed on the side. His head slumped over on his chest as he pretended to read a *People* magazine on his lap.

I read about Rothko's early works, mainly still-lifes and frowning nudes. Toward the end of his life, his subjects became floating blocks of color: oranges, reds, dusky maroons. "Silence is so accurate," he wrote. *And deadly*, I thought. Even his titles diminished over time from *Still Life in Front of Window* to just numbers and then to simply *Untitled*—huge nameless monochromatic murals. Did it all come down to just one color, one sentence, one word?

Thirty minutes later, I parked a block away from Alexandra's house, steeling myself for the inevitable. I watched the movers load a small moving van with her couch, a mattress, a chest of drawers, and then they closed the doors. She told me not to come, but I had to be there, to witness her belongings being physically loaded into the van to make it real. I had to watch her walk away for the same reason. Alexandra was closer to me than anyone. I vowed not to get that close to anyone ever again.

Her balding son emerged from the house with Alexandra

holding a yapping Tristan in her arms. Steadying his mother as she descended the porch steps, he carefully wheeled her oxygen tank behind him. I started the engine and turned the radio on. It was really over: the Jack Daniel's, the games, my weekly questions. Now the dénouement began right in front of me, with King Lear walking away in the final act.

<h1 style="text-align:center">13</h1>

<h2 style="text-align:center">FOR RENT</h2>

Things were always crazy busy on Fridays at the café, so I didn't have time to think about Alexandra or Ashley. I busied myself with hungry customers who couldn't care less what kind of day I'd had or if I'd been in a car wreck or if I'd been deserted by Joan of Arc.

Chase arrived after school. He was tired but couldn't stop giggling as he shoved a piece of notebook paper in my face—his spelling test. A big red "**A**" was scrawled in the top margin.

Carson peered through the serving window to see what all the excitement was. He was our substitute cook while Josh painted his boss's house. Carson loved kids and often worked two jobs to support his young family of four.

"Way to go, Chase!" Carson yelled.

"I think he deserves something special, don't you?" I asked, winking at Chase.

Carson's low whistle showed his approval before he returned to his smoking grill.

Chase climbed onto a stool and waited patiently for his early supper. He looked more like an eight-year-old than a boy of ten. I hoped he'd have a growth spurt soon and start putting on some weight. I didn't want him to be bullied.

"Where's Sam?" Chase asked, spinning around on the bar stool until it whined. I grabbed him by the shoulders and brought him to an abrupt stop.

"He had to take Cali to the vet this afternoon," I said. "I'll post your spelling test on the bulletin board, so you can show it to him when he comes in on Monday."

"He promised to take me to watch the alligators wrestling if I got an A," Chase whined.

"Don't worry. He will," I said, moving closer to the serving window.

Chase started spinning on the noisy stool again.

"Don't you tell on me," I whispered to Carson as I took a slice of Boston cream pie from the refrigerated case and set it in front of Chase. He instantly stopped spinning. "Since you got an A on your paper, you get to eat this first."

He shoveled forkfuls of pie into his mouth as I poured a tall glass of cold milk and set it beside his plate.

After work, I drove Chase to Sam's, and then I fell asleep early. I was exhausted. The sounds of a rainstorm with just a few flashes of lightning and no thunder guaranteed I would sleep for hours. My phone rang under my pillow, and it woke me from a Rothko black-over-gray dream, but I didn't answer the call. This week had worn me out; my feet hurt, my back ached, and I'd barely eaten since yesterday.

After a couple more hours of needed sleep, I finally slid my phone from underneath the pillow and read a text from Diana. She wanted to meet for lunch next week. Her treat. Then, I put the phone back under my pillow and pulled the covers over my head, I tried to re-enter an *Untitled* dream, but my phone rang again.

"Diana?" I asked.

"I must have the wrong number," a woman said in a muffled voice.

"Who is this?" I asked.

"I'm sorry I bothered you."

"Are you my *sister*?" I demanded, but the line went dead.

I was wide awake now, so I put on a sweatsuit, grabbed my phone and purse, and drove to Alexandra's in the dark. I turned on the headlights and windshield wipers in the steady rain. It wasn't even Monday, but I parked in front of her deserted house and just sat there, listening to the hypnotic rain and the whine of the wiper blades. I let the truck idle for a few minutes more before I switched off the engine. I had hidden a new bottle of Jack Daniel's under the passenger's seat as a thank you to Josh for the loan of his truck. He'd be surprised when he discovered it.

A *For Rent* sign had been planted in the front yard. I stared at it for a while and tried to think of a good question. *Any question*. No luck. Instead, I just whispered one of the words I had written on the index cards: "Saint."

"Sorry, Alexandra, I know you said everyone deserves a complete sentence, but it's the best I can do right now."

SUMMER 2011

PICTURES FOR SALE

Joy didn't come home for two days, and Chase started crying because he was hungry. I looked for a five-dollar bill under the ashtray each morning, but today nothing was there. I had colored some pictures in my coloring book with the new crayons the nice lady at the Baptist church had put in my lunch bag last week. I cut out the pages and stuck them inside an old magazine with a square of cardboard, so they wouldn't get wrinkled, and then I put Chase in his rusted red wagon with a bed pillow and pulled him several blocks until he fell asleep.

I parked the wagon at a bus stop and wrote "Pictures for sale - $1.00" on the cardboard with my black crayon. I held it up when people got on and off the bus, and I sold ten pictures. One man said he'd give me $5.00 if I signed his, so I did.

When Chase woke, I pulled his wagon to the grocery store and bought us day-old ham and cheese sandwiches at the deli and a quart of chocolate milk. The woman behind the counter gave me paper cups and a bag of chips for free. As soon as I paid her, we ate two of the sandwiches right there and drank half of the milk. I had some money left over, so I bought a loaf of bread and bologna to take home. I still had $3, so I stuffed the money inside my crayon box. If I saved enough, Chase and I could run away.

15

OFFER

U sed 1980 Chevette. $500. Still runs. *That's good to know*, I thought before I tossed the newspaper into the trash.

I don't have $500. Maybe I'd have some extra if I didn't pay the water bill this month. I wondered if I could afford a used motorcycle or even a Moped. I'd ask Josh about it. He said he didn't mind giving me a ride to work after he finished painting his boss's house, especially when we both had the same shift. But what about the other days? What about getting Chase to school? I couldn't keep asking Josh or Sam to bail me out forever.

Speaking of the devil himself, Sam sauntered through the front door of Calamity. He tipped his new Clint Eastwood hat, sat on a stool, and then hung his hat on a hook underneath the counter. I hoped he didn't start imitating Eastwood now. And I knew who he was, thank you very much.

"What's the Saturday Special, Twy?" he asked, handing me a large envelope.

"What's this?"

"Chase is legally yours now," Sam said.

"That was fast."

"I don't mess around," Sam said. "What's the special again?"

"Beans and cornbread and kale, with or without vinegar on the side."

"Okay, for my appetizer, I want a piece of lemon meringue pie. Without vinegar," he said, stalling for a laugh.

I wrote down his order and took a can of whipped cream from the refrigerator.

"What's wrong there, Buckaroo? You look like you're coming down with something. Have you had your flu shot yet?"

"I've got to find a second job. I'm going to call this morning and see if the newspaper will hire me back part-time. Or I could get a morning paper route and still work here."

"Jesus, Twy! You're serious, aren't you? What if there's not a route available near your high rise?" he asked. "Will Josh have to drive your route every day, too?"

I set the lemon pie in front of him, spun a fast tower of whipped cream in the bowl, poured him a cup of coffee, and put the creamer within his reach.

"Where's Cali?" I asked, trying to stay calm.

"I had to leave her at home today. It's too damn hot outside. She likes to sleep on my bed in front of the air conditioner," he said.

"The heat is relentless in the summer," I said as I Googled the main number of The Florida Sentinel and jotted it down.

"Hey, I know you're hurting, Twy. How can I help?"

"I'm just venting, that's all. Forget about it," I said.

"No, something is much worse. What aren't you telling me?'

I stood motionless for a second before I spoke.

"I think someone wants to kill me, Sam. It wasn't an accident when my car was rear-ended," I told him.

Sam studied me as I wiped off the countertop. After a few minutes, I automatically refilled his cup.

"You know what? I could really use a good house sitter this winter," he said casually. "I planned to advertise in the newspaper, but maybe you might be interested," he said.

"At your condo?"

"No, my mountain cabin. I haven't returned since Lydia passed away last year. It hasn't been easy on me. There are too many memories stored there."

"I'm sorry, Sam," I said, automatically handing him the tin of cinnamon before he asked for it.

"Thanks, Radar," he said with a curious grin.

"Radar?"

"From Mash. I guess that was before your time, too. It was a great TV series. Radar played a young psychic, you might say."

"Oh," I said.

"I just need someone responsible like you to stay and look after things. There's lots of snow and solitude. You could dog-sit Cali for me, too. What do you think?" he asked hopefully.

I stared at his bowl of whipped cream as he dusted it with cinnamon.

"Twy?"

"You're kidding, right? I couldn't leave Chase that long, and I'm allergic to poison ivy," I said.

"The pay is real good, and in a few short months, you'd be on your feet with money in the bank. If you don't take the job, I'll just offer it to someone else."

"How much money?" I asked, trying to sound casual.

"I'd more than double your salary. All the food and whiskey and movies are free. No utilities or anything for you to worry about. If you don't mind me asking, how much money do you make a month?"

"About $1,500, not counting tips," I said.

"Well, I'll pay you $5,000 dollars a month."

"You're kidding," I gasped.

"Would I kid you, pilgrim?"

"What about Chase? I wouldn't be here to protect him."

"He could stay with me. We'd come and visit you when the weather breaks. I'd take great care of him and make sure he did his homework and got to school on time. And I'd keep his mother and her boyfriend-of-the-month at arm's length. That part's easy," Sam said. "Money talks."

I didn't say anything. I tried to process this strange offer, tried to read his body language in case he was making it all up.

"What with Lydia gone and my son somewhere across the pond in Scotland, I get pretty lonely these days," Sam said in a sad voice.

"How long are you talking about?"

"Oh, maybe four months. Say, September 1 through January 1 and $20,000 would be waiting in your checking account," Sam answered.

"I don't accept charity. What's the catch?"

"No catch. It's worth it to me, Twy. The cabin was sacred to Lydia and me, and I don't want anything to happen to it. If not you, I'd just have to pay a stranger to watch it. Gotta protect my palace, you know. And Cali, too. She hates it here in sunny Florida—too blazin' hot. You could rest, get on your feet, and write that cookbook you keep talking about," he said.

"How do I know you're good for $20,000?"

"Trust me, Twy. I was a popular lawyer, and I'm good for a lot of money. Here, take this as collateral," he said as he slipped off his Rolex and put it in my hand.

"Joy would never agree to any of this," I said, staring at the watch.

"I have a way with women who've been in trouble with the law. Didn't you say she'd let just about anybody watch Chase?"

"She's pretty fucked up," I mumbled.

"Just think about it for now, Twyla. No rush. No rush at all."

"You got mice?" I asked.

"The place is tight as a kettledrum," Sam said with a laugh.

"No mice or wolf spiders. I have the cabin sprayed for pests every year."

"And electric heat?"

"Absolutely, and a wood-burning fireplace if things go haywire," he said.

"Haywire?"

"If all hell breaks loose and the power goes out, and you run out of firewood and booze," he said. "Cabin fever might be a problem, but if you keep busy, you'll be fine."

"I don't have a car," I said quietly.

"No problem. Chase and I can drop you off. You'll be sitting pretty after Caleb stocks in food and firewood. He lives at the bottom of the mountain and checks on things for me from time to time. He's a piece of work. Smart man, really smart, but he's a loner. A little strange, I know. Plus, Caleb's really good at a lot of things, especially asking questions. And he's a great handyman. You two would get along just fine."

"But my apartment?" I asked.

"When's your lease up?"

"September," I said.

"I'll take care of it. Anything else?"

"I've got a lot of credit card debt."

"Like I said, I'll take care of everything. It's your decision," he said.

"I don't want your watch, Sam."

"Maybe I could buy you a horse, so you could ride to school and to work. Chase would like that, wouldn't he? You could gallop to work just like Calamity Jane if you had a good horse."

"Why are you doing all of this?" I asked softly, studying his face.

"Hell, why does anybody do anything?" he asked. "I just want to help. No ulterior motive, if that's what you're worried about. When Lydia died, I was sucker-punched and got the wind knocked clean out of me. I need more time before I return to the mountains, and I think my cabin-sitting job might be the perfect solution for both of us."

"Do you have any maraschino cherries there?" I asked.

"Anticipating a craving, Twyla?"

"I might consider your offer if maraschino cherries were part of the deal," I said. "I like Pina Coladas."

16

FAVOR

Early the next morning Josh gave me a lift to work since we both worked the early shift—6 a.m. to 2 p.m. Calamity closed for supper on Sundays. We didn't talk much—just shared a cup of coffee and a cigarette. Josh wasn't much of a morning person, either.

I left Chase sound asleep in his bed, but Sam would be there at 7:00. I had set his alarm for 6:30 and put a bowl, a spoon, and a box of Cheerios on the kitchen counter with a note: *The milk is in the refrigerator and your clothes are on the couch. Don't leave until Sam texts you he's out front.*

"Are you awake yet?" Josh asked, while we waited at the stoplight. It was already hot outside, so he had turned the air conditioner on.

"Turn around," I commanded. "I can't leave Chase alone anymore. Not even for a few minutes."

Josh made a fast U-turn, and we were at the high rise in less than five minutes.

"I'm taking him to work with me from now on, and Sam can get him there," I said.

Chase lived with me full time now. I had bought two cans

of wasp stopper spray and kept one by my bed and another by the front door. I told him to use it if someone tried to break in again. It shot a lot farther than pepper spray and would blind the intruder until Chase could escape and call 911. The thought of another confrontation scared him to death, but at least he would have something to protect himself with. Like the derringer I kept in my purse. But none of this comforted me.

Josh waited out front until Chase and I hurried to his truck. We might be a little late for work, but no one would notice. I texted Sam and told him to pick up Chase at Calamity this morning instead of my apartment.

"Could you do me a favor, Josh?" I whispered after Chase dozed off.

"Depends," he said. "What do you need?"

"Do you know any cops who would do a background check for me?"

"Maybe."

"I'd pay for it," I said. *Eventually*, I thought.

"Who do you need to check on? Me?"

"No, not you. On Sam," I said.

"That ole guy? He's just full of hot air," Josh said. "You want a drag?" he asked, offering me a freshly lit cigarette. "You want me to buy you a pack of cigarettes?"

"I don't smoke," I replied. "Just jumpy."

"So, when do you need the background check?" he asked.

"As soon as possible. I have to make sure Sam's legit. People aren't what they seem anymore. He could be an ex-con or worse."

"You sound serious," Josh said.

"How much do you think it'll cost me?"

"My buddy Chris is new on the force. He owes me a big favor. I loaned him some money last year, so I'm sure he'd do it for nothing."

Ashley's bike still hadn't been moved, but when we pulled into the lot, there were more pink and lavender balloons tied to the handlebars and flowers and cards on the ground near the bike. I had hoped she and Brad had eloped, and Ashley was inside Calamity, wearing a smile and a wedding band, but the added balloons and offerings killed that dream.

We parked and Josh turned the engine off, but he switched the key to the battery, so we could listen to the radio until he finished his cigarette

"You wanna go to a movie tonight?" he asked shyly as he crushed the cigarette butt in the ashtray.

"I'm still not back to normal yet, Josh. Maybe next week," I quickly added.

I woke Chase, and we all entered through the kitchen door, where Carson worked. Chase's straight hair was wild, so I dampened it with a wet comb and smoothed it into place while he sat on a barstool. I put my cowboy outfit on in the restroom, made coffee, and topped off some of the containers of catsup and mustard. After I wrapped silverware in red napkins and set them on the tables, I turned on the overhead lights and the ceiling fan in the sunroom. Carson made Chase scrambled eggs and bacon before Sam pulled up out front.

Every so often, a couple of crying teenagers would walk over to Ashley's bike and leave another balloon or a pink carnation. Sometimes an oversized letter "A" that had been cut from pink felt hung from the spokes. Her photo was posted on telephone poles and bulletin boards all across town. The police had already begun their search and were using dogs to track her.

The morning seemed to last forever. Only a few regulars sat in the sunroom today, and at 8:00 a.m., Sam walked in the front door.

"That brother of yours sure likes to talk. He talks nonstop about school and marbles and riding his bike with a new kid. What's his name?" Sam asked.

"Bryce. He just moved into his grandmother's apartment on the third floor of Ocean View. Nice boy."

"Chase says they play video games and Skylanders. What's that?" he asked.

"It's a video game with action figures. What can I get for you this morning?" I asked, staring absently out the window.

Sam looked in the display case and pointed to a frosted cinnamon roll studded with pecans.

17

PROMISES

"Josh? It's me."

I heard his TV blaring in the background.

"Josh, can you hear me?" I asked, louder this time.

"Bad connection," he said. "Call me back."

I turned off my phone and tried again.

"Josh?"

"That's better. What are you doing up so late?" he asked.

"I can't sleep."

"What's wrong? Did they find Ashley?"

"No, not yet. There are two more search parties, though, and the police are following every lead."

"So what do you need?" Josh asked.

"Do you think you could do that big favor for me now?"

"Tonight?"

"It's an emergency. I'm about to do something insane or really smart," I said.

"Is that all you're going to tell me?"

"Once I make up my mind, I'll tell you everything. Sam's background check will help me decide what to do. Are you in?" I asked.

Josh didn't answer for a second.

"I'll call Chris right now," he answered.

"Thanks, Josh."

"I figure you're worth it," he said.

I began to worry about everything again. Was Sam a con man? Was his cabin really a palace or just a dumpy old trailer with cinder block steps and an outhouse in the middle of nowhere? I Googled Sam's name, and there were hundreds of hits. The pages were populated with law cases and raves about his generous humanitarian contributions to Doctors Without Borders and the Salvation Army.

His name also showed up in his wife's online obituary. I clicked on the link that took me to the funeral home's website. I stared at the photo of Lydia, an elegant lady with white hair and a warm smile. Friends, relatives, and admirers had left personal messages, as if she could read them from the great beyond. I wondered why people often saved their kind words and glowing praise until it was too late. My stint at the newspaper taught me that and other important things. Some people could afford a photo, most couldn't. Some paid for long obituaries, most didn't. One woman even wrote her own obit before she died. It struck me as meaningful and direct. I planned on doing that someday when I'm much older. Sam was described as a "loving husband and prominent trial lawyer." Maybe this validation might be premature, but I'd take it.

My phone rang, and I answered on the first ring.

"Chris will do it," Josh said. "He wants me to remind him again before he goes on midnight shift tomorrow. He said he could get it done for you faster if he had Sam's license plate number and his full name. Can you get those?"

"It's Samuel L. Ford III," I said, reading directly from the funeral home's website. "I'll get his license number for you late tomorrow morning. I only work until 11 since Chase has early release at noon. Sam's driving me to the school and then he'll take us home. I'll memorize his plate then. Anything else?"

"He said if you could find out his Social Security number, it would help, but he doesn't have to have it," Josh said.

"Yeah, that's a lot harder. I don't know how I'd do it without really snooping around."

"Don't worry, Chris said he'd call me right away if Sam has a record or any outstanding debt."

"Thanks a million, Josh. I owe you."

"You keep saying that."

"I always keep my promises," I said.

18

CAKE

After Sam pulled into the café's parking lot, I put on my sunglasses and went outside. Waves of sadness rushed over me as I stood in front of the bike shrine. Hour by hour, the trinkets kept growing each day she'd been missing. Prayer candles now encircled the bike and cute stuffed animals perched in the bike's basket. Ashley's mother couldn't bear to take the bike home, and none of us wanted to move it or put it in the storage building. It represented our hope she'd be found any day and became a sacred gathering place to pray for Ashley's return.

I walked slowly around Sam's truck before I climbed in so I could memorize his license plate number. I felt a little dirty doing that. It was a breach of trust somehow, but when I spotted his plate, I almost burst out laughing.

"Gonna be a scorcher," Sam said. "The weatherman says it will be a hundred degrees later with a heat index of 110. Hard to believe." His eyes were fixated on the bobbing helium balloons tied to Ashley's bike. "It doesn't get hot in the mountains. Not even close," he added.

"Thanks for coming on short notice. Could you come

inside for a few minutes after we get Chase? I made you a chocolate cake last night," I said. "Betty Crocker."

"I never say no to cake!"

"It's just a small thank you for helping me out while I was in the hospital and recovering," I said.

"My pleasure," Sam said. "It gives my life purpose these days now that my wife is gone and my son's jet-setting all over the world."

After Sam pulled in front of the school, he parked.

"Tell me about Joy," he said after a minute. "I saw her at the grocery store this morning. She was feeling no pain, so I hid from her until she left the store. I don't mean to pry or anything, but she's quite a character."

"What do you want to know?" I asked.

"Well, anything to help me understand her, but if it's too personal, we can talk about something else. I've gotten pretty nosey in my old age."

"Well, Joy's an alcoholic and a drug addict who goes through boyfriends like hot glazed donuts. She's always borrowing money from me, so I don't keep much cash on hand." I stared out the window at nothing. "I can't seem to shake her," I whispered.

"That might be the perfect reason to go to the mountains and escape your troubles. It's remote and beautiful and cool. No mosquitoes either! There's nothing more restorative, in my humble opinion," Sam said.

"I haven't forgotten about your offer. I just need a little more time."

"Take all the time you want. It's a huge decision, I know. But in the long run, it might be what you and Chase need. A fresh start."

Sam searched for a radio station, and I quickly texted Josh the words on Sam's vanity plate: "The Duke." It was a cinch to remember. Normally, I might have needed a trick or a mnemonic, like the one I learned in 10th grade biology class.

IPMAT: Interphase, Prophase, Metaphase, Anaphase, Telophase. Not this time.

Sam found a country station and then switched on the windshield wipers and sprayed a healthy dose of blue cleaning fluid onto the glass.

"Too many damn bugs in Florida!" Sam said, watching the dead insects turn his windshield into a gummy yellow mess. He kept squirting extra cleaner until we could see out. "Anything else I should know about Joy?" Sam prompted.

"She's been in jail and rehab a few times and is constantly looking for her next high. She'll sleep anywhere unless she has a new boyfriend who'll take her in. Joy's pretty and men are attracted to her. She looks younger than me."

"That's not true," he said.

"People think we're sisters. I'm the ugly older sister with a buzz cut and brown eyes, and she's the pretty younger sister with blonde hair and baby blues."

"Bullshit," Sam said. "I'm glad you don't resemble her. You're your own person, Twy."

"You'd think with all her years of drinking and drugging, she'd be haggard like the real Calamity Jane, right? Even after two kids, she still doesn't look her age," I said.

Just then, Chase ran out the school door and spotted the Silverado. Sam tooted his horn seven times and chanted along: "Shave and a haircut, two bits."

"What's two bits?" I asked.

"Twenty-five cents. I'm showing my age again, right?"

"I like people who act their age. More than you know," I answered.

Chase climbed over me and sat between us. He rattled on about the kids he played with at recess: a new kid who collects model cars and a girl who knows her multiplication tables up to 12. I smiled at him and squeezed his hand three times. It was our secret "I love you" code. He grinned and squeezed my hand.

"It sounds like you had a really great day," I said. "Guess

what? Sam's taking us home and then he's going to have cake with us."

"Cool!"

"I hope I can make it out of here before these damn school buses do," Sam said. "There's nothing worse than getting behind a bus—a ten-minute trip turns into an hour, and I don't want your cake going to waste!"

19

JOSH

"S am's clean," Josh announced when I answered the phone. "Totally clean: fingerprints, criminal record, traffic violations, everything. His wife died a year ago. He was a trial lawyer, and he's wealthy, so he didn't lie to you about his past."

"He's not a serial killer or anything?"

"From what Chris said he's not, or at least he never got caught," Josh teased.

"I can relax now?"

"Well, since I have no idea what you're talking about, I guess so," he said.

"Not even a parking ticket or a DUI?"

"Nothing, but remember, Sam was a prominent lawyer. I'm sure he had lots of connections," Josh said. "Chris will give me a copy of the full report."

"Thanks, Josh."

"Listen, you said you owed me. How about dinner tonight?" he asked.

"Chase is having a sleepover with his friend Bryce, so that might work. They're celebrating the last day of summer school. At least, Chase is. Bryce lives with his grandmother on the third floor of Ocean View. I have to be home by midnight since I work tomorrow."

"Don't start digging your escape hatch before I get there," he said. I held the phone away from me, so I wouldn't say something stupid.

"I don't do that," I said in a controlled voice.

"Just every time. I've watched you. Even if it's something you want to do, you're tunneling through to the other side in case you need an escape. "

"I just don't want to get cornered," I said.

"So, what's it gonna be, a real date tonight or a foxhole with a secret door?"

"A real date," I said softly. "What time?"

"How about 8 p.m.? That gives me plenty of time to take a long shower and dress up."

"Where are we going?" I asked.

"Wear something pretty," Josh answered.

"Okay, I'll try to find something nice to wear."

"No last-minute cancellations or sudden emergencies. Promise?"

"I promise," I said.

A swallow-tailed kite hovered motionless in the air and then gracefully landed on the top of a palm tree right outside my window. I'd seen them many times before, but this one seemed different. Its striking black-and-white feathers and deeply forked tail caught the sun, and the bird glowed almost iridescent as it slowly turned, like an elegant weathervane.

I slid the metal clothes hangers, one at a time, to the right side of the closet until I found Joy's sundress. I'd worn it to my high school graduation three years ago, but it seemed more like ten. The dress was powder blue—Joy's favorite color. It played up her eyes and hair, she said.

"Pastels do that for blue-eyed blondes," she told me, "but you might look pretty in it, too, Twyla."

I pulled it off the hanger and tried it on. It still fit. If I washed and ironed it, the dress would look like new. I had a pair of strappy sandals I could wear with it and dug them out of the closet and set them on the floor beside my bed. I felt better, almost excited.

Two hours later, I had taken a shower, dried my hair, applied some make-up, and put a few drops of my favorite cologne behind my ears. After I slipped on the freshly ironed dress and buckled the sandals, I put on a pair of sparkly earrings I found at a yard sale.

The doorbell rang right at 8:00, and I froze for a second. When I opened the door, Josh stood there dressed in a crisp white shirt and striped tie. He wore khaki pants instead of jeans, and his hair was neatly parted and combed to one side like a college boy. He handed me a small plastic box with a white orchid inside. It was a wrist corsage like high school girls wore to proms. I felt too old for one, but I opened the box and smiled at him.

"Thanks, Josh," I said, slipping the corsage over my left wrist. "It's beautiful."

"Here's Sam's background check," he said, handing me an envelope. "You can read it later."

I wanted to rip the envelope open right then, but I didn't need to delay our evening together. I took it to the laundry closet, stuck it in the washing machine, and closed the lid. Nobody would look in there, especially Chase, and he wouldn't be home until noon tomorrow.

Josh helped me into the cab of his newly washed and waxed truck. A new coconut air freshener dangled from the rearview mirror. He drove to a fancy nightclub called Club Flamingo. I'd never been there before but had heard it was expensive.

We stood in a long line for a while, since they were checking photo IDs. Music pulsed from the dance floor inside, and the bass was really loud. When we got a little closer, we could see through the entrance doors that had been propped open.

Strobe lights flashed from floor to ceiling and white lights snaked all around a fancy wood bar.

"Maybe we should come another night," I said. "The line is so long."

"No more hatch-door excuses. We'll get in. I *know* people," he boasted.

When we reached the head of the line, the bouncer shook Josh's hand.

"Hey, how ya doin' man? Just go on in," he said, not bothering to check our IDs.

The place glowed electric with music and laughter. I knew then I needed to soak it all in and forget my worries for a while.

"What do you want to drink?" Josh asked.

"Whatever's on tap, I guess."

"No cheap stuff tonight. How about a fancy drink? A martini or tequila?"

"With an umbrella?" I asked.

"You can have anything you want," he said.

"Okay, I'll take a pina colada with extra maraschino cherries. And an umbrella."

"Wait here," he instructed, after finding an empty table for two at the edge of the dance floor.

After a couple of minutes, a cute guy approached the table.

"You want some company?" he asked, pulling a chair out and sitting across from me. "Nice dress. And I like your little wrist corsage. You from Naples?"

"Yeah, I've lived here a while."

I hid my wrist under the table and wanted to take off the flower without hurting Josh's feelings. I felt childish wearing a corsage.

"I'm with someone," I said, nodding toward the bar.

The guy either didn't hear me or thought I was lying. He didn't budge and leaned across the table toward me as Josh returned with our drinks.

"She's *taken*, buddy," Josh announced in a loud voice.

"Sorry, man. I didn't know," the guy said, pushing his chair back from the table.

"Now you *do*," Josh said, staring the guy down.

I watched Josh take charge. Impressive.

"Already picking up guys, huh?" Josh kidded. "I can't leave you alone for a second, can I? You're honey to the bees."

That sounded old fashioned, like something Sam would say.

"Here's your drink with a pink umbrella, just like you wanted. The bartender added extra cherries," Josh said.

I touched the tiny ribbed umbrella that shaded my drink and felt like royalty. There was a pineapple wedge, plus four cherries pierced with a pink plastic toothpick. I lifted the tooth-pick to my mouth and sucked off the cherries, one by one. Juice dribbled down my chin, and Josh reached over and smoothed a drop away with his thumb. I remembered how embarrassed Sam was when I removed a dot of whipped cream from his nose, but I wasn't embarrassed at all when Josh did it. I lifted the umbrella out and carefully closed it before I took a drink. It tasted sweet and strong—definitely an eye-opener.

Josh sucked on a lime and then downed a shot of tequila.

He insisted on ordering steak dinners for both of us, and we sipped our drinks and shared an appetizer while we waited.

As the live band switched from hard rock to the intro for a ballad, a female vocalist walked to the mic. She was a tall redhead with blue streaks in her hair. The crowd applauded wildly. I figured she must be a local favorite.

After she sang "Dancing in the Dark," the lights dimmed and the band played another slow tune. A lone couple walked to the center of the dance floor. Soon it became crowded with lovers dancing under a mirrored disco ball.

After dinner, we strolled to the center of the room and carved out a space. Josh pulled me close, and I liked it. With my hand on his shoulder, the orchid tickled my nose. We danced with others all around, but soon it felt like just the two of us.

"You smell like cookie dough," he whispered.

"It's vanilla."

"Perfume?" he asked.

"No, just artificial vanilla."

"Hey, Cookie, enjoying yourself?" he asked.

"Yeah," I whispered. "I really needed this. Understand?"

"Completely," he said.

"You smell good, too, Josh."

"After a hot shower, I finally got the smell of greasy hamburgers and onion rings out of my hair," he said.

The music stopped, and the lights pulsed to the beat of a fast number. When the floor became twice as crowded, we retreated to our table. Our waitress took our plates and empty glasses and returned with two more drinks on a round tray. She looked worn out, like me after a double shift. I wanted to leave her a nice tip, but I couldn't afford it. Maybe Josh could.

"Caught in a maze of booze and flashing lights and midnight shifts, she lost her way," I whispered.

"What?"

"It's just a game my teacher Alexandra and I used to play," I said.

"How do you know who wins?"

"Nobody wins. We just liked to try to reduce people's lives down to one sentence."

"You need a new freakin' game. You haven't summarized me, have you?" Josh asked.

"You're much too complicated," I teased.

"Whatever. Let's dance," he said, reaching for my hand.

After three drinks or so, I'd lost count. We were dancing to every song, even the fast ones. I didn't feel out of place anymore or worry about Sam or Chase or even Ashley for a few wonderful hours. Josh finally took off his tie, unbuttoned his collar, and carefully rolled up both of his sleeves. It must have been a brand new dress shirt, but it was soaking wet now.

Close to 3:00 in the morning, the DJ announced the last slow dance, and the lights dimmed. Josh held me close, and we swayed in slow motion. With my hand on his shoulder, the wrist corsage tickled my nose, and it smelled delicate and exotic at the same time. I was thankful I hadn't taken it off.

"May I kiss you, Twyla?" Josh asked so softly I barely heard him.

Before I could answer, his lips brushed against mine. We walked hand in hand to our table, and then all the lights slowly came on. I closed one of the pink umbrellas and slipped it into my purse before we left and walked out into the night. The air seemed almost balmy for Florida after the frenzied heat of the dance floor. We took our time walking slowly, half-drunk, to his truck.

Josh lowered the gate and spread a heavy blanket on the bed's floor. He lifted me up, took off my sandals, and climbed in.

"I just want to sit here for a little while until my head clears," he said. "Too much tequila. I knew I shouldn't have had that last shot."

"Do you care if I turn the radio on?"

Josh handed me his keys, and I hopped out and found a Golden Oldies station. Then we lay together, singing along to *Desperado*, staring at the stars until he closed his eyes and fell asleep. I tucked the wrist corsage in my purse, and then I called Sam.

20

ASHLEY

Twenty minutes later, Sam pulled beside us wearing his new Clint Eastwood hat. He lowered his window and took one look at me and then at Josh, who was passed out in the bed of the truck.

"You're right, Twyla. You two definitely need a ride home. By the looks of things, Josh is wasted and you shouldn't drive, so let's try to ease him into my Silverado with a truck-to-truck transfer," Sam said, laughing at his own joke. "His truck will be safe here overnight."

Sam set his emergency brake and climbed in beside us.

"Josh, hey buddy. Wake up! It's time to go home," Sam said, nudging him.

He gently shook Josh by the shoulders until he opened his eyes.

"Sorry, Twyla. Did I ruin everything?" Josh asked in a groggy voice.

"No, no. Sam's just going to take us home. Are you too dizzy to walk?"

"No, I'm fine," he slurred.

Sam and I steadied Josh as he climbed down. He stood there for a minute, leaning against his truck until he got his sea legs. I felt a little dizzy, too, but nothing compared to Josh. He draped his arms over our shoulders, and then we helped him climb into the bed of Sam's truck.

Sam grabbed an old army blanket from his cab that I loosely draped over Josh. Then Sam turned off the radio, took Josh's keys, and locked the doors.

"Don't worry. I'll drive slowly," he reassured me. "If you spot any cop cars, though, lie down there beside Josh and hide under the blanket real fast. I don't want to ruin my perfect driving record," he said with a wink.

I thought immediately of his "perfect" background check, and how "perfect" didn't seem normal for anyone at all. I'd have to study the full report tomorrow.

"You're an easy target with that vanity plate," I cautioned.

"So you noticed *The Duke*? It took me over a year to get it, and now it's mine forever," he said proudly.

Sam leaned in closer and studied my eyes. "Remember to drink a lot of liquids when you get home, Twy. Do you have any Gatorade?"

I nodded my head yes, but meant no. I couldn't afford sports drinks. Water would do just fine. Sam probably thought I'd never been buzzed before. After he started his truck, he drove at a slow pace down the highway. It was a beautiful, clear night, and the wind on my face felt soothing. Josh turned over, and I wrapped the blanket around him again. After a block or two, he was out cold.

"I didn't dig my escape this time, Josh," I whispered.

He snored softly, a gentle hypnotic sound, and I struggled to keep my eyes open.

Sam headed to Josh's place first, got out, and knocked on his apartment door. A motion light came on, a dog started barking, and Terry, his roommate, came outside without a shirt on.

"Tied one on there, Ironman, huh?" Terry asked, peering in at Josh.

I got in the cab while Terry and Sam helped Josh stagger

across the yard and then up a narrow stairway just inside the entrance.

"I gave Josh's keys to Terry," Sam said when he returned. "I'm glad you two had a good time, but it looks like your hot date went a little sour."

I felt my face turning an angry red and felt grateful it was dark outside.

"You're my next stop," he said, pulling away from the curb. He seemed unnaturally quiet the rest of the way, and I didn't feel like talking either. He switched on the radio to listen to the weather report.

Sam parked out front and rode the elevator with me to the tenth floor. He lingered outside my apartment door while I got my keys from my purse. Pearl's door was cracked open, and I could feel her opera glasses zooming in on us.

"Can I make you a cup of coffee, Sam?"

"No, it's way too late. I've got to get home to Cali," he said, but he just stood there like something was nagging at him.

"Thanks again for everything, Sam," I said, hoping he would leave.

"My pleasure, cowgirl. You get some shuteye now," he said, tipping his hat. Pearl's door closed. The cowboy was leaving, so she must have decided to go to bed.

I watched him approach the elevator and then stop midway and turn. He cleared his throat before he spoke.

"I didn't want to ruin your evening, Twyla, but I don't want you hearing this from a stranger."

"Hear what?" I asked.

"Ashley," he said, steeling himself. "They found Ashley's body this evening. They think it's a homicide."

I couldn't move, and the words *body* and *homicide* hadn't registered. I just stared at Sam's moving mouth.

"She suffocated," he said.

"Why would anyone want to kill Ashley?" I gasped. "Maybe

it's not her, maybe it's somebody else. How do they know for sure it's her?"

"She matched the description, and they're 100% sure it's Ashley. Her mother identified her body at the morgue, but her DNA will be sent to the lab for verification."

I leaned against the stucco wall and barely felt its scratchy surface as I slowly slid to the floor.

"Sorry, Twyla. It's a damn tragedy! Ashley was such a nice girl. She had her whole life before her."

"Where did they find her?" I asked.

"I'll tell you tomorrow after you get some sleep. I just didn't want you to find out about this on the news," Sam said.

"No, tell me now. I have to know!"

Sam sat on the floor beside me and took his hat off.

"A family visited Corkscrew Swamp this afternoon, and their kids were throwing rocks in the water. One of them hit something that looked like a black mirror. They mentioned it to a clerk at the gift shop, and she called one of the tour guides to check it out. Nothing was suspicious at first, but after a ranger fished out a heavy metal footlocker, he called the police. A young girl's body was crammed inside. It was reported she'd been dead for about four or five days. Ashley's backpack was later found on the bank covered in mud, and her pink running shoes were still inside. Nobody deserves to die like that," Sam whispered. "Nobody."

I covered my face with my hands and felt myself retreating and sealing out the world. I tried to calm myself when the weight of Sam's words finally sunk in. A deep well of grief imploded inside of me.

"If it had been any other night except Monday, I would have been the one to drop off the money, and I'd be lying in that morgue right now. I was the target, not Ashley." I said.

"You don't know that for sure," Sam said.

"I've made up my mind."

"About what?" Sam asked.

"The cabin," I said in a rush. "I want to go to your cabin right now."

"Don't you need more time to think things over?"

"Ashley didn't know her time on this planet was up, so I'm not waiting here any longer. It's not safe for Chase or me," I said.

"Okay, but don't do anything you'll regret later," Sam advised.

But all I could think about was Ashley's angelic face, her mud-covered backpack, and her waterlogged cowboy boots lying somewhere on the bottom of Corkscrew Swamp under the shadow of a sleeping alligator.

"Let's talk about it again after you get some rest," Sam said, struggling to stand. "My knees are getting rusty, and they don't always cooperate."

"I'll make a reservation, fly to Maryland tomorrow, and get a rental car," I said, trying to plot my escape. "Where is your cabin located?"

"Slow down there, Twyla. I know you're upset, but I don't think you can get away that fast. Unless you can afford to rent a Hummer or a helicopter, you won't make it up Glass Mountain in a rental car," Sam said.

"What about a truck?"

"I don't think Avis rents out too many four-wheel-drive trucks. That is, if you decide to go through with this."

"I'll ask for the deposit on my apartment tomorrow morning, and then I'll have enough money for my ticket and the rental," I said. I felt lightheaded again, so I took a couple of slow, deep breaths.

"Look, if you have to leave right away, Chase and I can fly you there."

"What are you talking about?" I asked.

"I own a plane. A Cirrus. It's big enough for the three of us. I keep a truck in the hangar at the Garrett County Airport when I'm gone," he said.

"Who'll take care of Cali?" I asked.

"I'll just board her at a kennel for a day or two."

I tried to take it all in, tried not to look stunned, but I failed. He really must be rich, filthy rich. Sam smiled and patted me on the shoulder. He didn't look like a pilot—too old. Aren't there strict age limits to fly an airplane?

"How many trucks do you own?" I asked.

"Just two. One is here in Florida and one in Maryland. Both of them are red."

"I've never flown before or been out of Florida," I confessed.

"Just make yourself a drink before we leave. That'll calm your nerves. Here, take these whiskey miniatures," he said, fishing two little bottles of Jack Daniel's from his inside pocket. The thought of alcohol right now turned my stomach, but I put them in my purse anyway.

"What if I have a panic attack?"

"My plane has its own parachute if we need it," he said.

"But what if it doesn't deploy? What if we crash on takeoff? What if..."

21

ESCAPE HATCH

I lifted the wilted corsage from my purse, put it into a chipped coffee cup, and set it on the windowsill in honor of Ashley. I stirred a little sugar into the warm tap water like I had seen someone do on TV and filled the cup halfway. Maybe it would help bring the flower back to life. Then I gently opened the tiny pink umbrella and leaned it in the cup. Ashley's favorite colors were pink and lavender. Her running shoes and her backpack were pink. Her bike was lavender and pink.

No turning back now. I had made up my mind. I'd leave Florida tomorrow. My blind trust belonged to Sam, just like a lone hitchhiker on the interstate getting into a car with a complete stranger. Sometimes it's your only choice.

I got into bed and switched on the nightlight. Alexandra's favorite quote by Eleanor Roosevelt popped into my head: *Do one thing every day that scares you.* Leaving Florida and flying for the first time in an airplane made me an overachiever.

After Chase came home from his sleepover at Bryce's the next morning, I called in sick. He'd been awake half the night eating pizza and playing computer games, so he crawled right into his bed and fell asleep. I remembered I had hid the background check in the washing machine, so I went to the laundry room and put the print-out into my purse. Then I called my landlord and pleaded my case for breaking the lease. I told her I'd leave the place spotless.

"No worries, Twyla. I'll put your deposit in the mail next week. Where should I send it?" she asked.

"At this point, I'm not really sure. Any chance I could get it from you today or tomorrow?"

"Sure. Stop by anytime this afternoon and I'll have it ready."

I made more calls and canceled the utilities. My mail should be forwarded, but to where?

I decided I would leave Josh a note or a voice message. I knew what he'd say— I'd dug my final escape with a fucking bulldozer, but I didn't care.

My phone rang. It was Sam.

"I'll meet you and Chase in the coffee shop inside Naples Municipal Airport this afternoon. Are you packed?"

"Not yet. I'm worried about Joy. I can lie to her for a while, but she'll want to keep Chase when she discovers I'm gone," I told him.

"I'm a pro at getting my way, so she won't be a problem. Here's the plan. After we fly to Maryland, Caleb will meet you in the terminal of the Garrett County Airport, and then Chase and I will fly back to Florida. Caleb has a key to my cabin, and he can show you the ropes. The main thing is to turn up the baseboard heat, switch on the cistern pump, start a fire, and pour yourself a drink. The whiskey's in the liquor cabinet in my bedroom. It's the room with the big rack of antlers over the headboard. You can't miss it."

"Heat?"

"It's always a little chilly in the mountains, even in summer," Sam said. "I leave it at 55 degrees when I'm not there, so the pipes don't freeze."

"I don't have much to pack and what I don't need, I'm

throwing away. I have to buy a winter coat, though, but I can get one from Goodwill," I said.

"I've got closets full of clothes at the cabin—long johns, winter coats—I still have Lydia's clothes. I can't bear to throw them away. Some things take time, you know. She was bigger than you, but in a pinch, you'll have plenty to stay warm. Parka, gloves, boots, hats, scarves, flannel-lined jeans, that kind of thing."

"Do you have a phone there, Sam?" I asked.

"It's just for emergencies—a landline. You might even be able to use my dial-up if you're long on patience."

"Dial-up?"

"It's a really slow way to get on the Internet. Sometimes it works, sometimes it doesn't, but it's better than nothing, right?" Sam asked. "No cell service on Glass Mountain."

"Is it okay to have my mail forwarded to your Palmettos' address for now or do you have a mailbox at the cabin?"

"I do, but it's in Oakland. My box number is 214. The postmaster knows me. I'll call Bob right now and let him know your mail will be redirected to my P.O.," he said. "If you can't get off the mountain for a while, he'll hold it for you—a couple of months even. He puts a large cardboard box underneath my mailbox to handle the overflow."

"Instead of paying me all at once, Sam, could you deposit some money into my checking every week or so?" I asked.

"Anyway you want it, Twyla. There's just not much you'll need to buy—really nothing at all. I know you have a few outstanding bills, but I'll pay them for you."

"Don't say anything to Josh yet. He'll try and stop me from leaving. I'll call him after I get settled. Please don't tell him where I am. Can you keep our secret?"

"I was a lawyer, remember? I'm good at double-talk and keeping my mouth shut. I got top grades in Truth Bending 101. That's why I don't have to worry where my next meal is coming from. I'll hold down the fort here in Florida with Chase. If you need anything, anything at all, I'll take care of it. Leaving town in a hurry guarantees you'll forget something, but don't worry. It'll all work out," he said.

"After I empty the apartment, I'll drop Chase off at your place later this morning."

"I'll be here," he said.

I took a large duffel bag from the closet and a black plastic garbage bag from under the sink. I tossed everything I didn't need into the bag. My—I mean, Joy's— wrinkled sundress went first, followed by my sandals, shorts, flip-flops, and magazines and newspapers. I hesitated before I threw away my gasoline-soaked cowboy boots because they weren't paid for yet, but they reminded me of Ashley so I couldn't keep them. I carried all of Chase's stuff to the living room. He didn't stir one time.

I checked on him before I locked the door behind me. After I carried the plastic bag to the elevator and then to the alley behind the high rise, I remembered the floor mats I had thrown under the front hedge. I walked to the main entrance, pulled them out, and set them in the alley.

When I returned, Chase was still asleep. He looked so innocent lying there that a lump formed in my throat and my chest ached from trying not to cry. I gently closed the door, lay on my bed, and tried to muffle my sobs with a pillow. Then I washed my face with cold water, went into the living room, and began packing Chase's clothes, video games, and his Buzz Lightyear pajamas into my suitcase. It used to be big enough for all of our things, but now there was barely room for Chase's.

When he woke, I told him we were going on an airplane ride with Sam, but first I had to clean out the apartment. He got so excited, he didn't ask any questions, and he helped me strip the bed, dust, and sweep the floors. He was used to quick moves.

"Now that summer school's over, you might like to stay with Sam at his condo for a little while," I said. "I've got a new job, but I can't take you with me. I'll be back in just a few months and then we'll move to a bigger place, maybe rent our own house with a big yard."

Chase sat cross-legged on his bare mattress and took it all in.

"In Naples?" he asked.

"No, probably somewhere else. Maybe West Virginia or Ohio." I answered, trying to think fast because there wasn't time to dream of a future, a future that might not come true unless I lasted out the winter in Sam's cabin.

"If we move to Cincinnati, we could go to a Reds' game. Let me go tell Bryce!" he said, jumping off the bed.

"Not now. We don't have time, and anyway, it's top secret. I've got to take you to Sam's place, and then we'll all take a ride on his airplane this afternoon."

"Sam's a pilot? Cool!" Chase said.

"Would you clean the windows for me?"

"Sure!" Chase said, taking the Windex from my hand and grabbing a roll of paper towels off the counter.

"I'll take a taxi and drop him off in about an hour," I told Sam when I called him. "Josh's truck is still in the parking lot where we left it last night."

"I'll be here, Twyla. Are you getting a cold?"

"No, it's just my allergies. I've been dusting and that always stirs them up. I'm taking a taxi to get my deposit from my land-lord. Would it be okay if Chase rides to the airport with you? He's so excited."

"No problem," Sam said.

I emptied the refrigerator, wiped the shelves with rubbing alcohol, and scrubbed the sink. I did a quick walk-through and found a few things I'd forgotten. I tucked my bandanna-wrapped derringer inside my duffel bag.

I placed it and Chase's suitcase inside the apartment's front door, and then he went with me to take another plastic bag to the alley. When we returned to the empty apartment, my eyes strayed to the kitchen windowsill. The wilted orchid was still sheltered by the pink umbrella—a simple memorial to Ashley resting in a chipped cup.

22

SUMMER 2011

BROKEN CRAYONS

A nosy neighbor told Joy I was selling pictures to strangers at the bus stop. When she came home that night all drunk, she started screaming that if she lost her welfare money, Chase and I would be put in foster homes, and then we'd never see each other again.

Joy found my coloring books, ripped them apart, and threw my crayon box clear across the room. When the crayons fell out on the floor with my money inside, she grabbed it and said I'd stolen it from her purse. She said she'd beat the hell out of me for selling my pictures and for stealing. Chase started crying and tried to put the broken ones inside the box. I picked him up, but he cried even louder. Then Joy ran out of the house with three dollars in her fist.

23

OBITUARY

When the taxi pulled in front of Palmettos, Chase managed to carry his suitcase to Sam's porch, and I rang the doorbell. Cali started barking, and I spotted Sam's eyes framed between two parted venetian blinds. He opened the door and took the suitcase as Chase hurried inside to pet Cali.

"What if we all meet at the airport in an hour?" Sam asked.

"Sounds good to me, but I need to get there a little early, so I can calm down," I said. "I'll use an ATM to deposit my check and get some cash. See you two soon," I said, as I headed to the waiting taxi.

Sam saluted me, and Chase waved and sipped from a can of Coca-Cola. He was no stranger to Sam's apartment and his refrigerator.

I arrived at Naples Municipal Airport and put the strap of my overstuffed duffel bag across my chest. I felt like a grade school patrol girl but tried to look confident and worldly like I'd flown all my life.

After I ordered a cup of coffee and sat near the entrance of *The Landings* restaurant, I stared at passengers coming and going: weary businessmen, mothers with cranky children, vacationers wearing t-shirts printed with maps of Florida and

Florida is for Oranges. One man wore a bright yellow shirt with black paw prints walking across it. When he got closer, I read "Six-Toed Cats, Key West, Ernest Hemingway—the author of "write one true sentence." I wanted to go to Key West someday to see his house. I'd seen photos of it and the descendants of his cats, six-toed and otherwise, that still found sanctuary there.

I took out my phone and started to delete my old text messages. When I came to Diana's, I remembered I hadn't responded to her lunch invitation days before.

"Sorry I can't meet you," I wrote. "I just need to get away for a while. Don't worry."

Across the way, a small bar was crowded with men in expensive suits and starch-stiff dress shirts and silk ties. None of them looked too happy. I wondered how many business trips it took before the novelty of air travel wore off. I walked by a kiosk with designer purses and expensive perfumes, a newsstand, and a few leather reclining chairs. A man and a woman were getting neck massages, and they were oblivious to peoples' stares.

A young boy with dirty blond hair played a video game, and he sat at a table across from me. For a second, I thought he looked like Chase, and I felt myself shutting down, the walls going up. Joy used to call me Princess Stoneface. I learned years ago tears never helped, so I retreated, to turned to stone, so "stone-faced" was true, but not the fucking princess part.

I wished they had a crying booth in this airport instead of neck massages or expensive whiskey. The booth would be a soundproof space capsule with plenty of tissues for stockpiled tears. On layovers, you could steal away inside the capsule for a price. You'd push a button and listen to sad music or watch really old movies like *Sophie's Choice* or *Field of Dreams* and cry until your tears ran dry. Or you'd have the option to talk to an anonymous counselor who could milk the petrified tears right out of you and prescribe antidepressants you could buy from a pre-loaded vending machine. A sound machine would fill the booth with the roar of crashing ocean waves, and you'd take a nap on a down-filled recliner. When you woke, a pot of espresso and chocolate croissants would be waiting. There'd be a small sink where you could wash your face, red-out drops for your bloodshot eyes, a make-up mirror, and sample cosmetics if you wanted them, plus a disposable brush and a comb and a pair of dark sunglasses. You'd leave rested, purged, and stronger. I wonder how much a good crying booth would cost. Would there be a long line?

It had only been 30 minutes since I arrived. Slow-motion escapes didn't work for me. Since I had made the decision to leave Florida, I needed it to happen *now*.

I walked to the newsstand and browsed through the magazines and newspapers and best-selling novels. The books were too expensive, so I bought a copy of *The Florida Sentinel*, and the cashier dropped it inside a plastic bag.

When I returned to the coffee shop, I put the paper on the table. Ashley grinned at me in living color from the front page —she didn't know she was dead. I felt like the wind had been knocked out of me, and I couldn't catch my breath for a few seconds. I quickly turned the page, but then another photo showed her bike covered with balloons and stuffed animals piled in the bike basket. There were flowers and handmade cards, plus a circle of prayer candles lighting the darkness while friends and family held hands. Pink felt cut-outs of the letter "A" dangled from both sides of the bike's spokes. I spotted Ashley's mother on her knees, covering her face with her hands. Sam and Josh were standing close behind her. I wished to God that there really was a crying booth, one I could disappear inside of for a couple of days.

My picture should have been on the front page instead of Ashley's. If it had been one day earlier, I would have been the one headed to the bank in my white jeans and red bandanna. I tried to calm myself, breathe slower, but my body wouldn't cooperate.

Who would write Ashley's obituary? I couldn't possibly do it.

Maybe someday, when I'm thinking clearer, I could try to create a sentence for her—one true sentence. I found the obituary page and her smiling face was there, too, with a big write-up by one of the staff reporters.

Joy used to complain you couldn't afford to die because an obituary cost a hundred dollars an inch, and a color photo was out of the question. I remembered the voices of grief-stricken relatives when I'd called with a quote for running the notice about their beloved mother or father, son or baby daughter. I felt like a grave robber, but I was just doing my job. Joy said she could remember when obituaries were free. The high cost took one final stab, and the dead weren't even around to read it or cut it out and paste it in a scrapbook.

I started thinking about my own death. Since I didn't have much money, maybe Facebook was the answer. At least they didn't charge yet. I could create an Event, compose my own obituary, invite people to my graveside service, and have a friend click *Send* when I died. I'd even prepare a one-sentence distillation of my life and upload a color profile photo to be sent to all my friends.

People can be immortal on Facebook. It's a sin to unfriend them after they're dead. Maybe their Facebook page would keep their words and spirit alive for a century or more, as they continued to acquire more friends with family photos and inspirational messages and new happy birthday wishes posted on their Wall each year forever.

24

TAKEOFF

My hands were shaking as I stuffed the newspaper into a trashcan. I ordered another cup of coffee to-go and took one of the whiskey miniatures from my purse. I unscrewed the top, poured it into my cup, and took a sip. It tasted strong and hot, so I drank half of it fast. If I could afford it, I'd drink more. Not like Joy does, but I'd treat myself now and then.

Maybe it was the whiskey, but I daydreamed about taking Chase to Disney World. Even though we lived in Florida, the cost was more than I could afford. He begged to go because his buddy Bryce had gone over Christmas break with his grandmother. Chase wanted to see the Light Parade, the fireworks, Epcot, and buy a Dole Whip, just like Bryce did. I told him I'd save my money, and as soon as I had enough, we'd go stay in a nice hotel and ride the rides. He started dancing and hugging me like a six-year-old. Maybe I could make his dream come true next summer after I'd house-sit Sam's cabin for a few months.

I found my homemade card game in the bottom of my purse. It was the one with babies' names written on one side and one-word descriptions of my customers on the other. I removed the rubber band and shuffled them. After I closed my eyes, I pulled a card from the deck and set it on the table. "Intrepid," I whispered.

"Ready for liftoff?" Sam asked as Chase put his cold hands over my eyes.

"Shit!" I yelled, pulling his hands off and turning over my chair in the process as my coffee and the cards spilled onto the floor.

"Not funny, Sam!" I yelled. "You scared me to death!"

He seemed stunned and a bit sheepish at my reaction. Chase didn't know what to do. The customers seemed startled, and then ignored us when a fight didn't break out.

A waitress rushed over and mopped up the mess. The smell of whiskey filled the room, and the waitress watched while I gathered my notecards and put *intrepid* on top. Then I wrapped the rubber band around the deck twice.

"What were you thinking?" I asked.

"Sorry, Twyla. We just wanted to surprise you," Sam said.

"Well, you did," I muttered. "Where's Cali?"

"I'm boarding her at a kennel until we return. She'll be fine," he said, staring at my eyes. "You look sleepy. Angry and sleepy."

"It's the whiskey," I said.

"Oh, I thought I smelled something good," he said with a big grin on his face.

"You and Josh were at Ashley's memorial last night," I said. "I saw your picture in the paper."

"I'll buy one later," he said. "I just happened to be driving by and saw a crowd gathering, so I went over to pay my respects. Josh was already there."

As we made our way toward the hangars where the private planes were housed, I held Chase's hand, and he giggled with excitement. I felt a little spacy, but nothing more. After Sam opened the hangar door, he proudly pointed to his silver aircraft. *The Duke* was written in huge metallic letters on both sides of the plane.

Chase and I both gasped. It looked like something a movie star owned or a John Wayne obsessed movie star named Sam.

"Are you two ready to go?" Sam asked.

He positioned a small tow bar under the front wheel and lifted a handle that looked like one on a child's wagon. Then he effortlessly pulled the plane about 50 feet outside. After he returned the tow and parked his truck inside, he closed and locked the hangar door.

"I always leave my truck in there," Sam explained.

Chase raced to the plane, and Sam opened the gullwing doors. We watched him walk around slowly and inspect everything. Then we stepped on the footrest and entered the plane.

I sat beside Sam, and Chase had the bench seat to himself. The controls were all lit up, and there seemed to be a million gadgets and gauges. I hoped Sam knew what he was doing. To protect our ears, Sam gave us a pack of Teaberry gum to chew during the flight. *Where the hell does he find a flavor like that?* I thought. I chewed a stick as a precaution and to help mask the whiskey on my breath. The gum tasted strange. Chase made a face, spit it out, and handed it to me. I wrapped it in a tissue and stuck it in my purse.

We buckled our seatbelts, put on our headsets, and before I could change my mind, we were taxiing down the runway and lifting off into a cloudless sky. Instantly, I felt out of control with the world rushing straight at me behind the windshield.

Everything was magnified, and I couldn't adjust so I closed my eyes. When I was brave enough to look down, Naples resembled an alien landscape from the air, and the Gulf of Mexico stretched on forever below us.

After a few hours of nothing but clouds and blue skies, I finally relaxed and watched Chase, all smiles, as he rode on his dream amusement park ride. He looked out the windows and never once seemed afraid.

I must have fallen asleep until we hit some turbulence, and I jolted awake when I felt my stomach drop. The right wing tilted downward for a second, and Sam said not to worry. It was just a cross wind.

Before I knew it, the plane slowly descended toward the Garrett County Airport. I saw tree-covered mountains, checkerboard farmland, and a large body of water Sam called Deep Creek Lake. From the sky, it looked like a sparkly blue dragon with toy sailboats skimming its surface. He circled the lake twice to give us the million dollar tour. It seemed foreign and surreal. Not the water, but the mountains. I had read about them, seen them on TV and in the movies, but I hadn't been north of Tallahassee my entire life. From my birds-eye view, I looked down on the breathtaking Allegheny Mountains for the first time.

"We'll probably run into more turbulence as we descend. The airport is surrounded by mountains and sits on top of a mountain crest, so it can get pretty choppy," Sam warned.

I checked Chase's seatbelt and then mine again as a precaution. As we made our final approach close to the ground, we were being tossed from side to side.

"Hang on!" Sam shouted. "I might have to abort the landing and start over."

Sam turned the plane's nose toward the direction of the wind as we were pushed sideways. I thought we were going to die.

"Cross your arms over your head," Sam commanded.

But then in just a few seconds, the plane became stable, but it felt like a lifetime to me.

"What happened?" I whispered.

"Mountain turbulence. It happens a lot at this airport," Sam explained. "I'm used to it, but it's frightening for novice pilots and passengers. I just had to crab into the wind to counter the turbulence. Are you two okay?"

Chase's face was pale, and he held an air sickness bag over his mouth. I had already thrown up in mine.

"Caleb's not here yet," Sam said after we landed and slowly climbed out of *The Duke.* "I'm a little ahead of schedule."

Then Sam handed me a can of ginger ale to sip on. I tossed our air sickness bags into a nearby trash can. The airport was so small compared to the ones in Naples, and the terminal looked like a new double-wide trailer with picture windows.

"What's that?" Chase asked, pointing to one of the orange and white cones that looked like small kites.

"It's a windsock. It shows pilots the strength and direction of the wind. I always take off and land into the wind; it creates more lift," Sam explained.

We watched while Sam's plane was inspected and refueled for his return flight. I stared at the majestic mountains that rose up all around us. My ears were still plugged up, so Sam told me to keep yawning and chew more gum. If it didn't work, pinch my nose and gently blow until the pressure was equalized.

"The altitude in Garrett County will take a little getting used to," he said. "It's over 3,000 feet above sea level."

Maybe that's why I feel dizzy, I thought.

"Well, I hate to tell you this, Twyla, but we need to leave right away and head to Naples. I don't like flying after dark if I can avoid it, plus the weather can be unpredictable in the afternoon," Sam said. "We have 5 hours of flying time, more or less, ahead of us, but we'll stay overnight in Charlotte tonight."

Everything had happened so fast. My decision to leave Naples, the flight to Garrett County, and now it was real.

"Come and tell your sister goodbye, Chase," Sam called.

He ran over and hugged me. The longer he hugged, the more I wanted to go back home.

"I just spotted Caleb's truck behind the terminal, so he'll be looking for you," Sam said. "When we come for a visit, I'll drive my truck that's already parked in the hangar," he said.

When Caleb got out of his truck, Sam cupped his hands around his mouth like a megaphone and yelled, "Caleb! I'll see you in a few weeks."

Caleb waved in response. I tried to focus in on his face, but he was too far away.

"Come on, boy. My friend will drive your sister to my palace now, and we've got to head out. We have a lot of flying ahead of us, and the possibility of an afternoon storm I want to avoid," Sam said, gently taking Chase's hand. "You want to sit up front this time and help me navigate?"

Chase nodded, wiped his eyes, and tried to look brave as he walked away with Sam, turning every so often to see if I were still standing there. Just before he climbed in *The Duke*, Chase waved goodbye. I knew I couldn't be stoic anymore, and I hurried inside the small terminal. The windsocks pointed toward Sam's plane, and I watched through a large plate glass window as Sam accelerated his plane down the runway and lifted off. I had just left my brother in the care of a stranger, and I thought my heart would shatter when they disappeared behind a cloud.

Jazz played softly in the background, and I scanned the faces, trying to decide which one might be Sam's neighbor. He said I'd know Caleb as soon as I saw him. After I sat in a chair, a lanky man wearing a camouflage jacket, blue jeans, and heavy work boots approached and stood about three feet away from me.

"Twyla?"

"Yes, are you Caleb?"

He nodded.

"Nice day, isn't it?"

"So far, but the weather can change on a dime here. Is that your luggage?" Caleb asked.

"Yes, just the duffel bag."

"Helen's cooking dinner. Do you like turkey and sauerkraut?"

"Sure." I said, trying to remember if I'd ever tasted sauerkraut before.

He carried my bag, and I followed him to his truck. Every

time I attempted to catch up to him, he walked a little faster. He drove a beat-up Tundra that sat high off the ground. He tossed my duffel bag between the seats, and I climbed in. The bag acted as a soft barrier between us in the cab. Then he proceeded to the front of his truck and lifted the hood. I hoped he didn't have engine trouble. After about five minutes, he slammed it shut and climbed in.

"Do you like hairpin curves?"

He started the engine and lowered the electric windows down and up, and down and up again.

"Maybe," I answered. "Guess I'll find out."

We sat in silence for a few miles, and I felt uncomfortable. He drove slowly—not more than 30 in a 50 mph zone. At least the view was spectacular, with pasture lands and more mountain vistas. When I realized he never drove any faster, never even reached the speed limit, I knew I was in for a long haul.

"Did Sam tell you we get a lot of snow here? We average about 120 inches a year. Did you know Hurricane Sandy was our biggest snowstorm, and they had to send in the National Guard?"

Weary from the steady stream of questions, I stopped answering him. I knew we were about 30 miles away because Caleb had already told me three times, and at this rate, it would take forever to get there. I acted like I didn't hear his Hurricane Sandy question and checked my cell phone for messages.

"That phone won't do you much good. Lots of dead space. Did Sam tell you the mountains interfere with the signal?" he asked.

I checked my bars and "*No Service*" appeared like an error message on my screen. I put the phone in my pocket—already experiencing withdrawal.

"Do you have any good radio stations here, Caleb?"

I kept staring at his truck radio as if I could will it to turn on by itself.

"How long do you plan on staying at Sam's place?" he asked.

"Not sure. Guess it'll depend on a lot of things," I said, trying to be vague.

A blue car started tailgating us. The double line on the winding two-lane highway kept the guy from passing. Soon another car and a camper were trailing behind the blue car. Caleb turned on his flashers.

He was getting nervous and kept looking in his rearview mirror. The man in the blue car started honking his horn.

"Fucking bastard! Son of a bitch!" Caleb exploded.

He lowered his window and motioned for the cars to go around him. The occupants stared at us the whole time.

"I forgot to put my seatbelt on," I said, casually tugging at the strap and clicking it into place.

He motioned more cars to pass him.

"Have you noticed everybody's in a fucking hurry?"

We drove down the road in silence. At least his questions had stopped for a short while.

"You want some coffee?" he asked.

"Only if you do," I said, knowing I might need something stronger.

"There's a gas station about a mile down the road. How do you like yours?"

"Black."

"You want a snack?" he asked.

"No, just coffee. Didn't you say your wife made dinner?"

Caleb narrowed his eyes as he slipped an unfiltered cigarette out of a pack he had wedged behind his sun visor. He pushed the cigarette lighter in, and when it popped out, he lit his cigarette and lowered the window.

"Helen's my sister. How long have you known Sam?" he said, quickly returning to his questioning.

I started to say not too long but changed my mind. Maybe my arrival had raised a red flag for him, so I remained silent.

"I've known Sam for about 30 years now. Not a mean bone in his body. He hasn't been the same since his wife died last year. Did you know Lydia?" Caleb asked.

"No, but Sam speaks so highly of her. I wish I had met her."

"Lydia used to have us over for dinner on Sundays when they were here. She was a good cook just like my sister. Do you cook?" he asked without a beat.

"I, well, not very much. I'm a waitress, so I don't like to be around food too much these days. Overkill, you know."

Caleb took a drag from his cigarette and then tossed it out the window. Maybe he thought I'd have his sister and him over to Sam's cabin for dinner. Maybe he thought I was trying to replace Sam's wife.

"How old are you?" he asked.

"Twenty-one."

"You know you look older?"

"That's what people keep telling me," I said.

25

SUMMER 2011

UNCLE RICK

S ometimes when Joy ran out of whiskey money, "Uncle" Rick took Chase and me to a new neighborhood, and drove until Joy spotted the perfect house with old people sitting on the porch or working in the yard. We waited until he parked the car about a block away. Then Rick ordered us to get out. The first time I stalled until he lit a cigarette and held it close to my face. So close I could feel its red heat and the smoke made my eyes water.

"You want a cheap tattoo, kid?" he growled.

I shook my head and never hesitated again to do his commands.

Joy handed me a small zip-lock bag, and we followed her. Rick opened a new can of beer and watched for cops.

"I'm sorry to bother you, ma'am." Joy said in a rush "But my little boy has to use the bathroom and he just can't hold it anymore. Please let him use your bathroom. It won't take a minute, and I'll wait out here. My daughter will go with him."

If the woman paused even for a second, Joy stared at Chase like she was going to beat him. He always burst into tears.

After the woman quickly showed us where the bathroom was, I locked the door, climbed on the sink, and grabbed any pill bottles from a medicine cabinet. I took several pills from each bottle if

127

they were full and one if they were almost empty. Then I'd drop the pills into a zip-lock bag, stuff it into my pocket, and put the bottles back just like I had found them.

Then I flushed the toilet and Chase washed his hands. We left the house in a big hurry but remembered to say, "Thank you, ma'am" before we walked to the car.

"What took you so long? Give me that damn bag!" Uncle Rick yelled, and then he threw two pills into his mouth and swallowed them whole.

26

SAM'S PALACE

CALEB

"You like living alone?" Caleb asked abruptly as he turned right off of Route 219 and then left onto Second Street. His question was unsettling. I tried hard not to react.

With each question he asked, it seemed, more were generated.

"Sorry, I'm all talked out, and I'm a little nauseous," I admitted, unwrapping a stick of Teaberry gum.

He stared straight ahead as we drove down the hill past several beautiful Victorian mansions on a tree-lined street. One had concrete lions that guarded the entrance; another grand home had a stained glass bay window and a welcoming wrap-around porch. A little boy with light brown hair was standing in the front yard. He waved as if he recognized me, and I waved back. After we passed the library on the right, I could see a gold-domed courthouse, the spire of a stone church, and then a quaint old railroad station. From the top of a steep hill straight ahead, a huge American flag caught the breeze and an imposing wooden cross kept watch over the small town.

I wanted to ask Caleb more questions but stopped myself, in case it might make him ask more. Near the end of the block, he made a left on Alder Street and pointed to a small building: *The Old Curiosity Shop*.

"My sister works there," he said.

In the display window a white wicker table was set with bright place settings in every color. Two scary, toddler-sized dolls with huge unblinking eyes sat facing each other in the chairs. A large rocker sat out front on the sidewalk beside a sign that read *Red Tag Sale*.

When the light changed at the top of Alder, we drove for what seemed like miles into the countryside. We passed a horse-drawn buggy with an Amish family inside. I tried not to stare, but I felt like a time traveler in a strange and charming land. After a while, Caleb turned onto Route 50 near Red House.

"That used to be The Chimney Corner Restaurant," he said, pointing to an old log and timber structure. "The logs were made of chestnut and that's why it lasted so long. Even the dining tables were chestnut, but the blight wiped out all the trees by 1950," he explained.

I noticed a large black cross on the front door and realized it was a church now. I saw a newer sign that read *Fresh Fire*.

We drove by beautifully manicured farmland with crystal blue skies overhead, dotted with stark-white clouds. I spotted a farmhouse with a tin roof, an old barn, and a few chickens in the front yard.

"That's our place. Mine and Helen's," he said. "Do you have any sisters?"

"Not that I know of, but I have a half-brother named Chase. He's ten."

Caleb kept driving and I saw a sign that said Backbone Mountain, 3,360 feet above sea level. Soon we came to an unmarked crossroad, and Caleb parked and got out. A heavy wooden gate blocked the entrance to a dirt road. He unlocked the padlock with a small key, swung the gate open, and we drove through a dry creek bed and then headed up a steep hill. I wouldn't call it a road exactly since there wasn't any blacktop or gravel, just a rutted path wide enough for one car that was surrounded by grisly trees and thorny bushes. He turned on the 4-wheel drive, and we began the bumpy climb to the top of the mountain. Caleb lit a cigarette and offered it to me.

"I don't smoke," I told him, but I took it anyway. Then he lit one for himself and concentrated on the road ahead. After a couple of puffs, the cigarette seemed to have a calming effect, and I was grateful to have something to do with my hands.It must have taken us 20 minutes or more to reach the top. I kept thinking I had chosen my fate and now I was really stuck. The trees were thick with creeper and tangled vines, and although the sun had been shining just a few minutes ago, we were deep in shadow here. Caleb hit a pothole and I gripped the seat, but he seemed unaffected and kept driving.

A deer stopped in the middle of the road and froze. Its dark eyes riveted on mine. Caleb switched off the engine.

"Aren't you going to honk the horn?" I whispered.

"Might spook it."

After a few minutes, the deer sauntered to the other side of the road. Two more followed. Then, Caleb started the engine and drove even slower up the hill.

Finally, we reached a small clearing and things leveled out. I could see an old log cabin with a screened-in porch. The grass had been freshly mowed. Caleb pointed out patches of Black-eyed Susans, chicory, and Queen Anne's lace that bloomed in the ditch line. After we pulled in front of the cabin, he switched off the engine.

"Well, what do you think? It's authentic with chinking and butt and pass logs," he said, pointing to one corner of the cabin with criss-crossed logs that laddered up to the roof.

I stared at black logs with white mortar sealing them together like bricks and overlapping logs stair-stepped from the ground to the roof.

We both got out, and I felt sore and rattled. Even though it had been a little over an hour's ride from the airport, the last 20 minutes had been rough. The aftertaste of whiskey and coffee and cigarette smoke lingered in my mouth, so I unwrapped another stick of gum and chewed it until it burned my tongue a little. I ventured a few steps closer toward the cabin and then turned to soak in the incredible mountain views.

Caleb took the lead and pulled a keychain from his pocket. He managed to unlatch the screen door on the porch and then unlocked the front door.

"Someone left Raven a gift," he said, looking down at the thick welcome mat. "I'll start a fire. It's always a little chilly, even in the dead of summer. The nights get right cold sometimes," he said.

"Raven?" I asked.

He didn't answer and headed to one side of the porch and returned with a handful of kindling on top of an armload of shaggy split logs.

I waited for him to go inside, and then I tentatively stepped on the porch. I noticed an old quilt rack and two wooden rocking chairs and a metal glider, but I was distracted by the ethereal view. Mountain after smoky blue mountain crested on the horizon in the late August sky. I sat on the glider and stared at all the beauty. *Maybe I could stay here a while.*Except for the rattle and thump of Caleb putting logs into the fireplace, the air was heavy with silence. When he switched on the porch light, I walked to the front door and froze.

"It's just a dead mouse," Caleb said. "It won't bite."

"Why didn't you warn me?"

"I did. At least Marigold didn't bring it inside this time. She's a good mouser," he said.

I stayed on the far side of the porch until he grasped the field mouse by its fleshy tail, walked to the edge of the hill, and flung it into the woods. While he was busy, I stepped into Sam's palace for the first time.

The living room had deer antlers or the heads of wild animals on every wall. An ancient grandfather clock with a moon-face dial sat to my immediate left and a white Conestoga wagon lamp cast a spooky glow over a long side table filled with exotic knives and daggers. Sam had bragged that his jet-setting son got them from all over the world.

A guest bedroom to my right had two twin beds set at each end of the long narrow room. The entrance from the living room was separated by a thin curtain instead of a door. An old saddlebag hung from the exposed rafters and to one side sat a pump organ. Sam had told me once his father served as a Methodist circuit-riding minister, so the saddlebag must have belonged to his dad. I parted the curtain and scanned the room. No decapitated bears or deer in there, so I might actually get some sleep tonight.

I walked to the other side of the living room. A bedroom and bath were located at each end of an open floor plan kitchen, with a red Dutch door in the middle of the back wall that opened to the yard.

Sam's place would take a lot of getting used to, but the warmth from the burning fire felt cozy. Caleb had turned on a backlit painting of a regal 12-point buck standing in a lush green forest. The deer looked alive in the picture, so that was comforting. A gun rack mounted on the wall above the side couch was right where Sam said it would be. The guns were lying horizontal in the racks, trigger-side up. I knew I wouldn't need my little derringer with this impressive arsenal, but I'd always keep it handy.

I stared at his shotgun, the 30/30 rifle, and the 30/40 Krag. He'd inherited them from his father and had talked about them so much I already had them memorized.

"More killing power, the higher they are set on the shelf," I whispered, repeating Sam's words to the empty room.

Landing on a sturdy branch above the gun rack, was a beautiful red-tail hawk with a wingspan of about four feet. I knew it was a red-tail because its name was engraved on a small plaque. Frozen in flight, its russet tail feathers and rich brown wings with tips like ragged fingers seemed as if they could catch the wind at any second and soar out the door.

"I've checked everything and turned on the electricity, water pump, baseboard heat, the rotary phone, and all the mouse traps are empty and rebaited. Marigold and Raven do a good job, don't you think?" he bragged.

"Thank God," I said, thinking Raven must be Marigold's sidekick.

After a few minutes, he went outside and entered a small concrete building where the cistern was kept. He didn't stay long.

"You've got plenty of firewood, water, and provisions. Any questions?"

Questions? I thought. *No, not now*, but before he left, I blurted out two that just couldn't wait.

"The water?" I asked.

"Don't drink or bathe in the cistern water. It's not safe. Don't wash your hands or brush your teeth with it either. Use the jug of hand sanitizer most of the time," he said, squirting some into his hands and rubbing them together. "There's bottled water for drinking and cooking stored under this sink and in the cupboard," he said pointing to another door in the bathroom.

Caleb opened the metal cabinet under the deep kitchen sink, and there were cases and cases of bottled water. Next to the refrigerator that sat on one side of the bathroom were several green metal cans. He emptied half of one into a glass canister that rested on a wooden stand.

"This is pristine spring water," he said. "You can use it for drinking. When you run out, I'll refill them since the cans are heavy. They hold five gallons each."

"Where are the keys?" I asked.

Caleb reached into his pocket and showed me a key ring with a blue quartz stone attached to it.

"This belonged to Lydia, but it's yours, for now. She liked

pretty stones. I keep extras to the gate, the cistern, and the cabin. Nobody will bother you here, but you might feel safer at night if you lock the doors. Lydia always did. Even with Sam here," he said.

He held out the keys, so I took them from his hand. He recoiled from my touch and stepped backward as if I had burned him.

"When Helen gets home from the shop, I'll come and take you to dinner. She wants to meet you. We eat at 8, so I'll be here at 7:30."

"Thanks, Caleb. Did you put my bag in the guest bedroom?"

"I tossed it on the bed. Is that okay?" he asked.

"That's great. So, I'll see you in a couple of hours then."

"Did Sam tell you about the trash?" he asked.

"Yes, keep it inside until you can take it to the dump or I'd be visited by wild animals."

Caleb nodded. "Mainly raccoons and the occasional bear. You don't ever want to feed them your garbage. They'd come to expect more, you know. That's why there's a latch on the doggie door and protective bars on all the windows," he said pointing to a small square opening at the bottom of the Dutch door. "Lydia used to feed the raccoons until one followed the cat inside to eat the cat food. They destroyed the place."

"I'll be careful," I said, feeling uneasy, glancing at the metal bars on the kitchen window.

"Sam said to make yourself at home. If you like to read, there is a bookcase full of books. And the console radio works, too. If the power goes off, there are lanterns, candles, and matches in the pantry, land there's plenty more firewood on the side porch. If you need anything, I try to come every two weeks or so in good weather to check on things."

Caleb turned to go, and I watched him climb into his truck and head downhill. It felt eerie watching him leave, knowing I was completely on my own—if only for two hours until he picked me up for dinner. I locked the door and stared at the fireplace.

After I walked through the small cabin, I peered into Lydia's closet, studied the family photographs on the walls, and looked inside the nightstand's drawer. The Colt 45 was there just like Sam had said it would be, loaded and ready. His palace appeared to be a virtual fortress, scary and comforting at the same time. When I entered the living room, I took a few books down from the bookcase: a steamy romance, judging by the cover, and two Westerns by Zane Grey that must belong to Sam. No art books, sadly, but he did have an old set of encyclopedias. I took down Vol. #20 and immediately looked up Mark Rothko. No paintings of his were pictured, just a short summary of his life. I finally settled on *The Audubon Society's Field Guide to North American Birds* on the side table, a small green book filled with color photos. I wouldn't be able to focus on the plot of a story, but I might be able to handle photos of pretty birds and short descriptions after I made myself a drink.

Sam's liquor cabinet was set on one side of his bedroom. Inside I found expensive whiskeys and carried one to the kitchen and poured myself a double. I had earned it. I opened the refrigerator to look for soda water and was amazed. In addition to soda water, it had been stocked with brown eggs, milk, butter, beer, cheese, apples, potatoes, onions, celery, cabbage, two loaves of homemade bread, and unmarked packages of meat in the freezer. I knew Sam liked to hunt, so it might be venison or rabbit. Caleb must have been really busy stocking the place yesterday. On the side shelf were all sorts of condiments and four jars of maraschino cherries. Sam had put in a special request just for me.

I forgot to ask Caleb if the ice was safe to use. It had to be or he would have said something. I twisted the plastic ice tray until it released the cubes and added three of them to my drink, added the soda water, and four cherries. Then I walked out to the screened porch and soaked in the vista again. *This might be addictive*, I thought, as I sipped my drink and rocked in a rocker. Maybe I really could adjust. I noticed a dog bed on the porch and another at the foot of Sam's bed. I couldn't wait for Sam to bring Chase and Cali.

When I went inside to refill my drink, I remembered today was Monday. Unbelievable. A week ago today, Ashley was still alive. Her high school photo and the pink and lavender shrine flashed in front of my eyes. Too many painful goodbyes—some forever.

Out of habit, I tried to think of a new question, but it felt useless. I was tired and empty inside. Alexandra said life was all about loss, but I wanted life to be all about *life*. I wished I were still slow dancing with Josh and collecting more pink umbrellas, not isolated on this mountaintop.

Maybe I could go home tomorrow. I'd ask Caleb to drive me to the airport, but I can't afford a plane ticket and I don't have an apartment anymore. I can't even afford to buy food for Chase and me. Josh was barely making it on his own, so he couldn't take us both in. And Sam had become my only lifeline, and I prayed I could trust him. He had one son, one grandson, no outstanding debt, no criminal record, and had never been on social media. He went to Yale, graduated cum laude from law school at the University of Virginia, and became a prominent trial lawyer, humanitarian, and a member of the NRA.

"So, this is your palace, Sam," I said to myself, looking at the setting sun and the blue mountains in the smoky distance.

27

HELEN

Caleb parked and rapped on the Dutch door precisely at 7:30. The quaint door seemed out of place in this rustic cabin. Maybe Sam bought it to make Lydia happy.

I stopped reading about bald eagles and found a small piece of paper to mark my page in the bird book. When I opened the top of the Dutch door, Caleb took a step back.

"Are you ready?" he asked.

"Give me a second and I'll be right out."

I grabbed my purse where I had put Lydia's keyring. When I returned, Caleb was looking under the hood of his truck and adding windshield wiper fluid. I left the Conestoga lamp on and locked the door behind me. When I climbed into the cab, I noticed a shoebox on the seat between us.

"New shoes?" I asked when he got in and started the engine.

Caleb lowered the windows up and down two times, squirted cleaning fluid on the windshield, and switched on the wipers.

"Oh, nothing like that. Just candy. Want some?" he asked.

He removed the lid to reveal a boxful of old Halloween candy. Small packets of candy corn, peanut butter taffy wrapped in black and orange paper, and assorted bite-sized chocolates.

"No thanks. I don't want to spoil my dinner," I said.

"I always keep it on hand for Sam when he rides with me. He likes to have something sweet, so I thought you might, too."

"How thoughtful, Caleb. I just don't eat much these days," I said.

"Did you let the fire die out?"

"Was I supposed to? I've never had a fireplace before."

He killed the engine, walked to the door, and unlocked it with his key. In a couple of minutes, he returned.

"Everything's fine. It had almost burned itself out, and I just spread the ashes around," he said. "After dinner, I'll teach you how to build a fire and keep it going."

After he put the truck in gear, we slowly bumped our way down to the bottom of the hill and drove to his farm. His sister stood next to a pretty calico cat that wove between her legs.

"Hi, Twyla, I'm Helen," she said, extending her hand. "Sam says you're going to watch his place for a few months. He and Lydia used to live there until she died, so it'll be a comfort to have someone in it again. I know he wants to come and stay for good, but he just can't yet. He tries to hide it, but he's pretty eaten up with sadness. Are you hungry?" she asked quickly.

Another question. I felt a looming sense of dread, wondering if this might be a family trait.

Helen walked ahead of us to the house and held the door open for Caleb and me. The heady smell of roasting turkey drew us inside.

"It smells wonderful in here. You must have been cooking all day," I said.

"I took a day off to celebrate your arrival. I own an antique shop in town, so I didn't have to take a sick day," she said with a straight face. "Make yourself at home. I'm almost ready to put everything on the table.

Caleb disappeared into the house, and I sat in a platform

rocking chair in the living room. The calico cat I saw with Helen earlier jumped into my lap. I stroked her once, and her ears flattened against her head before she hissed at me and jumped to the floor.

"How can I help you, Helen?" I asked, a little wary of the cat.

When I stood, the cat took off and nosed her way out the screen door.

"Don't trouble yourself. The table is set, but if you want, you could pour the sweet tea. It's on the counter, and I've already put ice in the glasses. There's a plate of lemon slices, too."

I entered her fairytale dining room with a massive crystal chandelier hanging over the table. The elegant china was old and ornate, the cut-glass water goblets gleamed, and a pair of pink candles had been lit. Linen napkins and sterling silverware were arranged, just so, by each plate, and pink wine glasses with green stems that reflected the light—Ashley would have loved them. A bouquet of Black-eyed Susans filled a vase that sat in the center of the table. I couldn't help but think of the heartbreaking shrine next to Ashley's bike with its circle of tea lights flickering for hours until they went out.

Helen slid a pan of rolls from her double oven, and the turkey had already been sliced. Mounds of mashed potatoes were steaming in a serving bowl.

I filled the goblets with tea and set the plate of lemon slices on the table. A chilled bottle of Chablis waited for us with a corkscrew beside it.

"Do you want me to open the wine?" I asked.

"Yes, that would be lovely. Caleb, dinner's ready!" Helen called.

She struck three Chinese gongs suspended from an archway with a serving spoon. Each had a distinctive monastic sound that seemed to be an octave above the other. Caleb appeared in the dining room holding a photo album as Helen started carrying food to the table.

"Caleb, after Twyla opens the wine, go ahead and pour it. Twyla, you sit here next to me. Caleb likes to be near the window," Helen instructed.

I took my seat when Helen did as Caleb placed his album on top of the buffet table. Then, he filled the wine glasses halfway, careful not to spill a drop.

"I forgot the cake," Helen sighed, standing up and returning with a huge frosted cake on a glass pedestal which she set in front of me.

"I made this especially for you. Sam said to be sure and cut you a slice before we eat. But first, let's pray," Helen said, bowing her head. "Dear God in heaven, thank you for this most wondrous day. Thank you for friends, old and new, and for my family. Amen."

"Amen," Caleb repeated and then he served the turkey.

I couldn't remember if I'd ever had a real sit-down Thanksgiving dinner before. Joy rarely cooked, and Chase and I had eaten at Bob Evans restaurant on special occasions.

"Let's toast our new friend, Twyla." Helen raised her glass and Caleb did the same. "To life."

"To life," I repeated, and we clinked our glasses together. The candles flickered softly, and I smiled.

"We love good food," Helen said. "It's one of life's true pleasures."

I ate my slice of cake first in honor of Sam. The cream cheese frosting freckled with toasted pecans tasted wonderful, so I ate it all and downed my glass of wine.

Caleb and Helen ate two helpings of everything, and then she refilled our glasses. I wasn't hungry after the cake, but I took a spoonful of everything to be polite, even a little sauerkraut, but I didn't touch it. Caleb scooted away from the table and carefully hid himself behind the wildflower bouquet.

"How long have you been in the antique business?" I asked.

"Caleb pointed out your shop to me when we drove through Oakland."

He stopped eating for a second and seemed pleased.

"I've had my shop for close to 30 years now. It's a tremendous amount of work, but I enjoy it. Never a dull moment," Helen said.

"Where do you get your stuff, I mean antiques?"

"All over. Estate sales, auctions, and people coming in the shop to sell something. Caleb and I travel to New England in the spring each year to try and find unique items I know my customers would like. It's a challenge to haul heavy items home, but his truck holds a lot."

"I haven't been in an antique shop before," I admitted. "Why did you name it *The Old Curiosity Shop?*"

"After a novel by Dickens. I've read most of his work, and when I bought this place, I knew I had to use that name. We have quite an assortment of antiques and our fair share of odd characters here, so it seemed the perfect name. You'll have to stop by sometime soon," she said, gathering the plates and carrying them to the kitchen. "Coffee?"

"None for me," I said.

"Caleb?"

"I'll take a half a cup," he said.

"You always say that," Helen said as she switched on the Mr. Coffee.

"Well, did you get enough to eat?" Helen asked me.

"Sam says comfort food calms your soul, and I think he's right," I said.

"Amen to that," Helen said with a big smile.

"Everything was delicious. I may never leave the mountains now," I said.

"That's what we wanted to hear. Isn't that right, Caleb? We thought a late summer Thanksgiving dinner would be a special welcome. So, you think you'll stay a spell?" she asked.

"That's the plan," I said, drinking the last drop of my

Chablis and wondering if this might be my last supper before my isolation began.

"Caleb, pour her more wine," Helen said.

"No, I've had plenty. Let me help you clear the table."

"Sit still. I've got a kind brother who always cleans up after I cook a big meal, and I can't ask for more, can I? Let's sit in the living room for a while before you leave," she said, blowing the pink tapers out.

Caleb carried his photo album upstairs and then returned to work in the kitchen while Helen and I sat on the couch. Her face was flushed and damp with perspiration. Her graying hair had been pulled into a messy French twist, and she untied her butcher apron and folded it on her lap.

"Menopause," she said. "I'm either freezing or burning hot it seems, especially when I cook. Preparing a big meal can set off hot flashes. Not to mention the wine!"

"I'm sorry," I said. Not quite sure what the correct response should be.

"My mother didn't tell me a thing about it, but I remember she took Lydia Pinkham pills she hid in her jewelry box. I did a little research years later, and some thought it helped relieve the symptoms of menopause, but the pills were just pink sugar pills, a placebo. I guess change-of-life was taboo, something you didn't talk about even with your own daughter. Believe me, ignorance is not bliss. But, you're way too young to hear an old woman go on and on about female troubles and growing old," Helen said with a laugh.

Caleb walked into the living room with a cup of coffee for Helen. She set hers on a lace doily on an end table, and he went to the kitchen where I could hear him rinsing plates and loading the dishwasher.

"Tell me, Twyla, if you don't mind, what made you decide to stay at Sam's place? I knew he needed a caretaker and someone to watch Cali later, but I'm curious as to why a pretty young girl like you would ever come here. Nobody but Caleb and I go up on Glass Mountain anymore," she said.

Helen took a sip or two, and then she started to fan herself with a magazine. The wispy hair around her face rose and fell with each flap of her makeshift fan.

"I'm trying to do the right thing for me and my little brother. I can't explain it all right now, but it was a hard decision. Something tragic happened, so I knew I had to get away fast, plus I really need the money."

Sam said you were independent and strong. He likes that, Helen said. "I do, too. Nothing worse than a needy woman."

"I hope I made the right decision."

"Tragedy changes everything," Helen said. "It can derail your life in a split second."

28

GLASS MOUNTAIN

"Where's Caleb?" I asked.

"He's waiting outside," Helen said. "We're so glad you came. Don't be a stranger now."

"I won't, and thanks again for dinner and the leftovers," I said, holding up a paper bag.

Caleb leaned against his truck and held the purring calico cat. She flattened her ears when I tried to pet her and scratched my hand in one startling swat. After I yanked my hand back, he set her on the ground and she raced away to hide in the barn.

"Sorry," he said. "Marigold's a semi-feral cat; she only lets Helen and me pet her. I discovered her in the hayloft with her mother and littermates when she was about seven or eight weeks old. No human contact until then. She was a hard one to tame, but she finally made up with me," he said.

After we climbed in the truck, the drive up the mountain seemed even slower than the first time. Each divot and hole seemed deeper and the constant rocking made me wish I hadn't eaten anything at all or drunk a second glass of wine. At least Caleb wasn't asking any questions.

He turned on his headlights when we entered the shadows

of the canopy and overhanging trees. I held the paper bag on my lap and stared out the window into the forest.

"Do you have any pets?" Caleb asked, opening the lid of his shoebox. He took out some candy corn, bit off one end of the packet, and poured the candy directly into his open mouth.

"No, I can't afford one now, but I want to buy a puppy someday for my brother. He loves Sam's dog and can't stop talking about her."

"Cali's a good dog," Caleb said.

I remembered Chase's angelic face as he sat beside Cali and hand-fed her scraps. A wave of sadness washed over me just thinking about the two of them together.

"What kind of puppy would you get?" he asked.

"Not sure—maybe a mixed breed from the shelter. My friend Josh says they're the best dogs to own. They're not high strung or disease prone. Just good ole' dogs."

"I used to raise hunting dogs, but I don't hunt anymore." Before I could answer, Caleb asked. "Did you leave the front porch light on? It gets pitch black on top of the mountain. No light pollution. You can't even see your hand in front of your face sometimes."

"No, but I left a light on inside," I volunteered.

As we turned at the crest of the hill, the cabin came into view. It looked scary with the Conestoga lamp glowing through the front window like a Jack o' lantern. I felt grateful for Caleb's high-beam headlights that sliced through the darkness.

"Thanks for hauling me around today," I said, after he pulled into the driveway. "I guess I'll see you in two weeks?"

"You're not afraid of the dark, are you?" he asked, looking past me.

"I'm not afraid of anything except criminals and poverty, but if I'm ever cornered, I know Sam keeps his guns loaded. Most are in the gun rack above the side couch, and his Colt 45 is next to his bed inside the nightstand. He told me he even owns a rifle just like Calamity Jane's, but I don't know where he keeps it. Maybe it's locked in a bank vault somewhere.

"He said if I ever needed to make an emergency decision about which gun to grab first to simply remember 1, 2, 3. The 12 gauge shotgun was on the bottom rack, the 30/30 Winchester, the second, and the 30/40 Krag—just like the one Teddy Roosevelt and the Rough Riders used—rested on the third rack," I said.

Caleb's eyes widened a little, but he didn't say anything.

"Have you ever fired a shotgun or a high-powered rifle?" he asked.

"No, just a derringer, but I'm a quick study if you want to teach me."

"I promised to show you how to build a fire first," he said.

"I'm anxious to learn," I said, meaning it.

For the next hour, Caleb demonstrated, step by step, how to build and maintain the perfect fire. I was dirty and exhausted when we were done but grateful for the lesson.

"Thanks, Caleb," I said.

He nodded, and then I walked with him to his truck. He waited until I went back inside and flicked on the outside light. Then he made a U-turn and honked the horn twice before he drove down the mountain.

I watched through a side window as his headlights flickered through the leafy trees and then disappeared. After locking the front door, I turned on every light in the cabin. Then, I lifted the shotgun from the bottom rack, made sure the safety was on, and carefully propped it beside the front door. I put the bag of leftovers in the refrigerator before I poured myself a drink in one of Sam's shot glasses. No ice or soda this time. Just straight bourbon.

29

THE PANTRY

I glanced at my phone for the hundredth time and saw a text from Chase: *Miss you, Sis*. I tried to respond, but the screen said *No Service*.

I couldn't even send a damn text. I held the receiver of the rotary phone to my ear. It was dead. I was totally my own. I paced around the cabin and stopped in front of Sam's bed. It was on the left side of the kitchen, and his closet was stuffed full of clothes and shoes. Above his headboard, the casement window lined with steel bars made me feel like I was in prison. The walls were covered with old photographs and a couple of signed pen-and-ink drawings of a Scottish terrier. Although it was dark outside, it seemed far too dark inside the cabin.

I clicked on the big console radio and its moon dial glowed. The wooden console sat on a sturdy table and was about two and a half feet tall and two feet wide. When I moved the dial, I could hear the buzz of faraway stations playing jazz and classical music and a Spanish-speaking announcer all at the same time. Each turn of the dial brought a jumble of pitches and white static until I found a gospel station that came in crystal clear. A country preacher introduced a hymn and the choir sang. Better than nothing, I thought, so I turned the volume way up and the 4/4 beat of "Rock of Ages" filled every corner of the cabin.

The living room was furnished with two massive, red leather couches and a matching side chair, a camel saddle that Sam's son had bought in Morocco, and a couple of bearskin rugs, complete with furry, black heads, scary glass eyes, and snarling teeth. One of the bear rugs had been nailed to the wall like a dark tapestry, with the bear's open mouth ready to tear into any stranger's arm who came too close. An enormous moose head with dark brown eyes was mounted above the fireplace, and a stuffed pheasant perched on the mantle. Sam must have had a huge taxidermist bill.

The front porch light was on, and I could still see fishing tackle, red-and-white bobbers, bamboo poles hung on a rack, and different sized walking sticks poking out of an old wooden barrel.

It looked inviting, so I opened the door and stepped out on the porch. A dark object darted in front of my eyes. I froze. Maybe it was a small bird? In a minute, it was back. I waited for it to take off again and it did, but it wasn't a bird, it was a bat—something else to fear after dark.

I quickly went inside and turned off the porch light, so I wouldn't have to witness any more creatures of the night. Out of sight, out of mind, right? I locked the front door and headed toward the kitchen. The choir belted out "Nearer My God to Thee" as I stared at the steel bars on the window. They served as a deterrent for raccoons and the occasional bear, Caleb had explained at dinner. I wandered into the bathroom and opened the door to the walk-in pantry that was beside the Kelvinator refrigerator. When I tugged on a long string, a light bulb lit up floor-to-ceiling shelves of canned goods of every size on three walls. I spotted a well-worn dog bed next to a hundred pound bag of dry dog food.

"Cali's," I whispered.

I found my purse, grabbed an old afghan off a couch, and

went into the pantry, and closed the door. I sat on the floor beside Cali's soft bed as the choir started singing "Onward Christian Soldiers." It was a little muffled behind the closed door, but I heard the preacher shouting out the words to the song before the choir echoed him. It's called *lining*, the blue lady at Freewill Baptist church had told me once. No hymnals were needed, except one for the preacher who led his flock in song.

Sitting in the gully below cans of tuna fish, peaches, Campbell's tomato soup, and pinto beans, I began to cry. This was the crying booth I needed—a kitchen pantry in the middle of nowhere with a church-choir soundtrack. I had to be strong for Chase, but I could cry here all night if I wanted. I took my derringer out of my purse and set it on the first shelf where I could reach it. I curled up on the floor, wrapped the itchy afghan around me, and rested my head on Cali's bed while the lining preacher and his echoing choir sang me to sleep.

I woke to loud static on the radio that sounded like steady rain. As sunlight beamed under the pantry door, I stared at all the canned goods and coffee and jars of peanut butter that surrounded me.

I felt pretty stiff, but rested. I smelled like a dog and was covered in dog hair, but I didn't care. After putting the derringer in my purse, I folded the afghan and left it on the floor. I took a can of coffee from the shelf, carried it to the kitchen, and brewed a pot with the spring water Caleb had poured into the three-gallon glass dispenser.

After I turned off the radio, I saw a doe and two fawns grazing just a few feet from the back porch stoop. I watched them in awe until they disappeared into the leafy green forest.

I hadn't eaten much since last evening at Helen's and remembered I had a slice of cake in the refrigerator. I ate it all and licked the cream cheese icing from my fingers. When the coffee brewed, I filled a huge mug and sat at the dinette table.

I desperately needed a shower, but I remembered all the

warnings about the cistern water. Did Sam say I could shower in the polluted water? I wasn't sure, so I decided to take a sponge bath instead and used the bottled water to wash with and brush my teeth. Maybe next time I would boil some "good" water on the stove, add some cool water to it, and fill the bathtub up just an inch or two.

When I crossed to the guest bedroom, the snarling bear head in the living room kept his beady eyes on me every step of the way. After I unpacked my duffel bag, I grabbed a change of clothes and my toothbrush to take to the bathroom. I noticed the Conestoga wagon light was still on, and I switched it off.

After I climbed into the empty bathtub, I unwrapped a new bar of soap, put the stopper in the tub, and poured bottled water over a clean washcloth. I lathered up, and then I poured the rest over me to rinse away most of the soap. I used the last bottle to wash and rinse my hair. After that, I made one small goal for Day #1: Keep the fire burning.

I felt the weight of grief shadowing me, and I couldn't shake it. *This must be what real depression feels like*, I thought. Small goals, one step at a time, I kept telling myself. Tonight I'd try to sleep in the guest room bed behind the flimsy curtain for a door. I wouldn't leave the radio on all night this time, but I'd keep the derringer under my pillow.

I poured bottled water into a paper cup and brushed my teeth with Pepsodent—a brand of toothpaste I'd never heard of that sat beside a half-gallon dispenser of hand sanitizer. When I refilled my coffee mug, it was only 9 a.m., and I knew I wouldn't last a week.

30

STASH

Out of sheer boredom, I searched for the hidden tins of candy Sam had bragged about. I looked in the kitchen cabinets, under the beds, and finally went to the pantry. The cabin was completely different from my normal/abnormal life in Florida, and the pantry must have been close to what air-raid shelters looked like in the 1950s and 60s, only this one was not underground. Alexandra told us one of her neighbors had one in her back yard during the Bay of Pigs crisis that I learned about in social studies.

I began to turn some of the cans right side up so they could be easily read and made sure the labels faced front. One at a time, I moved the Campbell's tomato soup and Bumble Bee tuna to their own shelf. Crushed pineapple, peaches, and Bartlett pears were now arranged closer to the fruit juices and the cases and cases of bottled water on the floor. I shelved the canned dog food near the hundred pound bag of kibble. I spotted a small folding ladder tucked between two shelves and used it to relocate cans of olives, peas, dill pickles, lima beans, black beans, kidney, pinto, and sorted them by size and contents. I even thought about putting everything in alphabetical order, but didn't. I surveyed my work after I finished and felt a sense of pride.

I still hadn't found Sam's candy stash, and now I had a sudden craving for chocolate. Caleb's shoebox of stale candy even started to sound good, and I did a detailed room-to-room search, over and under, high and low. I even looked in the linen closet and a small metal cupboard where Sam kept his paper supplies so the mice couldn't get to them. I saw mousetraps everywhere, but so far, no mice. Sam told me if I ever caught one to use a snow shovel and pitch both the mouse and trap over the hill. He said he had an unending supply of traps in the cellar. I'd never met the mysterious cat named Raven, but as long as she kept mice out of the cabin, I didn't need to meet her.

After I wandered into Sam's bedroom again, I opened his liquor cabinet and sat on the floor, turning wine and whiskey bottles so their labels faced front. I realized I was becoming more and more OCD, but it was soothing and helped to pass the time. On the bottom shelf, I discovered a small latch, and I moved all the bottles over to one side and found a trapdoor. I opened it and inside were Christmas tins, large and small, and I lifted the closest one out. It was heavy and rattled when I shook it. When I pried the lid open, I found hundreds of rainbow-colored Jelly Beans.

I snapped the lid back into place and opened another tin full of Reese's Cups. I remembered when Chase was little and had stolen one from Joy. He was covered in milk chocolate when he found me on the side porch.

"I found your stash, Sam," I said with an evil laugh to the empty room.

I ate a candy bar right away and regretted it. Maybe I might turn into another Sam. Since his wife died, he must have tried to fill the hole in his heart with sweets. I put the tins back, latched the trap door, and moved the liquor bottles over on top.

Sam might have hidden the candy from Lydia, I thought.

Maybe she lectured him about eating too much sugar, or told him it would rot his teeth and shorten his life, and he just didn't want to hear it anymore. I imagined Sam watching a Western movie late at night, secretly popping jelly beans and drinking Sam Adams. I closed the cabinet door and went to get a glass of water but stopped when I smelled the foul fish-bowl water that poured from the faucet. I made a quick detour to the pantry, grabbed a bottle of water, and drank it all. I had only managed to kill five hours.

Sam's movies were stacked in a big box beside the TV/VCR, and I found his favorite, *True Grit*. Even the title sounded terrible, but I needed to hear some voices in the cabin and not another gospel choir. I jumped when the movie started, so I quickly lowered the volume and stared at the opening credits. Worn out from my sleepover on the pantry floor, I needed to stretch out on a bed and take a nap with a real pillow and blanket. But first, I gazed out the kitchen window at pine trees and a cloudy sky. Then I went to the guest room, got under the covers, and listened to *True Grit* until I fell asleep.

I dreamed about the stars and lightning bugs on steroids— huge ones that blinked in the vast darkness. A fantasy sunrise lit the sky from behind the mountains, and I spotted a tree that stood by itself in the distance. In the dream, Caleb said it was a den tree. Pocked with holes and nesting places for small birds and mammals, land owners prized them and considered them good luck, and never chopped them down. Just then I thought I heard Caleb's truck rumbling up the hill and watched as his headlights burned two holes in the nightscape, amid the shoot-outs and men bellowing from the TV in the living room.

I sat up, wide awake, in total darkness, looking for Caleb's headlights. There were none, so I turned on the light beside my bed. I slept 6 hours, and it was only 8 p.m. When I unwrapped myself from the tangle of blankets, the air felt cool, and I knew the fire had gone out. I padded through the living room in my stocking feet, turned off the TV, and stirred the ashes in the fire-place. A few glowing embers remained. I added one piece of kindling at a time, like Caleb had shown me, until they started smoking and burst into flame. Then I added two small logs and set a larger one behind them. I couldn't believe it was August. It had to be sweltering in Florida right now.

After I poured myself a glass of milk, I stepped on something furry that bit my ankle. I screamed and dropped my glass as a cat raced across the floor and jumped on a leather couch. It looked just like Caleb's cat, Marigold.

I called out to her, but she arched her back, hissing a don't-come-any-nearer-you-fool warning. I started to open the door, but she dashed out the doggy door instead. So, that's how the cat got in! I flipped on the porch light and watched her stalk something, maybe a bird, and then she disappeared. After I washed my bite wound with soap and bottled water, I cleaned up the spilled milk. *What a mess*, I thought. I'd better make a list of three simple things to do tomorrow before I forgot. Maybe I could walk around the cabin and sit on the screened-in porch during the afternoon when the bat was asleep.

I locked the doggie door, so Marigold wouldn't dart inside for another sniper attack. Now I was wide awake, so I attempted to read one of Sam's books and not look at the clock. Bedtime would be long, if ever, in coming tonight after my long nap.

I wondered if Sam had a calendar, so I could X off the days like prisoners do in solitary confinement. After my first full day by myself, the weeks and weeks that lay ahead seemed mind-numbing. I browsed through the books in the bookcase and finally settled in with a novel about cowboys and sharpshooters and nights alone on the lone prairie. *True Grit* must have made an impression on my subconscious somehow. I made a ham and cheese sandwich at midnight and poured myself a glass of red wine. Unless I went to sleep very soon, I'd eat myself into a coma before dawn.

31

HOMESICK

I woke at the creaking floor, a log settling in the fireplace, or the ticking of the alarm clock. When I heard a dog howl, or what sounded like a dog, I jumped up and grabbed the shotgun propped beside the front door. After I calmed down, I thought about playing another movie to fall asleep to, but I changed my mind. Instead I took the gun with me and slid it under my bed. The derringer was already underneath the other bed pillow. After tossing and turning, I finally dozed off, slept all night, and woke at first light.

I lay in bed for a while and finally got up at 8 a.m. and made coffee. I laid a change of clothes on the bed, folded the rest, and put them in an empty dresser drawer. In a deep bottom drawer, I discovered a crystal vase wrapped in an embroidered pillowcase. It looked expensive, and I ran my fingers over the etched grooves. Waterford Crystal was written on a sticker, and it reflected the sun's rays from the bedroom window. I also found seven wine glasses, two candlesticks, and a small bowl in the same drawer, each individually wrapped in pillowcases or fancy hand towels.

I set the vase and the bowl in the bedroom window and wished I had something to put in them. Maybe I'd pick a few of the Black-eyed Susans that bloomed near the cabin. I carried the candlesticks and wine glasses to the kitchen table and placed them in a circle with the candlesticks in the center. I remembered a big box marked "Christmas" in the cupboard. I carried it to the couch, and rummaged through it. There were handmade ornaments and a box of small red glass balls. Perfect. I filled the bowl with them and placed some in each of the wine glasses. I even found a pair of red candles inside the box and put them into the candle sticks. *Very festive*, I thought. The morning sun sparked the crystal and cast shimmering prisms on the walls. I carried the rest of the red balls to the bedroom and put them inside the vase and bowl.

The toilet had an iron stain that had probably been there for years. I knew no amount of scrubbing would remove it, and I wasn't going to try. When I flushed the commode, the water swirled and I remembered the warnings Sam had given me about touching, drinking, or even bathing in cistern water. Maybe Sam liked being a rugged pioneer or a wrangler who could conquer every challenge, even cistern water with a high bacteria count.

I put on a pair of fleece-lined slippers that were in the boot tray and a red and black hunting jacket hanging on the hall tree. It was a huge—probably Sam's—and I carried my coffee outside and sat on the cold metal glider.

My breath steamed the early September air, but the coffee tasted even better somehow sitting on the porch. The bat was nowhere to be seen, so I relaxed after a couple of minutes. Sam's coat warmed me, but my feet were cold. I should have worn socks with slippers. I tucked my feet underneath me and watched the sun move higher in the sky. The air was heavy with dew, and I pulled the hood up on the jacket.

A half-smoked cigarette and a pack of matches sat in a green glass ashtray on top of a wooden barrel. I wondered if Sam smoked.

I found a pair of white rubber boots on the porch that

looked like they might fit me. Maybe they had belonged to Lydia. I turned them upside down and thumped on the soles in case a wolf spider or mouse or a sleeping bat were inside. Just a little dirt fell out, so I took off the slippers and slid my feet inside the roomy boots, opened the screen door, and stepped off the porch into the yard.

There was a padlock on the door that housed the cistern, not that I even wanted to go in there. As I walked, I wondered what Caleb and Helen were doing on the farm today. Maybe she was feeding the chickens or polishing her sterling silver tea set or feeding Marigold after she found her way home. Caleb might be pouring milk into a saucer for her right now.

They were an odd but fascinating pair. *Isolation does that to people*, I thought, and if I stayed too long at Sam's palace, I knew I'd become obese and eccentric. I wandered to the side porch and opened the door. More firewood had been stacked there. Before I went inside, I slid off the boots, put the slippers back on, and took my to-do list out of my pocket. I had already forgotten the things I had scribbled down last night: brush my hair, sit on the porch, and take a walk and explore. You know you're in bad shape when you need a reminder to brush your hair.

I walked over to the bookcase and began arranging the books alphabetically by author, pausing to open each one and reading the opening paragraph. My newly acquired OCD wasn't going away.

Then suddenly my cell phone rang, and I dropped a book on the floor.

"Hello? Hello?!"

"How come you never answer your phone?" Josh asked.

"I left you a text."

"Your voice is breaking up," he said.

"Sorry, there's almost no service up here."

"When are you coming home?" he asked.

"I don't know yet, Josh, I..." was all I said before the phone went completely dead. I hit redial but nothing happened. I hurried outside into the front yard, hoping to catch a signal and tried again. No luck.

I reread Chase's text that must have slipped through when I was at Helen's.

"Miss you, Sis."

Those three words hurt like hell.

"I miss you, too, Chase," I whispered.

I hurried into the cabin and began to practice the words I needed to say to Josh.

"My voice is breaking up because I'm breaking up with you," I said with a catch in my voice.

Another three-cups-of-coffee morning was total luxury, but I felt like I was going stir crazy. I wondered what kind of pie Sam had for lunch today, what he and Chase had been doing since I left, and if they had found Ashley's murderer yet. An icy shiver ran down the length of my spine. Someone had mistaken her for me. They thought I was making my regular nightly deposit, but when they discovered their mistake, they made sure she'd *never* be able to identify her kidnappers.

I removed my boots and set them on the tray before I washed the dishes with the smelly cistern water and liquid soap. I wore a pair of rubber gloves I had found under the kitchen sink and boiled water to pour over the draining dishes.

I unplugged the coffee pot and stirred the logs. Maybe I'd listen to the radio this morning to pass the time. I tuned in at the first clear country station I came to and curled up on one of the squeaky leather couches, but it was cold. I got the afghan from the pantry floor and spread it over the couch.

When "Jesus Take the Wheel" started playing, it cut razor deep, and I turned it off. I wanted to drive all the way home, but I didn't have a car or even a bike. Or even a home.

I'm not tough enough for this shit — can't do it anymore.

When Caleb returns in a couple of weeks, I'll ask, no tell, him to drive me to the airport, and then I'll catch the first plane home. If Calamity won't hire me back, maybe the newspaper will.

32

HIKE

I slid the 12 gauge shotgun from under my bed and made sure the safety was on. I decided to hike down the mountain by myself, but I didn't want to startle any wildlife. Caleb told me to make some noise when I was in the woods, so I put a cord with an attached jingle bell around my neck. There were a number of them hanging from a hook on the front porch.

I was no stranger to guns. Joy always kept a loaded pistol to scare away unwanted boyfriends. She had taught me how to load and unload bullets when I was 8. We used to target practice at a local firing range and wore borrowed headsets to protect our ears, but bullets were expensive so we stopped going. I never wanted to own a gun when I moved out, especially with Chase living with me most of the time, so my pawn-shop derringer was just for an emergency.

After I stepped into Lydia's roomy white boots, I locked the front door and pocketed the key. I wanted to check off the goals from my new list. I had already drunk my coffee on the front porch, and now I needed to go down the hill to Helen's and tell Caleb I had to leave. I couldn't wait two more weeks to go home.

I lifted the hickory walking stick from the barrel and hung

the shotgun's strap over my shoulder, patrol-girl style. I slipped on a big jacket, grabbed an air horn, and headed toward the driveway. It had taken about 20 minutes for Caleb's truck to climb the mountain, so I guessed it would take me at least an hour or more to hike to the main road.

Small birds gathered like dark leaves in the tops of the trees. Maybe they were excited about their upcoming southern migration, and I was jealous. I spotted a pileated woodpecker, and it stopped hammering a dead tree trunk when my jingle bell announced my approach. The names of certain birds had stayed fixed in my mind, so the time spent studying the bird book worked. The sun slowly warmed the late morning air and light filtered through the lacy pines. I started down the steep road and picked my way over ruts and rocks, careful of my footing and watching for snakes. Caleb had warned me about the poisonous timber rattlers that lived in the mountains and liked to bask in the sun. He said I'd probably never spot one, but to always be on the alert.

I hiked for a while until I came to a thick canopy of hemlock. In spite of my bell, I startled a deer standing on his hind legs like some mythical beast nibbling the lower leaves of an oak tree. He stared at me as if he'd been spotlighted and then leapt into the woods flashing his stark-white tail before he disappeared. His glossy tan fur had patches of a darker winter coat coming on, and I spotted a few red squirrels and chipmunks that scattered across the dirt road in front of me. The trembling leaf shadows and the warmer pockets of air made me feel more welcome in this thick forest where I was an alien. I knew there could be a black bear watching me, but I never saw one. I kept my thumb near the air horn's button, though, just in case.

I wondered what I'd say to Caleb when I reached Helen's house. It wasn't noon yet, and he probably hadn't brought her home from the antique shop.

I wished I had taken the time to put on two pairs of socks so Lydia's boots didn't slip as much. I'd bet there might be room for my size six shoes to fit inside. *Lydia must have been taller than me*, I thought. Taller people usually have bigger feet.

The road curved sharply downhill for about a mile, and I lost my footing a couple of times and slid to a sudden stop. I landed on my butt and the walking stick went flying. No damage done, but my hands were scratched and dirty from trying to lessen the impact. Since I wasn't a good judge of time and space and dirt roads, I picked up the walking stick and guessed I might be near the bottom when I waded through a natural spring that still held Caleb's muddy tire tracks. I was glad I had brought the stick along as I carefully crossed the spring and slippery rocks. Fern and mountain laurel grew lush and green on either side of me, and the cool air smelled like pine needles and rain—the exact opposite of the oppressive oven heat in Florida. *At least there are no mosquitoes or alligators in these mountains*, I thought.

After I left the spring behind, I spotted the wooden gate ahead and the two-lane highway on the other side. I heard a semi's jake-brake gear down and saw a car zoom by, followed by a flat-bed truck. I slid my jacket off, pushed my stick and my gun under the gate, and then I climbed to the other side. I gathered my things and put my jacket on without buttoning it this time and hiked on the berm until I could see curls of blue wood smoke rising from a stone chimney. I knew Helen's farmhouse would be the next place on the right. I heard a cock crow in the distance. I was anxious to get there, so I walked a little faster and steadied the shotgun awkwardly under my coat. I didn't have a license to carry or even a hunting license. I hoped I wouldn't be stopped by the police.

Growing sore and weary now, I tried not to think about climbing back up the mountain if no one was home. It would take me much longer to make the return trip.

When I approached the farmhouse, the screen door was propped wide open with a big lava rock—there had to be a story about it. I knocked anyway, and Caleb appeared from out of nowhere.

"What's wrong?" he asked. I didn't scream but held my breath instead.

"A bad case of cabin fever. I'm not contagious," I finally sputtered.

He saw the barrel of the shotgun poking from under my coat and the air horn resting in my pocket.

"Those were Lydia's," he said, ignoring both and pointing at my boots.

"I know. They're way too big for me, but I didn't have anything else to wear. You don't happen to have an extra pair of socks, do you?" I asked.

"Can I take your gun?"

"I was afraid to hike down that road alone without protection," I said defensively. "Sam said there might be snakes or even bears." Then I took off my jacket and the bell around my neck jingled when I handed him the 12 gauge shotgun. "The safety's on."

"Buckshot won't stop a bear. It'll just make him madder than a nest of yellow jackets," he said, standing to one side. "Come inside and warm up, and I'll make a pot of coffee."

My boots were muddy, so I put them on the porch. Caleb unloaded my shotgun, put the shells in his pocket, and propped the gun in a corner.

"Helen's still at the shop. Have a seat in the kitchen. You like your coffee black, right?"

I nodded, and after a few minutes, he carried a cup over to me and just stood there.

"Aren't you going to have some?" I asked.

He shook his head no.

"The local newspaper comes out every Thursday. You wanna read it?"

He handed me the paper and watched as I leafed through the pages.

"You look like you had a rough trip down," he said, staring at my hands and hair.

"I meant to comb it," I said, dusting the dirt from my hands first and then trying to smooth my short hair into place. "It was on my to-do list."

"Is anything wrong?" he asked again.

"No, I was just feeling lonely, so I wanted to see if you or Helen were home. Is that okay?"

"Why wouldn't it be okay?" he countered with another question.

Caleb emptied the dishwasher and held each glass up to the light, checking for smudges.

"It takes some getting used to, you know, living alone in the country. Not everybody's cut out for it," he said, polishing the lip of a glass with a clean dish towel.

"Speaking of, will you give me a lift to the airport tomorrow? I'll pay for your gasoline and time and trouble."

Caleb filled his cup with tap water and took a long drink. It hit me that he and Helen didn't have a cistern. They must have a well or even city water.

"Sam told me not to take a bath in the cistern water," I said, waiting for him to answer my question.

"Sometimes Sam and Lydia came here to shower, but more often than not, they'd heat spring water and pour it in the tub for a sit-down bath."

"How'd they manage that?" I asked, as he stalled for time.

"They'd empty about a half a drum of spring water into the bathtub and boil a gallon or two on the stove and mix it in with the cold. I don't think they took a bath more than once a week, though. Sam never worked up much of a sweat since I did all the yard work and fixed the things that needed fixing. Lydia didn't leave the cabin much, so she didn't need a bath every day like some city folk think they do," he said.

"How tall was she?"

"Why?" he asked, raising his eyebrows

"Her boots are big, so I guessed she had to be tall," I said.

"I figure she was about five foot eight. I'm six feet one inch. She was shorter than me."

"I won't keep you any longer, Caleb," I said, giving up on him ever answering my airport question. "I just needed to hear a human voice and rest a little before I hiked up the mountain," I added as I glanced at all the antiques around me. "I guess when you sell old treasures, you can't help but fall in love and keep some of them."

Caleb disappeared for a minute and returned with two pairs of Helen's wool socks.

"Keep' em. We've got plenty," he told me.

I thought about asking Caleb if I could take a shower here since the drums of water were so heavy, but I changed my mind. If Helen were home, I might have been brave enough to ask.

"You want to look around our place before you leave? We've got two cows, a chicken coop, some pigs, a couple of horses, a field full of cattle, and a two-acre garden," he said proudly, watching me tug the wool socks on over mine.

"Sure," I said, going out on the porch and putting on the boots. "They fit much better now. Thanks."

Caleb handed me my jacket before he put on an insulated flannel shirt over his t-shirt.

"Mount St. Helens," Caleb said, gently moving the lava rock out of the way with the toe of his boot so the screen door would close.

"Helen?" I asked, confused.

"No, the lava rock was from Mount St. Helen's. We found it at an estate sale about 30 years ago. Nobody wanted it."

I followed him to the corral, and a white stallion with dark eyes walked toward us.

"He's gorgeous. How long have you had him?" I asked.

"I raised him from a colt." Caleb said, taking an apple from his pocket and cutting it in half with a pocket knife. "We have a black mare in the barn. She's ready to foal any day."

"What are their names?" I asked, as the horse lifted his head and moved toward Caleb's extended hand.

"This is Phantom." The horse ate the apple and nuzzled his hand for more. "The mare's name is Midnight."

"You want to feed him?" he asked, handing me the other half of the apple. "Keep your hand flat, so he won't nip you," he warned.

I did as I was told since I'd never been close to a horse before, and its size alone felt intimidating. Phantom sniffed the apple and then gently took it from my hand.

When we entered the barn, Midnight seemed skittish and stood at the far end of her stall. The cows had already been milked, and Caleb told me a large chicken coop was located behind the barn. It had been completely enclosed with chicken and barbed wire to keep predators out and the hens and rooster safe inside. The rooster strutted and watched us like a beady-eyed madman with a blood-red coxcomb crown.

"Spike's the devil incarnate. Don't get too close to the fence. He'll attack if you're not careful," Caleb warned. "He's very protective of his hens."

As if on cue, the rooster flapped his wings and landed on top of the coop, and he crowed a deep-throated warning. His shiny black feathers tinged with bronze gleamed in the after-noon sun. Spike's sharp claws and huge spurs looked like they could rip my face off.

As we walked through the vegetable garden, Caleb pointed out the late blooming bush beans, the dwindling heirloom tomatoes, and carrots.

"I'll be turning the garden under after the first frost, but my cabbage and Brussels sprouts will be fine for a while. Summer doesn't linger in the mountains," he said.

Caleb even had a grape vine and said Helen liked to make homemade wine as well as can vegetables. I remembered the elderberry jam from the other night, so I'm sure she had made it herself.

Caleb stopped and pointed to three elevated cages full of rabbits.

"They're black and white Californians," he told me proudly. "We like rabbit meat better than chicken," he said, as I stared into the scary red eyes of a white rabbit with black ears that fiercely guarded her kits.

"You hungry?" he asked.

"No, I'll eat something when I get home. The cabin, I mean," wondering how the word *home* had slipped out.

"Wait here," he told me.

He returned with a bottle of water and a lunch bag with a banana and an apple inside.

"Thanks, Caleb," I said, taking the bag. "Tell Helen I stopped by. Oh, I need my shotgun."

"You want a lift?" he asked, nodding toward his truck.

"To the airport?" I blurted out.

"No, I meant up the mountain," Caleb said.

"I need the exercise," I lied, trying to hide my disappointment.

Caleb showed up with the walking stick and shotgun. He loaded it with the shells he had stowed in his pocket and turned the safety on. An apple bulged from his other pocket, so he must be treating Midnight next.

"Be careful now," he said. I took my jacket off, and he watched me hang the gun strap over my shoulder before I put the jacket on.

"I'll see you tomorrow then?" I prompted. "Can you come about noon to take me to the airport?"

He didn't answer.

"You should sleep on it first," he said, handing me my walking stick.

"Okay, but come at noon, and we'll talk."

He nodded and took the apple out of his pocket and started peeling it with his pocket knife. The bright red peel spiraled down in one long unbroken piece, and then he offered me a slice from the blade.

"No thanks," I said. "See you tomorrow."

I was in unfamiliar territory and didn't know how to read Caleb. I learned long ago never to push too hard, especially with strangers on foreign soil. He seemed harmless enough, but his strange questions and total silence felt unsettling.

I crossed over to the main road and carried the lunch bag in one hand and the walking stick in the other. I followed the road until the wispy threads of blue smoke from the stone chimney scattered in the breeze until Caleb vanished from sight.

When I reached the gate, I hung my jacket on one of the rails, and slid the gun and walking stick underneath. As I climbed to the top of the gate, I could hear the jingle bell when it moved side to side. I sat there for a minute while I ate the banana. Once on the other side, I gathered my things, and slowly began the steep climb.

33

LYDIA

Before I reached the halfway mark, I found a mossy tree stump and drank the bottled water. I felt dwarfed under the towering pine trees and hidden by the briers and spreading ferns, but it wasn't quiet here at all. The wind rustled the tree-tops, and the piping of those birds overhead became a cheerful distraction. I rubbed my sore calves and tried to remember if I had ever taken a hike alone.

Suddenly, a huge bird landed in the canopy and a limb rocked overhead. The small birds immediately scattered, and I spotted a majestic bird with a white head and dark wings perched high above me. It had to be a bald eagle. I'd never seen one in the wild, and the caged ones in the Florida zoo didn't count. Sam told me he had spotted them on the mountain, but they only seemed to appear when he was alone. I tried to remain motionless, but when I moved my hand to adjust the gun strap, I accidentally tripped the air horn. It blasted its sonic boom, and the eagle shot into the sky. The empty limb rocked and creaked as the bird soared over the treetops and hitched a ride on the current. Its massive wingspan and stark white head and tail feathers confirmed my suspicions. It was definitely an eagle.

I set my apple on the tree stump and hoped a deer might

find it. An hour later I finally crested the summit of Glass Mountain. My feet hurt, my back ached, and I was out of breath. Road weary and bone tired, I carried my jacket over one shoulder. The air still felt a bit cool, but the climb had made me hot and sweaty. The cabin sure looked like a palace to me now, and I couldn't wait to stretch out on one of the cool leather couches.

After I entered the screened porch, I put my walking stick inside the barrel and propped the shotgun near the door before I rested on the glider for a minute and pulled off my boots. All three pairs of socks were damp now, so I removed them, unlocked the front door, and entered the warm and sunny living room. I started to perspire even more from the sudden change in temperature and exertion from my climb. I left the door ajar and opened the top of the Dutch door in the kitchen to get some cross ventilation. I hung my jingle bell pendant on the door knob and draped my jacket on a chair before I grabbed a can of cola from the refrigerator. When I finally stretched out on a couch, it felt great lying there, staring at the moose head over the fireplace while I cooled down.

The fire had gone out, but I was in no hurry to start a new one. I glanced out the front window toward the edge of the hill where a tall pine tree sparkled like a Christmas tree. Maybe it held the last of the heavy morning dew, and the afternoon sun must have hit it just right. Curiosity got the better of me, and after a few minutes, I had to check it out. I slid my bare feet into the boots, shuffled out on the porch, and headed toward the shimmering tree. When I got closer, I could see that green and amber beer bottles had been put on its branches. There must have been at least a hundred bottles on the tree. A pool of shimmering water encircled its base, but it wasn't water at all. It was shattered glass. I bent over and carefully gathered a few green and gold slivers in my hand. Sam must have decorated that tree and used the extension ladder I had seen leaned against the shed. The breeze picked up again, and when the bottles gently clinked together, rainbow prisms haloed the white pine, and one rippled across my shirt like a magic wand.

"You're one strange guy, Sam," I said out loud. "But, I like it."

Sam had secured the bottles to the tree with coated wire that was wrapped tightly around their long necks, and the end of the wire had been shaped into a hook. The vertical bottles hung from thicker branches closer to the trunk, and a few branches pointed skyward and those had been crowned with more bottles minus the wire. Green and gold alternated in a staggered pattern, and I imagined Sam hard at work, probably drinking a beer or two on the job, while he decorated and replaced any broken bottles. On some of the shorter sturdy branches they were hung horizontally. The tree looked like an exotic work of art in the middle of nowhere. I wondered if he spotlighted it at Christmastime. Maybe I could make him a glass star by gluing a few together, neck side out.

When a huge cloud covered the sun and snuffed out the magical lights, I wondered what happened when all the bottles shattered during a thunderstorm or a blizzard. I knew Sam would probably just say he'd be obliged to drink more beer to replenish them.

"You're having way too much fun, Sam," I said to myself as I walked into the cabin. I locked the door, latched the Dutch door, and moved the shotgun to its #1 slot on the gun rack. I wondered where Sam hid his stash of beer. It wasn't in the liquor cabinet or refrigerator, and I didn't see any stacked in the pantry beside the bottled water and drums of spring water.

I thought of Chase and couldn't shake an overwhelming sadness. If Caleb would drive me to the antique shop, I'd make a reservation at the Pittsburgh airport since there were no commercial flights at the Garrett County Airport. Mainly private planes. Or, I could call Sam and see if he would fly here again. The alternative would be an unending drive to the Pittsburgh airport with Caleb.

In any case, I was determined to go. I opened the hall closet and packed my light-weight jacket and scarf into my duffle bag. Then I stared at the rest of the coats and sweaters and vests of all sizes, weights, and colors that belonged to Sam and Lydia. I lifted out a stylish tan leather jacket that felt soft to the touch. It must be kid leather. One of Joy's old boyfriends had bought her a similar jacket she wore on special occasions. Hers was blood-red, though.

I slid it off the hanger and tried it on — size 6 — a perfect fit. Lydia must have worn this when she was much younger. The jacket smelled like Shalimar. The only reason I recognized that scent was because Joy had stolen a bottle of it once. I spotted the half-empty bottle of perfume on the dresser, dabbed a few drops on my wrists, and slipped my hands inside the jacket's silk-lined pockets. There was a pair of matching leather gloves tucked inside.

When I pulled them on, I felt something metallic inside one finger. I took it off and gently shook it over the dresser. A diamond pendant and earrings slid out, and they were beautiful. The settings looked like gold, and the large stones caught the light. When I turned the pendant over, it read 14 ct., so I knew it must be worth a lot, especially if the stones were real. Joy said if a diamond was the real deal, it would cut through glass, so I took one earring and scratched the corner of the dresser mirror. It left a tiny jag, so Joy had taught me something useful after all. I wondered if Sam had given them to Lydia.

I couldn't stop myself as I put the stud earrings on and fastened the elegant pendant around my neck. I glanced in the mirror and thought I saw a young girl staring back at me. For a second, she reminded me of Ashley wearing her birthday neck-lace with the gold heart. I quickly took off the jewelry that belonged to Sam's dead wife and slipped it inside the kid leather glove.

Bad juju, I thought, as I fumbled with the buttons on Lydia's jacket.

34

VISITOR

Insomnia set in, so I rearranged the clothes in Sam's closet and grouped the sweaters, shirts, and pants together by size and color. I pushed the leather jacket to one side and ignored a box in the corner, overflowing with wrapping paper, stick-on bows, and rolls of ribbon. Then I sorted all the shoes and boots, putting *his* and *hers* on either side of the closet floor. I found a small stack of shoeboxes, and four had new shoes inside: sparkly open-toed stilettos, running shoes, sturdy hiking boots, and pink toe shoes. The last one caught me off guard. I lifted them gently out of the box, stroked the satin slippers, and wove their long ribbons between my fingers. One of my rich high school friends had taken ballet since she was little, and I had watched a few of her classes.

The shoes might have been worn because the ribbons were sewn on, but there were no scuff marks. The toe pads, complete with lambswool, were tucked inside a small cardboard box. Had Lydia been a ballet dancer? No one buys toe shoes just for fun, unless they dreamt of being a ballerina and wanted to pretend.

I remembered another box filled with Christmas decorations was stored in the pantry. I guessed Sam and Lydia had spent many holidays here at the cabin. They liked being snow-

174

bound, and he had told me to relax and enjoy it like they did. *Just shovel the snow away from the doors and the doggy door*, he said, so I could let Cali in and out. I couldn't find an artificial tree anywhere. Sam probably chopped a pine tree down each year. I imagined him tromping through the deep snow wearing his Stetson and carrying a hatchet over one shoulder.

After working in the closet for over an hour, I got sleepy and went to my room to lie down, but I accidentally bumped into the end table beside my bed. I knocked over a couple of scented candles that were on top, and when I bent to pick them up, I discovered a small refrigerator hidden underneath an embroidered tablecloth.

"A new hiding place," I said out loud. Fascinated, I opened the door and saw domestic and imported beer stashed inside. There were at least 40 bottles, and when I looked under my bed, I found three cases of craft beer. No wonder I couldn't find Sam's golden brown and green beer bottles—they were right in front of me.

Clever, Sam, I thought. *You'll never run out of decorations for your glass tree if you throw a couple of big parties each year.*

I lifted out a bottle of Blue Moon and went to the kitchen to open it. As I nursed the cold beer, I washed the champagne flutes that sat in the kitchen window, seven crystal wine glasses, and the candle sticks and put them in the drainer to dry. Black ants were crawling on the window, and I squashed them with a can of tomato soup. I knew they came inside when the weather changed. Maybe Sam got a little behind on his cabin mainte-nance after Lydia died. I noticed a small army of ants crawling outside the window. At least they weren't inside yet. When Caleb comes tomorrow, I'll tell him.

I still needed to clean the bathroom, so I drank the last of my beer and set the bottle on the counter. I pulled on some rubber gloves and began to scrub the sink, toilet, and tub. I'd take the trash out tomorrow morning. Just like my apartment, I wanted to leave Sam's cabin as clean as I had found it.

Then, I heard the bell jingle that I had hung on the door-knob in the kitchen, followed by a soft thud. I hurried over to double check the deadbolt lock and secured the door guard on the Dutch door. Maybe a bird or a bat had hit the door or a window. I flicked on the porch light to check, but nothing was out there. Then a black shape loomed close to the door and began to climb the crisscrossed butt and pass logs. I froze in terror, hoping I was just imagining things, but when the shadow came down the same logs and moved toward the window, I knew it was real.

The creature stood erect and looked straight at me. Somehow I turned off all the lights and grabbed a flashlight from the counter. When I aimed its bright beam at the creature, two orange-red coals glared at me like the enraged mother rabbit who was protecting her kits.

It took a second before I realized those glowing eyes belonged to a gigantic black bear. My heart drummed in my chest, and I chose fight over flight. I dropped the flashlight, ran to Sam's gun rack, grabbed the powerful 30/50 Krag off the top, and turned the safety off. If the bear tried to break in, I would kill him. The sound of my heavy breathing filled the silence. After I switched on the outside light, I watched the bear clamber on a tall stack of firewood. When it reached the top, the logs crashed to the ground, and then the bear dropped on all fours.

The racket must have scared Marigold because the cat bolted through the unlocked doggie door. Her fur stood on end as she leapt on the countertop and then onto the narrow windowsill. She crouched low, her ears flattened as she watched the bear's every move while her tail twitched a warning. Marigold's sudden caterwauls terrified me, and the curious bear. It stood up again on its hind legs, looked at the cat, and sniffed every corner of the window.

The bear's breath fogged the glass as it pressed its nose through the steel bars. When it began to lick the ants into its mouth with its long pink tongue, Marigold exploded like a heat-seeking missile and attacked the windowpane. I lost my balance for a second, and so did the startled bear. It fell over backward, righted itself, and then lumbered away into the safety of the dark, cat-free forest.

Marigold began to groom herself as if nothing had happened. My heart continued to race as I checked and double-checked all the windows and doors. I tried to call 911 on my cell phone, but the *No Service* window appeared.

I grabbed the rotary landline and put my finger into the correct holes, and dialed 911. The receiver crackled with static as I waited for it to connect, but the phone was dead.

I turned the kitchen table on its side and barricaded myself as best I could, holding the rifle with my finger on the trigger. Cold sweat rolled into my eyes and down my back. The window was smeared with flattened ants and blurry from the bear's wet tongue. Marigold jumped down from the counter and began weaving between my legs. Her steady purr filled the room, but I was in no mood to let my guard down and wasn't fooled by her sudden friendship. I had no intention of being her frenemy.

"Hey, Marigold," I finally whispered. "Your new name is Killer. Got it? You get a treat if the bear leaves."

I stared at the steel bars that crisscrossed the window and felt grateful they had been installed. After about 15 minutes, I slowly ventured over to lock the doggie door and shoved the heavy leather chair in front of the door in case the bear returned.

I found my flashlight that had rolled under the table and turned it off, and then I rummaged in the refrigerator and found a pint of heavy cream. I quickly poured a little into a saucer for Killer.

After I carried my gun and a bottle opener to my room, I slid two more bottles of beer from the bedside cooler. *Should I sleep on the couch or in my room tonight,* I wondered. *Which was safer? Which would give me more time if the bear came back?*

Killer joined me on the bed in one graceful leap, and I didn't flinch. I didn't want to lose an eye. She seemed content and fell fast asleep. *Probably full of field mice*, I thought with a shiver. The fire had gone out, but it was hot in the cabin anyway. If I got cold in the night, I would pile on extra blankets.

I pushed up the legs of my pajama pants and bravely cracked the window above my bed an inch. I sat in bed and drank some beer until I got sleepy. Then I walked over, slid the guest room curtain shut, and kept my #1 rifle right beside me. It's crazy, but the closed curtain made me feel a little safer. If a bear really wanted in and managed to rip off a few steel bars, I couldn't stop him, but at least I had a loaded gun at my feet, and a watch-cat named Killer.

35

SMOKE & SQUATTER

I dreamt I was in my Florida apartment, and Chase had fallen asleep on the couch. I started walking down a spiral stair to the basement—even though we didn't have a basement and, obviously, no spiral staircase. When I reached the last step, a glistening lake appeared before me. I dove into its bath-warm waters and began to swim.

I kept smelling cigarette smoke but ignored it. When I finally made it to shore, I found a bottle of champagne nestled in a silver ice bucket and two crystal flutes. Mesmerized by the dancing prisms they cast, I started to open the bottle, but a flash of lightning ignited the sky, followed by a loud clap of thunder.

The cigarette smoke seemed thicker now, and a trumpet began to sound in short intermittent blasts until I woke up and started coughing. A smoke alarm, not a trumpet, was deafening and disorienting as I fumbled for the light switch. Rain pelted the tin roof, and I noticed smoke rolling in through my raised window, so I slammed it shut.

I didn't dare open the front door for fear of what might be lurking out there in the dark. I soaked a dish towel with water from the sink and covered my nose and mouth. Smoke could definitely kill you, but not cistern water, I hoped.

After I turned on the front porch light and the floodlights, I saw smoke billowing out from under the porch floor near my bedroom window. I had no choice now but to go outside. The high-pitched scream of the smoke alarm was relentless as I grabbed the Krag and a flashlight.

It was cold out, but I moved toward the source of the smoke, and Killer chased after me. I nervously bent down and peered under the porch. The cold rain beat down on my head and drenched my hair and pajamas. I quickly scanned the length of the crawl space with my flashlight beam. It smelled like a pack of wet dogs were under there, and then my flashlight glinted off something huddled in a corner, and six eyes glared at me.

I dropped my flashlight, raced into the cabin, and locked the door. Then I raised the bedroom window, stuck the rifle out between the bars, and pointed it skyward. I fired three shots and it bolted out from under the porch and disappeared into the night.

"If that doesn't wake the dead, I don't know what will," I whispered, rubbing my shoulder from the kickback.

I grabbed a broom and, after a few tries, knocked the smoke alarm off of the bedroom wall. Silence at last. I prayed someone at the bottom of the hill would come and save me, but for good measure, I fired three more times out the window. Then I locked it and stood guard by the door, hoping the pouring rain would smother the fire.

After 30 minutes of nervous pacing, I finally saw bouncing headlights and red flashers flickering through the trees. Caleb and Helen jumped out of their truck and raced toward the cabin. Both had handguns, and they pounded on the door until I opened it.

"There's smoke coming from under the front porch," I said in a rush. "And, there are bears or zombies living under there because their eyes glowed in the dark."

Caleb cocked his revolver, and Helen grabbed the small fire extinguisher from the kitchen wall and followed close behind him. They wore hooded yellow slickers over their pajamas and had work boots on. Killer was nowhere in sight.

"Where's your flashlight?" Caleb asked.

"I dropped it outside when I saw all those eyes," I said.

We walked outside into the rain, and I found my glowing flashlight by the steps. I grabbed it and held it steady for Caleb as he bent down to look under the porch. Helen covered him with her gun. They were a brother and sister SWAT team.

"Nothing under here except smoke. Get me a bandanna from the truck," he said, taking the fire extinguisher from his sister.

Helen ran to the truck with its flashers pulsing red in the mountain night and returned with his bandanna. No need to soak it; the rain already had.

"Move away now," Caleb said, tying it so it covered his nose and mouth.

I held the flashlight steady as the rain dripped into my eyes while he crawled on his belly, pulling himself forward on his forearms like a Marine. He held his gun in one hand and the fire extinguisher in the other. I heard a click when he pulled the ring off and then a whooshing sound as white foam exploded from the nozzle. He backed out and pulled the bandanna down.

"No animals under there, but something sparked the insulation, and it caught fire. Maybe an animal chewed through the wiring. It's under control now, but it's still smoldering," he said.

Caleb jogged to the shed and found a small spade. I held the flashlight for him again as he crawled under the porch and covered the insulation with dirt.

Thunder rumbled in the distance, and then a huge lightning bolt made the mountainside go from night to day and revealed three black shapes in Sam's bottle tree.

"What's that?" I shouted, as Caleb scrambled out from under the porch.

'Where?" he asked.

"In the tree."

I targeted my flashlight beam toward the top of the tall pine.

"Black bears. A mother and two cubs. She's treed them. The lightning and thunder must have spooked them all," Caleb said, looking up at the bears.

"Or six rifle shots," I said.

"They probably have a den under your porch," Helen said.

"Yeah, there's a big hole under there and lots of leaves. I thought I smelled wet dogs."

"That's what bears smell like," Helen said. "You're lucky the mother didn't maul you to death. They're fiercely protective of their cubs."

"What do we do next?" I asked, feeling shaky.

"We'll stay put until the volunteer fire department comes. It may take them a while to get up this road. Caleb will call them on his CB and then the DNR will come and tranquilize the mother and relocate them," Helen said. "He knows a guy who works there."

The rain beat down harder, and we were completely soaked, but the fire was extinguished and the smoke almost completely gone. I started to shiver uncontrollably and my teeth began to chatter.

"You might have lost power somewhere in the cabin—maybe to one of your kitchen appliances or your baseboard heat. Your lights are still working, though, and you'll have plenty of heat from the fireplace. Let's go inside while Caleb radios for help," Helen said, before we rushed into the safety of the cabin.

I got a change of clothes and towels for Helen while she took off her slicker and set her boots in the tray. After she changed, she built a fire, and I put on some dry clothes.

I went on the front porch and watched Caleb go to his truck. After a few minutes he backed it up, turned off the flashers, and spotlighted his headlights toward Sam's now dazzling beer bottle tree—the three bears didn't move. Helen said they'd stay put since there was so much commotion.

"How old are the cubs?" I asked when Helen joined me.

"Maybe a year old. They look like they might weigh close to a hundred pounds, and their mother probably weighs 250."

Helen walked to the bathroom to toss her sopping wet pajamas into the dryer.

Caleb left his slicker on the front porch glider and set his boots in the tray beside Helen's. Killer shot ahead of him and hid under my bed. I gathered a towel, a pair of socks, and one of Sam's old sweatsuits for Caleb. He changed in the bathroom and seemed uncomfortable afterward and kept tugging at the snug shirt and pants.

"A month from now, all this rain would have been snow," Helen said, staring out the window.

"How long do you think those bears have been sleeping under the porch?" I asked.

"Not long. We were here a week ago clearing brush and cleaning the place after Sam told us you were coming. No bears camping out then. Have you seen any?"

"Well, one looked in my kitchen window this evening. It must have been the mother bear. She knocked some firewood down, and when she stood up, she stared through the window at the cat. Killer hunkered down and then swatted at the bear. It freaked me out, and the bear!"

"Who?" Helen asked.

"Oh, Caleb's cat. I changed Marigold's name to Killer," I said. "I've been meaning to ask you about that other cat named Raven. I've never seen her around."

"Raven's not a cat," Helen said with a curious smile. "She's a black snake that visits the cabin—great for pest control. Sam spotted her one summer crawling on the moose's antlers over the fireplace. Later Caleb caulked all the crevices and holes where she might have gotten in," Helen said.

"Raven's an inside snake?" I asked.

"Not anymore, but she created a lot of excitement one summer when she decorated the antlers," Helen said, laughing at my stunned face. "Black snakes are harmless, just scary to some people."

We sat at the table while Caleb stared out the front door and kept watch over the glittering glass tree, all gold and green and blue with three unmoving shadows near the now barren top. I hoped more help would arrive soon.

"Can I get you a beer? I asked.

"None for us but go ahead if you need something," Helen teased.

"I could use a shot of whiskey," I said. "It's not every day I learn a black snake lives in my cabin and three bears camp under my porch. It's more of a nightmare than once-upon-a-time."

"So, are you going to stick around, Goldilocks?" Helen asked. "This isn't sunny Florida, but I can promise you won't be bored."

A siren's wail began to echo in the distance as our rescuers crept up Glass Mountain.

"I'm just grateful you heard my shots," I said.

"*What* six gunshots?" Helen asked, masking a smile.

36

TREED

The rest of the night became a rainy blur of flashing red lights, weary firemen, and three black bears, clinging to the top of a spotlighted glass tree. I wondered how often the firemen were called to a house fire and then put on high alert for treed black bears. It must be like a lifeguard trying to rescue a drowning victim with sharks circling the waters.

People rushed about until the DNR officers showed up, and then things came to a stop. After a brief consultation, one of them took aim and shot a tranquilizer dart into the mother bear. When the sow went completely limp, I watched in horror as she seemed to fall in slow motion to a waiting net held by four stout men. Then the bawling cubs scrambled to even higher branches as more beer bottles crashed and shattered on the ground below. The men checked the mother's vitals, put a radio collar on her, and scanned her neck for a microchip. After they recorded the data on a clipboard, the sow was strapped to a stretcher and lifted inside a waiting vehicle. Caleb said they would desensitize the bear first and relocate her at least 40 miles away in hopes she wouldn't return.

"But what about her cubs?" I asked, looking up at them.

"They might have to put them down," Helen answered.

"You're kidding? Right?"

Caleb crossed and uncrossed his arms while he stared at the ground.

"They won't survive without their mother, and nobody wants to raise bears—too many of them already," Helen explained. "They eat the farmers' calves and chickens, raid their orchards and cornfields, and sometimes break into homes. Once cubs have witnessed a break-in, they can't unlearn this new way to get food. Then they become a deadly threat to others."

"Is that why Sam has steel bars on all his windows?" I asked.

"He had a little trouble with two nuisance bears that tried to break in while he and Lydia were away one weekend. They broke out the kitchen window and tore the place up pretty bad. One even tried to drag Sam's venison-stocked freezer out the door."

"Couldn't the cubs be taken to a zoo or something? We had black bears in our zoo in Florida," I urged.

"No zoos here that I know of, Twyla, and even if we had one, no one's going to pay good money to stare at bears in a cage when all they have to do is look out their window," Helen said.

I saw the man with the tranquilizer darts take aim at one of the cubs. I closed my eyes this time.

"They've decided to tranquilize the cubs and relocate them along with their mother," Helen said matter-of-factly.

When the shots were fired I covered my ears, but I could hear the cubs crying until they suddenly went quiet.

"You don't see stuff like this in Florida, do you?" Helen asked.

"Never," I said.

"Don't they shoot alligators in Florida? Do they relocate or desensitize them if they eat family pets or toddlers?" Helen asked in a strange voice.

"Desensitize?"

"That's when you make a lot of racket, fire guns, and shoot

pellets at animals so they will leave the area for good," Helen said, studying my face. "Do they ever do that to alligators? Give them a second chance?"

I shrugged my shoulders. I didn't like her sarcasm. I didn't know much about alligators except they lived in swamps and people like to wrestle them for sport.

"Bears are omnivores, you know. They eat plants and animals, so when they're hungry, they're not choosy about what or who they eat. They're wild animals, Twyla. Most of the time, we coexist just fine, but sometimes things go haywire—like tonight. It's the right thing to do, but it may not seem like it now."

I watched the men check the cubs' vitals. They put ear tags on them instead of a radio collar.

"If the sow returns to Glass Mountain, and she probably will, they'll track her radio signal and the cubs will follow. Desensitization and relocation almost never work. It just wastes tax-payers' money, but it's more humane to try it this way first," she explained.

"What if they return?" I asked, already dreading her answer.

"Well, if they don't kill any livestock or try to break into homes, they'll be fine. Otherwise, they'll be put down the next time, not tranquilized."

Helen and I watched them lift the cubs onto stretchers and load them into a different van. They looked so small and innocent. The firemen worked for a while under the front porch, and made sure the smoldering insulation was snuffed out. Then they walked all around the cabin and finally went inside. They checked everything for the source of the fire: the wiring, overheated appliances, and the baseboard heat.

Helen found a bigger coffee pot in the pantry and carried it to my bedroom since the receptacle in the kitchen didn't work. After she brewed a pot, she poured coffee into several mugs and set them on a tray.

"Could you take these outside to the firemen?" she asked.

"Sure," I said, grabbing a jacket.

She opened the front door and then held the screen door open for me as I walked outside. Helen carried a cup over to Caleb who watched from the cab of his truck.

"Thanks," one of the men said.

"You're welcome, but Helen made it," I said.

He held the mug with both hands and took a big drink.

"Are you staying here at Sam's place by yourself?" he asked.

"Just for a little while," I said, weighing my words carefully. "It's been a huge adjustment."

"You're not much of a country girl, are you?" he said with a mischievous grin.

"No, but I'm a quick study."

"I'm Cory," he said, removing one glove.

"I'm Twyla," I said, shaking his hand.

"I've never heard that name before," he said.

"Not many people have. I'm named after a famous choreographer."

"Interesting. Maybe I'll run into you in Oakland sometime," he said.

"Maybe we will. Thanks for your help, Cory."

I carried the empty tray into the cabin, and after a few minutes, another fireman knocked on the door. His boots and rain gear were wet and muddy, and he looked like he hadn't slept in days.

"We're getting ready to take off. Everything's stable so don't worry. Caleb said to tell you he'll be here tomorrow morning to fix the wiring the bear chewed through. He's a good electrician," he told me.

"Thanks for coming all the way up here."

"No problem. It's our job, but Sam really needs to work on his road before winter. It's a real bear," he said with a wink and then he walked toward the flashing red lights that strobed the mountaintop.

I followed him out on the porch, and then Helen joined me.

"We're heading home now unless you want me to sleep here tonight," she said.

"No, I'll be fine," I assured her.

"Caleb will be here in the morning."

"Are you coming with him?" I asked.

"No, I have to work. Tomorrow's a weekday, you know. Some of us work for a living," she said with a laugh.

"Sorry, I forgot tomorrow is Monday."

"Don't make any rash decisions, Twyla. Give yourself plenty of time to adjust— some breathing room. The mountains are just testing you, that's all."

Caleb flashed the truck headlights twice.

"Well, I'd better go, Goldilocks," Helen said. "Are you sure you don't want me to stay? I could call in sick tomorrow. I'm best friends with the boss," she teased.

I didn't answer.

"It's no trouble at all, and my pajamas are in your dryer. Caleb could drive me home tomorrow morning after he finishes up here."

"Well, I do have an extra bed," I finally said.

37

KILLER

"I'm coming, I'm *coming*!" I yelled, as I slid out of bed and stumbled over Killer who was sleeping on the floor. She bit my ankle. Hard.

Someone continued to bang louder and louder on the door, so I grabbed the shotgun and limped to the kitchen. After peering through the window, I opened the door and Killer darted out. Caleb just stood there, smoking a cigarette.

"I thought something was wrong when you didn't answer," he said, looking at the shotgun in my hand.

"I overslept."

"Where's Helen?" he asked.

"She's still asleep," I said. "Don't you have a key?"

"I do, but I never come inside without knocking first," he said. "And, if I know someone has a loaded gun, I always knock."

"You made a joke, Caleb. Come on in," I said, rubbing my ankle. "I'm not ready to go yet. Let me pack a few things, but first I need coffee. You want a cup?"

"No, I've had plenty," he said, tossing his cigarette to the ground and putting it out with the toe of his boot before he stepped inside. "I haven't fixed the wiring yet."

"Oh, I thought that..."

"Here, I'll put it in the gun rack for you," he said, taking the shotgun from my hands, checking the safety, and carefully reloading the Krag. "Always keep your guns loaded when you live alone," he warned.

He noticed the hand-written note that was taped to the coffee pot and read aloud, "I decided to hike down the mountain early. A customer's coming to buy furniture about 9 a.m. Tell Caleb I put his pajamas on top of the dryer."

Killer kept meowing at the doggie door to come in, and as soon as I unlocked it, Caleb whisked her up in his arms and she began to purr. He fed her and then poured a saucer of milk before he took the coffee can from the refrigerator.

Meticulously, he measured spring water from the dispenser into the carafe, making sure the water sat plumb at the ten-cup mark. Then he put in a new filter and measured out five heaping tablespoons of ground coffee. I really could have used someone like him at Calamity.

When he pressed the ON button, the coffee maker didn't light up.

"Oh, Helen had to make coffee in my room last night. The receptacle in here is blown."

Caleb carried the coffee pot to my bedroom, set it on the refrigerator, and plugged it in.

"I'll repair the wiring and reset the breakers while you pack."

"Thanks," I said, as I limped toward the sink and looked at the empty spot on the windowsill where the champagne flutes used to be. I remembered my smoky dream the other night about swimming across a warm lake toward a silver champagne bucket and two crystal flutes.

"Did you know your face is bleeding?" he asked.

He dampened a paper towel with water and handed it to me.

I touched my face and smeared the blood, and then I pulled

my pant leg up to see my wound. Killer had definitely left her mark, so I cleaned the bite with soap and water. Caleb went into the bathroom and got some cotton balls, a bottle of hydrogen peroxide, and a box of Band Aids.

"Does Killer have all her shots? I'm not going to get rabies or cat-scratch fever or something crazy, am I?" I asked in a rush.

"Killer? Oh, you mean Marigold. She's mean-spirited sometimes, but completely healthy. Helen sees that all her inoculations are up to date," Caleb said before he doctored my wound and then returned the first aid supplies to the medicine cabinet.

The brewing coffee smelled heavenly, and I was ready for a cup. As Caleb headed toward the door, Killer scurried past him to go outside first. Nothing shy about her.

I watched him walk to his truck, open a toolbox, and step into a white paper jumpsuit. Then he went to the side of the cabin, and, in just a few minutes, I could hear tapping and thumping underneath the front porch.

I stared at the empty windowsill again. I didn't remember moving the champagne flutes, but they were there with the wine glasses and candlesticks in the drainer where I had left them.

I went to my room and noticed the empty twin bed Helen had carefully made before she left. I changed my clothes and packed what little I had. After smoothing the bed covers and tucking my pillow under the bedspread, I stood by the front door and drank a cup of coffee.

When I looked out the window at the top of the tree where the three bears had sheltered, the remaining glass bottles glinted and chimed in the breeze. When I walked outside on the screened porch, it felt like winter. I started to shiver, so I crossed my arms over my chest and tried to keep warm. Caleb was resting on the porch steps wearing his funny paper suit that was smudged with dirt.

"Do you want to see the fuse box?" he asked, unzipping the jumpsuit before he removed it. He shook it hard and then folded it into a small square. He joined me and set his suit on the glider.

"Give me a second," I said.

I opened the front door and unhooked Sam's heavy jacket from the hall tree and slipped on Sylvia's boots. Then we walked to the cinderblock building, and Caleb unlocked the door and turned on a light. It smelled musty inside, like the dirt cellar where I used to hide my money from Joy. There was a small padlocked trunk in one corner and gallon jugs of bleach stored in another. A Daddy Long Legs high-stepped it across the dirt floor and a couple of jumping crickets scattered when I entered. I wasn't afraid of bugs so much as snakes and uninvited bears.

Caleb opened the rusty fuse box door and showed me where everything was. He had neatly labeled everything, and I could see which fuse had blown. I watched as he simply switched it on.

He lifted the lid of his green toolbox, removed the top tray, and took a Phillips screwdriver out. I noticed at the bottom of the box there were several shiny glass doorknobs.

"Do you want to walk through the cabin one last time before we leave? I need to tighten the screws on this latch since they're starting to work loose."

"I'll wait for you to finish," I said. "I might need to know how to do this sometime."

We entered the cabin together, and he turned off the coffee pot and threw the grounds away. I checked the fireplace and stirred the ashes to make sure there were no embers. Then I poured a couple of glasses of water over the ashes and closed the damper. Caleb stuffed his pajamas inside a plastic bag, gathered the trash, and checked all the wastebaskets. I made one final trip through the cabin, making sure I didn't leave anything behind, and then I carried my duffel bag to his truck.

A few minutes later, he locked the cabin door, put his jumpsuit inside his toolbox, and slid it into the bed of the truck.

I handed him Lydia's blue quartz keyring, and we started down the mountain.

My tears caught me off guard as we made our way over the bumpy road and ever deepening pot holes. I was leaving a place I didn't really know, but I had called it home by accident a couple of times. I had never stayed in one spot for very long my entire life, so moving on to the next place and the next seemed normal. I was hardened and indifferent, or numb, I guess. This time, though, I was having trouble leaving, and I didn't understand why.

38

LICORICE

When we reached the main road, I opened the gate and locked the padlock after Caleb drove his truck through. I climbed in, and he turned on the flashers to let others know he was driving slowly. As we approached the main road, a long line of cars soon began to trail behind us. Caleb pulled off the road and signaled them to go around. It was going to be a long trip to the Pittsburgh airport.

"You want a piece of candy?"

He opened the shoebox that sat between us, took out a braided strand of black licorice about ten inches long, and bit a chunk off. I hadn't eaten licorice in a long time, but I remembered its strong smell.

"I've got strawberry, too," he offered.

"No thanks, I'm not hungry."

I glanced at my phone which was recharging in his cigarette lighter. It would take a while, but then I could make a plane reservation on my phone. I slipped my credit card out of my purse and worried I might have reached my limit. A grocery cashier in Florida had rejected my card one time while irritated people waited in line and scouted out faster check-out lanes. I hoped Sam had paid off my credit card debt like he promised.

"Helen told me to stop by the shop before we leave town. She wants to give you something," he said.

Caleb parallel parked near a sign displayed in the front window: **Cigarettes. All Brands 29 Cents.** I needed a cigarette right now, but 29 cents wouldn't buy one smoke at today's prices. That sign must be ancient, I guessed. He coiled the last of his licorice into a tight circle and popped it into his mouth. His craving had already blackened his teeth.

There might be just enough charge on my phone now to make a call if the reception was good. One bar. *Aren't there any cell towers around here?* I pocketed my phone and left my charger in the truck. Caleb held the door for me, chewing away on his licorice. It looked like he had a plug of tobacco in his cheek. As we entered the shop, the chime went off—that soft doorbell sound of two slow notes: diiiing—dooong.

I felt as if I were transported to another century with fancy wall hangings, painted china, silver tea sets, and crystal candelabras with slim white candles. The chandeliers caught the morning sun. Each section of this large room had been separated into distinct living quarters: a formal dining room, a parlor, a front porch, a kitchen, a master bedroom with a rosewood fireplace, mahogany dresser, and a highboy. It was nothing like the junk shops where I used to hunt for bargains.

An invisible pianist played sleepy jazz over the loudspeakers, and I closed my eyes for a second. In the living room section, an old stereo sat near a wine-colored sofa. I walked over and stared at the spinning turntable that played a 33 1/3 record. Josh had started to collect vinyl records and kept me up to date. He was always on the look-out for collectibles, especially from the psychedelic '60s and '70s.

Other than the music, the store seemed too quiet. I looked out the picture window when a motorcycle rumbled up Alder Street. The biker was dressed in black leather, and he had a long, white beard and handlebar mustache. He was followed by three cars that climbed the steep hill to the stoplight.

Caleb walked to the rear of the store and disappeared into the back room. I could still smell his licorice, but the fragrant pine boughs and baskets of cinnamon-scented pinecones took over. I needed to make a reservation and head to Pittsburgh soon, but I did wonder what Helen wanted to give me.

Helen's shop reminded me of color photos from art books I looked at in the Naples library. I noticed a Western saddle in the entranceway: a fancy hand-tooled one with visible signs of wear. The wool padding on its underside had a few bare places that had been rubbed off over the years. I wondered when someone had last saddled a horse with it. If only I could transport myself back to that moment, I could watch. Did the saddle belong to a prized horse or a thoroughbred? *The camel-colored leather would look great on a palomino,* I thought. Not that I knew much about horses, but I imagined a long blond mane and tail that rippled when the horse cantered or jumped over a gate in competitions. I wondered if Calamity Jane ever rode a palomino. Sam would know, but he'd probably say it was too fussy for her.

I looked at the tag and it read $225. I stroked the leather and lifted the shiny stirrups. I'd buy it if I owned a horse or give it to Calamity Café if I had enough money, but that was wishful thinking.

My eyes were drawn from the saddle to a couple of fancy mirrors and a white birdcage hanging from a tall stand in the living room. They all were missing the thing they were created for in the first place: a horse, smiling faces, or a bright yellow canary. *Canary* was Calamity Jane's real last name. I amazed myself when I remembered that fact. Sam would be impressed.

A man strolled by the shop singing in a deep operatic voice. I couldn't see him through the window, but several cars honked and waved. Who would sing on a public street in a small town?

I walked to the counter where a row of children's wooden ABC blocks spelled out M-e-r-r-y C-h-r-i-s-t-m-a-s. It was only September, but this greeting made me think about the holidays.

A few memories were good, but most were empty and sad: Chase and I alone on Christmas Eve, trying to entertain ourselves, me trying to be his substitute mother.

"Hey, Twyla!" Helen called cheerfully, stepping out of the back room. "We're having lunch, and it's almost ready."

Caleb was holding a glass of milk, so I walked to the small room. It was just big enough for a microwave, mini-fridge, and a couple of people. The spicy smell of barbecue mixed with the lingering smell of licorice didn't make me hungry. A plastic container of coleslaw and a bag of hamburger buns were set on top of a half-moon table. Helen pulled one of the two dinette chairs out and motioned for me to sit.

"Do you like your barbecue with or without slaw?"

"I'm not hungry, but thanks," I said. "May I use your phone, Helen?"

"You must be thirsty then. Caleb, pour her a Pepsi," she directed.

He filled a purple aluminum glass with ice and cola and set it in front of me. The glass was from a set of multi-colored ones I had once admired. Condensation formed quickly on the outside surface, and my hand became damp from holding the cold drink.

The little room felt too crowded now, so Caleb left and sat behind the cash register to work on Helen's ledger while he finished his sandwich. He was good with numbers and never made a mistake, she had told me.

"A man just walked in front of the shop singing really loud," I said.

"Oh, that's Henry," Helen said. "He's a retired policeman, and he's always singing. He's well known in our town and a crowd favorite at weddings and funerals. I think you caught him warming up for his solo this Sunday at St. Peter's Catholic Church. He's a friend of Cory, one of the firemen who came to Glass Mountain."

"Oh, yeah, Cory," I said, remembering his rugged good looks.

"What a crazy night, huh? I'm sorry I left so early, but I put a note on the coffee pot. I sold the teakwood dining room set with matching hutch and buffet table. I haven't had a minute to myself."

The door chimed as someone entered the shop; Helen peered through the curtained doorway.

"Do you need to leave?" I asked.

"No, Caleb can wait on her. He helps out a lot."

"It's like an enchanted castle in here, Helen. I guess you never get bored," I said.

"Never. There's always new stuff coming in and old stuff going out. It's a designer's dream actually. I'm always redecorating when I bring in things from estate sales or an auction. It's like when you buy a new sofa or bedroom suite for your home. The old things are gone, and the new take their place. Then you want to add newer pieces and accessories that complement everything. It's ongoing and demanding, but I love it," she said.

I didn't understand how a new sofa could make you add more things to go with it, but I liked the possibility of it all.

"It's like set designing, isn't it? After one play closes, you have to build a new set for a new cast of characters," I said.

"Exactly. I strike the set, and then I rebuild, redesign, and try to lure a new audience inside the theater to see the next show. I like how you think, Twyla."

"It's easy being surrounded by all your beautiful things," I said.

"So, you're leaving us?" Helen asked after a long pause. "I had hoped I could get you to work on Saturdays a couple times a month until bad weather sets in. I know it's a huge adjustment living on the mountain by yourself, and the three bears didn't help at all, but Sam said you really needed the money."

"I do, but it's time for me to leave," I told her, feeling guilty about my decision. "I need to make a plane reservation now and tell Sam I'm coming home. I can't get any cell service here, though,"

"I thought you were tough," Helen said abruptly, "but if you've made up your mind, you should go."

I am tough, but I know when I'm in over my head, I wanted to say.

"You can use my landline, but if you want more privacy, walk over to the restaurant on the corner. They have free Wi-Fi. Climb up to the top deck, and you'll be able to use your cell phone there," Helen said, looking up the airport's number and jotting it down on a piece of paper. "You may not be able to get a plane reservation on such short notice."

"Do you think they'd let me charge my phone at the restaurant?"

"Sure, they let tourists and bikers do it all the time. There are a few outside receptacles you can use as well. If anyone says anything, just tell them you're a friend of mine," Helen said.

I exited through the chiming door and waved to Caleb. He pretended like he didn't see me, but I knew he did. I grabbed my charger from his truck and hurried over to the restaurant. The wind cut through my thin jacket and I shivered.

The restaurant/motel was a three-story timber structure with outside stairways that led to each level. When I climbed to the third floor deck, I found an outlet and plugged in my phone. Three bars! I sat on the floor and called Sam.

39

MORE TIME

"Hi, Sam. How's Chase?"

"Where are you? We just walked in the door," Sam asked. "Here, I'll let you talk to him right now."

"Twy?" The sound of his sweet voice made my eyes tear up.

"How are you doing?" I asked.

"I'm great! Sam's going to take me fishing this afternoon and show me how to cast a fishing rod. A real fishing rod! Then we're going out to eat, and he's taking me to The Olive Garden, so I have to take a bath. He knows I love spaghetti, and he said I can have all the breadsticks I want."

"I'm glad you're having a good time," I said.

"There's no school tomorrow, and Sam's taking me to a movie at the mall. He's going to buy me ice cream first."

The excitement in Chase's voice was both good and bad. Good because I knew he was happy, and bad because he was slipping away from me. Fast.

"I'll see you next weekend. We're bringing Cali with us!"

"Hey, that's really great," I said. "I need to talk to Sam again for just a second."

"How's life on the mountain treating you?" Sam asked as soon as Chase handed him the phone. "Are you at the antique shop? We were just talking about what to bring next week. I really miss my palace, and I know you're taking good care of it."

"Sam, there's something I have to tell you," I said.

"Oh, I did what you asked," Sam interrupted. "I deposited the first installment of your pay in your checking account and paid off your credit cards. I wanted to wait a little longer, but you might need a little spending money when you're in Oakland."

"Thanks, Sam."

"Chase's doing great in school," he said. "He's going to bring a few of his test papers to show you next week, and he can't wait to go to Disney World next spring! Talk about putting a solid gold carrot in front of his nose. You did the right thing, girl."

Two bikers wearing knit hats and gloves climbed up the steps to the third level deck. One of them smiled at me and elbowed the other, and then they unlocked a door and disappeared inside their motel room.

"I'm going to come home today," I blurted out. "After I make a reservation, Caleb will drive me to the Pittsburgh airport."

"You gotta be kidding me, right?" Sam asked, his voice going flat.

"Your cabin is beautiful, but I miss Chase too much."

"You can't give up on us now," Sam said. "You've only been there a week. Give yourself more time. Please, wait a while before you decide. Once Cali's staying with you, you won't feel so lonesome," he said.

"I can't wait."

"Don't let me down, Twyla. Chase is doing great, and you've got to consider his future. If you still want to leave after next week, I'll fly you home the very next day. Promise me you'll think about it before you make your final decision," Sam urged.

"I can't promise anything," I said under my breath.

"Then wait one more day and decide," Sam replied quickly. "You owe it to Chase."

"Okay," I barely whispered, suddenly overwhelmed with guilt. "Let me talk to him."

"He's outside. Hang on and I'll go get him."

"Never mind, Sam. Just tell him I love him," I said, my voice cracking. "I'll call tomorrow."

I turned off the phone and buttoned my jacket. Then I leaned my head against the concrete wall and listened to the shushing sounds of the Little Youghiogheny River that flowed beside the restaurant. Helen said the river would be completely frozen over by Thanksgiving, but I won't be here to see it.

40

THE OLD CURIOSITY SHOP

I spotted Caleb's truck parked in front of the restaurant. He had the hood up and was busy checking the oil.

"How long have you been out here?" I asked, after I joined him.

"Just a couple minutes."

He wiped the dipstick clean with an old rag and then checked the oil.

"I'm supposed to drive you to the shop. Helen has something for you."

"Thanks, but I'd rather walk. It's just down the street."

"Suit yourself," he said, slamming the hood shut before climbing in and slowly pulling his truck away from the curb.

I walked to a nearby gas station to buy a pack of cigarettes. Just as I was getting my money out, the handsome fireman who responded to the bear incident came in to pay for his gas.

"Hey, it's Twyla, right?" he asked, smiling down at me. "So, are you in town for a while?"

"Good memory, Cory. I'm here for just a short time."

His blue eyes lit up when I said his name.

"Let me pay for those," he said, sliding my cigarettes toward the cashier and giving her his credit card. Then he handed me the pack and I quickly slipped it into my purse.

"I don't smoke," I stuttered. "I mean, they're just for emergencies."

"Like when you're visited by black bears that start electrical fires?"

"Maybe," I said, laughing at his quick wit.

"Next time you're in town, stop by the fire station. It's just there across the street," he said. "Maybe we could grab lunch at Englanders. They have comfort food and old-fashioned chocolate sodas."

"I might do that," I said, feeling myself blush as I turned to leave, considering his offer. After I waved goodbye, I quickly made my way to Helen's shop.

When I opened the chiming door, it felt like home, or what I imagined my dream home might feel like—a beautiful place with skylights and music and laughter. Caleb was sorting through a box of old postcards, and Helen sat behind the counter making entries into her ledger.

"Did you get to talk to Chase?" she asked, looking up at me.

"I did. He's fine. Actually, he's better than fine. He loves doing things with Sam, and they're going fishing later."

Helen smiled.

"Did you tell Sam you were flying home today?" she asked.

Caleb stopped his cataloging and listened intently.

"He asked me to wait one more day before I made up my mind. He and Chase planned to come here next week and bring Cali with them. I told Sam I'd let him know my decision tomorrow, so I won't need to go to the airport today, Caleb," I said looking over at him. "I guess I can handle just about anything for 24 hours, right?

"That Sam! He's such a persuader," Helen said.

Caleb continued sorting and cataloging his postcards. When the phone rang, Helen hurried to answer it.

The door chimed again, and I half expected to see Cory

standing there, but instead, a family of three entered the shop. Caleb nodded and left them alone to browse.

"Is that a Fenton lamp, Dad?" the daughter asked.

"Yes, it's beautiful, isn't it?"

The man moved in closer to examine the floor lamp.

"How much is this china cabinet?" the wife called, turning toward Caleb.

"It's half price: $200," he said without hesitation.

The family walked up and down each aisle, looking at everything. After they were gone, I studied the lamp. A note on the price tag said it was a brass torchiere lamp. It had a cream-colored glass globe etched with raised leaves. The heavy base inset looked like marble with gray and rust-colored streaks. It had been marked $395. No piano music fluttered from the wall-mounted speakers now. The stereo was off, and the buzz from the fluorescent lights overhead created the only sound. It was making me sleepy.

I watched as Caleb alphabetized the cards by year with colored tabs. Then he paused and silently read one that captured his interest. I could hear Helen talking on the phone, so I looked around and then stopped in front of an old electric typewriter—an Olivetti Lexikon 82, complete with its instruction manual. I wondered if it still worked. If the ribbon was intact, I could remove it and see the very last typed word.

"Do you want to buy a typewriter?" Helen asked, as she emerged from the back room holding a cup of hot tea. "You could write the Great American Novel on it, but it might take you a while. No spell-check or printer, but I could throw in a case of *Wite-Out,*" she said, laughing at her own joke.

"I'm just admiring it," I said, smoothing my fingers across the shiny black keys. "Maybe I could manage a chapter or two, or steal some of your secret recipes for the cookbook Sam thinks I'm writing."

"Speaking of recipes, do you want to stay for dinner?" Helen asked. "I'm trying out a new recipe."

"No, thanks, but I'll take a raincheck. I'm pretty exhausted."

"I'll have Caleb take you home early, so you can get some rest," Helen said.

"I don't want to be a burden."

"No burden at all. Isn't that right, Caleb?" Helen asked.

"Right," he answered robotically.

41

PAW PRINTS

When Caleb handed over Lydia's blue keyring, I noticed he had added a gate key to it. After I took it from him, I looked him in the eye.

"I don't have a car."

"You might need it someday," he said. "You never know."

He opened the glove box and, without a word, took out a small wrapped package and placed it in my hand. The tag said*For Twyla*. I thought for a second it must be from Helen, but Caleb said Sam had mailed the gift to the shop earlier this week.

After I entered the cabin and watched Caleb drive away, I set the package in my room on the dresser. Its mirror reflected the shiny gold and silver paper with a fat white bow on top. I wondered why Sam had given it to me. What more did he expect?

That night, Killer slept on my fleece robe which she had clawed from the bed. When the morning sun began to glint through the frosty window, I woke and realized I had slept all night. No bears. No fire. No excitement to wake me. Just country silence.

I sat up in bed and rubbed my eyes. The sun always lit the

208

crystal bowl and vase, casting prisms that shimmered off the walls, but I noticed they were missing. That's strange. Surely no one stole them. One of the firemen must have moved them to a safer location.

Something else was different this morning as well. I had slept in my pajamas, not in my clothes—another giant step for me. A loaded rifle rested at the foot of my bed, and I felt grateful Killer hadn't pounced on it and created a bloody crime scene.

I felt strangely calm, even though it had only been two days since the bear invasion. My room was chilly, so I gently tugged my robe out from under Killer. She hissed and ran away. I slipped it on over my pajamas and pulled on a pair of the wool socks Caleb had given me.

Killer meowed and scratched at the doggie door. I unlocked it and let her outside before I checked the fire. The leather side chair was in front of the back door where I had pushed it last night, and the pump organ still blocked the front. Not that those obstacles could ever stop a hungry bear, or bears, but they made me feel safer, just like the flimsy curtain in the doorway made me feel more secure somehow.

I added a big log to the fire and soon the cabin grew cozier. I carried the coffee pot to the kitchen, and then I sat facing the front porch. I watched the sunrise and pretended I was at a private drive-in movie. Joy had told me all about them—actually more than I ever wanted to know about her adventures with boys. She swore I had been conceived in a VW camper.

The silvery morning sky, backlit with gold-edged clouds, gave me a front-row seat to the universe as I watched the clouds turn coral pink and a pale feathery blue. I wanted to see the sunrise every morning if I decided to stay. Not that I was *going* to stay.

The pink rays became scarlet and then a blinding yellow orb appeared, as the sun moved higher in the sky. It seemed huge as it rose above the mountain peaks, and I had to shield my eyes from the glare. The glass tree became electrified, as if someone had thrown a power switch. Its dazzling light looked beautiful and alien at the same time. I needed to replace the beer bottles on it since the three bears had knocked so many to the ground. I'd have to get busy and drink more beer, and then I could leave the tree just like Sam had left it. I'd never become a drunk like Joy or Calamity Jane, but I was aware I was drinking more.

After the light show, I stripped my bed and changed the sheets. I wasn't sure how or if I could do laundry here, but I knew I had to have another bath. I carried the rifle and a change of clothes with me to the table. I decided to dump the water from one of the half empty drums into the bathtub, but first I filled the large tea kettle with water and turned the burner on high.

I inched the drum onto a throw rug and dragged it to the bathroom. Then I leaned it over the side and spilled a couple of inches of water into the tub. I added some of Lydia's bubble bath and then carried the boiling water from the stove and poured it in. The scent of lavender and steam was soothing, and I swirled the hot and cold water together with my hand until it felt just right. After I closed the bathroom door to keep the water from cooling too fast, I climbed in and washed my hair by lying down in the tub. I felt like a pioneer who conserved water for my family's Saturday night bath, only it wasn't Saturday, and, thank God, I was a family of one. I could imagine how cold and dirty the bath water must have been by the time the fifth or sixth person climbed in. They'd have to add another kettle or two of boiling water just to keep it warm.

I was wide awake when I heard Killer clawing at the doggie door, and I let her in, always careful now to lock it back now. I wasn't going to make that mistake again. She acted hungry, so I got a cup of dry cat food from the pantry.

I decided to study the glass tree up close where the bears had sheltered and do some exploring closer to home—I mean, Sam's cabin. I grabbed my keys, pulled on Sam's hunting jacket, another pair of socks, Lydia's boots, and a wool cap from the hall tree, and then came face to face with the pump organ. I decided it was much easier to shove the leather chair out of the way and go out the back door.

The thermometer read 30 degrees—really cold for mid-September, I thought, but Helen had said it wasn't uncommon. I guessed it must be 90 degrees in Naples, and Sam and Chase were probably floating on rafts in the condo's pool. Maybe I should talk to Caleb and Helen about preparing for winter, but no need, I'd be leaving today or next week at the very latest.

I carried the air horn and rifle with me like I always did. Nothing is guaranteed when you live in bear country. After I surveyed my surroundings for a minute, I felt acutely aware of everything. I walked around the cabin, noticing things I'd somehow overlooked. Something caught my eye near the knoll, and when I moved closer toward it, I saw the name Shep chiseled into a flat stone and an impression of a paw print. It must be a grave for one of Sam's dogs. He never mentioned anything about a dog named Shep, but I hadn't known Sam very long.

Even though the top branches were sparse because of the treed bears, the bottom of the glass tree glimmered in the sun. I pushed my coat collar up and walked faster to try and stay warm.

The Zen-like silence of Glass Mountain was calming, and I felt myself letting go. Maybe I really could make it to the end of the week, just like Sam had said. For a minute, I even considered working two times a month for Helen in her shop on Saturdays when the weather was good. Maybe she'd let me travel with her to an estate sale or an auction.

Even though I had gloves on, my hands were starting to go numb, so I didn't stay outside long. I hurried into the cabin to warm myself in front of the fireplace, rubbing my hands together. Above me, the stuffed moose stared at the opposite wall like he always did, but a bare lightbulb with a short chain attached to a log beam still blocked his view. I needed a ladder to turn the light on, but it would put me right next to the moose's nose. I knew it would freak me out to be that close, and I changed my mind. I double-checked the lock to the side door beside the fireplace and the locks to the front and back doors, plus the doggy door like I did many times.

On top of a towering bookcase, I spotted a wooden cigar box. My curiosity took over, so I carried the stepladder from the pantry to reach it. When I raised the brass latch on the felt-lined box, there were two neat stacks of letters bound together with thin blue ribbons. Intrigued, I brought the box down and sat on the couch with it opened on my lap. *This might hold more twists and turns than any novel*, I thought as I untied the first stack and lifted out the letter on top: *January 1965, Dear Lydia.*

42

LOVE LETTERS

The rest of the afternoon, I became a willing voyeur to Sam and Lydia's world during the 60s and 70s. Sam wrote to her every week when he was at law school in Virginia. He was smitten, that much I could tell, and told her everything from the moment he opened his eyes until he fell asleep at night. He described his classes, the notes he took, and how long he had studied. Sam told Lydia how much he missed her and as soon as he got his degree, they'd get married in a real church and dance to a live band that played the Beatles non-stop. He was saving all his extra money so they could honeymoon in Key West for two weeks, and he even sent her pictures of wedding dresses he had clipped from magazines and asked which one she wanted. It was so romantic to hear Sam go on and on about their wedding and future lives together.

Each letter was handwritten in green ink, and I wondered how he found the time to write while he went to school. It must have been a safety valve for him to plan their dream wedding late at night. True to form, Sam had even asked what kind of cake she wanted and what kind of filling between each layer. His sweet tooth was evident, even then.

"Maybe we could have fresh flowers and a porcelain balle-rina on top of the cake with white satin ribbons streaming down the sides. What do you think, Lydia? Too much?" he asked.

Instantly, I remembered the toe shoes in the closet.

Three hours passed before I slowly began to transition from the '70s to the 21st century in an isolated cabin on top of a mountain. I didn't want to leave the past Sam had created so beautifully in his letters, but my eyes hurt. I decided to return to them another day and neatly restacked the letters, tied them with the blue ribbons, and closed the lid.

What a romantic you were, Sam. No wonder Lydia fell madly in love with you, I thought.

The idea of them being married all those decades was foreign. I couldn't think of anyone I knew who wasn't separated or divorced or remarried at least once. Sam and Lydia were like dinosaurs, almost extinct these days, but I loved the idea of finding the perfect man. For a second, I missed Josh and wished he were here with me. Even blue-eyed Cory seemed promising.

I climbed the rungs of the stepladder and safely returned the cigar box to the top shelf. I'd never tell Sam I had read his love letters. Some secrets should remain secret.

When I heard Caleb pull in the back, I quickly descended the step ladder and put it away before he began to thump on the door.

"Are you going to stay or not?" he asked, when I opened the door. "Sam wants to know right away."

Caleb waited patiently until I finally spoke.

"I'm going to stay one more week until Sam and Chase come," I said slowly.

"I need to tell Helen," Caleb said, and for once, he got in his truck without checking under the hood first and drove away.

I had learned to expect the unexpected from Caleb. When he disappeared down the hill, I tuned into a soft rock station on the console radio, and then I opened a bottle of Blue Moon so I could hang it on the tree tomorrow. I was acquiring a taste for beer instead of wine. I sliced a couple of chunks of cheddar cheese onto a plate and found a sleeve of crackers in the pantry.

When I moved the ashtray to one side to clear a spot on the coffee table for my beer and cheese, I knocked over a stack of magazines and uncovered an old photo album. *More research*, I thought, as I made myself comfortable on the couch facing the fireplace. I propped my feet on the Moroccan camel saddle and studied each page: photos of Lydia in her wedding dress, on her honeymoon in Key West, hiking, swimming in the ocean, laughing, and riding a bike. She was taller than me but looked like a dancer or a fashion model. I watched her age and grow slightly heavier every few pages. In one photo, Lydia stood in front of the cabin and in another, she waited at the top of the gravel road. I loved the picture of her sitting on the front steps, petting a large brown and white collie. It looked like the dog on the reruns of *Lassie* that Chase and I liked to watch. The name Shep was printed in ink on the back of the photo—the same name etched into the stone marker on the knoll.

"So, that's Shep," I whispered, turning the page to discover more pictures of the beautiful dog.

I couldn't wait to see Cali again and wondered if she got along with Killer. Surely she did, or the cat wouldn't come in the doggie door. Where was that damn cat anyway? I hadn't seen her for a while.

I stared at Lydia in shorts and a tank top, in a sundress and sandals, and later dressed for winter, wearing the same white parka I often wore. From an elegant young woman in her early twenties at the beginning of the album, I watched the years slip by. Soon her hair was sprinkled with gray and before I knew it, her hair had turned almost white. In one picture a homemade banner was strung across the living room: "Happy sixty-fifth year around the sun, Lydia!"

I flipped past a few blank pages until I came to pictures of clocks and the grandfather clock with the moon face. They all were set at 3:17 p.m., and some of the mirrors were blurry because they had caught the glare from a camera's flash. On the last page, the same clocks and mirrors were covered with sheets. Maybe they were trying to protect their furniture and pictures from dust before they left. But, still it seemed odd.

After I drank my beer, I rinsed out the bottle and held it up to the light. I'd hang it on the tree tomorrow and add more later in the week. Just then, Killer clawed at the doggie door, and when I unlocked it, she raced into the pantry.

I looked out the kitchen window and didn't see anything at first. Then I spotted a huge beady-eyed bird perched on the bird feeder. It stared intensely at the doggie door as it teetered back and forth. The bird reminded me of the stuffed peregrine falcon on the mantel with its spotted chest and large talons. It must have singled out Killer for an appetizer. I stopped the swinging door with my foot and set the lock so nothing could enter or leave. I wasn't in the mood to fight off a hungry falcon.

I rapped hard on the window with a big metal spoon, and the startled bird took flight. Bears, falcons, cats, bats. At least there were no mosquitoes.

It was just 6 p.m., but I decided to shove the leather chair in front of the door. The radio had been playing oldies for over an hour, and I planned to turn it off after the news and local weather:

Tonight will be overcast and cold. There's a hard frost warning for Garrett County, so bring in your plants and your pets. Tomorrow's high will only reach 30. No snow yet, but I'm not complaining, the weatherman joked. *The Farmer's Almanac says we're in for a bad winter since the wooly worms are front and back-end loaded with coal black coats with just a little stripe of white in the middle. Our first snow will probably arrive before October. Get those generators fueled and your pantries stocked.*

I poured Killer some milk and set a bowl of dry food on the

floor. She waited until I left before she approached. I wasn't about to open another can of stinky cat food. Caleb said bears have an acute sense of smell and can sniff out scents on a molecular level. I didn't want to entice them with gourmet cat food and have the three bears jog 40 miles to break in my window.

43

GHOST

I X'd off the days on the calendar each night, patiently waiting for Saturday when Sam and Chase and Cali would arrive. I explored every inch of the cabin and went outside each afternoon to climb the ladder and slide new bottles near the top of the glass tree. It was addictive finding just the perfect limb, the perfect angle, and being rewarded with a light show when the sun rose. I looked at the tree each day, but I ignored Sam's small gift that remained unopened on my dresser. I wasn't used to receiving presents from anyone, especially strangers.

One day I flipped to the peregrine falcon's photo that had been dog-eared in the bird book. It matched the description of the stuffed bird on the mantel, so I had guessed right about the bird perched outside on the feeder, but Caleb said it had to be a Cooper's hawk, not a peregrine. It was just one of the many birds Sam or Lydia had spotted on the mountain, along with various woodpeckers, cardinals, thrushes, and barn swallows, among others, including an owl. I hadn't seen any owls, but I had heard one.

I'd never be a "birder," but I was beginning to understand what captivated those who were. Birds were everywhere in infinite varieties, but I hadn't paid much attention to them until recently. Being alone and bored most of the time had definitely heightened my curiosity about the natural world.

One sleepy afternoon, I returned to Sam and Lydia's closet to explore. Except for her shoes, some of Lydia's clothes were near my size, especially those she wore when she was young. The polyester pantsuits and blue jeans with elastic waistbands were way too big, so she probably bought those decades later.

I discovered a pair of white ski pants with a red stripe down each leg and a matching ski jacket hanging on a hook in the closet. Next to it were two large travel bags filled with dresses, slacks, sweaters, and fitted shirts. When I unzipped the first bag, the overpowering scent of mothballs made me sneeze. I lifted out one wooden hanger with an expensive red sweater and the other with a pair of black wool slacks. When I held the pants up to my waist, the legs were too long. I slipped the angora sweater over my head, and my hair crackled with static electricity. When I looked at myself in the mirror, my hair stood on end. I poured a little bottled water into my hands and dampened my hair to counter the static, but it just made me look soggy. The sweater must have cost a fortune in its day, yet it looked brand new to me.

As I grew even bolder, I discovered a long white box labeled "My wedding dress" on the very top shelf. I was now the trusted but very nosy neighbor who secretly read their mail, looked at photo albums, and snooped in closets while they were away on vacation. I'd never seen a real wedding dress this close—only in magazines and from a distance in fancy department stores—so I couldn't resist. I carefully set the box on the bed and removed the lid. The dress was nested inlayer upon layer of white tissue paper like an expensive Christmas present.

I gently lifted the silk-and-lace gown halfway out and held my breath. It was everything I was not: delicate, elegant, and sophisticated. When I slid it from the box, thousands of seed pearls glittered as the long skirt flowed onto the floor in a soft rustle. It reminded me of one of the wedding dresses Sam had clipped from a magazine when he was in law school. Maybe it was the same one.

I wanted to try it on, but I didn't dare. It was sacred, and I really didn't want to jinx my chances of getting married someday. I held it against me instead and imagined what it must have been like to wear it, to walk down the aisle toward a younger, handsomer Sam with The Beatles playing "All You Need Is Love." Even if I had tried it on, I wouldn't see myself in a full-length mirror, just the small one on my dresser. White ballet slippers, long white gloves, a circle of dried baby's breath attached to a filmy veil, and a preserved bouquet were nestled under the dress in a separate plastic box. I placed the veil on my head and stared at myself in the mirror. For a second, I felt like a fairy princess with it floating over my shoulders, but I quickly put everything back just as it was. It might be okay to try on one of Lydia's sweaters, even her veil, but not her wedding gown.

By the end of the week, I had settled down or settled in, I'm not sure which, but I slept better and woke refreshed. On Friday, the weather turned rainy with high winds, and the weatherman said there could be 60 mph gusts. I believed him. I felt safe inside with Killer curled in front of the fireplace. Still the wailing wind was unnerving. I worried about the glass tree, but I knew I couldn't save it from a violent storm.

The temperature dropped all day, and by dusk the weatherman predicted snow. Not much accumulation, he said, just an inch or so. Like a little kid, I started giggling when I spotted the first snow flurries. I kept running to the windows and finally sat outside, bundled up on the glider until I had to go outside in the snow.

It began with tiny flakes, almost like fragments of lost snowflakes. Then the flurries started to swarm and looked like albino gnats. Soon big, fluffy flakes began to mix with the tiny ones. The treetops started to sway in the wind and the ground became dusted with a coat of white. I looked up at the falling snow and white sky. The mountain range had disappeared completely when the clouds rolled in. Sam's glass tree was edged in white and the stiff wind made the colored bottles click together.

When the snow finally began to fall steadily and fine, the gusts blew the snowflakes sideways. I waited for as long as I could before I hurried to the safety of the screened porch and the glider. My face and hands were numb even though I had on mittens, and I was forced to go inside and watch the snow from the warmth of the cabin.

I worried Sam wouldn't be able to fly in tomorrow, so I distracted myself by making cookies. While they were baking, I straightened the cabin and found a pair of Lydia's silk long johns in the dresser drawer and put them on, along with my wool socks. They were warmer and thinner than my PJs, and they would be easy to layer under my clothes for extra warmth. I found a make-up mirror in one of the drawers, so I placed it on top of the dresser and plugged it in. I might fix myself up a little if Sam and Chase did show up.

The next morning I woke to a strange light. A heavy wet snow had blanketed the mountain, and it seemed to generate its own internal glow. There was at least six new inches of snow, and it clung to every tree branch like a glittery Christmas card. But my wonder quickly faded to sadness because I knew Sam, Chase, and Cali would never be coming now.

The thermometer read 24 degrees, but the weatherman on the radio reported the wind chill was below zero. I flipped the make-up mirror over to the magnifying side and smoothed on a layer of Chapstick. My jeans had gotten tight from my regular snacking, so I wore Lydia's black wool slacks and rolled up the pant legs to keep them from dragging the floor.

I thought I heard a loud rumbling noise. When I looked out the window, no one was there. And then a miracle: a little after 2 p.m., Sam's red Silverado, complete with noisy tire chains, appeared. The icy cold and the whipping wind were brutal, so I zipped on the white ski jacket and put on my boots. A pair of red mittens and a matching wool cap were still in the pockets of the jacket. When I pulled the cap on, it smelled like Shalimar perfume.

When Sam opened the truck door, Cali's tail was wagging like crazy, and then she leapt outside, making a bee-line over to me. When she jumped up on her hind legs and put her paws on my chest, she knocked me down and began licking my face over and over, whimpering and barking all at the same time.

She sniffed my jacket and gloves and started running in tight circles around me. I scrambled to my feet just before Chase slid out of the truck and plowed into the middle of a snowdrift. Then, he ran over and gave me a big hug. Cali kept dancing and barking and wagging her tail non-stop.

"She's nuts," Chase said, laughing at Cali's antics.

"She sure is happy to see me," I said. "You look great."

"Sam takes good care of me. He's the best," Chase said.

Then he shoved his hands into his pockets and started shivering.

"Where are your hat and gloves? Let's get you inside right now where it's warm," I pulled off my mittens and gave them to him. "Put these on. Now!"

Sam unloaded a small suitcase and a bag of groceries from the cab. He must have stopped at a store on his way in and purchased a few things. I could see a load of firewood and two black plastic bags still in the bed of his truck.

"You made it! I worried the storm would keep you all away. Here, let me carry something, Sam," I said, touching his arm. "It's freezing out here!"

For the first time, Sam stopped and looked directly at me with a big grin on his face. But then his smile faded, and his face turned paler than pale. He lowered his head, and I thought he was going to faint. I steadied him as best as I could, but a dozen eggs, a loaf of bread, and a box of glazed donuts tumbled into the snow. Chase picked up the bread and the donuts but left the carton of broken eggs on the ground. Cali started nosing through the eggshells and lapping up the runny yolks. Sam looked dazed.

"They're just eggs, Sam. Don't worry," I said, trying to reassure him.

"Lydia," he gasped. "Lydia!"

44

MARSHMALLOWS

"It's just me," I said, pulling him close and whispering in his ear. "*Twyla.*"

Sam didn't seem to hear me, and I could feel him trembling. He buried his face on my shoulder and hugged me tighter. I almost lost my balance but managed to regain my footing. After a minute, he slowly began to release his grip on me and cradled my face between his hands. His blue eyes were red-rimmed and glistened with tears.

"Don't ever leave me again, Lydia. You *hear* me?" he pleaded.

I pulled off Lydia's red cap and threw it on the ground in front of him.

"*Look* at me, Sam!" I yelled, trying to make him focus on me.

He didn't move, so I took his hands in mine.

"I'm not Lydia. I'm *Twyla* from Calamity Café. Twyla Townsend."

Chase, wide-eyed and scared, stood near us still wearing my mittens and holding a loaf of smashed bread. The three of us became a winter tableau with snowflakes floating about us as Sam tried hard to make sense of it all. After what seemed a long time, he bent to pick up the snowy red cap. He held it to his face and breathed in the memory of Lydia—a soft wool cap that still clung to the fading scent of her perfume.

"That's Lydia's cap, not mine," I told him. "I shouldn't have worn her clothes, but it's just so damn cold here, and you *told* me I could, but I never thought how it might look to you," I said defensively.

Sam began shaking harder now, and it wasn't from the cold but a haunting grief that held him captive. He seemed much older and frailer.

"Let's go inside," I finally said. "Sam, you go first. We can bring in the rest of your stuff later."

He didn't respond and stared through me until a big gust of wind blew the snow from my hair. Then Sam quickly snapped back to reality.

"You, you look just like Lydia did in her white ski jacket and red cap," he stammered. "You even smell like her."

"Chase, take Sam inside and sit in front of the fire. I'll take care of the broken eggs. We don't want to attract any more wild animals."

He obeyed and led Sam by the hand into the cabin. Cali was still licking the eggs. I grabbed some plastic bags from the glove box and double-bagged the remaining eggs that leaked their half-frozen yolks onto my bare hands. I was so cold my fingers began to throb, and my hair became wet from the falling snow. I checked the black bags in the bed of the truck and made sure there was no food in them. After I locked the door, I ran into the cabin. Sam and Chase were standing close to the fireplace, and the mittens, Lydia's red mittens, were still on Chase's hands.

"I'll make you a drink, Sam, just as soon as I can feel my fingers," I said, turning on the faucet and waiting on the water to warm up. I didn't care if it was contaminated or not as I let it flow over my hands.

"I baked cookies, Chase. They're in the tin on the table," I told him as I dried my hands and pumped some sanitizer into my hand. "Help yourself and give Sam as many as he wants. How about a cup of hot chocolate?"

Chase pulled off the red mittens, popped the lid off the tin, and crammed a large chocolate chip cookie into his mouth. I put the bag of eggs into a big zip-lock bag and threw it in the trash can. Then I poured a glass of wine for Sam, slipped off Lydia's boots, and hung her ski jacket on a chair. I vowed I'd never *ever* wear her clothes again.

"Sit closer to the fire, Sam," I said, pulling a chair over to him. Then I added more kindling and a split oak log. Chase offered Sam a cookie, and he took it robotically and held the glass of wine in his other hand.

"When you guys warm up, hang your coats on the hall tree," I instructed, as if I were the owner of this cabin. "And put your boots in the boot tray beside mine. You both tracked in a lot of snow."

Snow-covered Cali bounded through the unlocked doggie door and dashed over to Sam, sniffing at the red wool cap he still held in his hand. She then snatched his cookie from him before I could stop her.

"Let me have that cap, and I'll hang it on the hall tree to dry," I told Sam, gently taking it from him.

When Cali followed me, I grabbed her by the collar and led her to the bathroom to dry her fur. Snow had frosted her golden coat, and it was packed between her paws. I rubbed her dry with a big bath towel and worked on one paw at a time. When I finished, she licked my face once, just like she always did. Cali knew who I was, but I had totally fooled Sam.

"Hey, Cali, remember me. The marshmallow girl? Only I don't have any right now. Sorry," I whispered.

Cali's ears perked up at the word *marshmallow*, and then she proceeded to sniff my wool slacks, the ski jacket, and the white boots.

"I'm going to get Cali some dog food," I said, going to my

bedroom first and taking off Lydia's slacks and sweater. I kept the silk long johns on and changed into my sweatsuit before I went to the pantry and scooped two cups of kibble into a bowl. Cali had been trailing me the entire time, but when I set her food on the floor, she turned up her nose.

"It's pretty dry, isn't it, girl?"

I opened a can of beef broth, poured part of it into the bowl, and stirred it with a spoon.

"There you go," I said, as I covered the can and set it in the refrigerator.

I heated milk, sugar, and cocoa on the stove for Chase and made extra for me. Sam still stared into space and scratched Cali's head after she finished eating.

I poured the steaming hot chocolate into two mugs and handed one to Chase. "Thanks, Twy," he said, holding his mug with both hands. "Any marshmallows?"

"Sorry, I need to buy them the next time I'm in Oakland. You and Cali need a regular supply, right?"

"Sam has some in the truck. Do you want me to get them?" Chase piped.

"Of course he does! Where?"

"Behind the passenger's seat," he said.

"Any more food hidden inside the truck? I don't think Sam wants hungry bears ripping his Silverado apart to get to it."

"Bears?" Chase asked. "What kind?!"

"Didn't Sam tell you there are black bears here?"

"And ghosts," Sam whispered, staring at his wine glass. "These glasses were a wedding gift from Lydia's mother. I haven't seen them for years."

"I totally screwed up, Sam. I'll put them back where I found them," I said.

"I'll get the marshmallows," Sam said suddenly, setting his untouched wine beside the sink. "I need something to do."

He still had on his coat and boots, and before he opened the door, he gently stroked Lydia's wool cap I had hung on the hall tree.

"Who's Lydia?" Chase whispered after Sam left.

"Sam's wife. Didn't he talk about her? They'd been married for a long, long time, but she died about a year ago."

"But why did he call you Lydia?" Chase asked, taking two more cookies from the tin.

"I had on her clothes. I didn't have warm things to bring here, so Sam told me to borrow whatever I needed. But when I came out to the truck wearing her clothes, he thought I was Lydia."

Chase sat at the table and broke one of his cookies in half.

"You fooled Cali, too, didn't you? That's why she went totally nuts," he said.

I dumped Sam's wine down the drain and washed his glass by hand. Chase helped me carry the wine glasses and candlesticks to the guest room. I stowed them in the bottom dresser drawer where I had first discovered them, wrapping each in a dishtowel. In the process, I found the missing crystal bowl and vase inside a pillowcase stuffed with old newspapers. I lifted one out and looked at a paper that had a color photograph on the front page of a blackened home with its windows broken out. The headline read "Winter Sun Suspected in Caversham Fire." I wondered where Caversham was as I carefully put everything inside the pillow case and then put it back in the drawer.

When Sam returned about five minutes later, he held two bags of miniature marshmallows. Cali started prancing on her hind legs and begging for a treat. Sam ripped a hole in one of the bags, put a handful into Chase's cocoa, and made Cali sit before he rewarded her.

"It looks like we got off to a real ragged start today, Twyla, but things have to get better," he said.

After Sam removed his coat and boots, he tuned in a country station on the console radio. I added a generous measure of Gentleman Jack to my cocoa.

"I see you discovered my *good* whiskey," Sam said with a grin. "You deserve a reward, too, for taking great care of everything. Any trouble so far, other than me?"

"Didn't Caleb and Helen tell you?"

"Tell me what? We didn't stop at their place. You were our first priority," he said.

"Well, it's a long story about a mother bear and two cubs that were living under your front porch.

"You're kidding."

I was ready to tell him everything. I sat down in a chair and propped my feet on the camel saddle while Sam and Chase waited on me to begin.

"Well, a mother and two cubs were camped under your front porch, Sam. I didn't suspect anything until one afternoon the mother bear peered in the kitchen window. Killer frightened her away with one ferocious hiss and a lightning-fast strike of her paw that made the bear topple over and run into the woods. That night, smoke started coming in my bedroom window. Long story short, I found a flashlight, went outside, and located the source of the smoke beneath the front porch. When I shined the flashlight under there, six glowing eyes stared at me."

"Six?!" Chase asked.

"Yes, six."

I couldn't sit still any longer. I stood up and finished telling my story.

"A mother bear and her two cubs were bedded down. I didn't know what to do, so I got the shotgun, fired three shots out my bedroom window, and hoped Caleb and Helen would hear them. They did, but I had to get a rifle next because the shotgun only had three shells in it just like you told me. I fired the rifle three times for good measure. When Caleb and Helen got here, the bears had climbed to the top of the pine just over the hill—your glass tree. The smoke, the gunshots, or both had terrified them. Caleb radioed for the fire department, and, well, they finally made it up Glass Mountain."

"Now, that's no way to start your holiday. Did they relocate the bears?" Sam asked.

"Yes, but Caleb said they might return."

Chase didn't move, but Sam immediately walked outside in his stocking feet. He looked under the front porch and stared up at the pine tree before he hurried inside.

"After your story, Chase and I will just have to watch *True Grit* tonight for sheer fun. Have you ever seen it before?" Sam asked Chase.

"No, sir," he said.

"My wife and I used to watch it every year about this time. You go on to bed, Twyla. We can take care of ourselves now. I'll tuck him in after the movie is over. You might pull down the covers on the other twin bed, though, and make sure there are no wolf spiders or field mice under there having a party," he said mischievously.

"No mice, so far," I assured Chase. "If you guys need anything, just wake me," I said. "Lock the doggie door before you go to bed, Sam."

"I'll lock it down tight, and we'll be just fine. You know, you really gave Cali and me one hell of a scare," he said in a hoarse whisper, patting his chest. "Promise me, you'll never do that again. I don't think my old ticker can handle it."

"I promise," I said.

Sitting in my room, I finished drinking my cocoa and then set the empty mug on the nightstand. Cali had followed me and watched as I turned down the covers on the other twin bed. Killer was already asleep beside my bed. Cali simply sniffed the air and pretended the she-devil didn't exist.

45

POET & COWBOY

I woke to the smell of coffee brewing, but I turned over and made myself go back to sleep. An hour later, I found myself hugging the side of the bed with Chase sprawled out next to me and a cat and a dog lying at my feet. I almost managed to slip out of bed without disturbing anyone, but Cali lifted her head.

"Go to sleep, girl," I whispered. She put both of her paws over her nose as if she understood. The other twin bed had been slept in, so I knew Chase had gotten into my bed during the night just like he used to do.

"Arise, arise to greet the morn! The bird is on the wing! The bee his labor has begun! The woods with music ring!"

Sam's bellowing voice rattled the silence and now everyone was wide awake.

"Arise, arise to greet the morn!" he began again. "The bird is…"

"We're *awake* now, Sam," I shouted, as Chase jumped out of bed. We both peered cautiously to one side of the curtain. No one was out there. Then we heard the back door slam, and both Killer and Cali bolted from the bedroom and exited through the doggie door.

I rubbed a circle of condensation from the bedroom

window and looked out. Chase climbed back in bed and pulled the covers over his head. I didn't see Sam anywhere out front, so I hurried to the bathroom to put on clean clothes. The fireplace blazed and it was toasty warm inside. I heard the truck door slam and glanced outside. The woodpile on the side porch had been stacked even higher, and Sam walked toward the cabin like a lumberjack Santa with two black plastic bags slung over each shoulder.

"I'm glad you finally decided to get up," he said, after he opened the door and spotted me.

"I didn't have much choice. My human alarm clock is a performance poet," I said.

"That's how my father woke me and my brother and sister each and every morning," he said. "It's an old tradition."

"Well, what did you bring me? Two bags of toys?" I teased.

"No toys," he said, shuffling toward the kitchen and gently setting the bags on the floor near the couch where I sat. "This is *much* better than toys."

He took out a manila folder from one of the bags and then removed some papers.

"Thanks for making coffee," I said.

"Did you open the present I sent you?"

"I'm saving it for Christmas if that's okay?" I asked.

"Whatever works for you, Twyla. Pour me another cup there if you don't mind," he said, sinking into the leather chair. "I've been cutting and stacking wood and doing chores since before dawn."

"What's in the folder?" I asked. "It looks important."

"It is. *Real* important. I'm hoping you'll let me have temporary custody of Chase," Sam said in a rush. "Joy's been creating quite a stink, and then I could protect him from her."

I stared at Sam in disbelief.

"I know it's hard to comprehend, but he had a bad experience last week, and this would keep it from ever happening again," Sam explained.

"Let me read it," I said, taking the paper from his hand.

"It will simplify everything if you sign. Remember, it's only *temporary* custody."

"Did you watch *True Grit* last night?" I asked, trying to distract him while I scanned the document.

"We did, but Chase fell asleep on the couch and then I had to carry him to bed. I hope we didn't wake you."

"No, I was sound asleep. He got in my bed during the night along with Killer and Cali."

Sam's face brightened, and then he laughed until he started coughing. I got him a bottle of water, and he took a drink and quickly recovered.

"Four varmints in a twin bed! Now that could be a serious problem," he said. "But it's nothing compared to my home-coming yesterday."

"I found Lydia's clothes in your bedroom closet. I didn't have enough warm things to wear, and you said I could wear them," I said defensively, handing him the papers.

"I do remember, and it's okay, but you blindsided me, girl."

"I'm sorry. I just got used to wearing them."

"Any other surprises, Twy?" he prompted.

"No, but I did discover a pair of toe shoes by accident the other day," I ventured. "Was Lydia a ballet dancer?"

Sam hesitated and seemed both shocked and a little pleased.

"You've been snooping around, I see," he said with a laugh. "Not much to do up here, right? Lydia danced with the ABT. It was love at first sight when I saw her perform. She was just 17, but she stole the show and my heart along with it."

"What's the ABT?"

"The American Ballet Theatre in New York City. It's known worldwide for its artistic excellence," he told me.

"That explains the toe shoes," I said.

I didn't dare mention his love letters.

"She wore white ballet slippers on our wedding day," Sam said wistfully.

Killer scampered into the kitchen and Cali followed. The pecking order was strictly enforced. Cali nosed under Sam's hand so he would scratch her head.

"What's in the bags, Sam?" I asked.

"Let's wait until Chase comes. I want him to help open them."

I was really curious now. It wasn't food or firewood or marshmallows. They had already been unloaded.

I brought Sam a fresh cup of coffee with cream, the way he liked it.

"How long are you staying, Sam?" I asked, trying to decide if I should sign his document or not, and feeling pressured.

"How long are YOU staying? That's the question."

"I'm not sure," I said.

"You survived another whole week and passed the bear test. You'll do fine with Cali and Marigold here with you. What did you say you called her now?"

"Killer. She scared a black bear away," I said.

"Okay, then Killer it is."

I began studying the plastic bag closest to me.

"No you don't! No guessing Twy!"

Rubbing his eyes, Chase strolled into the living room in new flannel pajamas that Sam had bought him.

"Are you awake, son? Your sister wants to know what I've got in these big black bags. If you'll join us, I'll show you both at the same time," Sam said.

Chase perked up and sat beside Sam as he unknotted the first bag and peered inside. He pulled out a long box with a big red bow and let Chase unwrap it. His eyes widened. It was an expensive telescope.

"I thought we might do some serious star gazing while we're here. Are you ready to open the second bag?"

Chase nodded eagerly. With that, Sam sprang into action, opened the bag, and handed him another wrapped present. Chase ripped off the paper and discovered a tripod inside.

"We can look at the craters on the moon tonight if it's clear and even see Saturn's rings. Venus is always spectacular, you know. It shimmers and winks at us like it's alive. The first time I saw it, I thought it was a UFO," Sam admitted.

"What's a UFO?" Chase asked.

"An unidentified flying object," Sam said

"A flying saucer," I translated.

"Here on the mountain, you'll see shooting stars at night and a magical sunrise the next morning if you're lucky. And the constellations are crystal clear on cold cloudless nights. Look in the bottom of the bag. There's a book that identifies all of the constellations. Show it to your sister."

Sam began stuffing the plastic bags inside the empty boxes while Chase brought the book over to me. It had glossy, colorful pages and several unfolded like road maps to the stars.

"I'm going to take Cali on a short walk," Sam announced, slipping on his coat and hat before he secured Cali's leash and then they both set out.

"Are you going to stay, Sis?" Chase asked, spotting the folder. "Sam said if you do, we'll have enough money to go to Disney World."

"It's a tough decision," I said with a sigh.

"Cali will keep you company," he said.

I looked out the front window at Sam walking Cali. He lingered for a few minutes at the base of the glass tree, at Shep's grave, and then he leaned over and brushed the snow away from something on the ground.

"Do you like staying with Sam?" I asked.

Chase nodded.

"Do you think you'd be okay without me for a few more months?"

He turned away, so I couldn't read his face.

"I'll come home right this minute if you want me to," I told him.

"Sam says we won't ever have to worry about money or food or me being alone anymore," Chase said.

"What do you mean?"

"I had to stay with Joy last Friday. She said if I didn't, she'd call the police on Sam and say he had kidnapped me. When she didn't come home that night, I got real scared because I didn't have my flashlight. There wasn't anything to eat, not even crackers."

"Oh, my God! I'm so sorry, Chase," I said, feeling my rage boiling out of control. "Sam didn't tell me much. He just said Joy was being a pain in the ass again."

"When I woke up, Joy was asleep on the floor. Her face was blue and she didn't move. I thought she was dead. I was scared and I called Sam. He came right over and called 911. An ambulance showed up and they gave her two shots of Narcan, but she still didn't move. Sam took photos of her with his phone. When Joy finally opened her eyes, she started fighting with the EMTs. They took her to the hospital, and Sam said not to worry because he'd see to it I'd never have to go through that again," Chase said, fear flashing in his eyes.

"Something awful could have happened to you," I whispered.

"I know, so, *please* stay here, Sis," Chase begged. "Sam says I'm safe with him now, and Joy can't take me anymore if you sign the paper."

I glanced over at the folder.

"And before you know it, you'll be home again," Chase said.

"Wherever home is," I whispered.

46

PROVIDENCE

I watched snow flurries appear and disappear. Spitting snow, Sam called it. It looked like bits of ash scattered from a smoking chimney. I looked over at Chase, who slept in the other bed with Cali curled up beside him.

The floodlights were on and cast long shadows over the snowy drifts. I didn't see Sam anywhere, but I spotted footprints leading to the brow of the hill. Even though I had layered my clothing under Sam's hooded coat and put on two pairs of gloves and socks, I knew it would still be bitter cold outside. I refused to wear Lydia's clothes anymore, even if I froze to death. I took an air horn with me and hurried out to the truck. I tossed my duffle bag into the bed and found two Army blankets behind the driver's seat in the cab. I draped them over my head. I probably looked like a monk, but I didn't care. I needed time alone to think, and Sam was nowhere in sight.

He left his keys in the truck so I started the engine. It would take a few minutes for the heater to start blowing warm air on my feet. Just then, Cali bolted like a rocket through the doggie door and started scratching at the passenger side. I leaned over to let her inside. Her fur was already cold when she jumped in, and she whimpered a little. Maybe she thought we were deserting her. I covered her with part of my blanket as she nuzzled close to me.

The flurries quickly became light snow, and then the wind started blowing it sideways. It wasn't sticking yet, but the ground had already frozen, and I guessed it wouldn't take long for it to start piling on top of the last snow if the clouds decided to drop another six inches.

"What should I do, Cali?" I whispered.

She looked up at me with those soulful brown eyes and wagged her tail like she really wanted to tell me.

"Should I stay, or go?"

She tilted her head sideways before she stuck her head under the blanket.

"Should I give Sam temporary custody of Chase?" Cali didn't move. "It's a tough decision, girl. I didn't mean to upset you."

The snow came down in a sudden burst, and the cabin disappeared in a white-out. About an inch of snow quickly dusted the hood of the truck before the wind swept it away. If we were going to leave Glass Mountain, I knew it had to be soon. I clicked on the radio and tuned in an oldies station that blared "Running Scared" by Roy Orbison—Josh's favorite song, but it was interrupted by a breaking weather alert.

We'll only reach a high of 30 degrees today. A nor'easter is headed our way. After a brief clearing this morning, it looks like we may get a foot or more of snow by sunset. Those of you who live at higher elevations may get more. Be sure to fill your cars with gas, and stock extra food, firewood, batteries, and candles. Stay warm out there, folks.

"We've got to get the hell out of here, Cali. I don't want to be sliding down this hill in a blizzard."

She pulled her head out from under the blankets and started panting and nosing at my hand.

"Hungry?"

Her ears perked at the familiar word, and she gently rested one paw on my hand.

"Okay, let's go inside," I said, switching off the engine.

I walked to the cabin with Cali at my heels, and we entered the kitchen door.

"Chase! Wake up! There's a bad snowstorm headed this way," I yelled.

As Cali jumped on Sam's bed, I could hear the familiar jingle of her dog tags.

"Okay, okay, Cali!" Sam shouted, and I gasped. I hadn't seen him lying there earlier, but the room was very dark. Maybe he had gone to bed after he had made coffee and fed Killer. Strange things were happening here. Creepy things.

In a few minutes, Sam shuffled into the bathroom and emerged fully dressed. His white hair stuck out in all directions.

"You scared me, Sam," I said, still rattled.

"Are you cold?" Sam asked, staring at the blankets around my shoulders.

"I thought you were outside since the floodlights were on. They're predicting a foot or more by evening. We need to get out of here," I said, taking the blankets off and draping them on a chair.

"The floodlights are on a motion detector," he said. "Probably an animal."

Sam poured a cup of black coffee and drank it while he stood there staring out the window.

"You feed Cali, and I'll get Chase ready," Sam said, springing into action.

I dumped the last of the beef broth over Cali's dry food and poured the remaining coffee down the drain. I froze the loaf of bread, the rest of the marshmallows, and anything else in the refrigerator that might go bad. There was a quart of milk left, so I poured Chase a glass and then put the rest in a thermos.

When Sam walked into the living room, Chase was dressed and ready to go. I couldn't believe it.

"Can I build a snowman first," Chase pleaded.

"You haven't seen snow before, have you, boy? Well, you can play in it while Twy and I load the truck, but we're heading out right after that. The weathermen preach the gospel truth in these parts," Sam said.

I handed Chase the glass of milk, and then he put on all his gear and hurried outside. He immediately turned toward the sky, and his face lit up like it was Christmas morning. Cali gulped down her food, and after Sam went through the house carefully checking each room, he carried a suitcase and the blankets to the truck.

"I saw your duffel bag in the bed of the truck. That means you're going with us, right?" Sam asked when he returned, dusting the snow from his hair. "Cali needs to sit on your lap, though. It makes her nervous to be on the floor, and the cab will be too small anyway with the three of us and all our extra stuff."

I ignored his question and stirred the ashes in the fireplace. No embers, just cold gray ash. I got a pitcher of water and doused the ashes and then closed the damper.

Sam's eyes were red-rimmed; he wasn't awake yet.

"I filled your thermos with milk and put the bananas in a plastic bag. It should tide us over until we reach a McDonald's. What time did you make coffee this morning?"

"I didn't," Sam said. "Unless I've started walking in my sleep."

"I guess I must have set the coffee timer last night. I keep forgetting to do it most of the time. Did you feed Killer and open the doggie door?"

Sam shook his head no, and I hoped he was kidding.

Maybe this place is haunted by friendly ghosts who make coffee and hide Waterford crystal, too, I thought.

"The telescope and stand will wait on us until the next time we come to Glass Mountain," Sam said.

He carried the last load to the truck and called to Cali, but she leapt onto a red leather couch and covered her nose with her paws.

Chase rolled enough snow together to build a small snowman by the front door. He hurled snowballs at the glass tree, and a couple of bottles shattered into green confetti. Sam started the truck, and Chase climbed inside. The windshield wipers barely kept pace with the heavy snow, but I could see the two of them sitting together inside the cab.

Sam left the truck running while he turned off the cistern pump and the water. I saw him emerge from the building and lock it before he came inside the cabin to lower the baseboard heat to 55 degrees.

"Just enough heat to keep things from freezing," he said "Caleb will come and drain the pipes later and add antifreeze. You got everything?"

"I'm ready," I answered.

"Let's go, Cali," he called, but she stood her ground. She raised her head for a second, and then she curled into a tighter ball on the couch.

"She's being contrary. Get her leash from the pantry door and bring her out when you come. Don't forget to lock the doggie door."

When Sam climbed into the truck, I could hear the radio blasting. I got the leash and snapped it on Cali's collar.

"Come on, girl, let's go," I said, but she wouldn't budge.

I grabbed a handful of marshmallows from the freezer and tried to lure her to the front door, dropping them on the floor one at a time in a row, but she refused the bait.

"Are you trying to tell me something, girl?" I asked.

I finally lifted her from the couch onto the floor and dragged her a few feet by tugging on her leash, but she balked and clawed and slipped on the wet linoleum.

When Sam honked the horn, I ran out and he lowered his window.

"I need a few more minutes. I might have to carry Cali out if she'll let me."

"It's providence, Twyla," Sam warned. "Don't mess with destiny."

I felt a chill run down my spine and it wasn't from the cold.

"Where's that document? I'm ready to sign," I said.

Sam pulled the folder from the glove box and handed me a pen.

"You're doing the right thing, Twyla. Just sign on the dotted line," Sam instructed.

"Well, I guess I'll see you guys the next time if there is a next time," I said, after signing my name and handing him the folder. I hugged Chase, and then I grabbed my duffel bag from the bed of the truck and headed toward the cabin as the snow began to frost my hair.

"Hey, you're way too young to have white hair," Sam shouted.

"Platinum looked okay on Marilyn Monroe, right?"

"Ah, there's hope for you yet, Twyla. Now you just need to learn more about The Duke."

"Keep my little brother safe!" I yelled, trying hard not to cry.

"I will," Sam hollered. "If it clears in an hour, we'll be good to fly out of here. Do you still have your keys, Twyla?"

I lifted them from my pocket and ticked the blue quartz keychain in front of my face.

47

BLIZZARD

By mid-morning the wind had died down, and the snow stopped just as suddenly as it had begun. A brilliant blue sky replaced the dark clouds. A cardinal perched for a second in the glass tree—a burning flame in a snowy pine. The male species of any animal was more intelligent and beautiful, Joy always said. She despised women and that hate never faded. When I was older and sick of Joy's constant put-downs, I argued with her in front of Chase. He needed to know his mother was dead wrong about a lot of things.

The heavy silence felt strange. If this was the eye of the storm, then Sam and Chase might have a window of clear weather to fly home.

Precisely at noon, the sky turned a steely gray, and at least three more inches of snow fell within an hour. The wind created a spooky concert as it whistled across the mouths of the bottles in the glass tree. Cali hid under my bed, but Killer slept through it all. It sounded like haunted woodwinds in a horror movie. *Or, glasswinds*, I thought, and by dusk, over a foot of new snow had fallen.

After I unpacked my duffel bag, I set Sam's gold and silver

gift on top of the dresser. *It might be a turquoise bracelet or something Western,* I mused.

Sam had warned me not to go outside in white-out conditions. Now I knew exactly what he meant by those two words. This was my first mountain blizzard, or anywhere, for that matter, and I wondered if I would be snowbound. I had survived three Category 4 hurricanes in my life and had helped Joy board up the windows and doors of our rental before we headed inland to shelter at her brother's place in Tallahassee.

Cali whimpered when the wind wailed through the eaves, and Killer finally found refuge inside an empty cardboard box. At times, the radio reported gusts of 75 mph. When the wind started howling like a freight train, Killer hid under my bed with Cali, and they didn't come out. I hated doing this, but I finally filled a large plastic container with kitty litter since Killer couldn't or *wouldn't* go outside—another reason why I didn't want an inside cat, especially a feral one.

During tropical storms or Category 1 hurricanes in Florida, we went to the center of the apartment and sheltered in a closet or bathroom and sometimes inside the bathtub. The cistern was the perfect choice here with its sturdy cinder block walls and no windows, but there were spiders and jumping crickets, so it was a last resort. During a lull in the storm, I put the crank-up lantern inside the cistern just in case, plus a bag of long johns and warm clothes, a sleeping bag, blankets, bottled water, and pet food. I wanted to leave a can of Raid in there, too, but figured it might kill me instead of the bugs, so I left a flyswatter instead.

When Cali crawled out from under the bed and sat in front of me, I knew she needed to go out. I unlocked the doggie door, and she tunneled through the dry snow. In a few minutes, she was furred with tiny snowballs. She shook the snow from her head to her tail in a spiraling motion until she created a kitchen snowstorm. Then she found Lydia's ski jacket and dragged it over beside her boots and lay on top of it. Cali let me pick off the remaining snowballs, one by one, and then I gently dried her paws.

"You miss Lydia, don't you, girl?"

When the doggie door started swinging and banging, puffs of snow blew inside like clouds of confectioners sugar, I quickly locked the door.

That night I slept on the couch underneath the gun rack to be closer to the door in case the roof blew off and became a metal Frisbee. I kept the front porch and back door light on, so I could check on things and see how deep the snow was. The floodlights stayed on for hours. They revealed sculptured drifts several feet deep that formed soft prows on the stoop. The pines were laden with snow, and the glass tree blended in with all the other trees now. I found a snow shovel in the pantry and leaned it against the door. Nothing to do now but wait it out until morning and hope the nor'easter would blow itself out.

During in the night, the power went off, but I kept the fire burning and I had plenty of dry firewood on the side porch. Cali eventually left the comfort of Lydia's soft ski jacket and joined me under the afghan on the couch. The power outage made us fast friends once again, and Killer returned to her cardboard box to sleep. She liked heat of any kind: sunlight from a window, warmth from the hood of a car, and her cozy spot in front of the fireplace. I had a lot to learn about this heat-seeking animal.

I woke to bright darkness. It wasn't the porch light, but a strange iridescence gleamed through the windows. I tried to open the door, but it didn't budge: a heavy drift blocked the exit. I put on a coat and broke my promise and wore Lydia's boots since they were the only ones that came close to fitting me. After several attempts, I managed to shovel the snow away about six inches from the door and squeezed through sideways while holding on to the snow shovel. And then I froze in place. Not from cold, but from awe. The snowstorm had swallowed everything in sight like Kudzu does to trees in the South. The driveway had become a white sea with frozen waves; distant forests looked like cumulus clouds.

After an hour, I shoveled a very narrow path from the door to the driveway. I brushed the snow from the window with a broom and cleared the outside of the doggie door, so Cali and Killer wouldn't sink into the drifts. As soon as I came inside, Cali was ready to go out. I unlocked the doggie door and she pushed her way outside. Killer just blinked her sleepy green eyes at me from her cardboard room. After quickly adopting her new litter box, she wasn't in any hurry to dash outside anymore. When I added a couple split logs to the fire, Killer jumped out of her box. The power was still off, so I didn't dare open the refrigerator. Since I had forgotten to load the cooler into Sam's truck, I took out a block of cheese to slice for breakfast. Killer started purring and twining between my legs, and I gave her some milk. I reached down to pet her, but stopped myself.

Cali raced in looking like the abominable snowman this time.

"Stay!" I shouted, grabbing the same towel I had used on her last night. I dried her off, swept the snow into a dustpan, and dumped it into the sink. She didn't resist when I led her by the collar to sit in front of the fireplace.

"Stay, Cali," I commanded, and she did. I got her bed from the pantry and set it in front of her. She climbed in immediately and turned around and around until she made it her own.

I found an old percolator under the sink and made coffee on top of the gas stove. I knew how to do it because Joy had made it this way when our electricity was off. I turned on the burner and lit it with a wooden match. While I waited for the coffee to perc, I fed both animals. I wasn't suffering at all—even without electricity. I looked out the window and marveled at the huge icicles that had grown from the roof.

"This is my first blizzard. Did you know that, Cali?"

She cocked her head and wagged her tail.

The rest of the morning I worried about snow and gales and

gusts and ghosts and unending solitude. The snow had further silenced this already silent world, and I didn't have to go anywhere, plus no one could visit or even try to. No responsibilities except to stay warm, eat, drink, and think. I wondered what Alexandra would say about this white monastery, this chapel of sacred snow, this Fortress of Solitude.

I even considered Helen's invitation to work at her shop on a couple Saturdays each month. Maybe next week, Caleb could come and rescue me. Helen said I could stay overnight at their place, and he'd bring me home on Sunday.

I X'd off another day on the calendar and settled in with one of Lydia's mysteries and read by flashlight. If the power came on, I might even watch *True Grit* or write a little or open Sam's gift. Each choice tempted and terrified me like Pandora's Box—I didn't know what I'd discover. If the movie were bad, I'd just turn it off, but I could at least give it a shot. It would make Sam happy, and I could fast-forward through the boring parts. If the novel made me sleepy, I'd go to bed early.

Instead, I followed my flashlight beam through the house and found myself in Sam's bedroom. I opened the closet and felt proud about its new organization. I decided to open all of Lydia's shoeboxes again. I sat on the floor, removed the shoes, and arranged them neatly on Lydia's side of the closet. Then I nested the empty boxes inside each other, did the same with the lids, and carried them to the kitchen table.

I hoped Sam and Chase had made it safely to Florida. If this weather was any indication of heavier snows yet to come in Garrett County, I may not see them until spring. At least Chase seemed happy and safe, and maybe we really could go to Disney World this summer. I felt like a kid thinking about the rides and Epcot, The Enchanted Kingdom, Mickey and Minnie, the fireworks, and the light parade. All those magical things Chase talked about endlessly and all those brochures he had shown me that Bryce had given him. He kept them inside his pillowcase, so he could read them before he fell asleep. I always wanted a

Mickey Mouse watch and hoped to see The Magic Kingdom one day. I just wanted to be a normal kid growing up, and this might be a belated first step toward that goal. Right now, my Fortress of Solitude was here on Glass Mountain, but I missed slow dancing with Josh or flirting with fireman Cory. It would be nice to have a drink with a real-life Superman now and then.

48

CABIN FEVER

I sat straight up in bed and slid the derringer from under the pillow when the power came on in the middle of the night. Killer leapt to the floor, but Cali simply moved to the empty bed. When I realized what had happened, I lay in bed until I could go to sleep.

At dawn, I went to the kitchen and stared at the empty lids I'd left on the table. No brewed coffee was waiting for me this morning, and I had to unlock the doggie door myself.

Each morning, I shoveled fresh snow from the front steps, widened the path to the cistern, and the driveway. Nothing exciting, but it gave me purpose on this wintry planet. I built a snowman to pass the time and took a photo of him with my phone. At least it worked for taking pictures, just never connected to call or text anyone unless I happened upon a fleeting signal. When I finally finished, my snowman grew bigger and bigger—about eight feet tall and three feet wide. I brought the step ladder outside and stuck two pine branches where his armpits should be, and they became his fringy arms. I found one of Sam's old cowboy hats, a ragged bandanna, and a jar of assorted beer bottle caps I used to create the snowman's eyes, nose, mouth, and shirt buttons. My broom fit perfectly under his arm, and I put a pair of Lydia's rhinestone-studded sunglasses on him. He'd look more authentic if I could fashion a rifle out of firewood, but that was too hard. I just hoped my giant cowboy would last until Thanksgiving.

Some days I would spot a deer eating bark from one of the pine trees and nosing for grass in the places I'd cleared. One evening at dusk, I saw a black bear hurrying past the cabin, intent on his destination. It didn't faze him when Cali started barking because he didn't glance in our direction. He had more important things on his mind like hooking up with his latest lady friend or foraging for food before hibernation.

I finally began to write in my journal, and the entries grew longer each day. I added a few sketches, too. Not that I could draw or anything, but it kept me occupied. It wasn't the start of a novel but just a diary with crude drawings of birds, deer, and pine trees covered in snow. I even wrote down some of my weird dreams like the one where it rained pencil-thin icicles, and I grabbed one and began to eat it.

One long day after another and another. I often forgot what day it was, as if it mattered. I rummaged through the junk drawer and found packing tape, a pair of scissors, and a glue stick. After I removed the cap to see if it was still good, I sat at the table and drew a detailed floor plan in my journal. I taped two of the shoe boxes together, and then two more. Then I stacked them on top of each other and glued the first set of boxes to the second, so they resembled a four-room house.

I heard rolling thunder in the distance, and soon a truck with a snowplow mounted on its front fender rounded the top of the hill. It was Caleb. I put on my boots and waded through the snow to greet him with Cali at my heels. He lowered his electric windows down and up twice—his signature hello.

"Hey, Caleb! Come on inside, and I'll fix breakfast."

He turned off the engine and smiled his licorice smile but quickly averted his eyes.

"Helen wants to know if you'd like to help her in the shop

today. She's cooking this evening, and she's hoping you'll stay for dinner and spend the night."

"I have been going stir-crazy here," I admitted. "Can I bring Cali along?"

"Sure," he said, getting out of his truck and scratching Cali behind her ears.

"It'll take me a few minutes to get ready. Come on in if you want."

"I'll wait out here with your rhinestone cowboy," he said with a funny smile, coiling a new strand of licorice like a budding fiddlehead fern and popping it into his mouth. Then he walked to the front to check his snowplow and all four of the tire chains.

I laughed at his snowman joke as I packed a pair of pajamas and a change of clothes. After I checked to see if I had left any lights on, I set out a big bowl of dry cat food and clean water, and changed the litter box. Then I turned on the outside lights in case I got home late on Sunday.

Cali jumped in the cab of the truck after Caleb opened the door. She knew the routine and sat between us on the candy box. As we descended the mountain, Caleb lowered the plow and pushed more snow out of the way. The trees were white on one side from the blowing snow. A deer suddenly leapt across the road, and Caleb slammed on the brakes. I almost hit the windshield, and Cali was thrown to the floor. She wasn't hurt, though, and jumped in my lap, so she could bark non-stop at three more deer that raced single file after the first.

"There's never just one," he said. "People forget."

When we reached the hard road, Caleb raised the snow-blade. The two-lane highway had been completely cleared. Civilization ran like a top down here, but on Glass Mountain, it was the dead of winter. We drove to town, and it felt strangely bleak and barren without a blanket of fresh snow covering everything. Even the trees and sidewalks had been cleared.

"It's usually 10 degrees warmer at the bottom of the mountain," Caleb said as if I had asked. "Sometimes more."

He parked in front of the shop, and Cali jumped out when I opened the door. Just like always, as soon as I walked in, the bell announced my entrance into an eclectic mansion. I spotted a few new pieces: a solid wood dining set that looked like maple, a grandfather clock with an ancient moon face like Sam's, and white china with huge pink flowers painted on them. Eight place settings were already on the table, complete with crystal goblets, and pink cloth napkins rolled into silver napkin rings. A silver tea service glimmered from a mahogany side table.

"We're here, Helen," Caleb called, and she emerged from the back room holding a book.

"How did you survive your first blizzard, Twyla?" Helen asked, taking off her reading glasses that were suspended by a black cord around her neck.

"It was dramatic and scary, and stunning," I said all at once.

"Well, if you can make it through an electrical fire with black bears living under your front porch, I figured a snowstorm would be a cinch."

"I'd almost forgotten about the bears," I said. "They haven't returned as far as I know, but I did see a different one the other evening. He seemed in a rush to get somewhere."

"Make yourself at home. Things are slow today as you can tell," she said. She showed me the cover of the book she was reading. "Du Maurier. I love to reread a good mystery now and again. You want a cup of hot tea?" Helen asked.

"No, thanks. Your new place settings are beautiful."

"It's called Desert Rose. It was very popular in the early 70s and 80s. I always thought it looked romantic and charming, and I could just imagine a prospective bride registering for that pattern in a fancy department store. Couldn't you?" she asked.

I didn't know anything about fancy stores or prospective brides. I just nodded my head and wandered to the table, picked up one of the plates, and ran my fingers over the raised hand-painted flowers.

"I might buy this one day," I said.

"Thinking of getting married, Twyla?"

"No, I just want to own something impractical, you know. Just because it's pretty."

"I can't think of a better reason myself. As you know, I love elegant things, and I like to surround myself with them," Helen said, looking out over a sea of other people's memories and treasures and precious keepsakes.

"How can I help you?" I asked, after I stowed my bag behind the counter.

"Would you dust the glass cases and polish the tables?"

Helen disappeared into the back room and emerged with a feather duster, a bottle of Windex, lemon Pledge, and clean rags. Cali lay behind the counter on a braided rug. There were squeaky chew toys on the floor, and she had one in her mouth.

"Have fun," Helen said with a smile. She put on her reading glasses and disappeared. Caleb nodded at me on his way out.

"I'm going to get gas and run errands. You need anything?" he asked.

I shook my head.

The shop was quiet, just like the last time I was here. The only noise was the whirr of the furnace when it kicked on. I dusted a glass case and stared at its contents: costume jewelry and fancy rings with sparkly ruby and amber stones. The case was unlocked, so I guessed they weren't too expensive. The next case held a tiara studded with fake diamonds, gold sequined purses, a silver letter opener, and a magnifying glass decorated with a frog and emeralds, or at least they looked like emeralds to me.

On the second shelf, I spotted a child's tiny tea set with pink flowers and a pair of beaded moccasins with black fur lining that were made for an infant. I put the tiara on my head and glanced in the mirror on a nearby dresser. I carefully placed it back on the shelf and took out the moccasins next. I could hold both of them in the palm of one hand. I wished for a second I had a real baby to put them on.

After I stacked the Desert Rose plates together, polished the maple table until it shone, and gently replaced each place setting, adjusting the silverware and goblets just so near each plate, I admired my work. If this were my table, I would cook a fancy dinner, light the candelabra, and fill the flutes with pink champagne.

The furnace clicked on with its soothing white noise, and the dangling price tags on the furniture danced in the man-made breeze.

The door chimed, and I greeted a man and a woman. They looked around the shop, and then the woman sat at *my* dining room table and turned over one of *my* plates like she was looking for a mark.

"How much for the eight-place setting?" she asked.

"Let me check," I said.

When I walked into the back room, Helen was engrossed in her novel.

"How much is the Desert Rose china?" I asked.

"Oh, it's $500, but I thought you wanted to save them for yourself?"

"That's way out of my price range," I said, and then I walked toward the couple. "Five hundred dollars," I told the woman.

"Would you take $300?"

"No, but I'll take $450," Helen called, making a beeline over to the table.

"Let me think about it," the lady said, moving closer to her husband who held a switchblade with a fancy carved handle. When he opened the blade, it caught the light from the chandelier overhead.

"Thank you," the lady called as they left the store.

"Everyone wants something for nothing these days," Helen

grumbled. "Things look great, Twyla. I'm going to put price tags on a few new items now. Next time you can polish all fifteen of my crystal chandeliers."

"In two weeks?" I asked, looking up at all of them.

"Yes, that would be perfect," Helen answered.

When Caleb returned at closing time, Cali was ready to leave. I had taken her outside a couple of times on a leash that Helen kept behind the counter. At 5 o'clock, Helen flipped the sign to CLOSED, switched off the lights, and locked the door. After Caleb and Helen climbed into the cab, I got in last and held Cali on my lap. Helen held the shoebox full of candy.

49

LUKE

Gradually over the next month, I paced less and developed a new rhythm for the long snowy days. I still pushed the leather chair to block the door and wheeled the pump organ to the front door at night, but it was a habit now. I watched a few of Sam's VHS Westerns, but not the one he wanted me to watch. Procrastinating, I guess. Maybe I'd never watch it. I stayed up late and continued to make short to-do lists. It took me a while to adjust, but I started to enjoy the slower days.

Sometimes I worked on my four-room shoebox dollhouse and added a peaked roof and a cardboard chimney. I made them from box lids and cut one in half to make the porch floor and shed dormer. A box cutter created an opening for the front door and two windows in each room, upstairs and down. Then I carefully covered them with squares of aluminum foil to make the windows shiny. Killer kept a close eye on me and my cardboard creation, but she left me alone while I worked. At night as a precaution, I'd put the dollhouse on the pantry's top shelf and closed the door.

Like clockwork every two weeks, Caleb returned on Saturday morning, and we'd go to town. Helen always made me

256

feel welcome and found a new job for me to do. One sleepy Saturday in November, a husky teenager wearing a Navy pea coat over his hooded sweatshirt came into the shop and asked to speak with the manager.

"I heard you might buy this," he said, pulling a watch from his pocket. "It belonged to my dad."

"It looks like 14-carat gold," Helen said, turning it over and studying its markings. "But I'm no expert, you know."

"How much would you give me for it?" he asked.

"I don't normally buy jewelry—just estate furniture and costume jewelry—but if you let me keep it until Monday, I can find out if it's real gold or not."

"I need the money now," he demanded.

"Then, I can't help you, son," Helen said calmly, handing him the watch. "Anyway, I don't keep cash in the store, so I wouldn't be able to pay you today."

"Do you know anyone else who'd buy it?" he asked.

"You might try Red's. It's the pawn shop a couple of blocks over. Or if you're headed to Cumberland, there are a few pawn shops there. What was your dad's name?" Helen asked.

"Jed. Jed Plymale. Why?"

"I just thought I might have known him. Was he from Preston County?" Helen asked. "I used to know a Plymale who lived there."

"No, he's from up North. In, um, Maine," he said.

Helen followed him to the door and locked it after he exited. She watched him cross the street and climb into a faded green jeep. Someone was waiting on him, and they drove up Alder Street and made a left at the stoplight onto Route 219.

"He stole that watch," Helen said.

"How do you know?"

"The initials on the watch were M. A. R., not J for Jed or P for Plymale. I know when people are lying. After 40 years in the business, it's an instinctive gift, you might say. People come in here all the time with hot merchandise. They think they can get a fast buck for it, but I don't keep money in the shop."

"Are they locals?" I asked.

"No, they're almost always people on the run. I'm one of the first shops they come to when they pull into town, so I get a lot of traffic, good and bad."

"Have you ever been robbed?"

"Not yet, but I keep a Glock under the counter. Everybody in town knows that, so I never have any trouble. Caleb likes to tell people I sleep with a loaded machine gun, and they don't dare mess with a crazy old lady."

My phone beeped, and I jerked from the unexpected sound. It was a text from Sam.

Joy's looking for you, Sam wrote.

You're kidding, I texted back.

I felt a stinging surge of fear. *She'll never find me here,* I thought to myself.

That evening at Helen's place we sat down to eat, and Caleb ate in the kitchen.

When I helped Helen with the dishes later, and he left to bring the horses in from the field, I had to ask.

"Is something wrong with Caleb? He always keeps a spacer between him and me in the truck. A shoebox, a dog, or you," I said, trying to make light of it.

"Caleb is an extremely private person," was all she said.

"Is he autistic?"

"No, he's just been to hell and back, so I give him plenty of room and respect his ways," Helen said.

"How long has he been like this?"

Helen sighed and took a minute to respond.

"He was just my pesky brother when we were growing up, but after Luke died and his wife deserted him, he became someone different. Someone I didn't know. He shut down and stopped talking for months, stopped doing things that used to give him pleasure, even stopped taking photos of sunsets and working on his pen and ink drawings. Tragedy changes people, and the death of his only child ripped his heart out. He has suffered for years and coped the best way he knew how. If he seems robotic to you or a bit odd, it's called survival."

50

LOST

When my snowman finally melted, I moved his cowboy hat, bandanna, and broomstick to the front porch. I wore his rhinestone sunglasses while I dropped the bottle caps back into the glass jar. The robo weatherman said it would continue to be unseasonably warm with a high in the 60s today, so I only wrote one thing on my to-do list: *Take a hike this afternoon with Cali.* Now I knew intimately what people meant when they said they had cabin fever. Sam told me it could get bad. *Stay busy*, he warned. Being inside for days and weeks at a time can drive you mad. That, and obsessing over Sam's text message about Joy looking for me.

I carried the dollhouse from the pantry to the table and stared at it for a few minutes. I needed to make a staircase to the second story, paint the floors, and paper the walls. I brought the box of wrapping paper and bows from Sam's closet and set it beside the table. Killer ran over and sniffed the box. I was afraid she might jump on top of the table and destroy my dollhouse, so I took a new roll of red ribbon from the box and let her play with it. I rummaged through bright Christmas and pastel birthday paper until I found a green and purple floral design. It would be the perfect paper for my fantasy bedroom. I measured the walls and made a pattern by pressing white tissue paper from floor to ceiling, marking where the windows were. Then I traced the pattern onto the wrapping paper and cut out my wallpaper. I used a glue stick to make it stay on the walls and pressed it gently into place. When I finished, all three walls of my bedroom were covered. I'd paper another room later on and put aluminum foil on the windows. I carried my dollhouse to the pantry along with the box of wrapping paper and closed the door behind me.

The next morning the kitchen was a wreck. Killer had had her way with the roll of ribbon and had torn it to shreds. She didn't budge when I walked in, so she must have been exhausted from demolishing it. After lunch, I headed outside with Cali trotting right behind me. I had already packed two bottles of water, a box of raisins, and dog biscuits in my backpack and pulled the hickory walking stick from the barrel. I felt more confident about living alone, but because of the bears, I never let my guard down. I put the bear bell around my neck and the air horn in my pocket. I decided to take the Colt 45 from Sam's nightstand since the revolver was already loaded with six bullets and easier to carry in its leather holster. I buckled it on, and it hung low from my waist.

"Look out, Calamity Jane. There's a new outlaw in town," I told Cali.

Cali pranced and hopped because she knew what the walking stick meant. We headed straight into the woods from the porch and passed by the glass tree. I had a compass in my pocket and made sure I paid attention to landmarks. I remembered to break a branch now and then to mark my trail just like a Native American did in one of Sam's old movies. I guess I had learned something from them after all.

It was a sun-dappled afternoon with shafts of light streaming through the pines. The beer bottles created red and gold haloes as they clinked together in the soft breeze. I hiked a couple of miles, up and down steep hills. When Cali would take off to chase a squirrel or a chipmunk, I rested on a big rock to drink some water during one of her getaways. When she returned, I poured the rest into a paper cup for her. She lapped it up fast, so I opened another bottle and poured a little more into the cup and fed her a dog biscuit.

After about an hour, I was tired and ready to head home. I retraced my steps to the mossy glade and the oak tree that had been struck by lightning, but everything after that seemed foreign. I quickly realized I was lost when I circled back to the same tree. Twice. I took a drink of water and studied my compass. I headed due north, but the woods grew even thicker, and alien. Even Cali seemed jumpy. I spotted evidence of bears: a big pile of bear droppings. Cali sniffed at them but didn't linger. We were definitely in bear country, and I patted my gun from time to time to make sure it was still there.

"Okay, take me home, girl," I said, but she didn't take the lead.

The more we walked, the more confused I got. Nobody would know how to find us for days, maybe weeks. Several of the trees had been marked by bears with deep clawed gashes in them and the bark was rubbed off. Cali began to sniff the ground: fresh bear droppings.

I heard a loud crash to my right, and there was a massive black bear standing on his hind legs to get a better look at us. Sam told me they didn't have good eyesight, but their sense of smell made up for what they couldn't see. That, and their incredible speed. *Don't ever turn your back on a bear*, Sam had warned. *Stay your ground and then slowly back away. Never run.*

"No, Cali," I said in a hoarse whisper when she began to bark. I grabbed her by the collar, but she started howling and barking non-stop, shaking her head and wrenching her body trying to break free of my grasp. The bear instantly dropped on all fours and charged, stopping just a few feet in front of us. It happened so fast I was paralyzed with fear. I remembered that smell, that foul wet dog smell. My heart was beating out of control, but I managed to keep a death grip on Cali's collar and slowly moved away, sliding the Colt 45 out of its holster, cocking it, and aiming it at the bear's head. I held my breath and tried to steady my shaking hand. I couldn't afford to miss. My life depended on it. In one flash, Cali twisted herself free of my grip, growling and barking as she tried to attack the angry bear. It began to circle us, slapping at the ground and making a huffing sound. When Cali jumped on the bear's back, he sent her airborne. Everything moved in slow motion until a pine tree stopped her flight, and Cali limped into the brush, bleeding and yelping in pain.

When the bear charged me, I pulled the trigger and fired twice. The blast exploded like a cannon and the kickback almost knocked me flat. The wounded bear groaned in pain before it lumbered up the hill.

Cali was pretty messed up, but she was still alive. She cried out when I touched her, and blood oozed from the claw marks that striped her face.

"Let's get the hell out of here," I said, scanning for any movement. I turned the safety on and put the gun in its holster. Then I gently picked her up, and carried her around my neck like a shepherd carries a lamb. I half walked, half ran in the opposite direction until I came to a freshwater spring. Sam said if you're ever lost, go downhill or follow a creek, or both. The heat of Cali's body against my neck and the racing of her heart reassured me, but I felt her warm blood running down my neck.

"Hang on, Cali. We're almost home," I told her.

She didn't move, but began to whimper. After what seemed like forever, I exited the woods through a bramble of dead weeds and vines at the bottom of the hill. The hard-top road was right in front of us—the two-lane highway that led to Oakland. I could see the gated entrance to Sam's road about a half a mile away. A car whizzed by and honked but didn't stop. Another truck pulled over on the berm and backed up. Thank God, it was Caleb. I tried to run to the safety of his truck, but my legs gave out. I stumbled and fell to my knees, but I still held tight to Cali. Caleb lifted her from my neck and carried her like a baby the rest of the way. He rested her in the bed of the truck and checked her hind leg and the deep wounds on her nose. Then he swaddled her in a wool blanket.

"Jesus, what happened, Twyla?"

"A bear," I stuttered. "Cali tried to protect me, but it lashed out when she attacked him. The bear tried to kill her. And me. So I shot it."

"Did you kill it?"

"Just wounded it, I think. It took off up the hill. There's a trail of blood."

Then, Caleb carefully placed Cali in my lap after I got in the truck, and he made a U-turn and sped toward the farm. He carried Cali to the barn and laid her in a bed of straw. I stayed while he gathered bandages and disinfectant from the house.

"You'll be okay, girl," I whispered.

I held her still while Caleb cleaned her leg and wiped the blood from the claw marks around her nose. Cali yelped at first, but then she didn't move as he wrapped her leg in gauze and secured it with surgical tape.

"Are you okay?" Caleb asked me.

"Just rattled. Will Cali be alright?"

"Her leg isn't broken, just badly bruised with a surface wound. It will take a few days to heal. Those are bad cuts on her face, but she won't need stitches. She does need antibiotics, though," he said.

"I bet you've saved a lot of animals."

"A few," he said quickly.

"When Cali is better, take me to the cabin, so I can keep close watch over her," I said.

"I'll stay with you tonight, if you want," he offered, "but first Cali needs to go to the vet."

He wrapped her in a clean blanket and carried her back to the truck before resting her in the passenger's seat.

Knowing Cali was safe in Caleb's capable hands, I let my exhaustion and fatigue take over. I stretched out on Helen's couch for just a minute, but when I woke, it was 4 p.m. and Caleb was in the kitchen tending to Cali.

"She looks a little better," I said. "Has she eaten anything?"

"I hand-fed her some dog food and she drank a little water. She's slowly coming around," he said. "Are you ready to go after I get Helen?"

"Sure," I said.

I kept a close watch on Cali until Helen rushed into the house. She lay on the floor beside Cali until she opened her eyes and wagged her tail.

"She'll make it," Helen predicted.

We needed to get to the cabin before dark, so I walked toward Caleb's truck and climbed in the cab. He carried Cali to me and put her in my lap.

"Guess we'll have to wait a long time before we go on another hike, huh, Cali," I whispered.

I moved Caleb's shoebox and set it under my feet. Now there'd be more room for all of us.

Caleb opened the driver's side and glanced at the empty space on the console. He walked around a couple of times, pretending to check the tires and the oil. When he finally got in, he started to whistle. Not a sweet "Home on the Range" kind of whistle, but an ear-piercing tea kettle scream when water is boiling over on the stove. Cali panicked and tried to bolt from my arms, but I held on tight. Even when Caleb lowered the electric windows down and up, and down and up, the mind-numbing whistle continued to explode from his pursed lips, and Cali began to howl.

I blindly felt on the floor for the shoebox with my free hand, but I knocked it over and the lid came off. A little of the candy spilled onto the floor mat, but I managed to wedge the box onto the console between Caleb and me. Then I scooted as close to the passenger door as I could while still holding Cali on my lap.

And then, just like magic, the whistling stopped.

51

MIRROR

That night, Caleb slept in the living room beside Cali's bed. Even Killer stayed close by as if she knew something was very wrong. I slept on top of the covers, staring at the ceiling and listening to Caleb snore. My mind replayed the vicious bear attack yesterday that ended with Caleb's ear-piercing whistle. I thought about Chase, his fear of the dark, and being left alone. I thought of poor Ashley abandoned in Corkscrew Swamp. I worried Joy was looking for me and about all the things I'd never forget or unsee.

I felt a little safer because Caleb stayed the night, but knowing a strange man slept on the couch in the next room troubled me. He had saved my life and Cali's, too, but he was unpredictable, and scary sometimes.

The next morning, Caleb stood on the front porch smoking a cigarette while Cali slept in her bed. When I came into the living room, Caleb opened the door and came inside.

"Cali's going to be fine," he said. "Just watch her closely and take her outside on a leash from now on. She's already been fed, so she'll sleep a while longer. You should too," he said, looking at my bleary eyes. "Wanna cigarette?" he asked, taking a pack from his inside pocket.

"Remember, I don't smoke."

"Well, if you change your mind, I left a couple in the ashtray on the porch," he said, putting on his coat.

"I won't let Cali out of my sight," I promised. "Are you leaving now?"

"I've got chores to do," he said, "but I'll be back later to check on her."

I didn't watch him start the engine or lower and raise the windows like I usually did, but when I heard his truck rumbling down the hill and the suffocating silence settling in, I added four bullets to the Colt 45.

The days were colder now, and soon the black bears would be sleeping at least for a few weeks at a time Helen had said.Near the first week in December they'd find a cave or a shelter to sleep in undisturbed. Late autumn was their time to mate and fatten up for hibernation.

I worried Caleb might have a nervous breakdown one day, but Helen told me he was fine and his way of coping was totally foreign to me. Over time, she had accepted his ways. I hoped I could, too.

"We all have strange habits," she had said out of the blue one afternoon. "Some of us are just better at hiding them. I drink good whiskey to blow off steam, some people jog, others gamble or overeat. Caleb can handle his pent-up stress pretty well until he has to release it."

He reminded me of a boy named Noah in grade school who had Tourette's. He cussed sometimes and made coughing sounds along with weird jerking motions. Our teacher said he had tics that he couldn't control, but not the blood-sucking ticks that latched onto us in summer, she explained. Noah seemed perfectly normal, until he wasn't. He could only hold his emotions in for so long. He managed to hide his tics in public most of the time, and then he'd go to a safe room in school and let loose.

I vowed when Caleb showed up next Saturday, I'd never

touch his shoebox again. If it got replaced with a toolbox or a cooler, I wouldn't touch them either. They were his line in the sand.

I took a walk like I did every day now. I replaced a few beer bottles in the pine tree and checked on the cistern. I moved extra firewood to the side porch and carried some inside. Killer sat like an Egyptian queen in the glider and watched me work. She groomed herself and took a twenty-minute nap in the afternoon sun while Cali slept. It was a bitter cold December day, and as soon as the sun went behind a cloud, Killer darted inside.

The horizon was unobstructed with all the leaves gone now, and the den tree was the only one I could spot in the distance. The farmers left it there undisturbed, so birds and small animals would have a place to nest, plus it was bad luck to chop a den tree down.

The knoll where Lydia's dog, Shep, was buried had been swept clean by the wind. I looked at the marker and wondered about her collie dog. I needed to ask Sam about Shep when he returned.

None of my clothes fit now. My vow not to wear Lydia's clothes failed miserably. Sam's sweatsuits were my go-to uniform since I couldn't button my jeans. No one saw me anyway, and I had learned my lesson to never to wear Lydia's stuff if Sam might be coming or when I worked at the antique shop. There were no bathroom scales at the cabin, but I figured I had gained a good 10 or 15 pounds.

I put on layers of clothes and sat on the glider at dusk and watched the sun set lower and lower in the sky. I hadn't watched *True Grit* yet, so maybe this was the night to finally get it over with. At least I had listened to it weeks ago. That should count for something.

The fading sun glinted off of a shiny marker near Shep's grave, so I walked over to it. His stone lay flush with the ground, and I brushed away some pine needles and looked for the shiny object. The dog's marker was smooth white granite, so I walked around his grave twice and still couldn't find anything. I started to leave, but then I spotted part of a mirror when it caught the setting sun.

I bent over to pick it up but realized it was stuck in the frozen ground. I gasped when I saw my own face reflected in the mirror. I looked closer and kept brushing away dirt and dead leaves until I uncovered an oval mirror with a gold frame. My heart raced from an unknown fear.

I kicked the dead leaves back over the mirror until it disappeared again, and then I hurried inside the cabin and pushed the pump organ in place. The sun's afterglow dazzled the clouds with gold leaf and streaks of coral and cream from horizon to horizon, but I couldn't stop thinking about the mirror and why in the hell I had ever agreed to come here.

52

MRS. SPITZER

"It was made in Kentucky," Helen said, as she pointed out the date, 1885, embroidered on the lower right corner of the crazy quilt.

"Kentucky is horse country. There's an appliquéd riding cap and crop in that square," Helen said. "I bought the quilt from an elderly woman who lived in Lexington. She needed the money, so I gave her more than it was worth. I'll never break even, but, who cares, it was a thrill to see her reaction."

A set of new goblets filled two shelves in a china hutch along with Fiestaware in bright orange, aqua, and red. I was learning history and more brand names every time I came to the shop. I found myself drawn to a clay bust of a Victorian woman, almost life-size, displayed on a marble pedestal. She seemed right at home, and her expression was thoughtful and serene, almost wistful as she stared at the opposite wall. Her profile formed a silhouette on the painted cinder block, and I thought of Lydia, and how much Sam must miss his wife.

Near the picture window, Helen had placed a headless wicker mannequin dressed in a sexy white slip with a satin cummerbund. The slip had been pinned to make it look tailored. I touched its silkiness and wondered who wore it last.

Many secrets in this shop, and all those "last times" preserved forever. The last person to read a certain book, the last meal served on fine china, the last people to sit at that table. I wished you could flip a switch and see them—a talking exhibit like museums I'd seen on TV. If you stepped in front of a painting, a recorded voice revealed its history. Maybe you could watch a teddy bear or toy train being played with by that very last child, and see the last person to sit in the colonial Windsor reclining chaise lounge, circa 1800s: price $1,800. Maybe it belonged to the same lady who wore the sexy silk slip? White artificial petunias cascaded from a planter near the picture window to bask in the December sun. I touched the petals and was surprised that the delicate blossoms were very much alive.

A Geisha doll propped on top of a white bookcase surveyed the entire shop. She was a natural at keeping secrets, so I didn't dare disturb her.

I moved to the far side of the room and chose one book after another from the many packed bookcases: cookbooks, art books, poetry, first editions, signed and dedicated. I turned the pages and read a few with personal inscriptions. Sometimes it was heartbreaking. What happened to all those people?

The door chimed, and a young couple entered. They were not dressed for cold weather.

"May I help you?" Helen asked, her voice pitched a little higher than usual.

"Just browsing," the girl said, as the boy scanned the room until he zeroed in on a chest of drawers.

"Are you looking for anything in particular?" Helen pressed, her intuition on overdrive.

"I saw a cigar box in here the other day," the boy answered, moving quickly toward the chest.

He raised the lid of an old cigar box with his right hand as a diversion, and then swiftly lifted the stopper of a blue perfume bottle with his left, dropped something inside, and replaced the stopper.

"I want to buy it for my uncle, but I think I'll wait until closer to his birthday," the boy said.

"I'll give you a good price," Helen countered.

"Thanks, I'll wait," he said, and then they were gone.

I waited until they got into their car and pulled away from the curb, then I walked over to the blue perfume bottle with its white seashell stopper. When I lifted it, the rancid fumes of old perfume still remained. I spotted something at the bottom of the bottle and shook a clear packet into my hand. Inside it were white pills.

"That guy dropped this inside the perfume bottle," I said, handing the packet to Helen. "I was standing behind the bookcase, so he didn't see me. What do you think it is?"

"OxyContin," she said abruptly. "It's a drop-off. I could call the police now or wait until someone comes to get it and catch them on my surveillance cameras. Or both."

"Has this happened before? I mean, is there a drug problem in Garrett County?"

"It's everywhere, Twyla. We're not immune. Most are drug dealers from other states, but we have our own problems. Poverty, addiction, and unemployment just make things worse these days."

"I didn't know you had a camera," I said, scanning the room.

"Cameras," she corrected me. "I've got too much time and money invested in this shop, and I'm not going to let some freeloader steal it from me. I'll call Gary. He's on duty today," she said, heading toward the back room.

A few minutes later the door chimed again, and an elderly lady with curly gray hair started browsing. She wore a Christmas sweater with sequined angels and 3-D candy canes on the front. She had fuzzy pink Ugg boots on and looked a lot like my 3rd-grade teacher, Mrs. Spitzer.

"May I help you?" I asked.

"Yes, I'm looking for lace doilies," she said sweetly.

I remembered seeing linens and doilies stacked in a box, so I led her to it. She began unfolding a tablecloth first with matching napkins, and then she examined each doily.

"I'll be right here if you need anything," I said, walking toward the cash register where Helen was stationed.

Soon the lady carried a few doilies to the counter. She began digging through her purse and pulled out a ten dollar bill.

"That will be five dollars," Helen said.

"Oh, I really wanted to look at stoppered perfume bottles, too. Do you have any?"

Helen counted out five one dollar bills into her outstretched hand.

"I might have a few under this counter," Helen said, bending over and sliding a glass case open.

"I collect old Avon bottles. Do you have any of those?" the lady asked.

"No, just Evening in Paris. This taller one was for bubble bath and the smaller bottle held cologne," Helen said, placing the two cobalt blue bottles with silver caps on top of the counter.

"Do you have an old-fashioned glass bottle with a stopper? I love those," the lady said, casually glancing toward the chest of drawers.

"Yes, a light blue one with a faux seashell stopper. Let me get it for you," Helen said, tucking the packet of pills inside her pocket as she crossed to the chest of drawers and slipped the pills back into the bottle. She returned with the blue bottle and handed it to the woman who lifted the stopper part to peer deep inside.

"Phew! It stinks. How much?"

"It might be more than you can afford, I'm afraid. It's an antique, but I'll take a hundred dollars for it," Helen said.

Without hesitation, she pulled out two fifties from her purse and gave them to Helen. I carefully wrapped the bottle in newspaper and put it in a shopping bag. After I handed it to her, she promptly left the store. Sergeant Gary waited outside and watched as she fished the pills from the bottle and swallowed one whole, just like Randy used to do.

The last thing I remember was my third grade teacher dressed in her sparkly angel and candy cane sweater being handcuffed and put into the back seat of a squad car.

53

DEAD-END

"Open it," Helen said.

She handed me a gift bag with a pink bow.

"What's this?"

"It's not every day someone spots a drug dealer and a user in my shop. Gary located the car from your description and arrested that guy on Possession of a Controlled Substance. They had a trunk full of pills in their car."

I lifted a small box from the bag surrounded by white tissue paper and opened the lid. After I removed the top square of cotton, I saw a tiny tea set nested inside—the same one I had admired with the pink roses in the display case weeks ago: four cups and saucers and a teapot.

"I don't know what to say," I said.

"Just say, thank you. It's not the Desert Rose place settings you loved, but it's pretty special. That set is about 200 years old."

"Thank you, Helen. It's a treasure," I said, lifting a teacup out and pretending to drink. Helen picked up one, too, and we extended our pinky fingers and toasted an extra gentle toast.

That evening after dinner Helen said she wanted to show me Caleb's bedroom, but I had serious reservations about invading his privacy. He was in Frostburg picking up furniture that Helen had purchased at an estate sale a few days earlier and wouldn't return until late. She told me she had bought a black walnut table with a brown marble top, a huge chestnut corner cupboard, and a mahogany Eastlake dresser from the 1800s, complete with its own hat box.

"The dresser is from the grand old Deer Park Hotel. They catered to the rich and famous who vacationed in Garrett County to escape the city heat during the 1800s and 1900s. It finally went out of business and the contents were auctioned off. Sadly, the hotel burned to the ground decades later.

"Tell me more about Caleb," I urged.

Helen motioned for me to follow her.

A Persian rug in dark burgundy with a floral design graced Helen's living room along with the inlaid hardwood floors. A matching runner covered the length of the hallway. I marveled at the original signed paintings hanging on her walls. An abstract caught my eye immediately.

"Is it a Rothko?" I asked, moving closer to it.

"It is," Helen said, obviously impressed at my knowledge. "I bought it at a yard sale for practically nothing. I think I paid $5 for it. It's probably worth $200,000—a real find."

I stared at the monochromatic painting and realized just how far I had come in the last few months from depressed and overwhelmed to a budding survivalist with a Colt 45 I wasn't afraid to use. My transition from cell phones and TV to total solitude in a remote mountain cabin still amazed me. The prospect of being attacked by a bear drove my depression away faster than shock therapy. Not that I ever had shock therapy. It was just something I had read about, but one of my friends did say it had worked miracles for her mother.

It seemed forever since I had tried to reduce anyone down to a sentence or one word or one color like Rothko did. I hadn't forgotten how, but it didn't seem as important now. It was strangely calming now to watch a woodpecker, a field mouse, or the way the sunlight filtered through the pines. Or to fantasize how I would furnish my own dream house someday. My shoebox dollhouse became a miniature version of that fantasy. I had even drawn a detailed floor plan for my future home in my journal, carefully labeling where the furniture should be placed. I added a wrap-around porch, a heated swimming pool, and a roller rink for Chase and me. It would have a fabulous sound system, strobe lights, cotton candy, and a popcorn machine.

When we reached the top of the stairs, another long runner led us down the hallway; only this one was white with red and black flowers or tulips. I wasn't sure. Helen stopped in front of the last door on the right, turned the knob, and then reached inside and felt for the light switch. When she clicked it on, nothing was out of place. Caleb's room was hotel-room perfect. His bookcases were filled with photo albums and color-coded boxes.

"Caleb's a collector," Helen said matter-of-factly. "Most of his photos of dead-end streets and pen and ink drawings are inside those albums. He also collects old postcards from all over the world, and they're cataloged in those filing boxes. We find hundreds of discarded cards at estate and yard sales for practically nothing."

"I bet he loves collecting stamps, too," I said.

"No, but he's a whiz with numbers. He balances my checkbook and double checks my ledger every week."

"People think I'm a collector, too," Helen said. "I stuff my antique shop with things people don't want or need anymore. As soon as I sell an item, I'm looking for something to take its spot. I get enormous pleasure in giving cast-offs a loving home and sharing my finds with others.

"Does he read the postcards?" I asked, motioning toward the filing boxes.

"All of them. He often shows me the ones that are especially sad or touching. He organizes his cards by country, city, and year. It's a treasure-trove of recorded history."

"I like reading old letters," I said. "They make me feel like I really know the people who wrote them."

"I'm sure you have noticed, but Caleb loves to ask questions. You see, he doesn't have to answer any if he's always asking them. It's a brilliant way to keep people at arm's length and to verify what he already knows," Helen said. "It's his room, so he can collect as many albums and postcards as he wants. Nothing is ever abandoned or lost. I think his underlying fear is he might be abandoned again someday."

"Why does he whistle?" I asked before I could stop myself.

Helen raised her eyebrows in surprise.

"You've seen him really upset. Not many people have. The doctor told us he acquired Tourette's-like behaviors after Luke died. Have you heard of Tourette's?" she asked.

"A boy in one of my classes had it. My teacher said his tics were hard to control, but he was perfectly normal otherwise.

"Caleb is like that," Helen said. "Only when he's stressed, he can't stop whistling. Did he scare you?"

"Yes," I admitted. "It was terrifying."

"Any more questions?" Helen asked, changing the subject.

"Just a couple more if that's okay. Where do *you* sleep?"

"In the master bedroom at the other end of the hall," she answered.

"How long have you two lived here?"

"Caleb's my brother. When our parents died, there wasn't anyone left to take care of him but me," she said.

When we were ready to leave, I spotted a framed photo of a little boy set on an end table beside his bed. Helen turned out the light, and we walked in silence down the carpeted stairs, past the Rothko, and into her cheery kitchen

"Will he know you've been in his room?" I asked.

"Maybe, but I'm not a threat to him."

"Can I ask you a question about Sam's place? Something's really been bothering me," I said.

"Okay, try me," Helen said without hesitation.

"Who's buried in that unmarked grave?"

"How do you know it's a grave?" Helen asked, looking away.

"There's an oval mirror with a fancy gold border right beside another stone marked with the name Shep," I said.

"You know Shep was a dog, don't you?" Helen asked.

"I figured as much because of the name."

"He was Sam and Lydia's dog for fifteen years—a gorgeous sable collie. Real gentle. He was more Lydia's dog than Sam's, and she took him everywhere she went. Shep loved the mountains, so when he died, they decided to make it his final resting place," she told me.

"Then Sam found Cali soon after that?"

"That's right. Cali stole his heart just like Shep had stolen Lydia's," Helen said.

"What about the other grave? The one with the mirror?"

"It's a secret," Helen said.

"It's Lydia's grave, isn't it?"

"If you want to believe it's her grave, then it is," Helen said coolly.

"Then Lydia is buried next to Shep," I said. "In a way, Sam's wife never left the mountain at all. Why didn't he tell me?"

"What if I drive to the cabin next week and spend some extra time with you?" Helen asked. "I could come next Saturday after work and go home on Sunday morning."

"Would Caleb come along, too?" I asked.

"He might, but I'd need to give him enough lead time to prepare. He doesn't do anything on the spur of the moment. Listen, we better go to bed now," Helen said. "Caleb will take you home in the morning."

"C'mon, Cali," I called, and she followed me to Helen's guest bedroom. I felt like royalty with the color-coordinated linens and drapes in blue voile and the sky-blue crystal chandelier over my bed. I opened the window an inch and climbed into the queen-sized bed, and Cali slept beside me on the floor. The sailboat nightlight on the far wall cast a misty blue glow over the room.

I lay in bed for a while thinking about everything: Caleb's perfectly organized room, Mrs. Spitzer in handcuffs, Shep's stone, and the mirror. I had trouble falling asleep, so I stared at the blue chandelier until I finally heard Caleb's truck come to a stop outside my window. The last thing I remembered was his truck windows whirring down and up. Twice.

54

WHISTLING

I ventured a little further away from the cabin early one evening and saw a flock of wild turkeys for the first time. Cali started barking ferociously, wanting to chase after them, but I held tightly to her leash. When it started to rain, those strange dark birds, about two dozen, scattered down the hillside. I found their prints in the mud, and later I added those to my list of recognizable animal tracks.

My late night routine of furnishing my doll house had begun. I had papered all the walls, foiled all the windows, and painted the floors. I carefully glued kitty litter to the chimney to make it look like stone. I gathered small twigs, and after they dried, I cut them into small pieces with the box cutter and attached them to the house to look like a log cabin.

I fashioned curtains from quilt squares Helen had given me and glued them above the windows. I used a large matchbox for a table and covered it with a blue linen napkin. Then I placed my tiny new tea set on top with a cup and saucer at each end and the teapot in the center. I discovered four silver thimbles in Lydia's sewing basket and used them as stools. Two empty jewelry boxes with the cotton still inside became the beds, and I placed one upstairs and down. Lydia's

Irish lace hankies served as bedspreads, and I made two pillows from the quilt squares and rested them at the head of each bed. A small jewelry box beside the upstairs bed became a dog bed.

On Saturday morning, I put frozen deer meat, onions, green pepper, spices, and two cups of tomato sauce in the crock pot and turned it on low. Helen and Caleb were coming for an overnight stay after work and would leave Sunday morning.

I went to Sam's bedroom to apply a little makeup before Caleb arrived. The mirror was face-down on the dresser. It must have fallen over, so I set it up. The low winter sun streamed through the transom above Sam's bed, and the glare in the mirror made it too bright to see my face, so I gave up.

Caleb honked the horn and, before I knew it, we were parked in front of the antique shop. Snow had been predicted for Sunday, and the clouds were turning smoky lavender. I could sense that snow was on its way. It was an intuitive skill I had learned. Something about the icy chill, the silence, and the smoky sky always tipped me off. Helen said her migraines often predicted big snowstorms, so she never needed a weatherman to warn her.

The shop had been all decked out for the holidays. Home-made stockings hung from the mantel, a freshly-cut pine tree sat in the front window with a lighted star at the top, and cinnamon-scented pine cones were displayed in big wooden bowls. "Jingle Bells" played over the loudspeakers, and I could see the record player spinning and an old album had been propped up nearby with a picture of Bing Crosby on the cover. Sam would be happy to know I knew who Crosby was. *White Christmas* was a popular classic.

"I'm over here," Helen called. She stood on a tall ladder and draped silver garlands from the ceiling in long, generous loops. Caleb hurried over to help steady the ladder. "I should have waited until you came, Twyla, but I wanted to get a head-start. You have no idea how long it takes me to decorate this place!"

Cali sneezed and then hid in the back room—too much commotion out here for her.

"Let me help you," I said, noticing she had her sunglasses on.

"Sure. Grab that box of ornaments on the counter and decorate the tree in the display window. When you're done, Caleb likes to hang silver icicles on the tree, one at a time. It's old fashioned, but people always used to hang them like that.Labor intensive, but it looks amazing when it's finished," she added.

I held the box of glittering ornaments, and they were every size and color. Strings of bubble lights had been hung on each branch, and I couldn't wait to see them lit before Caleb began hanging the icicles.

"We go overboard at Christmas. Once the snow sets in, everyone's starved for color, so we do our part to brighten the shop," Helen called. "A number of people don't make it to town until the spring thaw."

Two children, a boy and a girl, peered in the store window and waved. They pointed at the toy train that blew puffs of smoke on its endless circles around a table lined with red and white poinsettias. Ceramic carolers holding lighted candles stood on the window ledge. When I finished adding the bulbs to the tree, Caleb appeared with a box of icicles and started to place them on the tree.

"Turn the bubble lights on first," I pleaded, and he did.

In just a couple of minutes the red and green lights glowed and began to bubble like champagne, only more magical.

I left him alone to place his silver icicles, one by one, and stood to admire the tree. It was almost as stunning as Sam's glass tree when the sun hit it just right.

An attractive woman came into the shop and let a gust of snow flurries in with her. She began studying everything in detail.

"Leah, what are you looking for today?" Helen asked.

"A special gift this time for a good friend. Her birthday is next week."

"I just unpacked two Belleek cups and saucers and an Irish linen tablecloth you might like," Helen said. "And I found a new poetry book by an Irish writer. It's a first edition."

"Thanks, Helen. I'll definitely take a look."

Leah took her time and browsed each section looking for the perfect gift. When she finally approached the counter with a framed pen and ink drawing in her hand, I noticed she had a triple-spiral tattoo on her wrist.

"Do you know who the artist is?" she asked, handing it to Helen. "I can't make out the signature."

"Oh, it's one of *Caleb's* drawings," Helen said proudly. "He just signs them with a C."

Caleb stopped hanging the icicles when he heard his name and slipped out of sight.

"I'll take it then," Leah said. "I love pen and ink. How much?"

"It's marked $50, but for you, $30," Helen said.

Leah smiled and handed Helen a fifty dollar bill.

"Keep the change," Leah said.

"No, that's too much!"

"It's worth more to me, Helen. My friend will treasure it. She loves photos and drawings of old barns like this, so an original pen and ink is perfect."

Leah left the store with her gift, and the door chimed when she stepped into winter.

"She's a regular customer," Helen told me. "Her husband was in a tragic car accident a number of years ago, and he remained in a coma until his death. Both he and Leah loved Ireland. I'm always on the lookout for something new for her. Caleb will be pleased she bought one of his drawings."

"I think he already knows," I whispered.

Caleb emerged from behind a corner cupboard and

resumed his tinsel ritual. He was a mystery man, and an artist, too, I discovered.

As I walked around the store, I noticed the Christmas books had been relocated from a shelf to a tea table near the front of the shop. A pair of glossy black bear bookends helped call attention to the holiday books. Vintage ornaments, jewelry, and festive brooches filled one entire glass cabinet. Holiday record albums were artistically displayed on the antique sofa and a reclining lounge chair. The Eastlake dresser had been festooned with snow globes and music boxes of all shapes and colors. The dresser's hat box was open and inside stood a miniature tree with toys and wrapped packages underneath. Children's wooden blocks were stacked across the dresser's flat surface instead of the usual comb and brush set, and they spelled out M-E-R-R-Y C-H-R-I-S-T- M-A-S.

The maple table I loved was still there, but now it had a green and red tablecloth on it. Christmas plates decorated with a log cabin under falling snow, and red goblets replaced the crystal ones. The silver napkin holders were filled with green cloth napkins tucked inside, and the centerpiece was a large music box with ice skaters wearing long dresses and hats and muffs. They skated to "Joy to the World" every time you wound the key. I wished Chase could see it.

"I need a cup of cocoa, Helen. Do you want one?" I asked.

"No, I've reached my limit. I've been drinking coffee all morning to ward off this headache. Caleb, how about you?"

He shook his head no and continued draping icicles on a branch. "Leah bought your pen and ink drawing of the old barn that used to be on Mayhew Inn Road," Helen told him.

I sat at the half-moon table, and Cali rested her head on my foot.

The door chimed, and I heard loud laughter, followed by Helen's familiar "May I help you?"

"We're looking for something special, and a guy at the gas

station said you might have it in stock," a woman said, winking at the man beside her.

"What are you looking for?" Helen asked.

"Well, it's not something you can keep at home, you know. It's precious but very hard to find," the woman said in a sweet slur. "Are you Helen?"

"I am. Are you folks local?"

"Not quite. I'm from Florida. Orange juice, sun and surf, and all that," the woman said shivering.

Her voice cut through me like a jagged razor. I peeked through the curtain in the back room and saw Joy holding a red cup with rum and coke inside, no doubt. Her blonde hair, flowered mini skirt, and sleepy eyes were all too familiar.

"What kind of antiques are you folks looking for? I have a large assortment," Helen offered.

"My semi-precious daughter," Joy answered, laughing at her own joke. "I hear you might know where she is. Roger, this is the shopkeeper Helen. The gas station attendant told us you might be able to help us find Twyla," she cooed.

I heard the man's heavy footfalls, and then the sound of a chair being dragged across the floor, and I spotted Randy. His hair was shorter and he looked a lot heavier.

"We never eat at that table, sir. It's used to display the fine china, but you're welcome to eat your pizza over on the Coca-Cola table if you want." Helen offered.

He must have been sitting at the maple table with the new Christmas place settings. *My* table.

"Do you know who Twyla is?" Joy asked.

"Unusual name," Helen said. "No, I don't know anybody by that name. Do you have a picture of her?"

"You got that photo of Twyla on you?" Joy asked.

"Hell, no! Why would I carry a photo of your kid?"

I could hear plates being stacked together and then something crashed to the floor and shattered.

"Jesus, you'll have to pay for the fancy plate, Roger. How much does it cost, honey?" Joy asked.

"It's a set, or *was* a set. Don't worry about it," Helen muttered. "Caleb, help me clean up this mess."

Caleb appeared with a fold of silver icicles draped over his hand.

"I'll get the broom," he said, handing his precious icicles to Helen.

I could smell the pepperoni pizza now. "Roger" must have brought in a whole pie. The smell of pepperoni and cinnamon-scented pinecones was not a good mix.

"If you tell me what Twyla looks like, maybe I could help you," Helen said.

I was impressed with her cunning while I stayed hidden from view.

Caleb entered the back room and got the broom and dustpan. I held one finger to my lips, and he knew not to say a word.

"Well, she doesn't look anything like me, does she, Roger? She looks more like her father, my first husband, Buck. Twyla's 21 years old, has short dark hair, and dark eyes. Kind of on the thin side. She's attractive, but not what you'd say pretty. She ran away from home a few months ago, and we were worried sick about her. We came all this way. It took us two days of hard driving to get here," Joy said.

"If your daughter is 21, then maybe she's not a runaway," Helen said sweetly.

"She *stole* money from us," Joy snapped. "I didn't want to involve the police, but someone at Calamity tipped us off and said she's living here in Oakland. My son, Chase, told me everything. He's been living with Sam, an old cowboy who's loaded from what I can tell. He's bailed me out a few times, but he's starting to get stingy. You heard of him?

"Calamity?" Helen said, playing dumb.

"Yes, Calamity Café. That's where Twyla worked in Naples, Florida," Joy said.

I could hear someone sweeping pieces of broken glass together.

"You missed some over here, buddy," the man yelled.

"Well, we'll keep a look-out for you, Joy. Come over to the counter and leave your name and phone number. If we run across anyone who matches that name or description, we'll be sure to give you a call," Helen said. "Where are you staying?"

"I said you *missed* some, buddy!"

A strange whistling—a shrill ear-piercing sound—began to fill the shop. Cali rushed out and started howling.

"Holy shit!" the man shouted.

Caleb couldn't stop, and his whistling began to hurt my ears.

"Let's get out of this fucking looney bin," the man barked, and I heard a chair crash to the floor.

"Let go of my arm. You're hurting me!" Joy cried.

The slamming door marked their exit, but the whistling didn't stop, and Cali kept howling.

"It's okay, Caleb. They're gone," Helen said in a soothing voice. "They're gone."

Bing Crosby started crooning the chorus of "White Christmas," and Caleb's piercing whistle kept exploding from his lips. I wanted to help, but I was afraid of being discovered if Joy and "Roger" decided to come back inside the shop.

"You're okay, baby. I'll get those new postcards for you right now, so you can finish organizing them. Follow me," Helen said calmly, still holding the spill of silver icicles in her hand.

Caleb walked to the bookshelves and then he stood facing a corner. His whistles echoed off the walls. Helen didn't touch him or try to make him stop. She moved a three-sided Chinese screen that stood near the bust of the Victorian lady and placed it around him. Then she carried a box of postcards and set it on the buffet table behind a sofa. I couldn't see Caleb now, but I definitely heard him.

"When you're ready, I've put the box on the table," Helen told him.

Gradually the whistling lessened and turned into a high-pitched hum. Cali stopped howling, and Helen busied herself with sweeping the splintered remains of Desert Rose into the dustpan.

"After you're done with those cards, Caleb, you can finish the icicles. I draped the ones you gave me over the Windsor chair," Helen called in a casual voice. "Don't worry. They won't be returning. You scared them off. Good riddance!"

Helen carried the dustpan to the back room and emptied its contents noisily into a metal wastebasket.

"You got your cup of cocoa just in the nick of time, Twyla," Helen said. "You just missed them. I think it's safe for you to come out now. I saw a beat up station wagon parked out front, and they just pulled out. Gary will catch them with his radar."

"Is Caleb okay?" I whispered.

"He'll be fine, but I think you'll need to comfort poor Cali. She's still shaking," Helen said, kneeling down to pet the dog.

"Chase would never rat on me," I said.

"Roger probably threatened him. Your brother is just a little kid," Helen said. "If he yelled at Chase, he would have been terrified and forced to confess."

"It was Randy," I said. "Not Roger. I'll kill him if he hurts Chase."

We didn't say anything for a few minutes, and Bing Crosby and David Bowie began singing their "Peace on Earth/Little Drummer Boy" duet in the awkward silence.

"I need to use your phone," I said.

Helen nodded and left the room. I called Sam, and he answered on the first ring.

"Randy and Joy are here. They said Chase told them where I was."

After a pause, Sam started cussing so loud I had to hold the phone away from my ear.

"I kept Joy happy by giving her money whenever she came begging, but she's like a horse that bites you when you run out of sugar cubes."

"I'm worried sick about Chase, and I don't feel safe, Sam," I confessed.

"I'm sorry I talked you into all of this. We'll come and get you."

"When?"

"Just as soon as we can get away."

I hung up the phone and walked behind the counter. "Jingle Bell Rock" was playing now, but it felt like a funeral dirge. Helen helped Caleb put the icicles on the Christmas tree, and it was soothing to watch their slow ritual.

I took some marshmallows from the opened bag near the tin of instant cocoa mix and sank onto the floor beside Cali, and cradled her soft head in my lap.

55

SKY

"Those damn silver squiggles," Helen said, pressing her fingers against her temples.

"Chrome gnats?" Caleb asked.

"Yeah, those," she answered. "I hate it when they swarm."

She always saw an aura or silver squiggles right before a migraine began and had taken an Imitrex as prevention. A big weather change was on its way. "I'm a human barometer," she liked to say, and I believed her.

I sat on the passenger's side of the truck with Cali on my lap. Helen had her sunglasses on and sat in the middle holding Caleb's shoebox. As usual, it was a tight squeeze for three of us, actually four counting Cali. In all the chaos, I forgot about buying licorice for Caleb, but I couldn't risk running into "Roger" and Joy—Caleb didn't need any more candy anyway. He did need a slow afternoon or two to sort his postcards and add tinsel to the Christmas tree.

"What's for supper tonight?" Helen asked when we reached the cabin.

"Spaghetti," I said. "The sauce has been cooking all day in the crock pot. I made it with ground venison I found in the freezer."

Once Helen and I settled in, I added a log to the fireplace.

"Did you finally have time to watch *True Grit*?" Helen asked.

"Well, no, not yet."

"Classic avoidance behavior," she said.

Caleb walked in and didn't remove his coat and hat.

"Is supper in the refrigerator?" he asked.

"Dammit!"

"What's wrong?" Helen asked.

"I forgot to plug in the stupid crock pot," I muttered, holding the cord in my hand.

Helen lifted the glass lid.

"Yep, it's not done yet. Not even close," she joked. "I wondered why I couldn't smell anything cooking. Don't worry, we'll help rustle up dinner, won't we, Caleb?"

"My life's so screwed up," I muttered.

Caleb surveyed the contents of the refrigerator and freezer.

"I'll make breakfast," he announced. "You two take Cali for a walk."

"Great idea! I'll get her leash and a flashlight. I don't want to be chasing her if she takes off after a squirrel, or another bear," Helen said with a laugh. "What time should we come back?"

"I'll need a half hour," Caleb said, setting a dozen eggs on the counter.

"Okay, we'll be here at 6:00 p.m. sharp."

We opened the door to bitter cold with a foreboding sky overhead, a bone-chilling wind, and a fine dusting of snow. *A hint of what's to come*, I thought as I zipped myself into Sam's heavy jacket and put an air horn in my pocket.

Helen took off her sunglasses and switched on the flashlight. After we walked a short distance, we crossed over to the glass tree. Cali began sniffing the ground, always on the lookout. I had replaced about 15 of the wine bottles recently, but more were in reserve if I needed them. Helen reached up and bent a branch toward her, and then she gently released it. The bottles clinked together in the falling snow and a strand of thin ribbons fluttered from a branch.

"I wonder who put those here. They're pretty, but pastel colors aren't Sam's style. At least the plastic ribbons are weatherproof," Helen said with a laugh.

"I never noticed them before. They're bicycle ribbons like Ashley had on her beach bike," I whispered.

"Who's Ashley?"

"A co-worker at Calamity Café where I used to work. She went missing one evening a few months ago."

"And?" Helen prompted.

"Her body was found in a swamp, Corkscrew Swamp, inside a metal foot locker. I still have nightmares about it, but being here in the mountains makes her death seem distant—as if it hadn't happened—but I never want to forget her."

Helen was silent as she took it all in. "You won't forget, but the pain will eventually lessen over time," she finally said. "As the months and years go by, you'll recover and move on, but you never forget, never stop grieving."

"My high school teacher, Alexandra, used to say every time the name of the dead is spoken, they become immortal. I hope she's right."

"I'm sorry about your friend. What a god-awful tragedy. Maybe those aren't bicycle ribbons at all, but just something Sam thought would look pretty hanging on the tree," Helen said, trying to reassure me.

"Or someone's trying to scare the shit out of me," I said in a rush. "And it's working."

"Forget about it, Twyla. It's just a coincidence. Maybe Caleb put them there. You know how he likes putting tinsel on my Christmas tree," she said, quickly untying and tossing the ribbons over the hill. I watched until the wind carried them away.

"That crazy Sam," Helen said. "He's always coming up with

something offbeat. Beer bottles, and now plastic ribbons. He told me the bottles could trap evil spirits," she said, rubbing her temples.

"Maybe that's why he keeps so many on the tree. They come alive at sunrise and sunset, but the bears and the wind have taken a number of casualties," I said, dipping my toe into the pool of shattered glass at the base of the pine.

"I know," Helen said. "His glass tree has been here for years, and it's charmed a lot of people, including me."

Cali started tugging on her leash, and we headed toward the knoll.

Helen stopped by the looking-glass grave marker first and brushed away a dusting of snow and debris. Cali lay between the two markers like a guard dog.

"That's Lydia's grave, right?" I asked.

"It could be, but it's not. Lydia is buried in a little cemetery in her hometown of Rockport, Maine."

"It's a pretty mirror," I said. "It scared me at first when I saw my reflection in it," I admitted.

"Hold this," Helen said as she gave me the flashlight.

She pried the oval mirror loose with a pocket knife. The ground was frozen, so it took a few attempts, and then she slid it over to one side. Cali sniffed the shallow hole that held a small draw-string bag.

Inside were marbles, three dimes, a toy ship, silver gum wrappers, two rocks that glinted like gold, a jingle bell, and pieces of colored glass.

"Who put those in there?" I asked.

"Luke loved shiny things," she said, carefully fitting the mirror back over the treasures. "He died when he was only four years old. Caleb and he liked to visit Sam and Lydia, and they used to lie together on this knoll in the summertime and watch the clouds. It was one of their favorite things to do," Helen said quietly.

"What happened to him?"

"He caught the flu one winter, developed pneumonia, and died the next day. It struck without warning. Such a tragedy. Sam let Caleb bury him up here, so he wouldn't be far away in a strange cemetery. Caleb never got over it. His wife left him after Luke died, and he had a nervous breakdown and spent a year in a psych ward. Over time, he developed coping mechanisms. Most people die if they get struck by a bolt of lightning, but Caleb managed to survive," Helen said, putting the mirror back into place.

"I'm sorry," I said, but I needed to know more. "Why isn't Luke's name on the marker?"

"Caleb couldn't bear reading his son's name on a gravestone. It made his death permanent, and he didn't want words and dates to block out sunrises and sunsets, clouds and rainbows, shooting stars and falling snow. It sounds a little crazy, but he wanted Luke to see the things he loved forever," Helen said.

The snow picked up and quickly coated the mirror, and Helen didn't brush it away this time.

"Time to go. Breakfast is almost ready," Helen said, as she rubbed her forehead and glanced at her watch, "and I need to take another Imitrex. Sometimes it makes me sleepy, but my headache is turning into a full-blown migraine. A sure sign that a snowstorm is on its way."

We walked to the porch and gazed at the knoll. I pointed the flashlight toward Luke's grave and captured falling snowflakes inside its narrow beam. The mountains had dissolved into total cloud cover, and the glass tree was flocked with snow.

"It looks like we'll need to leave right away after our breakfast because if I'm right about this storm, you'd be stuck with us for days. I'll take Killer home with us to give you a break. We'll stay longer next time, Twyla. I promise."

I switched off the flashlight, and we stood together in the snowy darkness.

"Sam said Glass Mountain got its name from all the ice

storms, but I think it's from the glass tree and Luke's grave marker," I said.

"You may be right," Helen said.

When we entered the door, we were greeted by a steamy kitchen and a country breakfast was on the table.

"Breakfast is Caleb's specialty," Helen explained, looking a little pale as she grabbed a bottle of water from the refrigerator and quickly swallowed a pill.

Caleb's flushed face reminded me a little of Chase's when he ran a fever.

"I've already eaten. You two go ahead," he said, drying Cali's paws with a towel. "I spotted an old black and yellow station wagon with Florida plates yesterday at the Comfort Inn in McHenry. One of the back windows was covered with black plastic and duct tape, and the front grille was smashed in. It looked like it had been that way for a while."

In that instant, I realized who had rear-ended my car months ago in Florida and put me in the hospital.

"Randy and Joy were going to rob me," I said, finally putting it all together now. "They both were high. That explains my mysterious "sister" call at the hospital after the wreck. Joy must have felt guilty, but she didn't want the police to find out who called, so she lied and said she was my sister."

"You never told me about this," Helen said, looking totally confused. "We'll have to have a long heart-to-heart."

"Are they still here?" I asked.

"McHenry is about 25 miles from Red House. I told Sergeant Gary to keep a close eye on them," Helen said. "Those two stick out like sore thumbs anyway."

"What if they find me?" I asked, feeling panicky.

"They won't, and they won't make it very far in that junker car of theirs. I'm sure they don't know anything about mountain roads and snow."

"I wish you and Caleb could stay with me."

"Don't worry, you're safe up here," Helen said. "Safer than in town."

Seeing Randy and Joy in the antique shop made it clear just how desperate they were for drug money, so desperate they terrified Chase into talking. I pushed the food around on my plate while Helen poured herself a cup of black coffee, and Caleb stepped outside to smoke a cigarette.

"Aren't you going to eat anything?" I asked.

"I'd better not," Helen said, fanning herself with a dishtowel. "The smell of food is making me nauseous."

56

FOOTPRINTS

When the snowstorm set in, Helen and Caleb were gone. One storm merged into the next with a day in between, and everything became white again. The ground. The trees. The mountains. Even the sky was white.

I bundled up and pushed the door open just enough to squeeze through and clear a narrow path, so Cali wouldn't tumble into the drifts. Even on a retractable leash, she might wander too far if I'd let her. I remembered to shovel a thin slice of snow off the top layer and work my way down. It took longer this way, but my arms and back wouldn't ache afterward. The rusted Esso thermometer registered below zero.

I brushed the snow from the kitchen window almost every day now, so I could see out. The bone-chilling air made it painful to breathe, and my eyelashes and eyebrows often frosted over. I tried covering my face with a wool scarf, but it didn't help much. Maybe Sam had a ski mask in his dresser. I spent more time layering my clothing than I actually spent outside. Snow was still falling, but not as fast. At least I had cleared a pathway.

The snow finally stopped midafternoon one day, and I bundled up once again to hang a cheerful wooden bird feeder outside. I discovered it in the cellar, and it had pink hearts and green shamrocks painted on it. A tin full of sunflower seeds sat beside it. Sam said birds had a hard time finding food in the winter, and I wanted to help, plus I was starved for color: cardinals, yellow finches, blue jays, actually any bird at all would brighten this arctic landscape.

I found a hook right outside the kitchen window and hung the bird feeder on it. It must have belonged to Lydia because an "L" and 2010 were carved on it. I filled the feeder with sunflower seeds and within minutes, a pair of cardinals magically appeared in Sam's glass tree as if they'd been waiting on me. The crimson birds quickly perched on the gently swaying feeder, fluttering their wings and cocking their heads to study me with their beady black eyes. The bird book had been invaluable, and now I wanted to learn more about cardinals. But first, I needed to finish my dollhouse.

I carried it from the pantry to the table and positioned myself so I could birdwatch and furnish the house at the same time. When I looked inside, I gasped. My matchbox table and thimble stools were missing and had been replaced with an elegant tiny table and four chairs, just like the dining set in Helen's shop. The tea cups were set around the teapot which was on a doily in the center of the table. A tiny chandelier was suspended above the table with a fishing line. A four-poster bed with a lacy canopy and bedspread replaced my jewelry-box bed in the loft. A new dog bed had been fashioned out of foam and tan corduroy, and a golden ceramic dog was sleeping in it. I quickly scanned the whole interior, spotting a double bed and matching dresser with a mirror in the downstairs bedroom. A fuzzy mohair calico kitten slept at the foot of the bed. Persian rugs or what looked like Persian rugs covered the floor in each room, and a spiral staircase led up to the loft. I knew it had to be Caleb's handiwork with Helen's help, but when did he come inside? He was secretive and unpredictable, like a nervous ghost.

The only things missing were two red leather couches, a

chair, and a stone fireplace. With any luck, maybe the shoemaker's elf would return and finish the job. I hoped he or she would make a tiny moose head with sad brown eyes and mount it over the fireplace.

After I held and studied each new piece, I gingerly carried my dollhouse to the pantry. Cali didn't open her eyes or move from her sweet spot on the couch. My afternoon and evening diversion to work on the dollhouse was finished, so I decided to hunt for a ski mask and go outside during the break in the weather. I dug through every drawer until I finally found one. I pulled on Lydia's stretchy ski pants over my long johns and wore Sam's huge wool turtleneck sweater and two pairs of wool socks. I decided I'd borrow Lydia's double-down jacket with the hood even though it would be snug. Just before I opened the door, I pulled the black ski mask on after I was outside. I didn't want to spook Cali and carried an air horn and my trusty derringer with me instead of the revolver since I would be close to the cabin. The bears were hibernating anyway, but Caleb said one blast from an air horn might send them running. Cali came over and sniffed my ski pants and boots and then jumped on the couch.

After strapping on a pair of snowshoes that had been hanging on the front porch, I tried to walk around the cabin in the snow. It was tough going with all my layers of warm clothes. I was glad that I had on the ski mask since the air was foul with the unmistakable scent of a skunk that had been cornered or felt threatened.

Awkward and slow going at first, I sank through the deep snow until I got the hang of it. I heard the distant buzz of a chainsaw—*someone must be cutting firewood; a lot of firewood*, I thought. The depth of the snow on the flattest place I could find, measured a little over three feet deep—the drifts were five and six feet high in places.

The roof seemed fine, and the heavy snow melted a little when the sun came out. Icicles glistened from the eaves dripping longer and leaner as each day passed. I spotted deer tracks and droppings. When I came to the front again and stood beneath my bedroom window, there were fresh bear or human footprints in the snow.

Fear sparked through me like electricity shooting through my veins, and I instinctively lifted the air horn and the derringer from my pockets at the same time. I followed the tracks that led over to the furnace intake pipe. Sam had told me to check it after a big snow to make sure it wasn't blocked, but it had already been cleared, so those had to be Caleb's footprints. They moved from the cabin, headed across the driveway, and disappeared into the shadows. Maybe he had hiked here early this morning to see if I was okay, but why did he stand beneath my bedroom window? Maybe he wanted to see if my light was on? That sounded like him. He hated to inconvenience anyone. He had a key if he needed to get in, but it was odd that he hadn't knocked. His behavior was definitely peculiar, but harmless, I hoped.

I wondered if he put the furniture in my dollhouse while I slept. The thought creeped me out, but Cali might have barked or made some noise if Caleb came in the back door. I remembered he had a lunch bag in his hand the other night when he went into the pantry to feed Cali and Killer. He probably had the furniture hidden in that bag and secretly put the furnishings inside the dollhouse. It was either him, or the illusive coffee ghost who liked to hide shiny crystals.

I moved to the rear of the cabin, and the bright winter sun made the colored bottles in Sam's glass tree look like they were lit from within. They cast wavering shadows of cobalt blue, green, and crimson across the sparkling snow. If it had been windy, the bottles would have crazed and cracked, but now they just clicked together gently in the icy breeze. It was a beer lover's Christmas tree. I remembered a pretty green bottle of wine in Sam's cellar I wanted to sample. I didn't know much about wine, but I did like the color of the bottle. Not a good reason to drink it, but I'd be sure to hang the empty bottle on the tree. A sudden gust rattled the dead leaves in the towering pin oak; its dry leaves sounded like rain and the bottles created a brief woodwind harmony.

I removed my snowshoes and gazed at the glass tree again. It was such a simple thing with colored bottles slid onto pine boughs, but it made me happy. I hoped the bottles really could capture evil spirits forever.

Just then, I felt as if someone were standing behind me. But nothing was there when I whirled around, except a lone cardinal who took flight and caused the bird feeder to rock. When my eyes began to water from the cold, I leaned the snowshoes beside the door and noticed Caleb had dropped a piece of licorice in the snow.

Cali didn't bat an eye when I opened the door with a ski mask on. She acted like this was normal. As usual, I tucked the derringer under my bed pillow. After I stripped off the layers of clothing and tossed them on my bed, I started to sweat profusely from the exertion. I drank a bottle of water and cooled down a little, before I put on my robe and slippers and shoved the leather chair in front of the door. I settled in with the bird book and read more about cardinals: the blood-red male with his bandit mask and the soft brown female with her subtle flashes of crimson. *Territorial. Accomplished songsters.* Maybe my bird feeder would attract even more cardinals now. I was delighted at the thought and read until I fell asleep. The next thing I knew, Cali was whimpering beside me. She needed to go out.

"Okay, girl," I said, shoving the chair out of the way. I wrapped the afghan over my shoulders before I hooked on her retractable leash, and she pulled it all the way out. I stood behind the door and waited for her to return. When Cali came inside, she looked like she'd been swimming in a vat of snow and shook the snow off in an instinctive spiraling motion from head to tail. After a mini snowstorm, my hair was slightly frosted, but Cali had become her usual golden self once again. I toweled her paws and coat off before I mopped the floor.

December 23rd, just two more days until Christmas, but it didn't seem very Christmassy. I opened the box of decorations in the pantry and hung a few things in case Sam and Chase returned. If it wasn't too cold tomorrow, I'd chop down a small pine tree with Sam's ax.

I slipped the ski coat over my robe and stepped into Lydia's boots, so I could make a fast trip to the spooky cellar to find the pretty green bottle of wine. After I cranked up the battery-powered lantern, I headed out. In the daytime, the cellar didn't bother me, but at dusk, my imagination played tricks on me. The wine was called *Blue Flame,* and it had a long blue and white flame painted on the front of its pale green bottle. The dark wine inside made the bottle look cobalt blue, and red coals speckled the bottom of the bottle. It would look great on the kitchen table or in Sam's tree. When I hurried inside, I turned the bottle over and read: *Blue Flame Pinot Noir. What is Blue Flame? A burning passion. The heat of the sun. The fire of discovery. All of the above."*

I poured a little into a champagne flute that sat beside its twin on the windowsill. Lydia and Sam must have used them for special occasions. All the other wine glasses were safely packed out of sight now, but I didn't see any harm in using one champagne glass.

The breeze picked up and the trees were bending in a driving wind. I could hear bottles crashing and banging together as the pine wrestled with the stormy gale, and then it went silent. I peered out the front window into the moonlit yard. When I looked through the binoculars, the glass tree was completely empty. Not a single bottle had survived. I'd have to add my bottle of *Blue Flame* sooner than I thought.

A shadow seemed to be nestled high in the branches of the pin oak. It was almost dark and the snow-covered leaves made it hard to see. I hoped it wasn't another treed black bear, but I couldn't tell, not even with the binoculars. I checked from time to time until it got completely dark, but the shadow never moved so it had to be my imagination. The bears were asleep anyway, I reminded myself. I lowered the window blind and poured a full glass of *Blue Flame.*

After I draped silver garlands over each doorway and hung sleigh bells on the doorknob of the Dutch door, I found several strands of blue lights. I got the stepladder, and looped them around the log beams. When I plugged them in— instant fairyland! A lovely buzz from the wine had kicked in, and I basked in the magic of the twinkling blue lights. I hung three different stockings on the fireplace mantel and tried to think of what to stuff in them.

An unopened box of silver tinsel kept tempting me, so I hung strands everywhere from the mounted bear's nose, the deer's antlers in the living room and above Sam's bed, to the moose's antlers above the fireplace. The glassy-eyed animals seemed less frightening with their silver tresses. I'd decided to hang a pinecone and holly wreath on the front door tomorrow and save the rest of the ornaments, lights, and tinsel in case I found a small pine tree to bring inside.

I bundled up one last time, switched on the front porch light, and then I opened the door for Cali to go out again before bed. I didn't bother with her leash since it was icy cold, and I knew she'd beg to come inside. I watched as she circled the barren glass tree a couple of times, sniffed the air like she always did, and sneezed. Sure enough, she scratched at the screen door, but she had something in her mouth and dropped it at my feet. It was one of Sam's daggers. I picked it up and hurried inside to examine it closely under the light. It was definitely one of Sam's. I studied the table where all the knives and daggers were displayed. Some were missing and a few had fallen under the table. Cali must have grabbed one or more and taken them outside, I told myself, and I tried to place them back on the table as if they hadn't been disturbed.

When Cali fell asleep in front of the fireplace, I tuned in the weather band on Sam's radio scanner: "Another December snow storm for Garrett County, preceded by freezing rain," a robotic voice said. "The wind chill will drop to 15 below tonight."

I wanted to read a novel, but the wine had made me sleepy. It wouldn't take long for me to fall asleep, so I studied my bird book instead. After a half an hour of nest building, fledglings, and migrations, I called it a night. The wind had stopped now, but freezing rain began to pelt the tin roof. I cranked the battery-powered lantern and added more logs to the fire in case the power went out. After I washed my champagne flute and filled both of the flutes halfway with bottled water, I set them on the windowsill. When the afternoon sun hit it just right, the added water threw brilliant prisms on the cabin walls. After I pushed the chair and the pump organ into place and remembered to pull the window blind down, I turned off the light and climbed into bed.

After a series of thumps, I was jarred awake by a loud crash and Cali's hoarse non-stop barking. I stumbled into the middle of the living room and then froze. The back door stood wide open and the chair was pushed to one side. A fat metal door with the word Kelvinator written on it lay on the kitchen floor. The refrigerator had been dragged from the bathroom to the middle of the room, and a rancid smell of fresh animal droppings and rotten garbage mixed with the contents of the refrigerator was sickening. Flour and sugar dusted everything along with shattered bottles of pickles, olives, and maraschino cherries. The chairs were overturned and crushed except for one, and a sea of smashed cans, water bottles, and the remains of dry dog food paved the floor.

Cali stood her ground with teeth bared, growling and barking like a rabid dog as the freezing air filled the cabin. I slammed the door and then raced to my room, grabbed the Colt 45, and cocked it. When I ran into the kitchen, I slid across the wet linoleum in my bare feet and crashed into the table. Rattled but not hurt, I was dizzy when I tried to stand. I held on to a chair and tried to figure out what had happened. To my horror, I remembered I forgot to lock the door, and God only knows what monsters were lurking on the other side.

There was little wind, the freezing rain had stopped, and a full moon kindled the cloudless night. Even though the window blind was down, the moon cast an eerie moving shadow onto the floor. The only sound I heard was Cali's mind-numbing bark thundering in my ears. I slowly peered outside the door, ready to kill the first thing that moved, but Cali raced in front of me and skidded to a stop on the stoop's icy surface. A dark shadow loomed above us, but it wasn't a shadow.

A black bear at least seven feet tall stood near the window gorging on sunflower seeds. Each time he pawed the feeder, it swung wildly as he continued his feasting. Cali went totally insane, snarling and snapping at the bear's feet, but she managed to keep a safe distance from the bear's menacing paws this time. Panicked, I ran inside to hide and turn on the porch light, but I heard Cali yelping in pain and forgot my fear.

"Cali! Get in here!" I screamed.

The bear lumbered away, but Cali sprang to life, like a wolf, howling and yipping as she chased after the bear. When I stepped on the stoop, I saw Cali loping across the deep snow. The bear's glossy coat was inky black against the white drifts, and the full moon made it horribly surreal, like a horror movie. Golden dog. Blood on snow. Full moon. Black bear. Pool of broken glass. The wind shattered beer bottles must have released their evil spirits into the world.

I tried to aim my gun at the bear, but it disappeared over the hill, so I pointed the revolver skyward and fired six times. The kickback knocked me down, and I fell on snow littered with sunflower seeds, bringing back painful memories of other bear encounters I had had during my short stay on Glass Mountain.

I could hear Cali's pitiful yelps growing weaker and weaker

in the distance. Each time she cried out, my heart stopped. I felt helpless and too terrified to follow her into the dark woods. I sat up and yelled her name over and over at the watchful moon and the mountains that held me captive.

"Cali! Come, girl!"

My frightened pleas echoed in my ears, ricocheting, empty and hollow. I called until I was hoarse, and then I cried an ugly gut-wrenching cry. My lungs ached, and I couldn't feel my feet and hands. The deafening gunshots still rang in my ears, and then something huge toppled from the top of the pin oak. I started shaking uncontrollably. God, not another bear! Petrified, I staggered and half-crawled into the freezing cabin. I bolted the door and prayed someone had heard the shots.

57

TREE STAND

I stared at a blue chandelier overhead. A pot of hot tea sat on the side table with a cup and saucer. Outside the window, the snow blew sideways. Helen was sitting in a rocking chair beside my bed.

"Cali? Where's Cali?!" I exclaimed.

"It's going to be alright, Twyla. We've been looking for her all night. Some of the firemen and Cory came to search," Helen said, taking my hand. "They boarded up the back door for you until Sam can have the door replaced."

"A huge bear was eating from the bird feeder and attacked Cali, and then it ran off into the woods. Blood was everywhere," I said in a rush.

"I know. We followed her tracks and a blood trail. If she's got any sense, she's nursing her wounds and leaving that damn bear alone this time," Helen said.

"Cali protected me. It's my fault she got hurt!"

"There's a hell of a lot to learn about living in the woods, and I never thought to warn you about bird feeders. Bears love birdseed almost more than honey, and they'll do anything to get at it. Where did you find the feeder?" Helen asked.

"It was in the cellar beside a huge tin of sunflower seeds. The feeder had hearts and shamrocks painted on it."

"Then it had to belong to Lydia. City folk never think twice about bird feeders—they don't have to. Let me pour you some tea," Helen said, reaching for the cup.

"Did you hear my gunshots?" I asked.

"Just me and the whole mountain. We found you passed out on the kitchen floor. Caleb carried you to the truck, and we drove you to our farm. Then we put you in bed, called the doctor, and alerted all our neighbors. Caleb gathered a search party, and they headed out. He's a good tracker and knows these woods. He didn't find Cali, but he did find something else."

"What?" I asked.

"Who, not what," Helen said. "It was your mother's friend, Roger. Caleb found him lying beneath the pin oak with a bullet in his head. He must have died instantly.

"I don't understand," I said.

Helen took a deep breath.

"Lydia's costume jewelry, a gold watch, and a few diamonds were stuffed in his pockets, and he stole Sam's Krag. Caleb found a few of Sam's exotic daggers stowed inside a plastic bag in the snowmobile, too. He must have been desperate for drug money and took whatever valuables he could find. The place was crawling with police and detectives after Caleb discovered Roger under the tree. It was an active crime scene.

"He shoplifted insulated boots, pants, and a down jacket, plus a lined knit hat from a shop at Wisp Resort a few days ago," Helen continued. "A detective said he left the tags and his shoes in the trash and exited the store, wearing the new clothing over his own underneath a long, baggy coat with pockets filled with beef jerky. One of the clerks remembered him because he smelled like booze and paid cash for a pair of insulated gloves, hand warmers and thermal wool socks."

"Randy watched me from that tree, ate Sam's food, and

stole the gun from my nightstand," I whispered. "He was the mysterious unmoving shadow."

"No, Roger watched you. Randy's twin. Detectives discovered his license, credit cards, and phone during their search. A background check revealed he had lived in Miami but moved in with Joy and Randy after he was released from prison. Randy helped Roger and Joy track you down before he took off."

"You're kidding."

Helen just shook her head.

"Where's Randy?" I asked, still confused.

"Good question. They're looking for him in three states."

"How did Roger get up the mountain?"

"Caleb discovered a snowmobile covered with branches piled on top of it in the woods. I'm sure he felt no pain and probably slept most of the time. That explains your unmoving shadow," Helen said.

"I thought Cali acted funny when I let her out last night. She kept circling the pin oak and sniffing like crazy but never barked," I said.

"She was sprayed by a skunk once and learned the hard way," Caleb said. "Hunters use the scent on their clothes and try to position their blind downwind, so animals don't detect them. Roger had gone to a lot of trouble to fool Cali, plus he had soaked sponges in a bottle of skunk scent he had bought and hung them from the pin oak. It masks the smell of humans and keeps anything away. He drank a lot of whiskey to pass the time, and it made him numb to the cold and the stench. We found his empty bottles buried in the snow. He must have put the tree stand up at night while you were sleeping," Helen explained. "He attached a long rope to a limb and tied big knots in it, so he could climb up and down unnoticed. The leaves still clinging to the pin oak gave him good cover, too."

"I always lock the cabin at night or when I leave the mountain. I didn't think I needed to during the day," I said, shaking my head. "That's why Cali didn't bark. She didn't smell danger at all—just a sleeping drunk who smelled like a skunk. That's almost funny, but I can't laugh right now—give me about ten years. How long do you think Roger had been watching me?"

"Not long. Two or three days max, judging by the receipt for the snowmobile and climbing tree stand. Just long enough to find what he wanted and when to get it, so he hung around awhile. He must have put Ashley's bike streamers in the glass tree just to torture you."

"It was an accident, Helen," I whispered. "I didn't know he was in that tree. I fired my gun to signal for help, not to murder anyone."

My teeth were chattering now, and Helen got two more blankets from the closet shelf.

I tried to understand everything that had happened, but my head swam with questions.

"Where's Joy?" I asked.

"Caleb said the police found her passed out at the Comfort Inn, and they had to give her Narcan to revive her. She didn't know Roger was even gone. The manager said she never left the room, and it was littered with needles. After Joy recovers, she'll be questioned. They'll need to talk to you as well."

Helen helped me into her fleece robe, and we walked into the living room and sat in front of the fire. The wind rattled the windows and a sudden downdraft swirled the ashes in the fireplace.

"It started snowing early this morning. There are a couple of feet on the ground already and more on the way. At least it's a dry snow, but the gusting winds aren't helping any. It's supposed to clear for a few hours later this morning, and then the forecasters said we'd get more snow after that. My head is throbbing, so I know they're dead right."

Killer came into the room and began purring and making figure eights between Helen's legs.

"What if they can't find Cali?" I asked.

"Don't worry about that now. All we can do is hope they

can locate her before the next snowstorm sets in. It's Christmas Eve, you know, and the firemen will want to get home to their families."

"I forgot all about Christmas. I'll bet Sam and Chase are grounded because of the weather. How can I ever tell Sam that Cali's missing? He's not over Lydia's death, and he won't be able to handle another loss."

The low morning sun started to inch out from behind the storm clouds, and I stared at the snow and watched the drifts explode when blasts of wind hit them. Snow devils formed and danced drunkenly across the field. Instead of hopelessness, a growing fury took over, and when my fury turned to rage, I knew what I had to do.

"Helen, take me to the cabin and help me find Cali," I said.

Helen took one look at me and began to gather extra winter clothes and boots. She gave me a parka, knit cap, gloves, and boots. While I dressed, Helen got ready to set out. She put a note for Caleb on the kitchen table, and we headed outside, squinting from the glaring sun as she swept new snow from her porch and stairs.

"This kind of snow doesn't make good snowmen or snow-balls, but it can suck the life out of you if you let it," Helen said. "Here, you'll need these."

She handed me a pair of sunglasses, and I put them on. Wearing them in the snow seemed strange. I only wore them in Florida at the beach. Helen grabbed an extra pair for herself from the glove box. We shoveled the snow away from the truck's tires that already had chains on them.

"It looks like we've got a few hours of sun before the second storm hits. It will take us longer to climb the hill because of the drifts on the road. I don't have a snowplow on my truck, but we can dig out if we get stuck. We've got plenty of gas and provisions and shovels. We're always prepared for emergencies. Help me load this firewood into the bed of the truck. The more weight we carry, the better our traction will be. It's 4-wheel drive, but we need all the help we can get," she said.

We hauled firewood to the truck, and then Helen got in the cab, started the engine, and we headed down the lane with no trouble to the main road. The snow plows had cleared it, but it remained snow covered since they couldn't keep pace with the blowing snow. The sleigh bell chime of tire chains made it feel like Christmas Eve, but it wasn't a happy sound today.

I got out and unlocked the gate's padlock for the first time with the key Caleb had given me. I had trouble shoving the gate open in the deep snow, but I finally managed and didn't bother to close it. Nobody in their right mind would climb Sam's hill on a day like this unless they had to. Nobody but Helen or Caleb or me and a desperate drunk on a snowmobile.

The winter sun helped us see better after we crossed over the frozen creek and headed toward the trees that formed an interlocking canopy overhead. We shouted for Cali every few minutes and listened for her bark, but the woods held her captive. The steady sun cast long shadows, and I kept a close watch for any movement or sign. After an hour of steady climbing with stops to clear the snow away, we were met by a barricade of fallen trees across the road. I looked at Helen, and she told me she had a chainsaw in the truck. Of course she did.

We got out, and she started it up with three hard pulls and began slicing through the tree limbs. I dragged them to the side of the road while she kept cutting. I remembered the distant noise of someone sawing firewood, but it wasn't a chainsaw at all. It was Randy's snowmobile climbing up Glass Mountain.

"I found a Christmas tree for you!" Helen shouted, as she cut a small pine tree down and tossed it into the bed of the truck. We kept clearing the road together, and pine sap coated my gloves. After about an hour, we were finally done.

We rested for a few minutes and each of us drank a bottle of water. Helen quickly swallowed an Imitrex, and then she jerked the truck in gear and resumed our slow climb up the steep road.

It must have been close to noon, and I was totally exhausted. I knew Helen was too, but I'd never turn back now. Slowly the winter sun began to fade, and the sky up ahead turned that dusky shade of lavender as if we were headed straight into the next snowstorm.

"I hope we can get to the cabin before the snow starts. At least we had a few hours of clear weather. The clouds are descending fast, and it will be hard to see the road ahead," Helen said.

A six point buck jumped in front of us, and Helen stopped and laid on the horn in case others were waiting to cross. I held my breath until the truck started jerking forward again when the chains dug in.

"Do you smell smoke?" Helen asked.

The snow clouds grew darker and became a sooty black above the trees. We were almost to the crest of the hill, and I knew the cabin would soon emerge. The clouds billowed and twisted in the wind, and then we saw licks of flame.

"The cabin's on fire!" Helen yelled.

Fire leapt from the kitchen window and shot clear through the roof. Angry clouds descended on Sam's empty glass tree, and smoke consumed the noon sky. Suddenly, it was as dark as midnight.

"Oh, my God," I whispered.

"It'll have to burn itself out. There's nothing we can do. I hope the wind doesn't spread the fire to the rest of the mountain," Helen said, kicking the truck in reverse and backing down the hill.

"We can't leave! Let me out!" I shouted.

"We don't have a choice," Helen said, ignoring me.

I shoved the door open and jumped into a snowdrift. Helen ordered me to get in, but I couldn't desert Cali. I stumbled uphill toward the cabin, and Helen turned on her headlights and started honking the horn. She lowered the window and stuck her head out.

"It's suicide, Twyla. Don't be a fool. Get in before it's too late!"

I started coughing and put my scarf over my mouth, so I could breathe. I felt the heat from the soaring flames as they lit up the sky. Helen kept honking, but it faded away like a distant lighthouse sounding its warning to ships at sea, and then it began to snow. First light flurries and then heavier and heavier. I wasn't sure if the snow or the smoke created the white-out. I threw my sunglasses off since I couldn't see more than a foot in front of me. I didn't know which way to go as Helen's horn echoed all around me.

Out of a bank of snow and fog and black smoke, a ghostly figure emerged and moved swiftly toward me. When it got closer, I recognized Caleb with Cali in his arms. She was swaddled in his coat, and when I reached out to touch her, Caleb pushed my hand away.

"Follow me," he ordered. "Now!"

I couldn't see, so I held tight to his shirt, and we made our way toward the truck's horn and the flashing emergency lights.

Helen jumped out and helped load us into the cab.

"We don't have much time. All the trees are on fire now," Helen said, looking up at the glowing red sky. She leaned out her window, so she could back down the mountain. The acrid smell of smoke and burning pines rushed into the cab, and I started to cough. The headlights bounced off the road in front of us while the truck's brake lights burned red holes in the snowy darkness behind.

Cali was alive. She had made it home to the cabin, and Caleb said he found her hiding under the front porch—the same place where the bears had taken refuge. Caleb carefully shifted Cali to his left side so his right hand would be free. He pulled an army blanket from under the seat and covered her.

"Is she going to be okay?" I asked in a small voice.

Caleb didn't answer but opened the shoebox and gave her a treat. I watched as he cut the bloodied fur away from one of her ears and applied an antibiotic cream. She didn't move or make a sound, and then she went to sleep. The chase had totally worn her out.

"Will she be okay?" I asked again.

"She will," Caleb said. "She's very lucky."

Cali's soft snoring and the rhythmical flick of the windshield wipers with the clinking tire chains were the only sounds as we slowly backed down. I watched the road slip away in front of us as the truck's headlights spotlighted the falling snow that covered our tracks.

58

SMOKE & MIRRORS

S am stood in the middle of ground zero and didn't say a word. He and Chase had driven non-stop all the way from Naples after Helen had called him. He parked his truck behind Caleb's, and Chase watched from inside Sam's truck. Helen stayed at the farm to tend to Cali. The vet gave her an antibiotic and said she'd make a full recovery. She just needed to rest after her bear adventure.

A huge charred spot surrounded by piles of dirty snow marked the scorched earth where Sam's palace had once stood. His cabin, the glass tree, his photo albums, his John Wayne movies, and all his mementos were gone. The skeletal trees had iced over with freezing rain and sagged from the weight. The smokestack, smashed appliances, broken porcelain sinks, and bathtub were all that remained. My shoebox dollhouse with its handcrafted furniture and tea set hadn't had a prayer.The cinderblock building and the cistern remained untouched. The blackened tin roof was still intact—a testament to fire-proof materials. Everything else had smoldered for 24 hours until the second snowstorm snuffed out any lingering flames and hotspots.

Caleb slowly walked the perimeter, searching for anything

that might be salvageable. He poked through the ashes with a walking stick and sometimes dug through the rubble with his bare hands. Not one love letter or photograph or shred of Lydia's wedding dress to be found. Just a numbing silence. No tall tales from Sam or endless questions from Caleb.

Caleb finally found something dark near the top of a snowdrift and held it up, turning it gently in his hand.

"This is yours," he said, placing a tiny wooden chair in my hand.

"Did you make it, Caleb?" I asked.

He nodded and then resumed his search for artifacts.

It wasn't a ghost or a magic elf who had crafted the dollhouse furniture. It was Caleb.

He combed through the ruins and searched several times, looking for fragments of Sam and Lydia's life. Finally, he bent over and picked up something a short distance from where the cabin once stood. He crossed over to us and held up two jagged pieces of cut glass.

"This started the fire," he said, looking straight at me. "The kitchen curtains ignited from the crystal flutes. The window exploded, and they became projectiles," Caleb said, placing the pieces into my hand.

"The winter sun can be treacherous. Not many people know this, but glass and mirrors and even glass doorknobs can sear a hole through curtains just like the focused beam from a magnifying glass," he said. "These fires can be triggered by glass objects left on or near windowsills. I know because I did a lot of research at the library after the first fire. Lydia used to keep her snow globes on the windowsill until her tablecloth caught on fire," he said. "Sam put it out with a fire extinguisher. They were lucky."

I stared at the broken pieces of glass and the chair. *This must be a lucid nightmare. I can go inside my dream and control what happens next, make it all disappear and then walk away.*

"Is that why you have a few glass doorknobs in the bottom of your toolbox?" I asked.

Caleb nodded.

"After I told Sam and Lydia about the cause of the fire, they put their crystal away, and Lydia locked the snow globes in a small trunk and stored them in the cistern house. I removed all the glass doorknobs and kept mirrors away from the sun."

His raspy voice was strained and foreign in the cold silence. I'd never heard him say more than a few words at a time, so his long explanation was painful.

"I killed a man, and then I set your palace on fire, Sam," I finally said. "An army of evil spirits must have been released from those bottles."

Sam just stared at me like I wasn't there. After a second, he wandered over to his truck and returned with Chase. He brought a couple of blankets and put one over my shoulders and the other around Chase who clung to me. I could feel his whole body trembling.

"I'm so sorry, Sam," I whispered.

"It was a freak accident. The Waterford crystal and those damn champagne flutes had been packed away for years, so I didn't think to warn you or anybody else about the winter sun," Sam said.

I looked at Caleb and then everything became clear.

"It was you, Caleb, wasn't it? You hid the mirrors and put the crystal wine glasses in the bottom dresser drawer. And you moved the make-up mirror and put it face down. It wasn't my imagination or a ghost, but it was you, all the time, protecting me, trying to keep me safe. You were the caring ghost who checked on us and hid the crystal."

Caleb stared at the ground, and then he took the pieces of glass from my hand and hurled them over the hillside.

"I'm sorry, Sam. I ruined everything."

"If it hadn't been for you, Twy, a murderer would still be on the loose," Sam said.

"What do you mean?"

Sam cleared his voice and took a deep breath.

"I haven't had time to tell you, but they found blood on Ashley's shirt and identified Randy's DNA under her fingernails. She fought a fierce battle but was overpowered by a monster. Randy panicked and took off when he found out he was a match, but it looks like karma found his identical twin brother Roger first," he said.

"Randy and Roger are identical twins?"

"Yes, identical. Crazy, isn't it? Sam said.

"They both deserve to die," I said.

"Randy is a hardened criminal desperate for drug money, and, sadly, Ashley was easy prey. He stole the bank deposit from her. When he realized that she recognized him, he bound and gagged her, put her in the trunk of his car, and drove her to Corkscrew Swamp. After he locked her inside a metal footlocker and dumped it in the swamp, he figured she'd never be found.

"A few days later, Ashley's cowboy boots were discovered inside Randy's car along with her gold necklace. The chain was broken, so he must have ripped it from her neck. I guess he thought he could pawn her boots and the necklace. He had sold her cell phone the first day, and it led the police to an empty house used by squatters. Randy was guilty of premeditated murder, and, sadly, your mother is an accomplice."

"Joy's a heartless murderer, too," I said. "They both need to suffer a painful death just like Ashley did."

Chase started crying, and I tried to comfort him. Nothing worked.

Sam reached over and squeezed my hand. I looked away but didn't let go.

Ashley's life had just started and just like that it was over. I tried to think of one true sentence for her, but I couldn't. I couldn't even think of one true word.

Caleb wandered away toward the blackened shell of the pin oak tree and found something shiny.

"Will you try and rebuild, Sam? What do you think will happen to Joy?" I asked in a rush.

"Easy there, girl. I might rebuild and I might not. Some things can't be rushed, and you just have to puzzle over them for a while. Especially tragedies like this one. Now, about that mother of yours, don't worry about her. She'll be jailed without bail until her trial. If she's found guilty of being an accomplice to a premeditated murder, she'll get a minimum of ten years in jail. I expect she'll get the maximum sentence since she's been arrested before. You'll keep custody of Chase. I'll see to it," Sam promised.

I drew Sam's words in slowly, trying to comprehend what he had said. I wanted to believe he could rebuild his palace, Joy would be in jail for the rest of her life, and Chase would be safe with me forever.

"There's nothing in the cabin I can't replace except old photos and mementos, but I can buy new movies. And I've got my memories of Lydia tucked away in my heart forever," he said, taking off his Stetson.

"How's Josh doing?" I asked, abruptly changing the subject when Chase pulled away from me.

Sam cleared his throat and put his hat back on.

"I hate to be the bearer of more bad news, but he got himself a new girlfriend," Sam said. "He pined after you for a while, and then he met a girl named Molly at the grocery store. Newly divorced with a baby boy named Ben. Josh was smitten, so I think it's serious."

"I'm happy for him," I said, meaning it. "He deserves happiness."

Caleb returned with fragments of silver and gold wrapping paper he found under the pin oak. I steeled myself for another calamity.

"Looks like Roger stole your gift while he was roosting in

that tree," Sam said. "It was a check, your pay, for $20,000, so it looks like I still owe you."

"You don't owe me anything. I owe you a cabin and a lifetime of lost memories."

"A deal's a deal, Twyla. No backing out now," Sam said.

Caleb continued his search for artifacts. He finally gave up and walked toward the knoll. He brushed the ash and soot away from Shep's stone, sat on the ground, and then he started drawing something with a stick and worked steadily at it for a few minutes. He motioned us over to see a crude floor plan etched in the blackened snow.

"I can rebuild your palace, Sam. I have every room memorized," Caleb said.

"Maybe we can figure out a better water system this time," Sam said with a laugh. "If I can have a water tower built up here, do you think you could have my new palace under roof by July?"

"With a lot of help, maybe by next September," Caleb answered.

"What do you think, boy?" Sam asked

"Would you take me fishing?" Chase asked in a husky voice.

"Anything you want. Maybe you could talk your sister into coming along, too," Sam said. "Well, we need to be hitting the road now. Helen will be worried sick."

I squeezed Chase's hand three times, and he squeezed mine back. Our secret code.

We walked to Sam's truck as it began to flurry, but Caleb lingered behind.

"You're going to need a little spending money until I cut you a check tomorrow," he said, handing me a new bill from his wallet. "It's not the original, but it'll have to do. Turn it over."

I've got your back, was written on it.

"It was you who left me a hundred dollar tip at Calamity," I whispered.

"I don't know what you're talking about, Twyla. All I know

is Rooster Cogburn would never let a brave young girl come in harm's way. You still don't know who Rooster is either, do you?"

"Was he in *True Grit*?" I asked.

"Just John Wayne's best role ever, that's all," Sam said.

"I'm sorry. I didn't watch it, but I will someday. I promise."

"Just like you never opened my present either. Never trust a gift horse, right? I can't fault you on that one," Sam said as we headed toward the truck.

"Should we wait on Caleb?" Chase asked, after we climbed in and Sam started the engine.

"He'll be joining us later," Sam said. "He needs to stay up here a little while. You know, Twyla, Caleb's one of the bravest souls I've ever known."

"I'm not feeling very brave right now."

"One step at a time, Twyla," Sam told me.

He switched on the windshield wipers, and we watched Caleb brush away the snow from his son's grave, and then he lay beside the mirrored stone and stared up at the sky, beside Luke.

ACKNOWLEDGMENTS

I want to thank Linda Riffe and Christina St. Clair for being my first beta readers who encouraged me to continue, plus Patricia Hopper who read a few early chapters.

My Trillium critique group members, Sheila McEntee and Cat Pleska, provided very important feedback as I revised my second draft. Melodee Hill went above and beyond by giving me invaluable context and advice, and she even created a cool collage that was inspired by my novel. Rick McClanahan helped me understand the basics of flying in a Cirrus airplane, and Dreama Craig-Buck gave me a vivid understanding of migraine headaches!

Thanks to Joanna Sexton for letting me explore her Hattie and Nan's antique shop in Central City and to Jesper Ferraris for sharing his expertise in cover design.

Finally, thanks to my brother Denny who read my novel three times and vetted it for accuracy. We both share many memories of visiting my maternal grandparents in their rustic cabin in Virginia called Sleepy Hollow Lodge. Many thanks to my editors Chandler Haun and Courtney Pierce for their artistic vision, support, and guidance.

ABOUT THE AUTHOR

Laura is an internationally published poet, novelist, and picture book writer from West Virginia who was born in Hagerstown, Maryland. She divides her time between West Virginia and a cabin in the mountains of Garrett County Maryland.

READ INDIE. STAY AWESOME.

MORE BOOKS FROM THE HENLO PRESS

Extreme Human Overload by Diana Johnson

The Mother of Monsters: Book One by M.A. Elliot

A Ghost of Spring by A.B. Hooser

304 Monsters by Stephen Bias

West By God by Tyler Bell

Deadly Choices: Will You Survive? | Camp Meltaway by Tiffany and Caitlyn Pace

Old Bones: Volume One by Various

A Shade of Winter by A.B. Hooser

Mumblings: West Virginia Horror Stories by Caitlyn Pace

Afterwords by Stephen Bias